JESS STEINBEISSER

Blood and Stone

Contents

I
Trigger warning

-alcohol consumption
-blood and gore
-blackmail
-bullying
-discussion of mental health
- death of family member (off page)
-death
-decapitation
-dead bodies and body parts
-desecration of a body
-description of a violent death
-death by fire (off page)
-foster care
-hospitalization
-hostage situation
-grief and loss depiction
-kidnapping and abduction
-knife violence
-invasion of privacy
-mention of (off page) rape
-mention of past domestic abuse and violence
-murder
-murder & attempted murder
-mention of serial killers
-mutilation
-stalking
-sexual assault
-sexism and misogyny
-sexual harassment

-suicide (off page)
-workplace harassment
-grief and loss depiction

The tone of this book is one of survival and growth for not only the main character, but also the people around her. If you or someone you know needs help and support please reach out. National Sexual Assault Hotline: Call (800) 656-4673

II

Playlist

I love music and listen to some of my favorites on repeat when I am trying to write a specific scene or want to get in touch with my character better. This Playlist was inspired by the book itself and carefully curated with a little help from Kaida! Hope you enjoy it.

https://open.spotify.com/playlist/2D5M2QEUBjyCzB1f2RXkfx ?si=VLj7YoPlQTqks8T6mIU6DQ

III

Dedication

To the girls who were told they were too much...you weren't really.
They just weren't enough and never would be. Go be amazing.

"She lights up his darkness, he quiets her mind."

To my own Mr. Darcy,
Most Ardently.
p.s. that gazebo in the rain...Yeah, it would be inappropriate to
talk about the things that would happen.
My grandma is going to read this.

Chapter 1

Mattie

I hate it here, Mattie. This is depressing.

Kaida whines sullenly in my head for the hundredth time today. This late in the afternoon, she usually got more and more antsy.

Dear god, it's a group meeting, not a party, I think to my darker half. She huffs her annoyance,

I could make this more fun.

No, babe you could make this bloodier, that's not the same. As usual, she has to insert her thoughts and opinions on everything, almost always unwanted. I was cursed, blessed, and stuck with her living rent-free in my head during the days, and she had to put up with my commentary during her nights. These last ten years, I had grown very accustomed to just ignoring half of her opinions. Attempting to ignore the gorgon altogether, I look to the room of women sitting around the circle, the low lighting casting shadows across their faces. Different races, ages, and backgrounds. That's the thing about being sexually assaulted; it doesn't matter who you were. Afterward, we realize it can and does happen to anyone.

I sat to the far left of the circle, back to the wall, so no one could come up behind me. Keeping my hands tightly clasped together in my lap, trying not to fidget with the one piece of my braid that kept falling forward.

The voices of the group ran together as I shamelessly was only half listening as a woman named Laura began to share her story of assault at the hands of a man who worked in her office. He followed her into their company parking garage after months of him harassing her.

"When I was in that parking garage, all I could think about was how I wanted my mom…I kept thinking that if she were there, then nothing bad could be happening to me. It was her voice in my head that told me to fight back. When I finally got away, I thought the worst was over. I was so wrong." Laura's voice wavered with emotion as she recounted her experience.

"The worst was not being believed. It was having to tell people over and over again what happened just for them to make light of it, to downplay it. I know from coming here that so many of you have had the same thing happen."

I looked up to study the tears clinging to her lashes. She was so young, it was hard not to think of myself at her age. She was right, many of the women had to tell their stories over and over again, only for people to never really listen. That's why these groups exist. My heart aches with anger at the trauma this girl had gone through, what all of them had been through. I held myself back from them not only because of what I was, but also, I didn't really know what they had gone through.

While my body had been used, Kaida had sheltered my mind and the memories from that night. Hannah had crossed the circle to wrap Laura in her arms and comfort her. A few weeks ago, when she came to her first meeting, she brought cookies that she had baked herself, smiling and greeting everyone. Laura is the kind of person who goes out of her way to make everyone's day better, even when hers is falling apart, doing those little gestures that speak of a kindness that I didn't have naturally.

That's because you are a terrible baker…you could burn water. Scoffing, thanks, Kaida, you are really supportive.

I am when you are good at something, but baking isn't one of your many admirable qualities. Her condescending tone was teasing, but I still mentally flipped her off.

Laura was talking about her fears of being home alone now and the other women in the circle showed their support by nodding in agreement and offering sympathetic murmurs. Remaining silent, fists clenched with my arms crossed I stare at the wall behind her head where the door is taunting me. My reflection in the glass of the door stared back at me and the withdrawn look felt more like my reflection was judging me for not being kinder, not paying these people more attention, not participating.

I had enough judgment from Kaida, I certainly didn't need it from my reflection as well. Unlike the rest of them, I don't come here for sympathy or support; it was a means to an end. The group leader stood and clapped her hands together softly to signal the end of the meeting. She always tried to meet each person's eyes as she spoke to the group, and I always avoided it like the plague. Hannah was sharp, and there was more to me than I wanted her to see.

I like Laura, she is so innocent. I vote we take care of this one. Kaida's excitement prepping for a hunt was palpable but I didn't disagree. I would like to make sure that she doesn't have to look over her shoulder anymore. Maybe she would have an easier time moving on then.

Laura shared that she had reported the incident and human resources only asked her what she did to bring about the situation. The guy convinced HR that she was angry after he turned her down and she retaliated. It wasn't the first time I had heard this story, and it certainly wouldn't be the last.

Between growing up in the foster system and later in my chosen "profession" of the past 10 years, I had heard the same tale many times, as my ancestors had no doubt heard for the last 3,000 years since we had first been cursed. They didn't do anything to try and change the tale for others, to protect anyone else. For many, many generations, they did nothing for the women who had stories that reflected their own. Then one day, I decided to be the one to change that.

We decided to change everything, little monster. Kaida purrs, her affection for me obvious as I picture her true form and mentally fist-bump her.

While there were things I wish I could change about the past, Kaida was one thing I would never change. She had always been more than a friend.

Surveying the plate of stale doughnuts and a pot of coffee on the side table was enough to turn my stomach, but then again, no one else seemed to have any appetite either. Getting up to go get a cup on my way out, I avoided meeting anyone's gaze both out of habit and so as not to encourage small talk. Avoiding talking to the women here made it easier to blend into the background. Since this was my hunting ground, the last thing I needed was to be memorable.

It was another hot day in New Orleans, but that was something I was fairly used to after all this time here. Hannah, the group leader and resident therapist, followed closely behind me, stopping next to the table too. The sad offering of food was missing cookies… and I found myself more than a little disappointed.

Studying her out of the corner of my eye, I took in her whole look, from the sharp pantsuit to the high heels that screamed professional woman. She kept her hair in a short, sleek, chin-length bob that accented her sharp cheekbones and elegant jaw. Her caramel coffee skin was just as warm as her aura. From the time she entered the church basement, she was always hugging people, smiling at them, or pressing hot drinks into their hands. I couldn't understand how she could let so many people with that much baggage near her without it wearing her down, but she seemed immune.

Standing almost shoulder to shoulder with me, she sighs. Maybe the weight of the group does weigh on her more than she shares. "I should just go and get something before work, but I never have the energy," she whispers under her breath, the weariness more obvious now.

Pushing my hair back over my shoulder and raising my cup, "Why do you think I just take the coffee?" I try to smile nicely at her, but my face feels like a frozen grimace. Taking a drink of the coffee, I immediately regret it and set it back down to try and doctor the bitter flavor out of it.

She turns my way and straightens her spine, looking me over, "Oh look, she speaks!" Her voice dripped with sarcasm.

I like her. She is funny. Kaida says, smiling to herself.

"I assumed you only came for the coffee in the first place…It's not like you ever share." Turning her sharp gaze back to the table, still, but I could still hear her therapist's tone chastising me lightly.

Your pain is your own, dear. You don't owe her or anyone else explanations. Kaida butted in, and I held back a smirk at her haughty attitude.

I do actually know that, but thanks for the reassurance.

Hannah picked up a doughnut and looked my way again with one expertly raised black brow on her dark face.

"Since the coffee is usually terrible, I can't imagine anyone crashing this super fun party just for that. Sharing is not a requirement; it's on the poster." I quipped back, "Or is that a new rule?" Softly stirring another sugar in the bitter coffee, like that will fix the burnt taste, while avoiding her eyes.

"We don't have posters, Mattie…if sharing is not your reason for coming, then what is?" Suspicion fills her eyes as Hannah reaches into her comically small and fancy bag, pulling out a piece of paper. Unfolding it, she places a newspaper clipping from two weeks prior right in my field of vision on the tabletop.

The story was covering the tragic accidental death of a man in the French Quarter who was bitten by a venomous snake while taking out the trash. My sister Alice had read it to me the day it was published over breakfast before giving me a twenty-minute lecture about being more cautious. While it had been more than enough for me, Kaida was less than convinced. It wasn't our first lecture about our nighttime adventures, and I am sure it won't be our last.

I think she is onto us, Mattie. Throw your coffee at her and run! Toss a doughnut too! Kaida yells dramatically. I have to resist physically rolling my eyes or slapping my forehead at her craziness.

I think you mean she is onto you. Last I checked, you're the one with the venomous bite and bad attitude, I think back at her loudly.

She huffs incredulously, *yeah? Because your attitude is just peachy. That's why you have so many friends, right?*

It wasn't like she was wrong or anything. I have exactly one friend, two if you count the snake lady cursed to live inside my body, but still rude to point out.

You're a bitch sometimes. Drinking the bitter coffee as most of the group says their goodbyes and files out, leaving Hannah and me here mostly alone.

I am your best bitch though. Just ignore her.

Pulling my attention back to Hannah as she taps her manicured finger on the clipping,

"I thought this man looked fairly familiar…Carol Shanks was a member with us for over a year. Do you remember her?" Casually, I shrug my shoulders, while internally I freak out and actually consider lobbing a doughnut at her forehead just to escape this conversation. Reaching to add a ton more creamer into the coffee, "Her husband was hurting her regularly, right? They had a baby a while back. Couldn't have happened to a nicer guy, then?" I asked, hitting the nonchalant tone perfectly, if I do say so myself, raising my brow questioningly, "Give her my condolences if you see her. Although she is probably pretty relieved." Hannah watches my shoulder rise and fall before studying my face, searching for guilt or deception, I guess, "I helped her and her baby get to a shelter a few days before her husband died."

Understatement of the century, I'm sure. It would have been better if someone had helped her before it came to us, Kaida, but I'm still not sorry. More effective than doughnut lobbing…

"Certainly, a mystery that a woman who comes to our group, looking for an escape, maybe even help? Then an animal attack makes her a widow fairly quickly after. That's pretty convenient, Mattie, maybe too convenient."

She waits patiently to try and meet my gaze, but I pull my sunglasses from my hair and slip them on, leading out the church's back door, and she is quickly following, her obscenely high heels clicking along the way.

"He was bitten by a snake, Hannah…. sounds like a tragedy of New Orleans proportions as usual." I say, shrugging my shoulders, keeping my shoulders relaxed as much as I possibly could, "A tragic comedy in the making."

Years of being on an even keel of temperament were the only way to survive so long in this world. I knew what it was to be afraid, but that didn't mean I had to show it.

Once upon a time, I thought that monsters were for storybooks, but I had been forced to change my mind about what and who the monsters were. My ancestor had turned to someone she trusted, someone she worshiped with her life, and was punished for that every single day. Then her descendants carried the curse for the next 3,000 years.

I had watched my older sister, Catherine, be punished for a crime she didn't commit, and it took her from me. I would have gone down the same path if not for the purpose Kaida and I made for ourselves; what started as self-preservation turned into something more. I had turned my curse around and made it my bitch. I had made friends with the darkness, loved it, and she loved me back.

Hannah reached out and grabbed my arm gently to halt my escape. Several of the women from the group walked around us, nodding or waving goodbye. We both gently waved and nodded our goodbyes until everyone was well out of earshot.

"Yeah, Mattie, and maybe it was a vampire attack. That would be classic New Orlean's but all I am saying is it's odd enough for there to be attention to the oddness of it, enough attention might lead back here."

She waited until she was sure she was actually looking into my eyes behind the glasses, trying to communicate without actually accusing me of anything. "Just be careful, okay? I have noticed this wasn't the first person attached to someone in this group to have something happen to them. If I have noticed, so has someone else. I don't know your story or why you come to sit with us each week, but I know that you carry the same look in your eyes as the rest of the women in the group. Just know that if you ever need more than this group, I am here."

She holds out a light green business card between slim fingers with her name and number.

Dr. Hannah Raines at Mercy clinic embossed on it in fancy letters. Taking it between two fingers and putting it in my back pocket, I nod gently with a small smile. Feeling the pressure of tears pushing through, "Thanks..." I turn to walk off to the gate to the cemetery yard.

I think I like her. She has a bloodthirsty streak somewhere in there, Kaida ponders. Hannah might think she knows what's going on, but the actual horror would be too much. She at least understands what it was to protect someone, even if we have different methods.

No, Kai, I think she is genuinely a good person. Too good to be around us.

"Please think about what I said..." Hannah says quietly enough that none of the others lingering nearby can hear but me.

Turning to capture one last look at her, I adjust my shades and nod before I cross the street. A silver sedan half a block down from the gate sits idling. I spot the flash of sunlight on the camera lens shortly before they cover it, but focus my eyes forward and open my senses as I hear someone softly curse from inside and sink into their seat.

Did you see them? Kaida hisses threateningly. I did indeed.

What the hell are they doing here is the real question. Hopping up the curb and walking calmly down the sidewalk, I pull out my phone, dialing the only person I trust to tell me why my women's assault group is being surveyed by police. After three rings, the receptionist at the station answers in her deep southern drawl,

"Hey, Detective Hester, please?"

"May I ask who is calling?" Lorraine drawls boredly.

"Tell her it's her sister." The line clicks over and starts to ring. Making my way around the block to see the car better from behind, Alice's voicemail answers instead, and I wait to hear the beep at the end, assuming it's only going to be bad news.

Chapter 2

Using the reflection of the elevator doors I straightened my tie and checked that my hair was pushed back neatly enough. It was always a little long for FBI standards, but my brothers would give me shit if I cut it too short. It was my little bit of rebellion, and the agency looked the other way as I always could be counted on to close my cases. Sometimes not as cleanly as they would appreciate but on paperwork it was neat as a pin and tied up with a nice ribbon. Walking down the hall to the regional FBI director's office I waved and said hello to everyone I passed.

Director Shaw had called me in to discuss an unusual case down in the French Quarter of New Orleans. It would be a welcome reprieve from Washington DC and the cold front moving in signaling the beginning of winter. I had heard about the third victim of a snake bite, all three men killed by the same type of venom, Montivipera Xanthina, or Ottoman viper. Flicking through the case file as I walked, preparing myself. The New Orleans police department was requesting our help on this rather than us asking which was somewhat unusual. Most places didn't want us involved at all until it's too late, but I guess three dead bodies in such a high traffic tourist area was cause for alarm. There was a report in the file flagging it as a possible animal trafficking case. With the snake venom being from a species that wasn't native to the area and the deaths happening in an area that was known for shady things, it was a possibility. Could be just a loose animal and three very unlucky guys but what were the chances. I really needed a win right now and a killer brought down is always a win, but I couldn't say how I was going to crack this.

Knocking on the office door with John Shaw's name painted in black on the front. I could see him through the glass, but it took a minute before he looked up from his desk and waved me in. The director had been my personal mentor for a few years now. He was a large man wearing a government black suit. He had served in the military for many years and when he was done, he turned in one uniform for another. You wouldn't be able to tell that he was covered in tattoos. On one of their few nights out drinking he had rolled up his sleeves and showed off the art. He was extremely proud of his military service and symbols of it decorated his arms in full sleeves. John smiled at him when he entered,

"Bennet, Come on in. This is a real strange one," Shaw said, pushing his own file over on the desk and spreading out the victim profiles on the desk. He was clearly studying it for this meeting. He wasn't going to waste resources on a wild goose chase.

"That's what you always say sir. It's a self-fulfilling prophecy and I think you enjoy that on some level." I said cheekily. He laughed, his eyes crinkling on the sides and nodded, "You're not wrong about that. I enjoy seeing you try and unravel the weird ones."

Gesturing to the chair in front of his desk, he walked around and sat on the corner edge of his desk facing me. I did too, I think because I genuinely believed that there was more out there in the world. Of course, you could chalk that up to the fact that I half joined the FBI out of loving unraveling a mystery and half because I grew up watching x-files so many times that I wasn't allowed to have control over the remote anymore as a kid.

"Did you get a chance to review the files already?" I don't know why he asks when he knows that if I get a case, I have to go over the files right away. My gut will nag me relentlessly until I read it at least once. This case had been one that dropped into my inbox at the end of the day yesterday, but

I was pulled in right away and took it home with me to review until 3 am. But I nod affirmative anyways and he continues.

"We have three victims, all men, from different ethnicity and backgrounds, all killed by the same type of snake venom in a small area of New Orleans. So far two of the three were contained to the quarter but one was found in an alley in the city proper. Some kind of weird viper from Greece."

I was nodding and looking at the crime scene photos. Each of the men had been found in isolated areas that were surrounded by busy places, theoretically they should have been able to reach help of some kind. Each of them was bitten on the neck, arm, or hand. It was odd that if it was a case of a loose wild animal, that they were all men, that they hadn't been bitten on the foot or leg, not on the upper extremities. The ME had said that the bite marks looked genuine.

I had read all this in my file over the course of my review the evening before. The crime scene photos were gruesome. The venom was hemotoxic, causing the red blood cells in the body to burst throughout the body. It poured out of the victims' eyes, nose, mouth, and ears. It was a quick death, but not pleasant. From what I had read, this particular snake's venom did not naturally cause this. It was potent stuff, but not known to be this fast-acting or effective.

These people should have had time to get to a hospital and get some treatment, but they all seemed to have died quickly after being bitten. One in an alley, one on a street corner in the quarter, and one outside his own home while taking out the trash. Shaw set down his file, and I shook my head to bring back focus to what he was saying, "I want you to investigate what is going on here. We want to know whether or not this could be the work of a serial killer."

I knew that was what he was going to say, but hearing it out loud got my adrenaline pumping and my heart racing. A thrill went shivering down my spine. I love a mystery, and this was shaping up to be the kind I loved the most, weird and twisty. I wanted to be sitting on the other side of this desk someday, but I also did this just because of the thrill of the chase.

"Yes, sir. I'll get right on it. Do you mind me asking why the local PD is requesting the FBI take the lead, instead of just handling it themselves? Normally, departments don't call us in unless they have to. I know the snake isn't local to the area, but like you said, there is no visible connection to the victims."

John sighed heavily and walked back around his desk, and sat down in his chair with a serious look on his face. He was studying me quietly and thinking over how much of his own theories he wanted to share and how much I could glean before he conflated my ideas with his own. John had been doing this for all the years I had worked under him. Trying to see what conclusions I would draw alone, and then even letting me fail if necessary, just so I could develop my ideas independently. He was a good teacher and was well known for mentoring and developing good agents.

"Will, I found something else, a detail that's not in the file. Let me be clear, I wouldn't be telling you this normally, but I know you will be respectful and sensitive about investigating it. Other than the venom, there is something else that connects the victims. My gut told me there was a piece missing here, so I had Tom, the intelligence analyst, do a deeper dive. You know he uses some colorful resources, but his information is always accurate. He had to dig for this info as it wasn't in the original request from the department. I don't know why they left it out, but for me, its absence was a red flag."

He took a deep, steady breath, running his hand over his bald head, and blew it out before he said, "Two of the men who died had been accused of assaulting a woman recently. It was in the background checks for their history, but the files were very thin, like they hadn't been investigated at all."

I reopened the file and flipped to the last victim's page, "Why didn't they look into it at the time? Seems odd that there is that kind of connection, but they didn't include it."

Shaw nods his head, "I got the impression that this kind of case wasn't a priority at their department. New Orleans, especially the quarter, has a lot of people in and out of the area. That's no excuse for shitty police work. We requested local PD to track down the last victim's widow, she was found at a women's shelter one state over. According to her, he had hurt her for the last time, so she took her daughter and ran, only for him to turn up dead a few days later. We tried to get a hold of her for more questions, but she went to ground. She returned after the notification of death a few days ago to grab a few things from their joint property, cleaned out their accounts, and disappeared completely."

This was not a connection I had suspected. I huffed out a breath and leaned back in the chair, studying the director, "So there is a possibility this was a reaction to those crimes? Any connection between her and the other two victims?"

It was a red flag that the department was requesting their help, but had left information out of the reports. Lucky for me, Shaw always does his own research before approving requests and assigning his agents to a case. The victims were both accused of crimes themselves, violent crimes. The wife's disappearance was suspicious. Was she running from something or someone else?

John looked straight past me, nodding. During all my years serving under him, I knew John took things like assault on women harder than most. He never shared why, but his being a father to 3 girls and in a job like this, it was something that always hit closer to home.

I gathered up the files and shuffled them back into the pile, taking the new ones the director provided as well. Checking my watch, I had a few hours to get to the airport if I left now. I still had to stop by my apartment and leave the key with the neighbor before grabbing my go bag.

"There wasn't anything in the preliminary, but it's something to look into. Maybe these are just assholes who got what was coming to them by virtue of karma, but maybe not. Weirder things have happened in that city of voodoo and vampires. We just need someone with an open mind to take a look, and if it is a serial, it would be the career boost you need here. Solve this quickly." He leaned back in his chair and turned his gaze to me as I tucked the file under my arm. He gave a sharp nod to both clear his mind and to dismiss me.

"I will travel straight there and let you know what I can gather from the local PD."

"Bennet? You need to meet with their captain first, but they have requested you work with one of their own, a detective Hester from their local PD's Special Victims Unit. I know you usually like to work alone or with other agents, not the local PD, but this time might be good to have someone who knows the area. Give them what they want for now, but if there are any problems you just let me know. I can get you another agent for backup down there. I am happy to go to bat for you with the captain there." His voice gradually grew harsher, betraying how annoying he found the requesting department's head officer.

While I usually worked alone or with another agent, I don't mind working with someone in their department if it means getting more access, and they don't slow me down. I tend to overwhelm others and then railroad my way into just doing all the work; that's why other agents didn't ask to be my partner anymore.

Smiling at the tone in his voice, I got the impression that he and the captain had gotten off on the wrong foot; never a good idea when dealing with Shaw. I was kind of looking forward to meeting someone who could get under his skin. Setting off to the French Quarter, I had a feeling this case would be more complicated than it seemed, but there was nothing I liked better than a good chase.

Chapter 3

Mattie

The police station was bustling when I arrived the next afternoon to meet up with my sister. Alice had been on shift all night, and now she could finally make time for me, probably only because I offered to bring coffee. I took up my usual spot on the steps of the building across from the station and stretched out my legs, getting comfy. There was no telling how long my darling sister would be, so like a lizard on a rock, I was going to soak up today's sunshine. Alice would come to meet up with us soon enough.

You did NOT just compare us to a lizard...that's just insulting Mattie.

Kaida's voice chastising my own mind wandering was annoying. Nothing was a private thought, even just a casual slip of the proverbial tongue. Well, you are green...and have scales...so really, am I that far off? Her only reply is hissing loudly like a white noise machine to express her vexation.

The police station, surrounded by a buzz of activity and the low hum of voices. I love being able to sit and watch people. The tourists stumbling out of the station had been out having a good time. Some of them, too good of a time so they had to sleep in the station, but it was comical. I sat on the hot concrete, feeling it seep through my clothes. I reveled in the sunlight like any other cold-blooded creature, while I sipped my iced hazelnut coffee with another sweating on the step next to me. Alice loved hers blended up and covered in tons of whipped cream and sprinkles. It was probably made fun of by the other cups of coffee while it waited on the counter, but it was the way she had always liked it, more dessert than drink.

The big double doors opened, letting out some girls who had too good a time at a bachelorette, and Alice. She exited the station looking pale and shaken as she waved at a car while she crossed the street to sit next to me. She picked up the mockery of a coffee and took a long sip before huffing sharply and falling into my side, so I had to keep her upright. I merely observed her while she decompressed. Alice had always been small, but since our childhood years, she had outgrown her round face of Asian descent; her sharp cheekbones, thin nose, and sweeping hooded eyes were all a combination that compellingly made her beautiful and exotic. Her long black hair was pulled back into a sleek pony. She sported her usual clean professional work wear, consisting of a variation of a white blouse and black slacks, exactly the opposite of what I wore, even though we were built the same in most ways, she had a more feline quality to her.

She moved gracefully in all ways, from her carefully winged eyeliner that accented her Japanese heritage to the classic red lip she loved. She carried herself like someone who was comfy in their own skin and knew she was beautiful, which she undeniably was. That, even after all these years, was not something that I could say about myself.

"Ow ow ow brain freeeeeeeeeze," she cried out, clutching her head and ruining her sleek pony. Even in the direst circumstances, Alice never failed to make me laugh. I leaned back on my elbows, smiling while Alice glared, going for another pull on the straw, her need for the sugar hit overwhelming her irritation at me momentarily.

"So, what's going on?" Alice asked, her voice tight with concern, "You didn't leave much info on my voicemail yesterday." Her eyes searched the crowds milling around us without pause, but her posture hardened as if she could sense my anxiety.

I sighed heavily, rubbing my hand over my face and setting down my coffee. "Shouldn't you know better than me? Yesterday, there was a car down the road from the church when I was leaving. Someone was on a stakeout, they were taking photos of the women, me included."

Alice briefly closed her eyes, collecting her thoughts, when she opened them again, they had darkened. The deep blue bags under her eyes indicated just how many hours she had been on her feet.

"Maybe it was a coincidence?" I could see her already planning on ditching this life we had built and moving on again.

It was a conversation every time she felt like I was in trouble, one ledge I had to talk her off of more times than I can count.

"Maybe it had something to do with Carol Shanks. Hannah asked me about that news article on her husband."

You better jump in there quickly because our sister is spiraling. Next thing you know, she will be faking our deaths and getting us dirty passports with names like Nancy or Gayle.

Kaida was right about Alice's thought spiral and her terrible choice in fake names.

I could spot when she started mentally rehearsing the conversation she would have with Brian Kemp, a fellow officer she had been casually seeing. Since I got the impression he was boring as hell, both in the bedroom and out, it wouldn't be the biggest loss, but she liked him, so I kept my opinions to myself. I just sat quietly waiting for her to process because there was no point in interrupting her while she internally melted down. She would wind herself down talking to her own internal voice, one that didn't harbor homicidal impulses.

She sighed heavily and slurped up a dollop of whipped cream, "I told you both that you need to lay low. Between this and the problem with the guy before, maybe it's time for us to consider moving on, Mattie."

Taking Alice's drink, I set it down and hold her hand in mine, "No. Just no. You love your job, you love the city, you love the house, and you could love…" I roll my eyes and fake gag, "Brian, too."

Shaking my head, "You don't have to make all the sacrifices, Alice. Let other people take care of you, too. I don't want to leave, and neither does Kaida. I love the library I work in, and we all love New Orleans."

Pausing to look at Alice's profile as she stared into space, anxiously chewing on her bottom lip. She pulled her hand out of mine looking seriously at the ground while she fidgeted with her pony, pulling it over her shoulder to twist the ends, staring at a dark spot on the sidewalk like she was hoping it would swallow her whole like a classic cartoon so she wouldn't have to say anything she thought would hurt my feelings. She took another sip of her coffee, then a deep breath.

"Okay, but this needs to stop. We can't keep going on like this…"

We were not born sisters, but since the day we met in our foster home, we had clicked. She confidently bounded up to me. I was gawky and shy and had taken to hiding behind my long hair. She started talking to me about nothing at all and never stopped. Her hands were waving erratically, and the next thing I knew, her arm was through mine. It sounded so corny, but it was like what people described when meeting their soulmate. It was a bone-deep understanding between two silly girls that they were meant to be.

Whatever it was quickly turned our friendship into sisterhood. Alice had always been on my side, even when I was cursed. The death of my older sister left me in the care of the foster system, and Alice became a port in the storm. I hadn't known just how much I would need that when, a few years later, my curse began. Now she was my very own partner in crime.

"Just let it play out and die down. I promise to switch it up if it makes you feel better. But I do need a little favor first?" I asked with hesitation.

Oh yeah, she just finished freaking out, obviously the best time to ask her about Laura's case.

Apparently, Kaida was done brooding about my lizard comment, and now we are back to criticizing me.

"You need to switch it up, like a lot. I saw the autopsy reports…. You can't just explain away why people are being killed by a rare snake that's native to another continent. The captain said he had flagged the last case to be sent up to the FBI, and now they are sending in an agent to come and test the waters for this being a serial killer. He is due to arrive sometime this week."

Surprised, "Why did the captain tell you? He can't stand you and has been trying to dismantle your unit since he arrived." Alice winced.

Captain Rayes had been the department head for the last few years. Alice had to work three times as hard to get stuff done and done right. She had volunteered to be the head of the SVU because she knew it was the only way that anything would be done right for the victims. Between my attack and years of listening to the same stories of women in the quarter, she had thick skin, but the captain still rankled both of us.

"Because when I found out it was being reviewed, I put in to be assigned to the case," Alice says softly.

"What? Why would you want to help them?" She sighs and takes a drink, watching people walk by, "Mattie, if I work it, I can steer the case. I can control the variables."

Alice thinks she can control anything and everything; it's one of her core traits. She has been doing it for over a decade. She made the plans for after we finished school, after the attack, what we would do, where we would go. One of these days, she was going to realize the chaos of the universe doesn't like being controlled or organized.

The FBI was going to invest time and energy into a serial killer that had claimed a few lives, but not into actually stopping the men who perpetrated the crimes that cost them their lives. They had their chance at justice, and they failed; I didn't. For the world, the matter of justice was black and white, but for me, it was a big, shadowy gray area where I did what it took so women didn't have their nightmares walking around.

Trying to deflect and lighten the mood so Alice didn't spontaneously combust, "That reminds me I have got to stop and get more Cinnamon Toast Crunch…." I pulled out my phone to type out a reminder for the shopping list. Alice huffed irritably, "Please be serious."

I looked her up and down, "I am. You love that shit too. I have to put this on the list now so we have some, or you'll have to eat oatmeal and deal with Kaida hissing over our lack of yummy breakfast essentials."

She smiled at the image of me parading around our big kitchen in my floral robe in my nighttime form, Kaida being mad at the lack of a children's cereal.

I do not parade about you, little witch, and everyone loves that cereal!

Yes, yes, we all love it, I think to her as I roll my eyes at her and finish typing in the note I didn't actually need, but I was already committed to this bit. An actual real threat, the only thing scarier than my monster was a hungry Alice.

"Fine, listen…" I put my phone back in my pocket and patted her knee gently.

"It is really going to be okay. I had a mark in mind, but it's not an emergency like the last one…maybe you could look at the guy a little harder and find a way to make something stick so it's not my kind of problem."

"Almost ten years doing this, and every time you say that, you end up handling it yourself anyway. Things are different here, and I don't want to leave, but if it becomes an us or them thing, we are hitting the road." Her dark eyes pleaded with me to be reasonable, a thing I was never good at, but she was begging me to understand that while we could leave again, she didn't want to, and she needed me to be the one to stop that.

I knew she was serious. She would drop her entire life to make sure I was safe and could do the hunting that I needed to keep hold of my sanity. It's been ten years since the night that I learned my entire maternal line had been cursed by Athena. She created the original gorgon, Medusa, an innocent and beautiful acolyte who was raped by Poseidon. As punishment for breaking her vow of chastity, Athena cursed my ancestor to exist as a gorgon. Eventually, her secret was uncovered by the Hero Perseus, who thought he was falling in love with a beautiful woman by day and got more than he bargained for at night. The legend was that he lopped off her head, but the story was a little biased towards the "hero".

Instead, he left her with a dagger in the already broken heart of a woman who couldn't die and a baby in her belly that would begin the long line of the curse that would become mine someday.

Generations of women in my line lived perfectly normal lives with no idea what they had hanging over their heads, unless of course the worst happens and they were a victim of rape like their ancestor, triggering the curse. By day, you live as a regular woman, by night, a gorgon, snakes and all.

Unfortunately, my gorgon, Kaida, had a mind of her own and a hissy fit if she wasn't allowed to hunt on the regular. I couldn't do much to keep her happy unless I let her loose. So I found people who were worth hunting, saving women like me and my older sister.

"I'm sorry. I promise I will figure out something soon." Alice leveled a long look at me, "You didn't ask for this, any of it, so you never need to apologize. You do what you have to survive, and you will continue to do just that. I will figure out what the FBI knows and if I can try and nudge it towards the weirdness of NOLA. An afternoon interviewing some Brujas, maybe a vampire or two? That should send anyone packing." Leaning over and nudging my shoulder lightly. Her face breaks into a smile too before she starts back in on that she calls travesty, she calls a coffee.

A large black SUV pulls into the spot in front of where we are sitting, and Kaida perks up. My senses go into overdrive as a gorgeous, tall man with wavy, dark hair gets out of the front seat. With his black suit and briefcase, he might as well be wearing a sign that says, 'Hi, my name is Mr. FBI, and I don't belong here.'

He's built like he should be pulling up in a long boat to conquer new lands like the Vikings. Handsome in a rugged kind of way with his formally straight nose that curved at the bridge a little, like he had broken it, the kind of handsome that could be devastating. He looked briefly around as he straightened his jacket, taking in the sights before his eyes settled on the two of us sitting on the stoop of the building and raised his brow under his sunglasses, nodded politely, and headed across the street into the station. I guess that the timeline for his arrival had moved up.

Alice squeezed my hand one last time, took her coffee, and leaned down for a quick cheek-to-cheek kiss. She started after him; I couldn't help checking out his fine-cut figure.

"I'll see you at home tonight and let you know what's going on. Be good!"

I rolled my eyes and waved her off before starting towards my truck. I had about 4 hours before sunset, so how much trouble could I get in? Slipping my sunglasses on, I felt someone watching. The hair on the back of my neck stood up, and goosebumps spread across my skin. Turning quickly, I saw the man in black watching me from across the street. He held open the front door of the station for my sister. He stared from behind his sunnies, and it sent my hackles up. I heard a hissing in my ears and knew even Kaida was rattled by this man. Lying low wouldn't be so much of a problem if even she was spooked by the idea of being caught, too.

Not scared, little monster, curious.

She says inside my head.

Scoffing, I turn around and walk off, "Great. Your curiosity is the last thing that we need. Have you ever heard the expression curiosity killed the cat?"

It wasn't curiosity; it was probably a snake. You should be more curious. It would do you some good.

Chapter 4

William

I knew that the NOLA police department was going to be a challenge, but I didn't realize that it would start in the parking lot. I was enjoying the sunshine and fresh air with my window down while I drove, pulling up across from the building. I saw two women sitting on a stoop sipping some coffee. I tried to flash them a charming smile, but it came across more as baring teeth. One of them left me with the feeling of the world circling down to a pinpoint, overwhelming me.

There, leaning back on one hand casually, she was fair-skinned and petite. Her heart-shaped face was surrounded by long reddish-brown hair pulled up into a ponytail. From the black tank top to the ripped jeans, she was like a wildflower, pushing up through the cracks of the city to make her place known. She turned her green eyes onto me, studying with the kind of assessing gaze that made me feel like she could see into me. It was more than disconcerting.

Something in my brain screamed that women like her were predators and to back away, but for some reason, I found that attractive. She reached behind herself, pulling out a ridiculous pair of blue-lens heart-shaped sunglasses, slipping them on. I didn't want to be the first to look away, so here I stood just warring with myself like a real weirdo.

She finally caved, looking away to the Asian woman drinking her coffee.

I actually do have a job here in the city and should probably go into the station before I make the questionable decision to ignore my instincts and ask her out. The smaller woman got up, and I observed as she kissed her companion on the cheek and quickly walked past me, yelling back at her companion, "I'll see you at home tonight and let you know what's going on. Be good!"

Shrugging off the disappointment that hit like a ton of bricks at their obvious affection…Apparently, I had been admiring a woman who was taken by the small Asian officer who followed him to the precinct.

I reached for the heavy door and held it open for her as she turned a thousand-watt smile to me and entered the building. I couldn't stop myself from glancing back to see the other woman get up and dust off her jeans, adjust her heart sunglasses, and flip her hair over her shoulder. She was walking down the street with determined purpose when her shoulders tensed. She turned so quickly that her long hair swung around her, and catching me staring, I felt a little jolt of electricity as our gazes met and quickly turned into the building behind the woman's girlfriend. Obviously, I need to get my head in the game.

The station was busy with officers escorting people back and forth between the main reception. The bullpen and offices are to the right, and storage and cells are to the left. Quite a few people were sitting in chairs surrounding me; most looked like they had a rough night here in the Big Easy and would give anything to just go back to their hotels.

At the end of the room sat a large desk with a high top; behind it was a larger African American woman wearing a headscarf and big reading glasses hanging by a chain around her neck. She had the phone resting against her shoulder as I approached and waited to be acknowledged. She put a hand over the bottom of the phone and quirked her eyebrows at me expectantly, so I introduced myself, flipping open my badge holder, "Agent William Bennet, FBI, to see a Detective Hester" The receptionist took a glance at the flashed badge and pointed at the quickly retreating Asian woman's back yelling, "Allie! There's a Fed for you!"

The detective stopped short and turned slowly, her warm smile fell away. She had the same assessing gaze as her girlfriend. A quick up and down, and it seemed like she had measured me up, and from the scowl that slipped on her face, she found me lacking. Changing her coffee to her left hand, she wiped the right on her pant leg before she came back and offered it out with a strained smile, "Detective Alice Hester at your service."

Her handshake was quick and firm, but the slight tremble gave away her discomfort. She was a short but curvy woman; her sharp suit matched her thick winged liner. Her red lipstick had been slightly rubbed off on the straw of her coffee, "Agent Will Bennet. It's a pleasure."

Releasing my hand, she stepped back and leaned on the desk to her left. She leveled a glare, finally demonstrating how so slight a woman became a detective at her age in a city like this, at the receptionist who was deliberately ignoring her, "Lorraine, please don't yell about feds in the office…or call me Allie."

Lorraine was wearing a colorful silk wrap on her head, sitting behind the desk. She hung up the phone and looked directly at Detective Hester with a scary smile. Women of this city were built differently. "Yes ma'am," she drawled sarcastically, "But since you are already here taking breaks for coffee and not bringing me one, do you want to take the Fed back or should I show him directly to the captain's office?"

Alice pinched the bridge of her delicate nose, frustrated, "Next time I will have Mattie bring an extra, I promise. I will show him back. Nice new Gele by the way." She smiled softly at Lorraine, then turned her gaze back my way, and I could admit appreciation and respect for the receptionist who could hold her own.

The pretty woman with heart-shaped sunglasses was obviously Mattie, whose face was echoing in my head with flashing green eyes. I shook my head to clear my mind of some dirty thoughts trying to form before I had to go into a meeting, while thinking about a woman who had been in front of me for only a moment. I didn't usually get distracted, but something about her was pulling my attention.

"Follow me, please," she walked off without waiting for an answer, her confidence clearly returning. I walked after her down the hallway into the bullpen. Weaving through the desks that cluttered the room, she waved at several officers as they passed, and they smiled and waved at her, too. She picked up a file from the corner of one desk without even looking at it and set it in the inbox of another a few desks away. She made eye contact with an officer who was talking to another by the window and gave him a flirty finger wave with a smile before she led me to the back.

There, on the far wall, was where the captain and detectives had offices and a main conference room. She led the way into the latter and gestured to the large table. On a big white board were the three victims' names with a photo and a brief on each. The detective was purposely not looking at the board. She looked very uncomfortable, standing with her back to the board, facing away from the crime scene photos. "So is there anything I can get you, coffee or…" She trailed off before looking up, "The captain will be here shortly, I'm sure."

I looked up at her; she was trying to find a reason to leave, my gut jumping to attention. Maybe she noticed me watching her girlfriend. I should apologize, but how do I without admitting that I was in fact checking her girlfriend out? Deciding to go for casual and charming, "Sorry I interrupted your lunch date with your girlfriend. I don't need anything in particular. I just need a rundown with you and the captain. Maybe a physical copy of your files on the case." Putting my own bag on top of the wide table, removing my files and water bottle. Alice's eyes dart over the stickers on the side, locking in on one in particular, a UFO that reads "I want to believe".

"Lunch date?" She looked up from the floor and cocked her head to the side, studying me with narrowed eyes, her long ponytail swishing with the movement. For a minute, I watched her expressive face work through what I had said, then her eyes lit up with mirth.

"Oh, you think…" she trailed off and laughed loudly, a blush flushing across her cheeks. Her shoulders relaxed, and she seemed to warm up a bit. Feeling the heat of embarrassment rise on my neck while she trailed off into giggles, the door opened abruptly, revealing a large man who could only be described as rotund, like in that movie Shrek, when they blow up a frog as a balloon. He was older than even director Smith, with a serious comb-over of gray hair and a thick mustache. He had small features for his face with little beady dark brown eyes. I instantly disliked the man even as he strode in and shoved his hand in my face, "Welcome to my precinct, Agent Bennet. I'm Captain Rayes. Your superior didn't let us know you would be arriving so quickly."

Glancing over to the detective's face, she wasn't smiling now as she stood off to the side, stiff again. I shook his hand and then sat down in the nearest chair and gestured for him to do the same while I pulled the files I had brought closer to me. I stacked them neatly, one on top of the other, and when the captain was seated, I looked at the detective out of the corner of my eye. Captain Rayes never looked at his officer, and she didn't appear to mind his ignoring her. She positioned herself with her back to the wall next to the door, watching the two of us. I turned to catch her eyes and gestured to the seat across the table from me, where she could keep her back to the wall.

She didn't move for a minute, like she was thinking, and then walked to the other chair, farthest away from the captain. It left her back exposed, but it was a statement since the captain hadn't said a word about her staying or sitting. I decided to just move on, "Well, I'd like to get to work before we have any more bodies."

The captain nodded, finally acknowledging Detective Hester. He gestured to her and, in an aggravated tone, said, "I'm assigning Detective Hester as your liaison."

I notice he doesn't call her my partner or even look her way while talking about her.

"She isn't normally involved in homicide, but I felt she would be the best fit for you to get the ins and outs of the city and the case. She, at least, isn't one of the more superstitious officers." He sat back, rubbing his face; his dislike of her was as obvious as her own for him.

"Normally, she works on our special victims' unit. In a city like this, most of those are false reports, but she keeps busy. It won't be a problem to pull her over for this, if you would rather have someone more experienced…"

I looked at her again as she tensed, clearly gritting her teeth. She looked like she was going to put her fist through the captain's face. Her eyes flashed like she was running a computer calculation in her head of 100 different scenarios. Her shoulders suddenly relaxed, and she leaned back in her chair, purposely trying to appear casual. She gazed across the table at me and smiled brightly, which brought to mind a mask keeping her real feelings locked inside. The saying 'the cat that got the cream' popped into my head when she looked back over at the captain.

"Captain Reyes, I know you are approaching these cases like homicides, possibly that they are even connected, but you know where I stand on that. I would be happy to walk Agent Bennet through the case and make my argument for animal trafficking and see if he agrees with my previous suggestion." She met my eyes across the table again and smiled in that very feline way.

The captain scoffed, barely restraining himself from laughing in her face, "I know you have this harebrained exotic animal trafficking idea, but we all agree that this is all the hallmarks of a hit or maybe a serial killer. After what the surveillance team put on my desk this morning, I am even more certain. I'll send over the images from what we have tracked down asap."

His condescending tone seemed like he was excited to knock the detective down a few pegs and get a serial killer on his books. Someone was trying to make a name for himself. The disrespect towards his officer was weird. I couldn't help but wonder why he had even assigned her to the case with me if he held her in so little regard.

"I am sure Detective Hester, and I will get along just fine." Gesturing my hand towards the well-organized evidence board, "She has a good handle on the case. I work alone most of the time, so having someone from here will be great." The detective was watching me with a guarded expression.

Captain Rayes gave a nod in my direction, "If you have any trouble with her, just let me know and I will get you someone else." He pushed away from the table, leaving as abruptly as he came.

I looked at Detective Hester again. She seemed to have a paler, almost green look to her now, like being in the same room with him cost her energy. I didn't particularly like being ordered around like I worked for him, either. I made a mental note to call Shaw after this and berate him for not giving me a better warning about the odious man. "Is he always such a dick?" I asked.

Her head whipped towards me with wide eyes, and she smoothed out her hair before she huffed out a laugh, "That's him being pleasant. Don't pay him any mind, Agent. I follow facts, not crazy theories or wild goose chases."

The detective wiggles her fingers playfully in the air, "The truth is out there, Mulder".

I can't help but smile at the reference to my favorite show growing up. While I loved the idea of it being something fantastical, it always turned out to be explainable...so far.

"I'm good at my job, even if most people here think it's a waste of time. I close cases, even if the captain dislikes me. He still knows I am the best here, Agent Bennet." Alice's mischievous smile crinkled her almond-shaped eyes.

"I thought we were chasing snakes or maybe a snake charmer?" I mimed a man playing a lute her way, thinking of the old movies my brothers and I used to watch. She was studying me, trying to figure me out. Maybe deciding that I wouldn't be horrible to work with? Perhaps I am a little less lacking than she thought. She moved over to the board and grabbed her own set of files.

"Alright, so let's review the case. I have an actual dinner date I don't want to miss…with my boyfriend." She looks at me very pointedly across the table and then smiles.

I stared at her for far too long, processing what she was saying before it finally dawned on me…ohh, so not her girlfriend then. That makes this warm, fluttery feeling in my gut feel a bit stronger now. Maybe I could find some fun here after all.

"Yep, yes, we wouldn't want you to miss out on that." Both of us are settling into our own files to review the facts and hopefully find some answers together. Looking up at her, concentrating on the papers seriously, her lips pursed, it finally caught up to me how long it had been since I had worked with someone, anyone, I could feel comfortable with. I hadn't even realized I was missing it until today, and now I kind of crave the idea.

Chapter 5

Mattie

Darkness was creeping in with the sunset, the swamp-like land surrounding the old two-story house that Alice and I had spent the last three years revitalizing. Now the house was painted black with cedar shutters. A brick walkway wrapped up from the driveway to the front door and wound its way through the gardens. A white fence wrapped the front yard, separating it from the large gardens.

Alice had insisted on some kind of fence since she always wanted a dog and was terrified of alligators wandering in from the swamps and spooking her. The woman carried a gun everywhere and lived with a bona fide monster who killed people but was scared of overgrown lizards in the yard. I had tried and tried to convince Alice that the swamp puppies were the same thing. I secretly loved them, so I would bring home chicken legs for them sometimes.

We had bought the house after it had been uninhabited for over 30 years, and it showed. The first six months had been the two of us cleaning and throwing out everything inside while sleeping in the living room on blow-up mattresses. It had been a painstaking process to renovate the kitchen to be modern, but in our dark color palette. The upstairs was the real priority, with the bathroom and bedroom floors unable to actually hold any real weight. Eventually, through trial and error, we had managed to get all 4 rooms fixed, at the top of the stairs, the hallway split and wrapped in each direction.

Alice took the left with her light, airy, soft bedroom and office, with a bathroom separating the two rooms. My own room to the right with a bedroom overlooking the garden and swamp out into the distance. My bathroom is filled with a large claw-foot tub and plants to make it feel like a jungle. The other room was where I had crammed all my books on floor-to-ceiling shelves across every wall except one, where there was a sort of daybed for the guests we didn't ever have, just in case.

The grounds could finally be seen after many weekends of burning brush and cutting down weeds and trees that had encroached on the house and driveway. It was a small 3-acre place outside the city limits, but it afforded a quick commute into the city and privacy to avoid prying neighbors. I had thought Alice was joking the first time she wheeled out one of Kaida's "statues" from the garage and placed it among the old garden beds. Over time, she trained some vines to grow on it with large purple flowers. Kaida had been way too excited about that. We were down to 5 now after reminding my worst half that keeping them all wasn't the easiest since they weigh a couple of hundred pounds, and after sunup, it was just me and Alice cleaning up after Kaida.

I take great offense at that.

Now that we were alone, I could speak to her out loud without looking like a crazy person,

"Good, you should! You're not the one stuck trying to figure out how to move them around when the morning comes."

She always purred proudly when we passed the statues, so as long as it kept her content, we would keep a few, even if it was a little morbid.

Maybe I am just making sure you keep our figure up. The way you two snack on junk food, you should really be thanking me.

"As someone who needs food to survive, how about I worry about my figure, and you just shut it? I broke three fingernails last time trying to load the damn dolly. Next time, I am just calling someone else."

Dear goddess, could you complain anymore? Fine, next time I will just bite them and then no bodies to have to move...well, at least not stone ones. We could just let the swamp puppies have them then!

Rolling my eyes at her, knowing she is only half joking because she actually believes that soft bodies are less inconvenient than the stone ones.

"Well, we'd better get cleaned up while we can..." I say to absolutely no one and start up the back door and into the kitchen.

It was a small space, but the dark blue lower cabinets and open shelving uppers made it feel a little more spacious. There were always bundles of herbs hanging by the window over the apron sink and an oversized fridge for snacks. The one thing my sister and I could always agree on was that a lack of snacks was never acceptable. I hung the gardening apron by the door, going upstairs for a shower. Although Kaida wouldn't hurt Alice on purpose, it made me feel better knowing that the possibility of accidents was removed. It wasn't that I had no control when the sun set, but Kaida operated more on instinct than reason. Sometimes we were in complete agreement, other times instinct took over, and I wasn't always the nicest. I washed my body quickly and efficiently with my favorite lilac-scented soap.

There was no point in going through all the girly steps just to crawl into bed. Stepping out to wrap a robe around me, I knew that the sunset was quickly closing in now. In the distance, I could hear the gravel crackling as Alice's car came up the drive. A solid oak door kept us inside, where we were supposed to stay for the entire evening.

You do realize that I could leave if I really wanted to, right? I'm basically a goddess. Why couldn't I just flip the lock?

My phone started ringing, and a number I didn't recognize flashed on the screen. "I know that, but you won't because we literally just promised to save Ali from an ulcer and stay at home for now." She huffed quietly but didn't respond. I slid my thumb over the green answer button on my phone while staring out the window. "Hello?" I asked hesitantly. No one called me except Alice, and I could hear her parking her car outside.

"Mattie? It's Hannah from the group…listen, I know you haven't given me your number, but you gave it to Meredith last fall, and she passed it on." Hannah sounded winded and like she was walking quickly. Of course, she gave it to Hannah. Meredith's ex had assaulted her, then he broke into her new apartment in the city and threatened her for siccing the police on him. They had been broken up for a while, but he kept cornering her at work over and over again, stalking her for months. He wouldn't take no for an answer when they were together and certainly didn't after she left him. The police were no help.

Sure, she had gotten a restraining order, but a piece of paper didn't make her any safer. I slipped Meredith my number after a meeting where she showed up with bruises all over her arms and cried the entire time. I could taste the fear rolling off her. Kaida made sure he went away. Her ex left her apartment that night, but he never made it home again. She was free, and my monster was happy, so it was a win-win.

"It's fine, Hannah. What can I do for you?" Trying to get to the point quickly as darkness fell. "Laura's roommate called me to let me know that she didn't come home after the group meeting. We've been calling her repeatedly with no answer. I just stopped by her office; she hasn't been to work either. Neither has that man she was having problems with, a Mr. Dan Reynolds, according to the front desk secretary, who likes to gossip and was a little worried about her." She huffed out a breath, "I am on my way to the police station to try filing a missing persons report, and you said your sister works there. They might not do anything yet, but maybe she has the resources to try and find Laura?"

I didn't remember ever telling Hannah that my sister was an officer. I didn't share in the group. It wasn't therapy for me; it was a hunting ground. However, she found out it didn't matter as much as finding the girl. I drew in a deep breath as the hissing in my head started to grow louder, Kaida pushing forward,

We could find the girl...I would make sure she is safe. Safe from this, Dan. Just like we discussed before.

No. No, we can't because we promised Alice we would lay low. I thought to her while chewing on my bottom lip, worriedly. Laura probably just took off for some alone time and forgot to tell anyone. I knew that wasn't the truth in my gut, but denial was all I had at this point.

You're lying again. You lie to everyone. Mostly, you lie to yourself. Someday you'll realize that the one person you can't lie to is me, and when you are ready for that truth, I'll be waiting.

Her usual snarky and teasing tone, replaced with an aggressive one, made my gut rebel. I rolled my eyes. She was always telling me that I just had to ask for the truth, like she knew me just because she and I shared a body. There were some truths she did know, and I had no desire for her to share. I was happy to keep living in blissful ignorance where I wasn't insane.

"Hannah, I will ask my sister what she can do; it's not much until she is missing for 48 hours. She is an adult after all, try to make a report, and I will ask her to follow up. Hopefully, she will pop back up long before the police need to be involved. She is probably fine, but no reason not to at least have more eyes looking out."

"Thank you, Mattie!" She sounded so relieved. I almost felt sorry for her taking it on herself to find Laura. This girl might have held my sympathy the other day, but I hate that she was worrying Hannah so much. It was just selfish. "No problem. See you Friday." I clicked off the phone and threw it on the bed quickly. The thought of the police station made the FBI agents' face flash before me. He was unfairly good-looking.

Unlocking the door and grabbing my sunglasses off the table next to the door, I yelled down for Alice to come up and shoved them on. As long as I wore these and didn't make direct eye contact, people around me were safe-ish. As safe as you could be hanging around an ancient, cursed creature who could turn you to stone or bite you. Okay, so not at all safe, but Alice never cared.

The transformation wasn't painful as the sun set beneath the horizon, washing over me. It was just like being inside skin that was too tight, and her voice and thoughts being at the forefront instead of my own. The hissing grew louder as the snakes shook themselves free from between my locks. Looking in the mirror over the dresser, that familiar creature stared back with soft green skin, you could still see the speckling of my freckles across the nose and cheeks. Blazing green eyes were covered by my sunglasses, and snakes were writhing like a halo around our face. She looked like me and didn't. Where I was soft with high cheekbones and a Roman nose. Kaida was all sharp angles. Where I would be described as cute, she was a predator, a stunning predator, but death was a guarantee with the fangs that tipped on our bottom lip.

"And now we go hunting…" Kaida hissed out her fangs, giving us a little lisp.

Hold your horses. We have to pass the message to Alice, and then we promised that we would lay low while the FBI is in town.

I say harshly inside our head, so she gets how serious I am about not leaving tonight. "Fine. But then we can go hunting." She moved away from the mirror to grab some clothing out of the closet.

No, we don't. You know what it means to be hunted, and that man we saw at the police station is here to do exactly that.

I tried to picture his face again, his dark hair flopping over his forehead, drawing attention to his crinkles at the corners of his striking gray-blue eyes. Focusing hard so she would mentally see it, I pictured him with his gun in hand and aiming it at us.

You don't want Alice to get hurt, I thought harshly.

Hoping to stress the fact that I was trying my best to keep us all alive and out of prison. Prison would be the end of us and so many other people. We had both decided long ago we would end it before it came to that. It would be best for everyone that way, but neither of us had an actual death wish.

"We could use another statue, and he would make a nice face to admire by the back door with the purple flowers I like! I like Alice. I will keep her safe."

I rolled my eyes and pinched the bridge of our nose.

It's called clematis. I told you that. No, if we turn him into anything, there will be far more of them, and then we will have to leave and never come back. Also, as far as we know, he is here to just do a job, we don't kill innocent people, babes.

She seemed to think about that hard when Alice came up the stairs and turned towards my wing. She appeared in my doorway with her hand over her eyes protectively and a smile on her face.

"Kaida, you have sunglasses on?" She asked for safety purposes. We were always cautious, but Alice had decided years ago that she had no fear of the gorgon. She had held to the promise she would stand by me no matter what.

"I am all good, Allie." She lowered her hand and smiled even more broadly. "Hey sis. Hello, gorgeous." She addressed Kaida, too, and the bitch actually preened, running our hands through the little snakes. She was as vain as could be and loved anyone complimenting her. I guess, being seen as a monster by most, she liked any positive attention.

"So, what's up?" Alice asked, settling herself in the chair at the corner of the room. It wasn't the first time that she came to keep my monster and me company. Sometimes she would read to us, or we would watch shows together. We had learned ways of being together over the years, and the genuine affection my other half felt for Alice was obvious. Not even instinct would get her to hurt our sister.

"It has to do with that favor we were talking about earlier. This girl from the group, Laura, was being harassed by a man at work, and he attacked her in the parking garage by their office. Laura didn't make it home from group the other night. Hannah, the woman who leads it, got a call from her roommate, panicking that she couldn't find her. She asked if you could see if there was something you could do," Kaida said. Her lisp from the fangs was fairly pronounced now as her anger grew.

Alice leaned forward, resting her elbows on her knees, "Technically, she has to be missing 48 hours before I can do anything official, but I can take a look tomorrow and see if there are any signs she might have taken off." She sighed a deep breath out. Obviously, she had more to share and wasn't looking forward to it.

"I was assigned the case with the FBI agent, who was pulling up while we were having coffee. His name is Will Bennet, and he isn't a total tool." She laughed, "We spent a while going over the paperwork, he seems to see my logic in the animal trafficking angle I'm spinning. I even threw in a file on Corbin that I put together last year when we arrested him for importing those weird weeds."

Kaida and I both laughed at her putting together a file on my friend, Lucian. He was a shameless flirt and maybe dabbled in some less-than-legal practices, but he wasn't a bad guy. He had a huge crush on Alice ever since she had busted into his apartment above his family's Voodoo shop and arrested him. There had been some hullabaloo about plants for his shop and how he procured them, but this was New Orleans, and his family was Quarter royalty. A charming smile and a small fine were all it took to make it all disappear. Now he tries to get Alice riled up whenever they cross paths. It was hilarious to watch him push all her buttons like a 5th-grade boy with a crush. One of these days, she might notice that gleam in his eyes and realize it was more than fun and games for him.

"Alright, I am exhausted. I am heading to bed, you two…love you both." She got up, blowing a kiss our way and wandered off to the other wing of the upstairs.

"Good night. Love you too, Ali!" Kaida shouted out. The shower started shortly after. I wish we could come home after a long day and sit down to dinner together, have a glass of wine under the fairy lights we strung up, and talk through our day. Tonight, we needed some space with the past being stirred up for both of us.

Having to revisit what happened to me ten years ago in college, even just the small details Kaida had shared, was enough to turn my stomach. It was horrid to see the physical marks after it happened. I can't imagine having the memories of it, too. Together, Kaida and I made the best of the bad situation and kept each other safe, but we are more symbiotic than we thought we'd be.

There was no one alive in my family line to tell me any different, but the women who stood out were because of the curse, and they all ended up dead, often tragically young. My mother and father died in a car crash when I was 10. It was tragic, too, but thankfully not anyone's fault.

After their deaths, I lived with my sister, Catherine. I was 10 and she was 18, just living her life and working a bartending job she loved. One night, she didn't come home until the sun was up. She sat in the bathroom crying the full day, and I guessed something terrible had happened, but she pretended so well that she was fine. My gut had been in knots for all those hours, the anxiety palpable in our tiny place. Two days later, she disappeared again. It wasn't until the social worker showed up that I realized something worse had happened.

They never told me what happened to her, and I didn't know either until a decade later, when I was walking in her footsteps. She had been cursed, but her other half killed three men at the mental institution she had tried to check herself into. They died of a snake bite, and with no one but a crazy girl in the room, they thought she had done it, but nobody could explain how. She slit her wrists that night and let the facility discover them all together with no explanation for what had really gone down. I wanted to hate her for so many years, but after my own curse, I couldn't help but feel sorry that she had no one to hold her hand.

When I was cursed, Alice had been there. She had washed the blood off me and held me while I cried. She hid me for a week in a hotel off campus while we tried to figure out what the hell was going on. It wasn't like normal people woke up one day and turned into a vengeful creature who hunted men. Kaida made her introduction and filled us in on the curse playbook.

We came to an understanding of what she needed and what I needed. While I had a full-blown panic attack at another voice in my head, a creature of lore taking over my body at night, Alice and her practicality served as a steadying presence. Instead of freaking out, she threw herself into research and writing down everything Kaida knew. Alice was friends with her before she and I had even made peace. Now we didn't keep anything from each other, except what happened the night I turned. Kaida blocked the memory, and I guess I should be grateful. I could have pushed the issue, but there were some things I didn't need to relive. I took the gift of peace over the truth that she offered and got on with my life. Alice had changed her major to Law Enforcement, and we moved on with our lives as we knew them.

My ancestors had not been as lucky; their creatures had driven them mad, and eventually, someone took them out like Perseus claimed to have done all the years before. When I had been cursed, I had two choices - To let the darkness consume me and end up dead like the rest of them or to make friends with it. Kaida and I decided that being friends was better for both of us. So, she taught me, and I did what I could to make the world a better and safer place. It was a darkness that I could live with for now…we both knew it was going to catch up to us one day.

Chapter 6

William

I walked into the station bright and early the next morning, greeting Lorraine at the desk with a coffee tray, sliding an iced vanilla coffee across the top of her desk with a smile. She looked up at me with a surprised gaze and then narrowed her eyes suspiciously, "What do you want, Agent Man?" She asked, her southern drawl deepening.

My smile grew wider, and I shrugged my shoulders. "Can't a man just bring a beautiful woman a coffee in the morning?" Her face turned blank while she reached out and took it from the top and sipped, "A man could, but I'm sure that there is something else you want, agent?" I smiled and chuckled because the shrewd woman saw right through me.

"Can I get those surveillance photos the captain mentioned yesterday?" She looked to the right side of her desk to a blue folder set off to the side, and I followed her gaze, "I might have them, but I am supposed to give them to Detective Hester, and only Detective Hester."

"How about you let me take a peek while we wait for her to get here?" I held out my hand, wiggling my fingers. She took another long drink and then slapped the folder into my palm.

"I didn't give you this, got it?" She turned away and answered the phone's shrill ringing. I winked at her, "I'll make sure Hester sees this right away. I promise your secret is safe with me." I head toward the conference room, flipping open the folder.

The report at the top detailed the surveillance team's account. They had followed the widow, Carol Shanks, to several stores and her home, which she previously had shared with her husband. She came back out with a small duffel bag and a rolling suitcase, presumably filled with her and her infant daughter's things, whatever could fit and nothing else.

Then to Mercy Clinic, a local hospital. A note in the file says they would head there later to try and confirm her patient status. Then she disappeared, not a single trace of where she's gone to ground. There was a phone record with a few numbers highlighted and a bank statement with some notes, but no large payments or withdrawals in the last few months. Reviewing the file, I couldn't see any reason to think she paid someone to get rid of her husband.

The doctor in question that she visited, Dr. Raines, claimed confidentiality in even answering if she was a patient or visiting someone. Carol had reported to the initial detectives who informed her of her husband's death that she had been at a church on Friday, but there was no service at that time. They staked out the church the next Friday morning.

Carol didn't attend, but they grabbed photos of everyone there in case someone was helping her hole up. I can't see why they are so convinced the widow had anything to do with her husband's death. She was a stay-at-home mother who had been attacked by her husband. Based on past hospital reports, it had been viscous and frequent. But she had left, she was out; gone with no other reason to return. She had no notable connection that I could see to any of the other victims and an alibi for not only her husband's death but the other two as well. The only thing suspicious was that no one could find her. Who was she hiding from now that her husband was gone?

I flipped through the photos casually until the last one caught my eye. A woman dressed in oversized tee, jeans that hugged her shapely ass, high leather combat boots, and unique heart-shaped sunglasses, the same woman from across the street that ensnared me the day before. Lorraine and Detective Hester had called her Mattie.

She was talking with a beautiful, dark-skinned woman in a business suit and high heels. She appeared to be handing her something while they talked. Mattie's face was tight, and she had her head angled towards the street on guard. She was watching something out of the corner of her eye. The next photo showed her walking across the street alone, and she looked directly at the camera. The next shot was her rounding the corner; she saw them. How did she spot trained pros so easily? Did she know Carol Shanks? What would all these women be doing at the church midday? Maybe it was just a coincidence, but my gut said nothing was a coincidence about this.

Alice Hester walked into the office with a large smile, a much warmer welcome than yesterday. A sleek French braid holding her mass of black hair back, dressed in another business suit in dark blue, and an iced coffee with a whipped cream top in her hand. She walked up and took a seat. "Good morning, Bennet. How was your hotel…" Zooming in on the table, spotting the layout of photos. Her color drained quickly out of her face, and her coffee fell from her hands, splashing on the floor and soaking her pants and his shoes.

"What is that? These surveillance photos were supposed to be turned over to me. How did you get these?" She whispered harshly and pointed directly at the photo of the woman in sunglasses she had been with the day before, the one I falsely assumed was her girlfriend, noting how visibly rattled she was. I answered.

"I just asked for them. The FBI asked for these in the first place. These are the surveillance photos of the widow of our last victim. Took a lot of effort to find her after her husband was killed. She came back into town and left again just as quickly to go back into hiding. They couldn't find her for further questions, so they started watching the places she said she had gone the week before her husband was killed. One of them was apparently an afternoon meeting at a church. We don't know what for, but maybe you can provide some insight since you know one of the people in attendance? We should bring her in and ask about Carol and this meeting." I tapped the photo of the woman in sunglasses, angrily staring down the surveillance car.

Alice stood silent and frozen, the only part of her moving was her eyes darting towards the door. Watching her as I gathered the photos with one of the women she knew directly on top and tapped it again, holding it up to her, "She was across the street with you. The world is a small place, but that seems too convenient. Who is she, detective?"

Finally, she shook herself free of her panic and grabbed a pile of napkins from the table beside her. Ignoring my question, she started wiping off her pants, reaching for more. She glanced up at me and then went back to wiping the tabletop methodically. "She doesn't have anything to do with a serial killer or a trafficking ring or anything else we might come upon. She might know Carol Shanks, but she is irrelevant to the case." She reached over, snatching the photos, flipping the folder closed, and set it on the table in front of her. I had a feeling that if she walked out of here with those specific photos, no one would see them again.

I didn't want to be the bad guy, but there was obviously something to this, or she wouldn't be so shaken up. After yesterday afternoon, I knew Alice to be professional and sharp. She wasn't the kind of person easily rattled, and now she looked like one wrong move could shatter her. I want to trust her, but I barely know her. Until I do what choice do I have except to ask questions? "Detective, I didn't ask if you thought it was relevant to the case. I asked who she was. How do you know this woman? And what is going on in that church?" I said it with a calm coolness that did not reflect what I was feeling as the knot in my stomach started to tighten, warning me that I wasn't going to like anything I heard next, but I was on the right track. She swallowed harshly and huffed out a breath, not looking at him, "She's my sister."

Reaching past her to grab the folder, I flipped it back open again and spun the top photo around to look at it again. There was nothing in their appearance that connected these two women as family. Between her lack of Asian heritage and different facial structures, there was no way these two came from even one shared parent. "Your sister?" My voice was full of suspicion.

"Yes, my foster sister, Mattie. We grew up and stayed together once we aged out of the system, if you must know. She didn't have anyone else, and neither did I, so we just stuck together." She sat back down in a chair as far from him as possible. "I'm not telling you what is happening in that church, but trust me, it has nothing to do with the case." She leveled me with a serious stare that said she wasn't going to be budged on the point.

Two could play that game; if she wasn't going to help me, then I would just have to check it out for myself. The sudden urge to go now had nothing to do with wanting to see the woman, Mattie, again.

"Why would I need you to?" Trying to sound as casual as possible, "They'll all be there Friday morning, so I could just pop in myself and see if Carol shows up or if anyone knows where to find her. Maybe your sister will be happy to come in and answer some questions I have about Carol," I shrugged my shoulders nonchalantly as I started to round the table to leave and call her bluff with my own.

Alice's whole body tensed, and she glared daggers at me through narrowed eyes. A whole medley of thoughts raced through her eyes, and I was certain that at least once she contemplated just killing me, feeding me to alligators, and being done. "Stop. I am just looking out for their privacy. These women have had enough taken from them. Their safe place shouldn't be another thing." Her glare was a little scary. "It's a sexual assault survivors' group." She bit out, avoiding looking directly over at me.

I had some ideas about the church being a meeting ground for Carol to see the hit man, or maybe that was where she was hiding out. Churches were known to sometimes have places for people in trouble, but I hadn't considered a group meeting for survivors. The implication that her sister was a member of the group gave it a whole new gravity. My shock must have been clear as I turned and faced her head-on. Mattie's face stared out of the photo, still sitting between the two of them on the table.

"I'm trusting you to make sure that fact doesn't leave this room, especially with my sister's face tied to it. If I had been informed about this ahead of time, I would never have allowed them to set up outside the church. I get that we need to know where Carol went, but if these women found out how many, do you think would continue to go there? How many distrust the police already? This isn't right." She was so serious and firm, I found myself nodding along, agreeing while I strode closer. I took the two pictures of her sister from the folder and slid them over to her.

"Anything she can tell us about Carol or the group? Off the record? Maybe there is something we are missing about the group. Maybe someone in the group helped Carol get rid of her husband?" The silence stretched between the two of us as she weighed how much she wanted to tell me against how much she was willing to trust me. I wanted to reassure her that I wasn't the kind of man to harass these women and make their lives worse. I was the kind of man who believed that sometimes justice happened outside the purview of the law, but eventually, people like this went too far, and innocent people got hurt.

"I doubt it. These are traumatized women who lean on each other for support, not to plot murder. This is NOLA. If you want someone gone, there are easier ways to kill someone and not leave a body." I contemplated the fact that she clearly already thought of that avenue, too, which was very different from the bullshit trafficking theory she had presented yesterday.

"And your sister?" It was impossible to hide the curiosity that colored my voice.

"I'll ask her what she knows. Privately." She left no room for argument, and as much as I wanted to see the gorgeous woman again, this new information meant taking a slightly different approach. A softer tone.

A knock at the door sounded, and it opened to reveal a young, fresh-faced, beat cop in uniform, "Alice, sorry to interrupt." She waved him in and used the moment to collect herself. "Did you flag a missing person report for a Laura Turner this morning?"

She looked at him curiously, "It wasn't an official report yet, just a favor. Why?" The kid gulped and looked at me before clearing his throat, straightening his shoulders, and addressing her. "We just got a call from St. Augustine's in the quarter. They have a body."

She looked a little sick. "It was ID'd as Laura Turner?" The officer nodded quickly as Alice stood and started putting on the jacket that was hanging on the back of her chair. She shoved the two photos of her sister into her bag.

"Apparently, yes. From the preliminary ID at the scene. Since you flagged it, I thought you should know, ma'am," She nodded along.

"Thanks, Officer Oliver...You might as well come, Bennet." She gestured to me, "Laura is from the group, too." She started out of the room, weighed down visibly.

"Detective?" Oliver called out.

"Yeah?" She stopped us short, waiting for some worse news.

"The body didn't have an ID on it. Your sister reported it; she is still there with the first responders. They reached out as soon as they recognized her," he said sadly.

She tensed up completely, frozen and contemplative for a moment.

"Fuck…thank you." She started stomping off quickly, with me trailing behind her, trying to keep up. She was clearly concerned about her sister being at a crime scene. Scrambling after her as quickly as possible, "I'm sure she is okay," I said as we slipped into the front seat of my SUV, buckling in and starting towards the crime scene.

She chuckled darkly, making the hair on the back of my neck stand up, "I'm not concerned for her." She turned stiffly to look out the window, mumbling under her breath, "Just everyone else."

Chapter 7

Mattie

The chapel was a huge grand dame in the French Quarter; the site of the historical war of the pews. Both the church and I had seen plenty of bloodshed before, but the beautiful girl draped across the front steps with her head almost sliced clean off was more than I could handle. Laura's blood was a macabre painting across her neck and chest, now drying dark and crusty on her skin.

After being hounded by Kaida for most of the night and spending the rest tossing and turning, I texted Hannah for Laura's address and went to her apartment to find only her unhelpful roommate. I made it clear that I had not been there, and she read between the lines, agreeing to keep my visit to herself. Doing this at night would have been easier, as my senses were better, but the risk of being seen in the Quarter was too high. I would probably just find her at some bar or friend's house, I thought, but there was a growing sense of unease about her every hour that passed.

Her roommate was certain that Laura had just left town and was visiting a friend or maybe staying with a new guy for a few days. Their apartment didn't tell me much, other than I was lucky that living with Alice was better than most roommates. While the common spaces of their apartment were a mess of laundry and dishes, Laura's room was impeccable. Thank goddess for that, because we had gotten a good sense of Laura's smell to help track her down.

Alice texted me Dan Reynolds' address early this morning so I could take a quick peek around. Dan's place was locked up tight and looked deserted. I was starving, exhausted from tossing and turning all night, and desperate for a moment to decompress. I took a break and started in the direction of our favorite shop to get coffee and beignets for my sister, when suddenly I caught a whiff of Laura's clean, lemony scent. Following our nose, those few blocks to the church steps, I was trying to keep calm and focus on the idea that maybe she had come this direction seeking safety or comfort. That thought was abruptly dashed when the coppery scent of blood hit my tongue. Pulling my phone out, I was dialing the station before I had even rounded the corner. Kaida started angrily hissing in my head.

I told you so.

The steps were still draped in morning shadows, shading her body. She was lying like she had been dumped on the steps carelessly. I was so focused on her body that the world blurred around me. It was hard to concentrate on your surroundings when you were arguing with yourself.

We could have saved her. We could have gotten to Dan before he got to her.

"We don't know for certain it was Dan," I thought.

Who else, Little Monster? If you had listened to me last night, we wouldn't be here. We could have done something.

She was right...it was Dan. Who else had this sweet, 25-year-old, beautiful girl upset? She had just left college and was working her first grown-up job when she had been attacked by Dan, but no one there really believed her. She was strong, stubborn, and wouldn't be scared away from a job she had worked so hard for. She had agreed to stay on while they investigated her claims. None of us believed anything would be investigated, but it was her choice.

Something funny happens to time when you are waiting for someone to get to where you are. My mind always seems to wander to places, significant and insignificant. Just over a year ago, Kaida went after a mark I had picked alone. We ended up getting hurt and stuck; if it hadn't been for Lucian, I really don't know what would have happened. More and more, I was taking risks, letting Kaida have full control.

I didn't tell Alice about what happened because I didn't want to listen to the lecture. Now I was trying to make better choices, to think things through, to stay detached, and this happens. Kaida is right, if I had listened to her, then Laura would still be alive, but would we? I'm sure it was only ten minutes before the first officers pulled up, but it felt like hours alone with Laura and Kaida. Sitting a few feet away from her, I watched the city wake up. No one looked this way. I was torn between a desire to walk away and wait for them, but I couldn't leave Laura alone…no matter what happened, she had spent her last hours devoid of anyone who cared for her. I could at least do that now…

The first car pulled up calmly, like they didn't believe the call was genuine, but when they saw the body lying there, the first officer stopped in his tracks and turned green. While he struggled not to lose his breakfast, the other spoke with me. They began questioning me, but once they realized who I was, they radioed for Alice. After a couple more basic questions, they left me waiting by the cruiser while they set up the initial perimeter.

We could have stopped him before. We could hunt him down now and stop him before he gets away.

I get it, okay! Don't you think I feel enough guilt about this? Let's wait for Alice and do this her way for now. I don't disagree with you, but just let her try. She hisses her displeasure and quiets down to pout at me for losing my temper with her, but I can't bring myself to care right now. Suddenly, she perks up inside my head, sensing something coming up behind us. Turning, I could see the large black SUV come to a stop a short distance away. Then Alice was out and barreling down on me quickly with the flustered Special Agent trailing behind. He looked like he got stuck in his seat belt trying to follow her out so quickly. Alice hugged me tightly.

"Are you both okay?" She whispered in my ear.

"No. We are negotiating, but I'm winning." The hissing in my head became louder.

HA! The day you win anything is the day I am dead.

Oh, what a day that will be. Finally, I'll have some peace and quiet. Inwardly rolling my eyes.

You would miss me, little monster.

I smiled, knowing it wouldn't reach my eyes, and squeezed Alice's hand as she stepped back and the Special Agent approached our little party. His jacket was stretched around broad shoulders, and his face was tight with frustration. He stared at me a little too long, trying to see past the sunglasses I always wore. I couldn't harm anyone in the daytime, but it left my eyes a little more sensitive and my gaze a little too bright green to be normal sometimes, so I tried my best to keep people from noticing. He was watching my face closely. Up close, he was far better looking than he initially appeared, too good-looking with combed-back wavy dark hair and icy gray-blue eyes. They tinged more towards blue now that he was actually looking at me up close, and I noticed his pupils dilating slightly. He licked his lips, cleared his throat, and shook out his shoulders, offering his large hand, "Agent William Bennet at your service, ma'am."

He can serve me anytime...

I barely repressed another eye roll while shaking his hand. My creature was born into the world to be a literal man-eater, which means that she should hate any and all men, but to be honest, she had a voracious appetite for good-looking gentlemen in period romance shows. Kaida and Alice loved regency shows and the spicy books that I kept the library stocked with to keep her busy on nights we actually had to stay put.

Hey, no judgment! You love those shows too... I am feeling attacked now. I am going to tell Alice that you are making fun of us, her voice teasing me.

We both knew she didn't actually care about me making fun of her. Taking his hand was like a jolt to the system. As soon as my fingers grazed his, a current shot through me. It was nearly impossible to focus on anything but his blue eyes. "Nice to meet you, Agent Bennet. I wish these were better circumstances." Letting go of his hand, I realized I had unconsciously gotten closer to him. Facing Alice, I watched out of the corner of my eye as he inspected his hand curiously.

"You need me to stay, or can I go?" I really want a few moments to not be surrounded by people, to process all this before I have to call Hannah...to call in a few favors.

"You were just walking by, spotted the body, and called it in?" Alice asked while looking me directly in the eye and nodding as she said each part. The pep in her step and smile on her face from this morning were a distant memory.

"Yep" I popped the p extra hard. I already gave a statement to the first officer on scene, although you might want to check on the newbie. He was having a hard time keeping himself together. Poor kid wasn't expecting this first thing in the morning."

Nodding back to where they stood, holding the now gathering crowd back. She followed my eyes and cringed slightly, seeing the young officer still avoiding looking this way. I know she will make sure to pull him aside and check on him later. Moving to go past her, Agent Bennet reached out to stop me by the arm. His fingers were warm and firm, wrapping almost all the way around my bicep. I stopped and looked harshly at the large hand, then back up at him. He quickly corrected himself and held up his hand in the air instead, my skin still tingling where his hand had been.

"Did you know the victim?" He asked, sounding like he already knew the answer. I nodded before crossing my arms defensively, "Yes, I knew her from around town. NOLA is basically a small town." I was going for casual, but my stomach was twisting in anxious knots. He narrowed his eyes at me and then looked over at Alice, who was watching nervously.

"You just happened to be walking by the murder scene of a woman you knew? The same woman that you asked your sister to look into yesterday? That seems like more than a coincidence. Did you know Carol Shanks as well?" He was walking on thin ice now, and my hackles were up. Neither I nor my monster liked being cornered. He knew too much already.

We could just kill him.

Suppressing a sigh, we can't just kill everyone who annoys you.

What about everyone who annoys you? Whose list would be longer?

Looking over at Alice, I tried to communicate that I did not like how much he knew. She was trying to apologize back with her eyes, and I nodded softly so she knew I wasn't angry with her. An officer called out for Alice, and she and the Bennet looked that way. Alice started to say something about my leaving, but Bennet spoke first.

"Can you please wait here for a moment? I have some more questions."

Chapter 8

William

The cathedral loomed over them, standing alongside Detective Hester. We inspected the body, but I kept an eye on Mattie to make sure she stayed put. Before us lay a young woman, sprawled on the cold stone steps, blood smeared across her skin.

Laura Turner's lifeless form was a stark contrast to the solemn beauty of the smooth stone surroundings. The vibrant red of her dress clashed with the pallid gray of her dark brown skin, highlighting the abrupt end to her existence.

Her eyes, frozen in a haunting gaze, stared into the abyss. There was a subtle tension in her limbs, betraying the sudden violence that had disrupted the serenity of the cathedral steps. The delicate features of her face, now tinged with the coldness of death.

Laura's hands, once elegantly manicured, were now stained with the darkness of dried blood and were at her sides. The killer had left a gruesome message, bloodily etched onto her forearm, the words stark against the canvas of her skin. It hinted at a deliberate act; a macabre calling card left for those who would come to investigate. The air carried the scent of tragedy; the location seemed to accentuate the brutality of the scene. Laura's body was a tableau of unanswered questions and unspoken secrets, each detail inviting speculation into the motives that led to her demise.

I surveyed the scene, eyes narrowed, taking in the details in the beaming sun. "What do we know so far, Detective Hester?"

Alice, her eyes scanning the surroundings, perhaps searching out her sister's face still in the crowd. She replied in a hushed tone, "The victim is Laura Turner, 25 years old. Her throat was sliced clean through, almost far enough to be an attempt at decapitation. Probably the cause of death, but I'll confirm with the ME later. The killer left a message." She gestured toward the cryptic words carved into Laura's forearm.

I leaned in for a closer look. "What does it say?"

Alice hesitated before using a probe to pull up the cloth covering parts of her, straightening her arm so we could read it together easily. "Liar in lace. Whatever that means."

My brow furrowed. Whoever did this was angry, and anger was personal. "Any leads on who would want to harm her? You flagged her before she was officially missing, why?"

Alice sighed, her gaze flickering toward the cathedral. "Mattie asked me to look into her after a member of their group wanted to report her missing. We all assumed she was just with a friend or maybe left town to blow off steam. From what Mattie told me, Laura didn't have enemies; she is just a kid. A man from her office assaulted her in a parking garage a few weeks back. She managed to get away but there was minimal physical damage, so it ended up being a he said, she said kind of case. She was still fighting her way through it.

When she left the last group meeting, she didn't make it home and never reported back to the office the next day. People in her circle were worried and reached out to others. That's why she asked me to look into whether or not she was missing. Neither she nor the man she accused showed up for work yesterday, and no one could get hold of her. I pulled the original case file last night just to look into it, see if there was anything I could do to help. The original case had fallen apart, though. I got the impression that her supervisor believed something happened, but the press would be bad, so the company covered it up."

I nodded, absorbing the information. These cases were hard to prosecute without much evidence. I'd like to look at the original report when we get back, so I can get an idea of what kind of people Laura and Dan are. "So, someone might have taken matters into their own hands."

Alice stood and popped her gloves off before handing them to a tech to dispose of. She was watching him with a serious expression. "So why do you want to talk to Mattie? More questions?"

Raising an eyebrow. "What do you mean?" Glancing over my shoulder at Mattie, standing separate from the gathering crowd. Her arms were still crossed defensively as she watched both the people around her and the officers on the steps. To someone else, she looked like another casual observer, but the tension in her jaw gave her away. While she was stiff and the grumpy look on her face made her unapproachable by everyone else, after that handshake that jolted me to the core, I wanted nothing more than to get back over there.

Alice hesitated again, "My sister, Mattie, found the body of someone she knows this morning. She's got her own shit to deal with, and she doesn't need some FBI agent sniffing around." There was a threat and a warning in the tone. "Do what you want, Agent. She isn't the kind of woman who needs rescuing. So, if that's what you're into, here is your warning that she doesn't need it." I couldn't tell if she was trying to scare me off or just be honest about what to expect from her sister.

"Just give me a little credit, Hester. I'll tread lightly." The two minutes of her acquaintance were all I needed to know Mattie didn't require saving, and if she was, I'm sure she would do it herself. I could talk to the woman about the case or anything else if I damned well pleased. I was about to tell her just that when I briefly saw the worry that was settled on Alice's shoulders. I didn't have any sisters, but plenty of female cousins and baby nieces now. It wasn't hard to understand that after a childhood in foster care, and from what little I had gleaned about Mattie's past troubles, she was protective of her for a reason. From observing their interaction earlier, it was like a goldfish being protective of a great white shark.

When my hand took hers, I knew she felt that same shock; it was in her eyes. For a moment, I felt like there was no one else standing there, and for the first time in my life, I genuinely thought about grabbing a woman and kissing her red, plump lips at a damn crime scene. That would have been awkward as fuck. Especially when she and Alice inevitably beat the crap out of me in front of the other officers. Now I'm here, standing over the body of a murdered woman and having to force my feet to stay still when I want to go back over there. Something unnatural drew me to her, just like the first time I saw her; it was like she was a magnet for my eyes. I couldn't keep from searching for her out in the crowd again, still standing and brooding where we left her.

I took the warning silently because I wanted to work on this case with Alice. I planned on pitching it to Shaw as soon as we were back. I already thought these cases were connected, too much overlap not to be. Choosing to steer the conversation back to the case, "We need to find out who Laura pissed off enough to end up like this."

Alice crossed her arms, a hint of frustration in her eyes. "I'll ask Mattie for more about the guy from work because he is the obvious suspect. We need to bring him in immediately. Her manager should be helpful now that the bad press is a dead body instead of a sexual assault, harder to cover up. We could bring up releasing a statement about the assault and murder of one of their employees."

I nod in agreement while thinking of how to get it done in time to be free for dinner. "Agreed. Let's track down anyone with a motive. And let's look into the message on her arm. It might be the key to unraveling all of this and finding her killer."

"This isn't related to your case, Bennet. You are here for an entirely separate reason." She said, pointing out the obvious.

I scoffed, knowing it wouldn't be hard to get Shaw to back me up on this. "Three men whose only link is a survivor's group, and then one of said survivors ends up dead and sliced up? I don't believe in that big of a coincidence."

As we walked away from the cathedral steps, the shadows shortening as the sun rose higher in the sky. The weight of the investigation hung heavy in the air; a tangled web of relationships and secrets surrounding Laura Turner promised a challenging puzzle. Down in the crowd, Mattie was waiting for us. The sunlight rising above the steeple of the church caught her face; her green eyes blazed brightly, unnaturally green, like shining emeralds. I stopped and stared. Mattie broke eye contact first and looked down. I was still chomping at the bit for the chance to talk to her alone.

"Detective Hester, why don't you go meet with the officers, and I'll ask those questions I have for your sister since we are already here." I left no room for negotiation. It was an order, not a request. Making my way over to her, she watched me without making an effort to meet me in the middle.

Alice looked like she was going to protest and follow me, but stopped short, met her sister's eyes, and briefly tapped her finger next to her eye. There was a lot of silent communication between the two of them. If I didn't know better, I would think they could read each other's minds. Mattie adjusted her shades and rolled her shoulders back before looking in my direction with a mischievous smile.

"You had more questions, Agent?" She asked, her arms protectively in front of her. It shouldn't have been provocative, but her cleavage was pressed up and together, spilling out of her tank top. I forced my eyes back up to her face to see her still smirking; she knew exactly what she was doing.

"Did you know Carol Shanks?" I started with what I assumed was an easy question since I already knew that she did. If she lied about this, it would set a bad precedent for the rest of my questions. She looked around for a moment and then answered, "I did." Not offering anything else. No deeper explanation, but she wasn't lying. She didn't move at all, just staring, poised to strike. It was frustrating; most people overexplained and, in doing so, usually gave away more than they wanted. Not Mattie, she seemed determined to see how long she could talk to me with as few words as possible.

"How?" Reaching into my pocket, I pulled out my little notebook I kept for such occasions and looked at her expectantly.

"How what?" Shifting her stance, she raised a brow surreptitiously. Now she was just being difficult. Why was that hot? She knew what I was asking for, but getting her to answer the actual questions was starting to feel like pulling teeth.

"How did you know Carol Shanks?" I gritted my teeth to keep some of the exasperation from slipping into my voice.

"Well, she briefly worked in my sister's favorite coffee shop." She said plainly, again being deliberate about not elaborating.

Fine. If she wanted to be difficult, then two could play at that. I was going to push and probably piss her off. That was fine with me, though, because she was starting to piss me off as well. "A coffee shop? So, you didn't know her from the Friday survivors group meeting you both attend at St.

Patrick's church over on Camp Street?" She stiffened, uncrossed her arms, and stepped back instantly, going on guard.

"Clematis," she huffed under her breath. She was talking to herself now…that was interesting. Maybe the reason her sister was so overprotective was that she had other issues.

"What was that, Miss Hester?" I asked, more suspicious by the second.

"Cutler." She spat out, pursing her lips. "My sister is Hester. My name is Mattie Cutler. We aren't biologically related," she gestured to herself, "obviously."

She was frustrated to be here. Her friend was dead, and she had found the body, which would upset anyone, and here I was acting like a dick. I tried to reach out to comfort her, but she took a large step back and balled her fists defensively, taking a deep breath and blowing it out slowly. I watched her build back her wall, "Yes, Agent. Carol was in our group after being repeatedly raped and beaten by her piece of shit husband. She was chased and tormented. No matter how hard she tried to get away, he always found a new way to victimize her and her daughter, while the police did nothing. So yes, I knew her, and before you ask, I don't have any idea where she may be, but I hope wherever she has gone is far away from here and she never has to look over her fucking shoulder again." She was tense as stone now. I was going to ask more questions, but I just couldn't bring myself to. I agreed with everything she had said and felt bad that she had to be the one to put me in my place. I swallowed slowly before closing my notebook gently and replacing it in my jacket.

"Did you know Laura as well?" I asked softly. It grated on her, her jaw tight and eyes avoiding me.

"You already know I did," she said, exasperated.

"And it's just a big coincidence that Mrs. Shanks' husband ends up dead, she is missing, and now this woman, Laura from your group, is also dead?"

She looked over my shoulder again, finding her sister bent over examining the body under a sheet and talking with a uniformed cop. I waited to see if she was going to walk away or if I was going to have to wrangle her back to the office to get any answers. Maybe if I had just let her sister handle it, then she would have cooperated, but the second I was standing next to her, this feeling started to take over my brain. It wanted Alice to stay away so I could talk to her alone. She was suspicious as hell, but I wanted to keep talking to her in a way I had never before.

"It's not my job to decide what is and is not a coincidence, Agent Bennet. Now I really must be going, I have some work to get done." She moved around him and off into the crowd of gawkers, all angling to get a view of the body.

"It's Will…" I said quietly. Her step faltered for a second, and she looked half over her shoulder back at me, then she slipped through the crowd and vanished like a wraith.

The crime scene was bustling with activity, a chaotic symphony of flashing police lights and hushed conversations. My instincts were finely tuned by years of investigative work and living with a grandfather who drilled into me that the gut never lies. My gut was tingling, trying to tell me that Mattie and Alice knew more about the murders than they were sharing with me. Alice was trying to watch out for her sister, but I didn't get killer vibes from Mattie, except when she had smiled, then I felt the predator appear. I couldn't shake the feeling that Mattie held a piece of the puzzle, a detail crucial to solving this particular case, at least.

I was fighting an internal battle. Torn between duty and a magnetic pull towards the enigmatic Mattie. I knew I should stay at the crime scene, coordinate efforts, and gather evidence. Yet, the allure of chasing after her was too strong to resist.

With a quick decision, I turned away from the unfolding investigation, footsteps echoing against the warm pavement as I took off after Mattie. As I caught up with her, she was just rounding the next block, walking quickly. Clearing my throat to announce my presence, "Ms. Cutler, just one more thing," I called out, trying not to let her know how curious I was to get to know her better. She turned, her brows rising with surprise. She scrunched her nose slightly, the shadows playing on her delicate features. I saw the green of her eyes shine a little more brightly as she pushed her sunglasses up on top of her hair.

"I'm sure Alice would be more helpful than I could be, Agent. Whatever you need from the group, let Alice handle it. They'll respond better. There are privacy issues which I'm sure you understand, and just a general distrust of outsiders," Mattie replied, her guard was up, but with a flicker of uncertainty in her eyes. She tilted her head oddly, like she was listening to someone else.

"I'm Will, just Will, okay?" I tried to re-introduce myself again, I gestured to the badge hanging from my neck before I slipped it beneath my shirt out of sight. "Let's start over and take what I know about you and the group off the table for a minute."

I watched her reach for her sunglasses on top of her hair and finally look up at me, meeting my gaze with the greenest eyes I had ever seen. They were the personification of the Emerald Isle, which my grandmother had originally come from. They were filled with a mixture of curiosity and wariness. She seemed to be assessing whether I was friend or foe.

Mattie's lips curled into a half-smile, and she tilted her head slightly again. "Will, then." She repeated, her voice wrapping around the letters of my name, sending a shiver down my spine. "What brings you chasing after me then, Will?"

I studied her for a moment, "Listen, I know this might sound strange, but would you mind grabbing a coffee with me after this? I could use a break, and I'm curious to hear your perspective on what happened to Laura. You might see some connection that we're missing." Mattie's gaze lingered on my face, quietly contemplating. "Or we don't have to talk about the case at all. You keep popping up in my investigation, and that usually is enough to put me off, but for some reason, I want to know more about you." She took a step closer. "Curiosity killed the cat, Agent. As you just stated, against your better judgment, you can't say why." She stepped out of the shade of the overhang balcony and came into my bubble of personal space.

I felt a flush rise to my cheeks as I smiled back, surprised by her boldness, but I didn't step back. She was trying to throw me off, and it was working. Mattie was like a tornado, and I was being pulled in. She smelled lightly of vanilla and lilac. If I thought I was attracted that first day, this was much more powerful. Up close, she had blazing green eyes that crinkled at the edges when she smiled. A soft dusting of freckles across her high cheekbones and nose. She was tanned, the lines on her shoulders said it was from lots of time in the sun rather than a natural coloring. The sunlight highlighted the red in her hair, pulled up, and it showed off her shoulders and slender neck. She knew she was beautiful, confident in her skin. I wasn't going to contest that; I loved a woman who liked herself. Now that I knew Alice wasn't her girlfriend, there was no reason I couldn't get to know her better.

"I…well, I just thought maybe you saw something, you know, that could help with the case. Something that could help to find who hurt Laura?" She raised her hand slowly and pulled at the chain that held my badge, lifting it out of my shirt and putting her hand over it and my heart.

She chuckled, a low, melodious sound that seemed to dance in the air. "Help with the case, huh? I'm sure Laura will be avenged soon enough."

Caught off guard, the word avenged stuck out. There was a curious way of wording it, and it came across as a thinly veiled threat that made me more curious about what she knew about the dead girl. But this was the first time I had talked to her since I was drawn to her. Even through my shirt and the weight of the badge, my chest burned where her hand still rested while she spoke softly and stared at him through her lashes. Sure, she was a little rough around the edges, and while I might not know her whole story, she was the kind of woman who was worth the effort to get to know.

"You could help me here, Mattie, you could help your friend, get her the justice she deserves." Clearing his throat, "Or maybe I just think you are stunning, and I want to get to know you. Is that crazy?"

Why the hell was I stuttering like a 15-year-old? She made it difficult to swallow past the nerves as she looked up at me through her lashes.

Mattie silenced me by holding up a finger, a mischievous glint in her eyes. "Will, justice means different things to different people. Maybe you should focus on your investigation instead of running around after me? Aren't you busy solving crimes, catching killers, and all that?"

I was usually composed in the face of interrogation, but she was throwing me off. I shoved my hand through my hair nervously and found myself trying to think faster than my mouth, which kept saying the wrong thing.

"I… Well, I just thought a break would be nice. And maybe you have a perspective on things that could be helpful." That wasn't stupid at all.

Mattie leaned in, standing on her tiptoes, her lips dangerously close to my ear. "Perspective, huh? Will, I don't think you're ready for my perspective. It's a dark and twisted place."

I huffed out a breath and shifted my weight back, taking her wrist in my hand. I pushed her away lightly while leaning my weight back onto my heels. She was trying to rile me up, and I didn't know if that made her more intriguing or threatening, but it was working.

"You've got quite a way with words." She smiled, "Keeps things interesting, don't you think? Ever think I might just be more trouble than you bargained for?" She quipped slowly.

Brushing my thumb along the inside of her wrist, I could feel her pulse thrumming wildly. She wasn't as calm as she appeared to be.

My cock throbbed with the thrill of the challenge and intrigue, combining with her soft vanilla and lilac scent. I was way too interested in Mattie Cutler, and my brain was flashing a DANGER sign in bright neon. "Trouble? I'm a federal agent. I thrive on trouble. It's practically my middle name."

Mattie arched an eyebrow, a playful glint in her eyes, and a sly smile. "Agent Will Trouble Bennet has a nice ring to it. But don't say I didn't warn you."

I matched her playfulness, "Well, Mattie, it seems we're both playing with fire here. What's life without a little risk?" She stepped even closer this time, pressing her softness into my chest. There was a wall behind me, so I had no room to move. The air was charged with an undeniable tension. "True enough, Agent Trouble. But let's not forget, sometimes fire can burn."

I dropped my eyes to her lips and couldn't help but smirk. "I've been burned before. I always come back for more."

Mattie laughed, a throaty sound that sent shivers down my spine. I realized we were standing in the alley, practically chest to chest. Nothing about our position said professional. "You're a bold one, Agent Trouble. I like that."

I was a ball of amusement and desire now. She was the most exciting woman I had talked to in years. This back and forth was so fun, it was easy to forget what she meant to the investigation. "Well, Agent Trouble, you might just be in for more than you bargained for."

I couldn't help but feel a surge of excitement. "Bring it on, Mattie. I'm up for the challenge." The banter flew between the two of us so quickly it was like my mouth had a mind of its own, well, that, or I was only thinking with my other head. It would all catch up eventually, but not while I was standing here, drowning in the emerald eyes of the engaging Mattie.

Nervous excitement rode me as she spoke, unsure of how I had lost control of this whole situation. Wherever this conversation was heading, now I had lost and was just along for the ride at this point.

"I'm willing to take my chances," I said louder, voice steadier now.

A sly smile played on Mattie's lips, her tongue quickly darting out to wet her lips before breaking our long eye contact. "Well, I'll think about it. But I'll need a way to contact you, if I decide to."

I stepped around her, finally releasing her wrist so I wasn't against the wall anymore. The space gave me a minute to clear her scent from my head. Fumbling in my jacket for my wallet, I extracted a business card and handed it to her. She took it gracefully, her fingers brushing against mine. The surveillance photo I had seen of her earlier, taking something from the other women at the church, popped into my head; it had been a business card.

"I'll be in touch, Agent Trouble. Until then, try not to let the darkness catch up to you. NOLA can be dangerous in more than one way."

With that, she walked away, leaving me standing in the bright light of the morning sun, but feeling like all the air had stopped and was suddenly cold as she stepped away. My mind buzzed with anticipation. As she disappeared around the corner, I couldn't shake the feeling that I was on the verge of something both thrilling and dangerous, and the desire to kiss her lingered in the air like a maddening, unanswered question.

Chapter 9

Mattie

I paused at the furthest point that I could still see back to the mess of flashing lights, seeing the outlines of Will and Alice bent over Laura's figure. I know it was wrong to look back and wish we had murdered someone, but if it could have prevented her from ending up dead, I would have jumped at the chance no matter what it cost me. Knowing what we would do to save Alice...there was no line I wouldn't cross. Saving Laura should have been no different.

Turning away finally, people filled the street doing tourist things, my chest was heaving, and my cheeks were blistering as I thought through everything Will and I had said. The back and forth was electric, not to mention the rush of warmth I felt in other places. I was fighting the urge to fan myself, or swoon, or whatever woman in Bridgerton did when a man was even the least bit forward. Dear god, he hadn't even started it. I was driving that bus. Straight off a cliff... Then it was as if Kaida up and took over my body and stupid mouth, pushing me to say the dirty thoughts inside our head.

Oh no, little monster. You know I can't do that. That was all you, and I must say, I am so proud.

Groaning loudly, I was more and more horrified over the fact that I was downright seducing the man a block away from a dead body. Even Kaida was becoming more intrigued by Agent Trouble.

Agent Trouble...think of all the trouble that man could get us into.

She was tempting fate by pushing like this. "No, no, no! Think about all the real trouble that man could do to us, he is here investigating murders. Murders we committed, remember? He's standing over Laura's dead body while you're plotting about how we are going to track down Dan and make him pay. Honestly, we'll be lucky to keep our head on our shoulders, young lady!" I mumbled that last part to myself. Trying to chastise a creature with little to no conscience was impossible.

We will track down Dan the dick and make him pay for what he did to poor Laura, and then we can play with Agent Trouble. Whatever happens after, at least we can guarantee to die with a smile.

I quickly unlocked my truck, climbed in and slammed it shut behind me. Sitting back in the seat, trying to calm down. I caught my reflection in the rear view mirror; my eyes were so bright they were glowing, and I was flushed from chest to cheek. I pulled the business card he gave me out of my pocket and ran my thumb over the embossed letters. Shaking off the temptation I tossed it to the floorboard on the passenger side.

"No. We will not be calling him, and we will leave the police to find Dan. Alice will make sure justice is done for Laura."

We have different interpretations of justice, little monster. We were not created like this for nothing. I know you think it is you who tempers me, but have you ever considered that you use me as an excuse? I am a comfortable scapegoat for your urge to act in ways that you think Alice will disapprove of.

Kaida was right. As much as I hated to admit it, sometimes it was easier to let her have control and claim it was all her, rather than acknowledge that we agreed more often than not, especially to Alice… I was torn right in half. Torn between doing what I wanted and what I knew was the right thing. Right now, the right thing would be to let Alice do her job, to stay away from Will, to never go back to the group. So why did all those things make me feel like I was going to throw up?

"We have different interpretations of most things, Kai," I said, staring into the rear-view mirror like it was a way to look in her eyes through my own. Backing out of the space and slamming the truck into drive, I headed towards home, determined to drown myself in so much work at the house that we would have no reason to cause trouble for my sister to be worried about.

Pulling into the driveway 20 minutes later, I realized that Hannah was still looking for Laura. Pulling out my cell to call her, I took a deep breath. I climbed out of the truck and leaned over the hood. The burn of the truck's metal hood stung my skin. It was a good way to keep focus. I was listening to the ringing on the other end, silently wishing that she wouldn't answer, giving me a reason to chicken out and avoid telling her the bad news. The line clicked on, and Hannah's voice cheerily answered. "Dr. Raines, how can I help you?"

Closing my eyes, disappointed, I took a steadying breath. "Hey Hannah. It's Mattie Cutler. Are you with a patient right now?"

"Oh, Mattie! No, I'm free. Did your sister have any luck finding Laura? I was so sure we were all overreacting and the girl would show up in no time. That's the way of New Orleans. Especially when you are young and not tied down. Sometimes people worry for nothing while you're out having a grand time." She chattered happily, and I let her go on for a few more seconds, not wanting to interrupt her wishful thinking. My skin was growing tighter, and the pit sitting in my stomach got heavier as I tried to think of a gentle way to tell her the news without bungling it and just blurting it out in the worst way. My signature move.

"Hannah," I said sharply. "Hannah," I tried to say it more gently. "Laura is dead." I cringed at myself. Blurting it out had not been my intention. This was uncomfortable, and I just wanted to get it over with.

The light breeze carried the scent of the gardens through the air while I waited for her to process. There was dead silence on the phone. "Hannah, did you hear me?" Suddenly, I could hear her gasping for air. I had bungled it. I gave the woman a heart attack or an anxiety attack…signature move, alright.

"What happened?" She asked shakily, her voice raspy like she was crying now.

"She was murdered. Sometime in the last 24 hours. My sister is on the case, and I'll tell her everything we know about this Dan guy from what Laura shared with the group. They'll figure out what's going on soon, I promise."

"Good…that's good," she whispered more to herself than to me. Suddenly, she gasped, "Mattie, we need to have a meeting ASAP. We can't have the women finding out through the news what's happened to one of us." I rubbed my hand across the back of my neck. I hated going to the usual meetings. An impromptu one that's sure to be filled with tears and hugging sounds like literal hell. I couldn't leave Hannah to deal with this by herself, but she would need to do the talking; sensitivity was clearly not my thing.

Understatement of the century. If I am a sword, you are a battleaxe.

"I'll call a couple of girls I know and ask them to spread it to the rest of the group. Hannah, I'm really sorry. I know you were worried, and it turns out you were right to be." I sighed heavily. "I need you to do something, okay?" I needed information from her, and this isn't exactly the best time, but who knows when I will get another?

"Call Carol Shanks. Just check on her. I'm not saying she's involved in this, but her name came up today, and I just want to make sure she's safe."

She needs to stay out of town, both for herself and her daughter, until the FBI is done here. If Will has a chance to question her about the days leading up to her husband's death, I don't need her telling him that she gave me her home address.

Silence fell over the line again before she quietly replied. "I'm not going to ask questions I don't want the answer to. My gut is never wrong. I just wish I trusted it more often. I'll see you soon, Mattie…don't do anything before then, okay?" Then the line disconnected.

I stared at my phone for another few seconds before opening a message from Alice. It was a photo of Laura's arm with words carved in it. Liar in lace. My blood boiled at someone violating her body in such a way. As if killing her wasn't enough? And calling her a liar? Anger grew inside, silently doing its best to will the sun to set early to unleash my monster on the city… eager to hunt Dan down. Trying to breathe through it, in and out deeply, I attempt to channel the anger into something productive. I walked over to the shed, gathering the house-painting supplies, and started on the garage we used as an extra storage space. I'd paint the whole damn thing if it would keep me busy enough to drown out the loud hissing in my head and give back at least some semblance of control.

I painted a whole side of the garage before my hands started to cramp and my arms ached. The painting got sloppier; it was splattered all over the trim and ground, maybe with more covering me than the building. Between Kaida hissing in my mind so loudly and this red haze of anger refusing to go away, I gave in to my frustration and threw the paint brush into the bucket and screamed into the empty sky. It tore out of my throat no matter how hard I tried to contain it.

All I could see was Laura sitting in that damn chair, wringing her hands nervously while sharing her story, or smiling sweetly while she set out her stupid cookies. Those stupid, delicious cookies. Whomever hurt Laura had basically decapitated her and then desecrated her body, dumped her like trash…what about the world has changed in the 3,000 years since the beginning of the gorgon curse? Nothing.

Someone had taken advantage of her, abused her, and then violently murdered her. In the end, Laura was the one punished, having her life taken before she even really got to live it. Even now, thousands of years after Medusa, victims are those who pay the price. The anger was all-consuming at this point, and when the tears slipped down my cheek, it startled me for a second. I couldn't remember the last time that I cried.

I screamed again and kicked the paint hard, watching it flip and splatter all over the grass. My judgment may be clouded, but I don't care. What I promised Alice would always matter, but I was making a promise to the universe for Laura now. The world had failed me, and now her. I wasn't going to just let it go. "We are not going to fail her, too, Kaida."

We won't fail her, little monster. We cannot right the wrong done to her, but we can get her the justice she deserves. Kaida tried to reassure me.

Our shared anger dissolving in determination and the focus needed to do what we knew to be right.

I don't want to agree with her if it means going against Alice, but there was no way I could let this go. It didn't matter that Alice and Will were on the case. Only one form of justice would do for Dan, and I was the one to dole it out, consequences be damned.

Chapter 10

Mattie

The sun hung low over the labyrinth streets of the French Quarter, casting eerie shadows upon the cobblestone. I had left before dark with my sunglasses and oversized hoodie in the passenger seat. My phone rang again. Alice had called five times already, but there's no way I'm going to explain what we're doing. Throwing the truck in park, I grabbed the hoodie and pulled it on in preparation for the change. My sunglasses are resting in the front pocket for now. My senses heightened and would get even sharper once night fell. We had to find Dan for Laura. We wouldn't kill him, but we could make sure he was found faster. Allowing Alice and the law to handle him.

The last of the sun's rays slipped behind the ocean, and the transformation washed over me painlessly. We pulled the hood up over our snakes and put on our sunglasses. The curse granted power and ferocity, but it also brought a relentless hunger for vengeance. Dan had wronged Laura, and now we would hunt for him through the silent alleys and deserted squares of New Orleans. We'd make sure he knew what fear felt like. He was going to pay for what he had done to Laura.

The hours slipped by as we searched fruitlessly. The frustration gnawed in my gut. Dan's home stood empty with no sign that anyone other than the police had been there. Alice's business card was still stuck in the door jamb. She must have come here right after leaving the church. His office was abandoned as well. He had vanished without a trace, leaving no trail for us to follow. Kaida's frustration grew into a gnawing fear. It took a minute for our minds to catch up with our instincts. Someone was watching us.

My ridiculous idea of a disguise was basic, but it worked. It disguised the snakes that were lightly tickling the back of my neck and ears. We wore the sunglasses, even in the dead of night, as a precaution against the sudden appearance of other people. Other than a green tinge to our skin, we looked normal enough from afar in the dark, but I still didn't like the feeling of being watched, no matter the distance. Neither did the monster,

Be careful. Someone's following us.

"Of course. It is I who sensed them first, but hush now or they may catch us," Kaida whispered.

Fine, I'll just shut up since you know everything.

Being sassy wasn't helpful at all, but I liked giving her a taste of her own medicine… A shiver ran down our spine as unseen eyes watched us, cold and malevolent. Every shadow seemed to shift and writhe with hidden menace; every sound echoed with ominous intent. Quickening our pace, heart pounding in our chest.

Then, as if by providence, I turned the corner and stumbled upon an old friend casually sitting on a sepulcher in the cemetery. Dark-skinned with long dreads, he smiled my way from the darkness. Silver rings on every finger, a piercing through his eyebrow, several in each ear, and highlighting his smile in the shadows was the glint of a hoop through the center of his bottom lip. His pitch colored eyes flashed in the shadows, recognizing us. Kaida breathed out harshly, relieved to find ourselves face to face with Lucian. His gaze lingered on us with a mix of amusement and curiosity. He was a welcome reprieve; teasing with Lucian would help Kaida's frustrations.

"Well, well, Mon petit," Lucian said, his voice low and playful. "What's a gorgeous creature such as yourself doing out prowling the streets again. Should I be concerned, or are you simply out for a midnight stroll?" He was teasing us, but she purred. She was always thrilled to see Lucian and his complimentary personality.

You know he is like this with everyone. You aren't special, babe. I teased, knowing how vain she can be.

Kaida chuckled at his teasing tone as he bowed mockingly and reached out a hand pulling us closer. A sense of comfort washed over, making the cemetery feel less void of life.

"Oh, you know me, Lucian," She teased, matching his banter with ease. "Just taking in the sights, enjoying the ambiance of the city by night. What about you? Are you here to keep me company, or do you have some other nefarious purposes tonight?"

Lucian's eyes twinkled with mischief. "Oh, I assure you, my intentions are entirely noble. There was someone following quickly and quietly behind a beautiful young woman strolling around NOLA, so I had to make sure they were safe…from you," He quipped. With a grin, he jumped down to stand at our side. Lifting our hand, he kissed the back gently. "But if you require some company, I'm more than happy to oblige. After all, it's not every day I get to flirt with a beautiful gorgon in the dead of night."

Warmth spread through us despite the chill in the air, a sense of camaraderie born from years of shared experiences and encounters. Lucian had discovered my secret quite by accident, but being born and raised a native of New Orleans, he wasn't one to be scared of monsters. We had been hurt during a hunt and were just about to call Alice because our DNA was all over the crime scene when Lucian appeared. He barely blinked at what he saw, just shooed us off with a promise to meet me at Murphy's the next morning. I never asked what he did with the body, and he never asked why I killed him, but no one ever came knocking at my door about it.

The next morning at Murphy's, we had a lovely breakfast as he told me his story, quickly becoming friends. His grandmother had been a real voodoo practitioner and taught him that the monsters you can see are far less dangerous than the ones you can't. She was a lovely woman who was buried in the very cemetery we stand in now. Lucian hadn't cared one bit once he understood why we do what we do. He offered to help haul statues to various cemeteries and out onto the swamp when Kaida would get carried away.

"Flattery will get you everywhere with me, Lucian, but Mattie is a harder sell." She winked at him playfully. "Did you get a good look at who was following us?"

Lucian's grin widened, his eyes alight with mischief.

"Ah, pas de chance. I was too busy following the woman of my dreams. You are too irresistible, my dear," he said, his voice laced with charm.

He waved those long ring-covered fingers at her, "A woman of mystery and danger, with a heart as wild as the night itself. Tell me, Kaida, do you ever tire of being so captivating?"

We both laughed at his flirting. This is why we loved being around him in either form. We weren't a monster to him, no matter what we'd done. "Never," Kaida whispered lightly. "But enough about me. You are being extra charming tonight. What is the occasion?"

Lucian bowed theatrically before taking a seat upon one of the headstones around them, a playful twinkle in his eye. "No occasion needed," he said with a grin. "But enough talk, charm, and beauty. Tell me, Kaida, what can I do to assist? Are you in need of a partner in crime, or simply a friendly face to watch your back?"

Considering his offer for a moment, my mind races with possibilities.

If Lucian can help, we would be stupid not to let him, Kai. He has more resources than we do.

Lucian was not just a familiar ally, but a kindred spirit, someone who understood the dangers that lurked in the shadows and the thrill of the chase. "We could use all the help we can get, Lucian," she finally replied with a sigh, grateful for his offer. "But promise me this: no matter what happens, you'll be careful. Someone killed one of the girls in my group…My Friday group."

He studied her before reaching out a hand. We took it, and he squeezed our fingers reassuringly. I had told him years ago, shortly after the infamous breakfast, what happened to me and explained the awakening of my curse. It was only fair to give him the truth after he cleaned up our mess. All flirty banter washed away, and he just looked with those caring, dark eyes.

"I'm sorry about your friend Mon Cher," he said softly. I couldn't meet his gaze anymore without crying. She wasn't my friend; I didn't even try to be hers. I ate the cookies she brought and listened to her story without offering even one kind word of support. This was the first time I felt guilty about my behavior at the meetings. It wasn't really sadness, but guilt, that ate at me now.

"The man who assaulted her has disappeared, and her body ended up on the church steps, almost decapitated. If he did this, then the justice Alice can provide might not be enough, but we… Mattie wants to do this her way. It might be up to us, regardless of her wishes."

I am trying to be better, Kai. Alice has made more sacrifices than I can count to be our friend; to love and shield us. She asked us to do something for her. She asked us to protect our home and safety for her. Is it too much to ask for us to grow?

Kaida's frustration and guilt rise. I know she loves Alice too, and only wants to be a protector. Lucian nodded solemnly; his expression was serious.

"I promise both of you," he said, his voice tinged with sincerity.

"I'll watch out for you and your group, and I'll do whatever it takes to keep you safe. But in return, you must promise me the same. Promise me you'll be careful and that you'll never lose sight of who you are, no matter how deep the shadows may grow; you both need to protect each other." He reached out his other hand to pat my cheek and grazed the side of one of the snake's bodies, quickly pulling his hand back, narrowly missing a nibbling fang.

"You aren't a monster, Kaida, don't let this world turn you into one." Lucian always pushed the bounds with the gorgon, but he was truly unafraid of us and had never been bitten. Thank the Goddess for that, because he grew on you, like moss on a stone. I couldn't imagine him not being around. He kissed our hand on the back of my fingers and smiled again.

Meeting his gaze, a sense of determination burned behind our eyes. "We promise, Lucian," Kaida said, her voice steady. "We will be careful. Thank you for always being there for us. You are one of the few people we know who likes every bit of us, even the dark bits."

"Oh, Mon Cher, what are we without our dark bits?" He chuckled. Together, we stood beneath the watchful gaze of the moon, two souls bound by fate and circumstance.

Chapter 11

The pursuit was going nowhere, so I went to the only person who could make me feel like I wasn't a total failure, my best friend. Even if I couldn't go inside and hug her, just being close calmed me inside. Hiding in the shadows, parked across the street, I knew if I got out of my truck and walked up those steps and went inside the police station, that I would find my sister slumped over her desk, asleep. It would be covered in Post-it notes and cutesy pens with a cold cup of coffee next to her. She shouldn't even be on shift tonight, but she wouldn't leave until she had answers for Laura's family. The doors to the station opened, and Agent Bennet walked out of the station. His mind was elsewhere; he didn't see my truck as he approached his SUV. Before I could even begin to talk Kaida out of it, she threw the truck in drive and began following him discreetly.

Rolling my eyes at her, *this is a terrible idea...*

"I only have good ideas. I just want to watch him a little," She spoke into the darkness of the truck, shadows playing over her features as the streetlights illuminated the space briefly as we drove.

Yeah, cause that's not creepy. We should be avoiding him like the plague right now.

This little crush was going to be the death of us...I thought hard about when Anne Boleyn got beheaded in that show, The Tudors. We had been watching it obsessively, and it was the part Kaida had hated. Since Alice and I had taken history classes in high school, we knew how the story went down, but Kaida had been caught off guard and had loved Anne. The off-with-her-head part always struck a nerve.

"That was rude. Agent trouble is a mild inconvenience, not the killer of millions of people... or that pompous asshole, Henry." She huffed, turning without using her blinker.

Hey, Blinker! The last thing we need is to get pulled over. I get that you think his banter is fun, but we could be killed if anyone sees you.

"Do not be a backseat driver, Mattie..." Our fingers wrapped harshly around the steering wheel, and she looked into the rear view like she could see me too. "He did seem considerate and kind...Maybe we should stick to a coffee date instead. I will call him," She threatened, reaching for the phone in our jacket pocket.

Do NOT call him. Dear goddess, you are a pain in my ass... between the fang lisp and the green skin, I think the date would be awkward as fuck.

"And you are what? A ray of fucking sunshine? I can't believe you just made fun of my lisp...you know I am self-conscious about that." Kaida rolled her eyes and stuck out her bottom lip, pouting.

I might not be a ray of sunshine, but I seemed to be the only one in this relationship who didn't have a damn death wish. I would keep making fun of her lisp, green skin, and anything else I had to exploit to make sure we kept our head attached.

Arguing back and forth with her had given me a migraine. It felt the same as banging my head against a brick wall. We followed him back to his hotel, hesitating now. I was torn between a desire for vengeance and those feelings he gave me earlier. In the alley, Kaida had been talking dirty in my head the entire time. It was basically impossible to say the words I wanted, rather than what she thought loudly in my head. While I could try and pretend that we were only interested in following him to see where he was staying, I would just be lying to myself. We got ourselves out of the truck, leaving it parked in the alley, and climbed the fire escape on the side of the building to get to the rooftop. Once up there, we scanned the open windows. There were only a few with the blinds open. We got lucky. We had a perfect view down into the Agent's room just as he came inside. He tossed his keys and badge on the table next to the door as he flipped the light on.

Kaida giggled and bit her bottom lip with those sharp fangs, thinking back to his soft gray blue eyes and full lips. Yeah, she wanted to devour agent trouble, but not in the way I was thinking, which was more of a problem than I needed. Fuck it, if it was going to be a shit show, then it would be MY shit show. I pushed for control, and surprisingly, Kaida let me have some. Usually, this was her time, and I only did this for emergencies, but this was close enough and better than letting her engage the agent herself. I pulled out my phone, intent on arranging a meeting for the following day.

Looking through her eyes, I guided my fingers across the phone screen. I'm not sure why, but I wanted to see him again badly.

"Oh, you know why, but keep lying to yourself, little monster. It's very entertaining to me." Rolling my eyes again, I typed out the message and hit send before I could second-guess myself.

Mattie: On second thought, maybe a coffee wouldn't be so bad…but if you order tea, I'm out.

That was casual, I think. I saved his number in my phone as a new contact and changed the name. The phone buzzed with a reply quickly.

Agent Trouble: Who is this?

I scoffed, wondering how often women texted him about getting coffee. The Viking in a suit? Probably fifty a day. This could be a fun chance to mess with him. Kaida smiled, reading what I typed out, and I couldn't hold myself back from grinning too.

Mattie: Oh, Agent, I'm hurt. How could you forget about me? What are we to do with you?

Inside, he turned on the lamp next to his bed. I could see him staring at his phone with a goofy but endearing smile as he typed his response. His response came through in three separate messages in quick succession, a hint of nervousness on his face as he tried to find the words he wanted.

Agent Trouble: Hello Mattie…we could get coffee tomorrow
  -and talk like normal people
  -and of course I wouldn't get tea on a date

I smiled at his reply. Normal people. If only he knew what was texting him. Watching him slide off his tie and undo the buttons of his shirt, I flushed, suddenly flustered. When he looked out the window, the light illuminating him from behind gave me a front row show. I could see the dusting of hair across his chest, a trail leading down…Shaking my head, I want to blame Kaida, but even I could admit he was attractive, classically rugged. "Yummy. I love it when I am right." Kaida teased, admiring the view too. I clenched my thighs together. Kaida sighed and leaned against the wall next to the rooftop door.

Mattie: Yes, I want to. I don't know why, but I want to see you again.

Why had I admitted that to him? He sat on the edge of the mattress typing back. Kaida loudly exclaims, "You should invite him back to our place for sex!" I blushed so hard it would have been noticeable even with Kaida's green-tinted skin.

Agent Trouble: I think you know why, but I won't pry.
  -Want to know something funny?
  Ignoring Kaida as she tried to take over again, I typed back.

Mattie: What? You already changed your mind?

I wasn't going to admit out loud that I found him adorable. His slight stammer when he was flustered had charmed me more than it should have.

Agent trouble: No! Of course not. I was going to tell you that I saw you the day I arrived, with your sister outside, and I idiotically thought that you were together.
   -As a couple.
   -I thought Alice was going to kill herself laughing at my expense!

Smiling, I looked up from my phone to his room, where he was pacing around holding his phone, his shirt draped open. Our eyes lingered on his chest. We had to stop now, or we were going to find ourselves in his room, and I wouldn't be able to totally blame Kaida for it. "That's because you like him… Mattie and Trouble sitting in a treeee," She sang to herself.

Are you freaking 8?

We should leave now. Accidentally killing the man wouldn't exactly help the situation. Kaida whispered, "No. I am ten…Mattie, you know when I was born." She spoke as if concerned my brain was deteriorating. Kaida really didn't get sarcasm when it was directed at her. Usually, it went right over her head. She often thought like a 10-year-old with no social skills. If I were the Ego, then she was the Id. I decided to see if I could get more information out of the Agent so I wouldn't have to push Alice for it. What's the worst that could happen? He decides I'm a true crime buff? Maybe really upset about Laura?

Mattie: Any new leads on Dan Reynolds? If he did this, it's going to be hard to find him.

I wondered if he would give up anything I could use to get to Dan first. He was scowling now and lay back on the bed, his shirt open and splayed out on either side of him.

Agent Trouble: You sure know how to kill a vibe, Mattie.
   -Why don't you leave that up to me or your sister?
   -The best thing you can do is stay out of this and let us handle it.

Well, he's not an idiot. He won't give me anything on Dan, but nothing he can say will get me to stop.

Mattie: If you really think I'm going to walk away, you didn't get a very good impression of me. You don't understand what she went through, but I do. I am not going to leave it be.

Agent Trouble: I know I don't know what you both went through, and I imagine it bonds people together. I get why you want to help her, but this man, if it was him, is dangerous.
   -Will you meet me right now? You pick a place, and we can talk. You want to talk about you, I'll listen. You want to tell me about Laura, I'll listen. We can talk about anything but the case.
   -I don't like you being alone tonight.

Kaida scoffed and pulled back for control again. She was frustrated with him, by him. Just frustrated in general, so I let go and gave her control again.
   It's not like I could tell him that I wasn't ever alone. I always had someone to keep me company. There were several hours till dawn, and unless his favorite color is green, I don't think he would take it well if I showed up for a date as a gorgon. Kaida started to text back when my phone began to ring. Alice's face, sticking her tongue out at me, appeared on the screen.

She isn't going to give up; you might as well answer.

I felt our shoulders drop as she swiped across the answer button and raised it to our ear. "Hey sis," Kaida's signature lisp carried the final s further than needed.

"I know you guys aren't at home, Kaida. You might not have promised me anything, but you know Mattie did when she said you guys would lay low and stay out of trouble. Someone triggered the alarm at home. I was about to head that way, but got called out to Mercy clinic instead. Dr. Raines had a note on her car this evening in the parking garage." From the sound of the echo, she was in her car now. She sounded worried and pissed off.

"What? Is she okay?"

Calm down, Kaida. Focus. We can't do anything if we are busy freaking out.

While I assured her, I was silently swearing to the gods that if something else went badly today, I'd quit life.

Alice sighed, "She's fine, but I'm talking to the captain about assigning a protection detail to her. The note was a threat, a creepy message like the one on Laura's arm. She was pretty shaken up."

"Thank you for calling. We will head home now, so do not go there after the hospital. I can handle anyone there if necessary."

"What if it's Agent Bennet? Alice asked. "He seemed to be too interested in Mattie this morning. He left early today. Plenty of time to make it out to the house." There was a lot she wasn't saying. I'm sure Alice had warned him off, thinking it was the best for both of us, but even now, I was reluctant to leave the rooftop and stop flirty texting with Will.

"It is not him." Kaida bit out as he pulled the curtains mostly closed. We could still see him stripping off his shirt and walking towards the back of the room.

"And if it is? There's no more room in the garden…especially for such a large statue." She sounded concerned but was trying to lighten the mood.

"Is that a comment on his size or my inability to control myself?"

She laughed, "Well, he is a big man. I don't know that Mattie and I could move him by ourselves, and you conveniently always leave us with the cleanup."

"Well, it is not him, unless he can break into our home and take a shower at the same time," She huffed out.

There was a very long pause before she giggled, "Oh, and how do you know what he is doing right now? Are you spying on the Agent? Which one of you had that idea?"

"We both know it was Mattie's. She just can't stay away...I was helpless against her nagging. Sometimes it is better to let her have her way.

You guys are both bitches...I'm not friends with either of you anymore. Tell Alice she is my least favorite sister now.

Kaida giggled and rolled her eyes, "The sun is coming up soon. We will go home, check out what's going on, and text you when it is safe. Mattie says she loves you!"

"Sure, I will go back to the office after this and wait. Be careful," Alice replied. Hanging up the phone, I started to feel the slight heat under my skin, telling me the night was coming to a close. She looked one last time at the hotel window and slunk down the fire escape, walking along the empty sidewalk towards my truck.

He wanted to meet me tonight, not me AND my monster. To indulge in flirtatious encounters could spell disaster for us both. The hard part was that it would never be just me, and I can't imagine a world where anyone was to be our third wheel... I knew I had to refuse, to retreat into the shadows before my curse was revealed. As much pull as he had over me, he was someone who got to walk in the light while I was relegated to the shadows. It wasn't all bad, but there was no point in fighting fate.

With my heart aching in our chest, I let my mind drift while Kaida drove towards the house, her mind consumed by the ever-present threat that loomed over us. Even as we hunted Dan, I knew that something worse might be hunting us.

Chapter 12

William

Walking into the police station the next morning with another coffee tray in hand, I smiled warmly at Lorraine sitting at the receptionist desk and set one of the cups next to her. She was talking on the phone to someone, but smiled back and covered the mouthpiece, whispering a thank you. Nodding, I started for the detective's office at the back of the bullpen. Officer Kemp, a younger blonde beat cop, was coming out of the back room with a dark and stormy look on his face. "Good morning, sir." He said, a little tightly. He straightened his spine too much and smiled, but it was fake all the way around, and didn't reach his eyes.

"Morning, Officer. Is Detective Hester in yet?" He looked at the coffees in my hand, inspecting the one covered in whipped cream for the detective, and sighed. "Since she never left, I'd say so. If she would just drop this crappy case, maybe she could have a life outside the office. Well, if that sister of hers would let her." He was rambling and oversharing. As he mentioned Mattie, I glared at him.

"Detective Hester is a talented officer and is essential to this department. I am sure she can manage her time and family just fine." Officer Kemp narrowed his eyes at me, a red flush of color flooding across his face and neck in anger.

"Of course, Agent. She is very talented." Before he can say anything else rude and condescending about his superior officer, I push past him, jostling him with my shoulder on the way.

I was a little shocked she hadn't gone home at all. I assumed she would be right behind me when I left the night before. If she hadn't gone home at all, maybe she hadn't heard from her sister about how I had practically begged her to meet up, and she had ghosted me. I knew even last night that I was pushing too hard, but there was just something about Mattie Cutler that drove me past boundaries. Boundaries like chasing after a woman whom I had been warned to steer clear of by not only her sister, but herself. Boundaries like not chasing women when I was supposed to be chasing a serial killer. Boundaries that I blew to pieces when I was in the shower the night before, jacking off to my memory of her gorgeous green eyes and her smart-ass smile like a teenage boy.

Pushing open the office door to the darkened room, I saw Alice lying across the sofa with her arm thrown over her eyes. There were folders and files spread everywhere with tons of papers pinned directly to the wall. She appeared to have run out of room on the two large white boards. I could see some of the crime scene photos from the church on the table in front of her. The file on Laura seemed to be what she was pouring over before she fell asleep. I cleared my throat so as not to startle her with my presence.

"Brian, I don't want to fight with you about this anymore. I am not moving anywhere, and you aren't coming to stay with me either," she huffed out. Clearly, she thought her 'friend' Brian had come back to keep fighting with her.

"Totally understand. You should never live with someone unless they bring coffee, can pick up their laundry, and don't act like a twat waffle when you don't do what they say. Isn't the officer still living at home? Seems a little young to settle down," I said jokingly to lighten the mood, but I was still aggravated by the anger and disrespect in his voice.

Alice drug her arm off her face and sat up with a groan, "I thought you were Brian."

I lifted a hand to my chest, faking a wound like I would when playing with my brothers' kids, "I'm wounded, Detective…. I'm far better looking…and not a twat waffle."

She picked up a wadded piece of paper and threw it at me with a chuckle. She smiled and turned away. "Fine, if you're going to assault me, then no coffee for you."

Walking to the large table, I put down the carrier and picked up my drink. Alice pouted for a second and then looked around the empty room conspiratorially, "Fine, you're a handsome crime-solving genius. Now, share the coffee?" She whispered. I handed hers over with a self-satisfied smirk. I wasn't going to risk not giving her the coffee, but it's always nice to start the day off with some fun, and to my surprise, I found Alice fun. "Why are you sleeping here anyway?"

Alice drank deeply and set it down, pushing her hair back.

"Little problem at the house. So I slept here instead."

What kind of problem would mean she needed to camp out in this office while Mattie was dealing with it alone? What if she got hurt and couldn't call me or Alice?

"And left your sister to deal with it alone?" I asked, trying not to sound concerned or intrigued when I was both.

Maybe she hadn't been ghosting me last night and was too busy to reply. She laughed quietly.

"There's no problem that Mattie can't handle…she has all she needs to keep herself safe."

I studied her for a moment. She seemed a little hurt by the idea of her sister being able to handle anything alone. I suppose that no matter who you are, it's nice to know you can lean on someone and they can lean on you. Mattie wasn't the type of woman to lean on anyone. As if summoned by his thoughts, Mattie appeared with a knock on the door. She walked in with a smile and her hands filled with a bag that smelled sugary and a coffee that had enough whipped cream and sprinkles that he wasn't sure it could be called coffee anymore. Unlike every other time I had seen her, this time she walked into the room with a blinding smile, lips painted bright red, her hair down and flowing over her shoulders. She had no walls, no defenses up, and it was beautiful.

"Allie bug! I come bearing gifts and…" She stopped short when she saw me, and just when I thought I could kick the idea of this woman, she ruined it all by blushing deeply. The red stain started on her cheeks and flushed beautifully across her chest. I was a sucker for a woman blushing, and Mattie turned the prettiest color.

"Hello, Agent Trouble." Her voice was as soft as the pink spreading up her neck. I couldn't hold back my smile as it stretched to match hers.

Alice looked between her sister and me with concern written all over her face. "Agent Bennet, could you give us a moment?" She asked. Gathering up my coffee and going to the door, "Of course, I'll go bug Lorraine to see if my office sent those records requests yet." I walked out, but the door was still ajar, so I sat in the seat outside the door and prepared to eavesdrop like a 13-year-old boy outside a girl's locker room.

Chapter 13

Mattie

I set my peace offering on the table in front of her sister.

"The house is fine. I reset the alarms and checked all the points of entry. Nothing but the electronic alarms were triggered. Someone tried to get on the property but didn't make it past the driveway. They must have gotten spooked and took off."

Alice didn't say anything, crossing over to the table and digging into the bag of beignets.

"Well, thank the gods for small favors. Spooked by alarms is better than scared to death…literally. I thought for sure I was going to be getting in a workout in the garden this morning." She shoved a large bite of beignet in her mouth, the powdered sugar dropping on her already rumpled button-down shirt.

I chuckled at her and moved to the table covered in crime scene photos. A photo of Laura staring up into the sky with dead eyes was on top. Her story wasn't going to get any kind of happy ending. I'm not sure when it was that I started trying to bargain with the gods for any kindness. I know personally they aren't capable of it, but I would trade anything to go back to that last meeting and walk out with her. Alice stood watching me, her hair falling out of her braid, her clothing rumpled, her face drawn and pale. She needed to go home and shower, and just as I was about to insist, she coughed on some powdered sugar.

"So, you and the agent, huh? Something happened last night when you were being less than reasonable?"

Without meeting her eyes, I respond. "You know that would be a terrible idea as much as I do. Kaida is an incorrigible flirt, and I wanted to make sure she didn't get carried away."

Oh yeah, Mattie darling...it was me who was texting all flirty with the Agent last night.

Kaida's voice was full of humor. Well, it was your hands, darling, I thought to her, emphasizing the word darling the same way she did.

I can't even blush, so if I am the only one attracted to the agent... then why are you that color?

Alice smiled. "Whatever you say, Mattie...just know that he is still here investigating, trying to justify connecting Laura's case to the possible serial killer."

Which is why we should do the sensible thing and avoid him. He can chase the ghosts of this case for a few weeks and then head home so I can be free to track down Dan and get justice for Laura, if Alice hasn't accomplished it by then. "I did have an inkling about that. I'll watch my back, and other parties are watching my blind spots."

She studied me for a moment before connecting the dots, "Oh, has Lucian taken an interest in crime fighting, or just trying to talk his way into your pants again?"

I tried but failed to hold back my chuckle. No matter what I said, she wouldn't believe that I never slept with Lucian Corbin. The man was the definition of tall, dark, handsome, and charming as hell. We were both huge flirts, and he was one of those physically affectionate people, like a friendly stray. He was one of the few people I could stand being touchy with me. Naturally, people assumed that we had a past or even a messy present. He had his reasons for never entertaining the idea, and our relationship had evolved to be more like siblings.

"There's a meeting today. I'm going there right after this. Hannah called to tell everyone about Laura before it made the news. It will shake up a few members, so hopefully we can get ahead of it if anyone needs extra support." Alice got up and started flipping through papers, looking for something, "Dr. Hannah Raines from last night? Yeah. It would be helpful if I could talk to someone about where Laura went after the last meeting, or maybe someone knows more about her personal life."

I was shaking my head preemptively, "No one is going to talk to you if you come in like a police officer. I could probably get a few of the girls to talk to you outside after the meeting. You can't bring the agent." The large and imposing man couldn't help but put off a law enforcement vibe, and most of the women in our group didn't have a good experience with law enforcement or men.

Alice handed me a file and started re-braiding her thick black hair for another day on duty. I flipped it open to see pictures of Hannah's SUV and a copy of her statement.

"The threat was a note card left under her windshield wiper before someone dumped a bucket load worth of what I am hoping is animal blood. The note card was too damaged to read the writing, but they were processing it anyway in case there were fingerprints or DNA left on it."

Alice was looking away as she continued to finish weaving the braid ends through her fingers.

"She implied in her statement that it could be a threat from her brother or father." Sighing, she tied the end off.

I knew both had molested her as a child, and she had testified against them years ago. Her father had gone to prison, but her brother had been relegated to juvenile detention and released at 18. She had no idea where he was and had not heard from him in several years.

Over the years, I had heard some of the details from her at the group meetings, but reading it so plainly was painful. Hannah was one of the few people I considered a friend, but really, we knew very little about each other. That was my fault. I could have shared bits and pieces and still saved my anonymity, but I chose to remain invisible for myself. She had been trying to convince me to do therapy with her for years, but she didn't know that therapy couldn't help me process what I didn't remember.

Hannah didn't need to know that the men who assaulted me were long dead. I had gotten justice for myself without even knowing. It was the first thing that happened when the curse was triggered. Alice watched me read the file and then slide it back across the table. The silence stretched out between us.

"I don't know what you want me to say, Alice." Crossing my arms, I wouldn't look at her. "They should both be dead for what they did to her…"

"I know, but they have been punished…not in your way, but that's not always for you to decide. From what I gathered, Hannah has made her peace with the past, and that's what matters."

I know she's right, that in some ways, punishment isn't always black and white. Alice loved black and white answers, while I loved gray. Gray was like a comfy blanket. Grey was guiltless. She knew I had little control over whether I stepped away or not. I started back toward the door.

"What makes you think it's me who decides anything?" Alice stood closely behind. "Just be safe. I can't stop the train here…"

Nodding, I walked to the door, noticing it was still slightly open. I closed the door behind myself as I exited. Agent Trouble was scrolling on his phone with a coffee on the floor next to his chair near the door. He looked entirely too good for this early in the morning, with his messy dark hair swept back, his face covered in an appealing stubble from not shaving for a couple of days. He was missing the usual tie, and his white shirt had the top few buttons undone, apparently settling into the more relaxed air of NOLA.

"Have a good day, Agent," I said, smiling.

He looked up at me with a serious face. No sparkle in his eyes, no cute dimple in his cheek, just flat "professionalism," and I hated it.

"Have a good one, Ms. Cutler." All the warmth from earlier was gone as he quickly looked away again. I tried to catch his eye to talk more, but he just leaned back in his chair and went back to whatever he was doing on his phone, his dismissal obvious. He was the ultimate in hot and cold. I was shocked at how he could sound so formal, but I just smiled and walked out. I had better things to do than worry about a grown man's feelings. Reaching the main hall, I looked back, and he wasn't typing anything now; he was watching me with a dark look in his eyes. A shiver ran across my skin as I turned away and moved out of the building faster.

What are we running from? Kaida asked curiously.

I'm not sure I know anymore.

As soon as I got in the truck, I dialed Hannah's number, the ringing drawn out and annoying.

"Hello, Dr. Raines' office," she answered.

"Hey Hannah, it's Mattie. I just talked to Alice, and I wanted to check on you." The silence stretched out, "Hannah?" She coughed into the receiver, "You're calling to check on me?"

I'm a little insulted that she sounds so shocked that I would call just to check on her…I'm nice… Sort of.

"Yes…I just…well, you had to talk to Alice about your family, and I know that must have been hard. I wish I could do something." I huffed the last part while I reached down to roll the window down. The fresh breeze coming off the water is just what today needed to chase off the stuffiness of the weather.

"I wish there was too, but I don't need your kind of help, Mattie." Her voice was calm and cool while my heart jumped out of my chest. She had asked questions at the last meeting, but I had convinced myself she was just fishing.

"I don't know what you mean, Hannah…I just meant I wish I knew some words of comfort, but we both know that's not my strong suit."

Her chuckles echoed in my ear, "Mattie, I'm not a dumb woman. A dumb woman would have missed you talking to Carol after her last meeting and quietly getting her address. A dumb woman would have missed you talking to that girl, Amy, last year, who stopped coming after her ex was killed in a mugging in the city. A dumb woman wouldn't have questioned why, not once in two years, you haven't shared anything about your reason for being there. I'm not a dumb woman, just one who cares more about you than your actions."

Somehow, in all the time I had been watching the group, Hannah had been watching me more closely than I suspected.

"Hannah, I can explain…" No, the hell I can't. I don't know why I said that…there is no explanation she will believe. I was about to lie my ass off when Hannah spoke again.

"Mattie, just know that when you need me, I'll be there. Until then, stay safe, okay?" The call disconnected. I just stared at the phone in my hand. Stay safe? That's it? She heavily implied that she had pretty solid evidence that I was a killer, and she is choosing to ignore it? What the hell just happened? Hannah knew about me…well, at least the human part, and she wasn't going to do anything?

See, I told you she was a little bloodthirsty.

Maybe Kaida was right about the Doc after all.

Chapter 14

William

After Mattie left, I had a lot of questions about what they were up to, so I sent a text to another agent back at headquarters, asking for whatever he could dig up on her and her sister. As soon as I sent the message, I felt sick with guilt. Alice had filled me in on the report about Dr. Raines at her office the night before, but we couldn't find any evidence that the threat was connected directly to Laura's case or any reason for Dan to go after the doctor. Security footage showed someone in a hoodie enter the garage, leave the note, and leave. Other than a shadowy figure, there was nothing to point to a certain person. They had officers tracking down the doctor's brother, just in case.

After hours of pouring over files, phone calls, and three pots of terrible coffee, Alice and I were fed up with Daniel Reynolds. He had contested the accusations from Laura, and it seemed to have been swept under the rug. It didn't seem there would be any reason for him to keep going after her. We couldn't track his phone, and he hasn't used his credit cards in a week. He wasn't at home, hadn't been to work, and had no cars registered under his name. More dead ends. The whole police force was looking for him but had turned up nothing.

It was mid-afternoon when Alice checked her phone for the 100th time, sighing harshly. She got up and started to pack up her stuff.

"I have to go," she said.

"Home?" I asked, since she had slept at the office last night and hadn't yet left. She sighed and rubbed at the back of her neck, trying to work out a knot, "I wish. No, Mattie and Hannah are having a group meeting to talk about Laura, so I'm meeting her at a coffee shop around the corner from the church to get more info after."

I started to put on my jacket. "Great, maybe we'll catch a break. Perhaps someone else has an issue with Laura…"

She was staring without blinking, looking apprehensive. After a moment, she finally blinked, winced, and mumbled, "You can't come. Mattie said I couldn't bring you along, specifically."

I tried not to look put off by that. Alice clearly wanted to discourage me from talking to her sister, but this was my case, and I wasn't going to do that without good reason.

"If this has to do with our investigation, then I need to go." Whether I had a thing for Mattie or not, she was not going to interfere in this case. Alice responded sharply, "My investigation. Laura's case is a local PD matter."

"Not anymore. I turned in my evidence about the case to my boss, and he spoke to the police chief. The FBI will be taking the lead on the investigation from here." I didn't want to pull rank, but I wasn't going to back down on this. Alice looked like she wanted to scream. Or punch me. Or both.

"Excuse me? So, you just railroaded my case and swept it out from under me?" I held back a sigh and kept my eyes on hers.

"I sent the file on Laura up the chain. Based on my initial observations, my boss wanted a file opened on your sister as a possible suspect. I told him that I wanted you to remain on the case, that you could remain impartial and professional if you were allowed to stay." I hadn't told him anything about Mattie. If Mattie was involved, then Alice would do whatever it took to get her out of it. Better to keep her close, where I could keep an eye on her.

Alice threw her coffee in the trash can and walked out without another word. I followed, but the guilt I felt about how I spoke of Mattie sat like a weight in my stomach. The drive was filled with silence and tension. Alice pulled up and got out of the car without a single word. She sharply motioned for me to stay in the car and be good, cracking a window for me before walking to the cafe. The car beeped, locking me inside like a badly behaved dog.

Outside the coffee shop, I could see Alice, Mattie, and Dr. Raines. Mattie hugged the doctor when she walked up to the group, but her smile was tight and forced. She met my gaze in the car and nodded once before ushering everyone inside. They went inside and sat at a large table near the window with a few other women. They all sat chatting solemnly while Alice took notes. My phone ringing brought me out of my daydreaming stupor, Tom's desk number popped up, and I answered.

"Hey, Benny! I got the info you wanted, and boy was it a doozy." Tom sounded so excited, so it was probably a successful fact-finding mission. My guilt grew and started to choke me as I swallowed hard. I hoped that there was nothing to find regarding Mattie Cutler when I messaged him this morning.

"Okay, hit me." I tried to sound casual.

"Alright, Matilda Cutler, born Matilda Wallace, March 30th, 1993. Her parents both died when she was 9. Car accident. Sister took custody of her; she was only 18. Killed herself about a year later in a mental facility. Lots of weird stuff in the local paper about that, but the file is sealed. After that, she bounced around foster care for a bit. Spent 6 months at a state university before she dropped out and changed her name to her mother's maiden name. Then she was basically off the grid. No credit cards, no phone bill, no home in her name, no car, literally nothing. Kind of suspicious, considering."

It was a shitty way to get the info, but it wasn't like I was getting anywhere with either sister on getting the real story. Eavesdropping on them this morning left me with more questions than answers. I was hoping that maybe she was talking to Alice about me, but now I had this gut feeling that Mattie was more involved than I could imagine.

"Considering what?" I was afraid of the answer. I'm not sure I really want an answer at all, and I didn't like snooping like this. Looking through the window, Mattie was silent, leaning back in the booth with her arms crossed across her chest. She was just watching her sister with a dark, concerned look in her eyes. She glanced out the window and looked straight at me like she could sense me watching or sense me talking about her.

"Well, her roommate, Alice Hester, reported her missing that first year at college. According to the campus report, it was the same night four guys at the college went missing from a party. Everyone assumed she had gone missing with them. She turned up a week later with no memory of that night, supposedly, and they never found those four guys. She and her roommate were questioned multiple times, but no evidence was found. The case went cold."

I swallowed the rapidly growing lump in my throat, starting to connect some pieces and wishing very much that I hadn't opened this can of worms. There was no putting it back now.

"So, they never found any connection to her and those men, other than that she was reported missing the same night?" It was college, people pop in and out, some people decide not to come back. It is weird that four men would decide not to come back at all at once.

"According to the police report, that's a no. The police were suspicious, but with no bodies and no crime scene, there was no hint as to where they could have gone. It was hard to connect four guys disappearing to a girl who was a hundred pounds soaking wet and maybe 5'5. It had to be a coincidence."

I wasn't as sure that it was. After knowing Mattie and Alice, I could tell that nothing was impossible for them. But would they kill four men and lie about it for 10 years? Could this be why Mattie was in the survivors' group?

"What about after that?" They both left their college and did what? How did they end up here in New Orleans and so involved in this case now? I couldn't stop wondering if maybe the connection was more than it appeared to be. I don't think that Mattie would have hurt Laura, but I also can't say for certain that her being killed isn't a result of something else she's involved in.

"Then nothing. She's a ghost. A legal ghost. Pays her taxes, although she doesn't file a W-2, so no idea what she actually does for a living. She has a driver's license and a Social Security card with her legal name on it. Nothing else. I had to dig deep to find all this info. Someone worked hard to make sure she was hard to find. You think she is the killer with the snakes?"

I pondered how much to share, but Tom was still an agent, a desk agent, but still. "No, just an anomaly in the case I wanted to get a clearer picture of."

Everything was coming together, but not in the way that I wanted it to. Was it possible that Carol Shanks had hired Mattie to get rid of her husband? Was that what she did for the group…or, maybe they worked together to go after the men who attacked them? I can't believe that Alice would be a part of that, but I saw the look on Mattie's face outside that church. She would do whatever it took to keep those women safe. I decided to try and get off the phone before Tom could pry even more details out of me.

Suddenly, there was a sharp rap on the window. Jumping in my seat, Mattie stood just outside the car, watching me through those heart-shaped sunglasses. Hanging up quickly without saying goodbye, I rolled down the window with an easy smile that I didn't even feel. I started to say hello, but she interrupted.

"I work at a library. I catalog and repair manuscripts. All legal, just commission work." My smile fell, and I stared as she crossed her arms and leaned on the car door. Shit. She had heard at least part of the conversation and now knew I was suspicious of her and invading her privacy. Not the best look for a guy interested in her, or as an investigator.

"Mattie…I'm sorry. You've got to understand, we have to look at everyone in an investigation like this, and having a big gray area around your life makes us look longer and harder."

She nodded without breaking eye contact and giggled to herself. I'm not sure what was more disturbing: that I wanted to kiss her, or that I needed to bring her in for questioning. I barely restrained a low groan when she cutely bit her bottom lip, "Agent Trouble, you are really living up to your name. If you had questions, you could have asked. Can I pose a question to you?"

She was smiling, which made me nervous. She should be pissed off, not laughing. I thought I could guess anything she would ask, but nothing prepared me for what came out of her mouth.

"Want to get breakfast tomorrow?"

Trying not to swallow my tongue, I was stunned, speechless. My jaw dropped. She asked me to breakfast. Not anything else? For some reason, whenever she was in front of me, it was like my brain froze. She looked over her shoulder at her sister, who was leaving the cafe and heading toward us, "Monty's, tomorrow morning at 8."

She waved to Alice and then disappeared around the corner while I was still trying to wrap my head around what had just happened. Was I going to meet a possible serial killer for breakfast, or finally get to sit down with the woman who had been consuming my every thought since arriving in New Orleans?

Chapter 15

Mattie

I wanted to spend the entire night searching for Dan Reynolds again. After talking to Hannah today at the cafe and watching her struggle with her demons, I wanted to vanquish some of those for her, too. But instead, I had stayed home, locked up inside, watching over my sister. Alice had slept the previous night at the station and was truly exhausted. I, and my other lovely personality, had decided that staying put tonight would be best. We had both cuddled up on the couch watching Netflix until the sunset, and then Alice dragged herself up to go pass out in her room. Unfortunately, that left a lot of alone time to argue with Kaida.

I think this is going to be a lot of fun.

Arguing with her on whether we were courting danger by having breakfast with Will, to trying to suss out how much he knew about us, wasn't worth the waste of breath. When he looked at me through the window earlier, I could see the worry and guilt written on his face. I knew I had to go, to find out what he knows. After overhearing part of his phone call in the SUV yesterday, I knew he was at least assembling some of the pieces. He wasn't a stupid man, so it wouldn't be long before he at least guessed part of what was happening. Unless he was super into believing in myths and monsters, he probably would just think I was a typical psychopath. No matter what, I couldn't allow any of that to come back on Alice.

Monty's was near the water and had the best beignets in the city, with the advantage of not having the huge crowds that were always in line at Café du Monde. Give someone any kind of clout on Instagram and watch the crowds roll in...

I was sitting at a small corner table with my back to the wall when the ridiculously handsome Agent Bennet walked in. He met my gaze with his stupid, bright eyes and a dumb grin on his face. It was impossible not to smile back when you saw him, seriously, impossible.

Smile back Mattie. You have terrible resting bitch face.

She was right... I did, but I didn't need a reminder that I sucked at being normal.

"Agent. I was hoping I hadn't been too vague when I said Monty's. I figured someone at the station could point you in the right direction."

He shook his head, disturbing his hair, before pushing it back and taking the seat across from me.

"Just Will and just Mattie, okay?" He pulled his chair closer to the table and looked at me seriously. He had tired, dark marks under his eyes.

Maybe he stayed up late thinking about us?

I had taken extra care this morning, redoing some of the braids that ran through my hair, before pulling it half up and securing it with a silver hairpin shaped like a snake. Anytime Alice found something related to snakes to wear, she bought it for me. At first, it had been a joke to try and be lighthearted about the situation we were both trying to understand, and then I loved it, so she kept it up.

"No problem at all." He seemed very wary now, guarded, and was fidgeting in his seat like he couldn't get comfortable. I picked up the menu and looked at it to keep from staring at him, "The beignets here are the best in the city...Alice and I get them often."

Do you get them often? You sound ridiculous. Going to ask him if he likes the weather next?

I tried making small talk, but it's never been my strong suit. Usually, I ended up saying something off-putting or rude. He must have been trying to figure out what to say, too, because he just held the menu in one hand and stared at me over the top. The waitress came by and took our order. Two coffees and two orders of beignets. She was cheery as usual when she patted my shoulder, "Hey, you!"

"Hey Sabine," Her smile broadened, lighting up her whiskey brown eyes.

"I was wondering if we would see you today. Lucian left a package for you last night at closing and asked me to make sure it got to you. I'll grab it really fast and bring it with the food," I cringed at her mentioning Lucian in front of Will, but it was too late now.

Glancing over at him, there was confusion on his face. We frequently left packages or notes around the city, and Lucian Corbin was well known locally, so it was easy to pass them along that way. When I looked back at Will, he had arched one eyebrow up and looked more curious, less guarded than before. After the waitress walked away, he finally spoke up.

"So did you kill Dan Reynolds?" He asked bluntly.

"No." I looked up at him and answered succinctly.

But we are going too, Kaida singsonging in my head.

I didn't even blink at his accusation. He asked if I HAD killed Dan, not if I was going to. There it was, that lovely shade of gray I call home. Looking back at my menu, I fought a smirk as he continued to just stare at me.

Setting down his menu, "No? Just, no? Most people would be appalled at lying to an FBI agent and being accused of murder," he said quietly, folding his fingers together and leaning forward on the table. His eyebrows were scrunched together over his blue-gray eyes, a mixture of concern and frustration.

I just couldn't help myself; I had to mess with him. Looking over the top of the menu briefly, I raised it to cover my smirk before answering him. "Most people would lie to the FBI even if they didn't do what they were accused of. You guys don't have the nicest reputation. If they did do something, it's not like people walk into your office and say, 'excuse me, I've committed fraud and killed my friend Joe.' So, I don't think you're making the point you think you're making." I tried to laugh lightheartedly, but it was coming out strained.

Reaching for the water on the table, my heart was starting to race. While I knew I couldn't turn in the daytime, Kaida could make herself known when I was panicked, usually by making our eyes glow brightly. It was too unnatural for people to write off. Usually, her droll commentary was just a pain, but today at least, it felt like she had my back. His watchful gaze was intense and off-putting while I waited for him to make the next move.

His gray-blue eyes felt like they were digging into my mind, "You're looking for Reynolds, too. You think he killed Laura. We haven't found a single trace of him, so my question still stands. Did you kill him?" He asked, totally ignoring my attempt to lighten the mood.

Well, Agent Trouble, you are no fun if you are not going to play at all.

No, he is not being fun at all. Whether I liked it or not, I plan on honoring my promise to Alice, but if Mr. Reynolds crossed Kaida's path, I couldn't be responsible for her actions…and I certainly wasn't going to apologize for it. "My answer is still the same, agent, no, but I do think he murdered Laura." I paused to look around at the tables near us.

"I know he did, and so do you." Setting down my menu, I leaned forward to rest my elbows on the table, getting closer to him.

"I didn't kill him, but that's not to say I don't want him dead. That's my curse, Will, I can't let things like this go." Anyone watching would think this was more a date than an interrogation, which was what I had actually been hoping for. A little info on my past, and Agent Trouble was done flirting. His gray-blue eyes clashed with my green as he absorbed what I said and thought it through.

"I came to New Orleans to investigate three men's deaths, two of which I can prove are connected to your Sexual Assault Survivors group, and now Reynolds is missing, and a group member has been killed at the same time. All that is adding up to a serial killer, and from a Law Enforcement perspective, you could look good for at least a couple of those deaths..." He huffed out the final part and broke eye contact to look down at the table.

"Just tell me you're innocent. Tell me you had nothing to do with this. I don't get murderer vibes from you, but maybe my judgment isn't so sound right now."

Oh, he likes us. He doesn't want us to be evil, which is totally adorable, Kaida squealed.

She was right. His neck was flushed, his pupils dilated, and he kept swallowing nervously. "Let me ask you something," I said.

He looked back up, meeting my gaze. "I figure that you got most of my story from a background check yesterday. In all that, did it scream I was a psychopath? Most of that story involves Alice. Do you think so little of her that she would cover up for me if I were some kind of psycho murderer?" I sat with my eyebrow quirked while I let him contemplate.

He stared quietly, studying me. Finally, he shook his head slowly and leaned back in his chair. "No, Detective Hester is nothing if not a professional. I have worked with very few officers of her caliber. But you're her sister...what wouldn't we do for our family?"

That was the question, wasn't it? What wouldn't we do for our family? Medusa considered her fellow acolytes and her goddess her family, but she was cursed anyway. The curse didn't take my parents, but it had stolen more women in my family than I would ever be able to track. Alice was my only family now, and there was nothing I wouldn't do for her.

"Nothing. There is nothing I wouldn't do for her. Nothing she wouldn't do for me, too; that's her curse. For some reason, my sister chose me to be her family; she chose that no matter what, she would stand by me. Here's the thing, though: Alice is kind and passionate about justice. You might look at me and see darkness, but Alice is the light. One can't exist without the other, and neither will snuff each other out. Alice is too good to let me be evil and do nothing about it, but you know that already. Let's make a deal."

He looked around suspiciously to see if someone was listening in, "Okay?"

I smiled again, so hard that my cheeks hurt. "I swear on any and all gods you believe in that neither Alice nor I had anything to do with Dan Reynolds' disappearance. Let's put that to the side for now. You wanted a date, right? So, just talk and ask what you want to. If I want to answer, I will…just like regular people do. Maybe we will learn more about each other, or maybe I'm a stupid criminal, and I'll slip up and give you all the info you need to hang me out to dry."

He was trying so hard not to smile that it was causing crinkles next to his eyes. Who would have guessed you could laugh with nothing more than your eyes? He was adorable. Even if I was courting danger sitting here, I couldn't have walked away at this point if I wanted to. This was almost fun, except that he may walk away any second now and probably get an arrest warrant for me by sundown. "Fine," he said, his eyes still smiling at me.

I sat back in my chair, a little startled that he agreed. "But if I'm treating this like a date…" He hooked his foot around the leg of my chair and pulled me closer to his side.

"Then you sit here, and I don't expect you to slip up and hang yourself on anything, Mattie. We both know you're not dumb, criminal or not."

Now he was very, very close. His voice had dropped an octave, making everything he said sound sexier, even the idea that he still thought I could be some kind of criminal.

Sabine appeared out of nowhere with her space buns bobbing on top of her head. She reached over his shoulder with our coffee, food, and a large manila envelope with my name written in elegant calligraphy across the front.

"Here y'all go! Is there anything else I can get ya?" She asked happily. Will answered for us both without looking away from me, "No thanks, we're all good." He glanced at the envelope curiously.

"Never been on a date with a woman where she gets a love letter from someone else." I tucked in under my thigh furthest from him and looked back at him.

"Lucian isn't writing me love letters, I can promise that. Although it's sure to contain flowery compliments. It's not like that between us."

"He's a friend?" Hearing the slight tremor in his voice, I reached out and patted his forearm.

"One of my best. He owns a few businesses around town. The voodoo shop just down the street is his, although he's rarely there during the day since he hates tourists." I giggled at the image that popped up in my head of him trying to answer people's questions about spells and potions with any kind of seriousness. "He is from one of the original families in New Orleans. His grandmother opened the shop decades ago, and the family keeps it going, with him taking care of the handsome and mysterious owner bit."

Will smirks, "Interesting people you know here."

"Some people like to be interesting, and some people like to be invisible. New Orleans is good for both," I replied, shrugging my shoulders. "I see why you chose to live here."

"We picked it because it's where Alice could be a detective. We have lived in plenty of places before this. It was what was best for her. Okay, Agent Trouble, tell me the kind of things you share on a first date, when you're not in interrogation mode."

He took a drink before answering, "Well, I grew up the oldest of three boys in Idaho. My dad was a logger, and my mom worked odd jobs in town. We ran wild and caused plenty of trouble. I went to college in Boise and then applied to the FBI. Moved to DC and I've been chasing bad guys ever since." I nodded thoughtfully; He was just so wholesome. I could picture him with a dark mop of messy hair and big eyes, all gangly and awkward, running around the countryside with a set of matching brothers, causing chaos. "And your family doesn't miss you?"

He smiled when they came to his mind, "My Dad passed away a few years ago. Mom moved to Boise with a friend, and they travel and keep each other company now. Both my brothers are married with kids now. Living our own lives keeps us busy, but we never miss a chance for family calls. We text often enough to keep up with each other's lives, and I go back to Idaho to hunt with them every fall." I smiled at his description of his hallmark family. I had no idea what that was like anymore, but once upon a time I had. "That sounds nice."

"This is where I would ask about your family, but that would be awkward, I guess," he said sheepishly.

"No, it's okay. My parents met in grad school. Both were studying archaeology, specifically Greek history. They married and had my sister, and then I came along years later. They died when I was just a kid, and I lived with my sister, Catherine. Your background check fills in the rest."

Now he blushed, "I'm sorry about that. I swear I don't usually do background checks on women I ask out."

I lean back, sipping my coffee. "Just the women who might be crazy killers," I smile to lighten the words.

He smiles back, "Well, yeah. I loved Dexter, but I would rather not end up in a real-life episode." He had no idea how right he was comparing me to the popular TV serial killer who targeted bad guys.

"Dexter wasn't so bad. He cleaned up the world's mess for them." I knew I was pushing, but I couldn't hold it back. Maybe it was sick to tempt fate, but I knew I was going to disappear at some point, and I wanted him to at least know if he put it all together that it wasn't some mental illness that drove me.

"Justice and vengeance are just two sides of the same coin. It's always a toss-up on which you're going to end up with. Dexter understood that for some people, justice wasn't enough; vengeance was the only answer."

He wouldn't be able to wrap his head around the truth, but if I were exposed, then maybe some of it would make sense to him because of what I say here. He reached over and took my hand gently, "Mattie, you know I would help you, right? Alice, too." He spoke quietly with a very serious tone. "You can tell me anything and I'll do right by you." He said it so sincerely, I was tempted to lay it all out for him.

For the first time, I wanted to explain and let someone know everything, but Catherine had tried to tell people to get help, and it ended with her being marked as crazy and locked up. Then it was too late to save her or anybody else. I squeezed his fingers and then tucked my hands between my legs.

"Of course you would, Will, I'd expect no less." I couldn't keep the sadness out of my tone, and he noticed.

He picked up the menu and waved over to the waitress. "I'm still starving, so I'm ordering more."

I laughed, "Go ahead. I live off these and coffee." I picked up one of the beignets and took a big bite. The waitress walked up and pulled out her notepad. "Hey, love, what can I do for ya?"

Putting my hand on his forearm, I butted in. "He'll take the Pet gator and I'll take the po' boy, dressed and boxed up." I took both the menus before he could argue and handed them over to her.

"You ordered me a pet? I don't think the hotel I'm staying at will go for that." He was smiling, so he must not have minded my high-handedness. "It is like eggs Benedict but with gator sausage. It sounds weird, but it's one of the best things to eat in the city. I promise you won't regret it."

"And if I do?" he asked

"Then you can have Alice's po' boy. No one can dislike a po' boy."

He was smiling but looked worried again, "Do you do that all the time? I've never seen you show up at the station without something for her to eat or drink."

I smirk at the comment. "Alice is a genius at crime solving, not so much at taking care of herself. She loves to eat, but totally forgets when she's busy working. I remember to keep her fed for my safety. You're welcome, since it's for you too. Trust me, a hungry Alice is a mean Alice."

He laughed at that. "Well, thank you for keeping us all safe from the hangry Alice Hester. The whole of New Orleans is in your debt."

Our waitress returned with his food and a bag with my sister's. I set it next to the table and watched him dive into his food. While he was distracted with his food, I pulled out the envelope Lucian had left for me and opened it. Most likely, it was a note setting up a time and place to meet. To my surprise, I pulled out two old Polaroid-type photos. The first was a dark photo of a bayou; I flipped to the next photo, a closer view of something on the bank. It was a muddy driver's license with some blood on it. There wasn't anything to determine where exactly this was, but my stomach was rolling and sinking at the same time. The license belonged to Dan Reynolds. I quickly and shakily went to put them back into the envelope, swallowing the lump in my throat. Will's hand reached out quickly to stop me. "What's wrong?"

I shook my head, "Nothing," but my voice was strained and sounded off even to my ears.

"Bullshit." He reached past me for the photos in my hand.

I harshly shoved them back in the envelope, out of reach. Digging into my pocket, I pulled out a few twenties. Throwing them on the table, I stood up, "This was great, but I have an emergency."

I tried to move past him, but his suave move he pulled earlier, tugging me and my chair to his side, made it harder to get past him now. He twisted around in his chair, trying to block me in.

"Mattie. Just stop! I can help. I WILL help." He sounded a tinge desperate, and if I were a better person, I would offer some comforting words to make him feel better. I wasn't that type of person, and he couldn't save me, so why bother?

"Just tell me what's going on, I can help you." I slid between him and the wall, "You would if you could, Will."

Partly giving in to the feelings I've had throughout breakfast, I leaned in and kissed his cheek just above one of his adorable dimples.

"Problem is, nobody can really help." With that, I slunk between two new patrons, finding their table and quickly out to the street. I didn't look back, even when something inside me was begging to. I knew he was just standing next to our table, watching me as I left. No matter what he said, it wasn't like he could help. Showing him pictures of Dan Reynolds' bloody driver's license was highly unlikely to inspire him to believe I wasn't a serial killer.

Now I had no idea how to help get justice for Laura. I quickly stopped in Lucian's family voodoo shop and left a note, asking him to meet me tonight at sunset in the cemetery. I sent him a quick text saying the same. He rarely had his phone, so I was covering my bases before heading to the library for work. Nothing to do between now and then. I stopped on the sidewalk, looking at my hands. I was holding just the envelope from Lucian, meaning I had gotten Alice lunch and left it by the chair at Monty's. Fan-freaking-tastic.

Chapter 16

William

Somehow, in just a short week, my whole world had been turned around, and I wasn't even sure what I was doing in this city anymore. I came down to investigate a serial killer, whom I wasn't really looking for, now that I had a gut feeling leading down a road I wasn't ready to walk down. I was supposed to be investigating Laura's murder, but that meant walking into the station and meeting Detective Hester when I had just been on a date with her sister. The same sister who might be at the end of every single path I had laid out in front of me. I should walk in and demand some answers, demand that we drag in Mattie and question her, or maybe call the head office and request a transfer. John would respect my opinion without asking too many questions if I told him this wasn't a serial killer. He'd also respect my choice to pass this off to someone else. That option would be filled with questions, too, as I had never just walked away from a case.

Thinking back to the last half an hour, I was sitting across the table with a woman who had captivated me since I first saw her. She was smiling down at the table, telling a story about some trouble she and Alice had gotten into when they were 17 and being rebels. It was adorable that she thought a day of playing hooky and taking a bus to the beach was being a rebel. This was a woman who was a literature major because she loved the classics. She bit her lip when she was nervous and constantly tucked her hands into the seam of her thighs, so she didn't fidget. I couldn't wrap my head around the idea that she was brutally murdering men with snake venom.

The why made sense, kind of, just a few times meeting Mattie had me convinced she would do anything in her power to help those around her, especially the women in her group. Laura's death was the anomaly. Nothing would convince me she had done it…unless Laura knew something she wasn't supposed to. I shook my head to clear the dark ideas forming. No, there was no way she would have hurt the girl. Those two types of people just didn't coexist within one person.

This city was crawling even at this time of day, but nothing compared to the people who would crowd the quarter when darkness fell. I could appreciate why the architecture and feel of the city made people think of ghost stories and legends. Jazz music followed me past several street corners and restaurants. With the sun shining bright and having spent the morning trying to charm Mattie, I should have been flying high, but I was confused instead. I didn't enjoy this feeling.

Walking into the precinct, Lorraine's warm smile greeted me, making the morning's failure feel slightly more tolerable.

"Good morning, Cher. How was Ms. Mattie today?" She teased.

How the hell did she know I had been having breakfast with Mattie… "How did you know?" Her smile grew like I'd just confirmed something.

"Well, my nephew Lucian meets Mattie at Monty's quite often …and my niece was your waitress. She texted the group chat as soon as she saw Mattie on what appeared to be a date. Now that girl doesn't date and certainly not law enforcement, so it was the news of the Quarter." She wrapped it all up like she was explaining something that should have been obvious.

"Now I, for one, won't be the one who has to deal with Ali." She pointed a red fingernail at me before picking up an iced coffee and taking a drink. "That would be your problem. Those two are a package deal, trouble all around, so I hope you know what you are getting into."

I wasn't going to stir up more gossip or encourage the receptionist in any way, so I just nodded and started back to Alice's office. I knew I was in trouble with the detective before the door was even open all the way. Her back was to me as I stepped inside. She was on the phone with someone. Probably someone had just left a guy holding her food in a restaurant that she had invited him to.

"Mat, I know you are frustrated, but I'm going to insist on your thinking this through. You are making rash choices, and I don't know if you are in the driver's seat anymore. You want to go tonight, fine, but I'm going with you. I don't trust anyone else to watch your back, or hers. I'll meet you at the number one gate tonight after my shift. Just wait for me, okay? Call me back, please." She paused her pacing and huffed out a deep breath.

"Be good. I love you."

She set the phone back on the table, leaning forward, resting her head in her hands. She looked like the weight of the world was on her shoulders. As a brother, I could understand how, sometimes, even when there was nothing you could do for your siblings, their burdens weighed you down too. Even just the pressure of not being able to do anything was hard. Clearing my throat and pushing my hair back off my forehead, I broke the silence.

"Detective. Good morning."

She whirled her head up to pin me with a scrutinizing gaze. Trying to be casual, I smiled and closed the door behind me. The last thing I needed was her catching on to me dating, slash investigating her only family. All of a sudden, it crossed my mind; Alice would do anything for her only family member. She had said so herself. How far would she go for her sister?

"I called the main office today, and we are putting protection details on the women of the S/A group. After the threats to Dr. Raines, I would rather we keep an eye on them." I sat down and watched her for a reaction. Alice watched me get settled across from her desk and start going through the files we had on each member. Setting down the file for Carol Shanks, Dr.

Raines, and Mattie Cutler, I looked at Alice.

"These three will have full surveillance and background checks." She took the stack of files and read her sister's name.

"I can take care of the night shifts with Mattie. No reason to waste resources there. She stays in every night, and there is no way to watch her at our home without someone noticing. We're all alone out there."

I studied her while spinning the ring I wore on my right middle finger. "She stays in every night? All night? That's a little odd for a 30-year-old woman."

Alice shrugged her shoulders. "She's a homebody." Deciding to push the detective a bit, "That's fine, then I'll take the night shift. Gotta be sure you're both covered, partner."

She met my eyes and narrowed hers sharply. "Agent, you are NOT going to do that. I can protect myself and my sister just fine. I'll take this to my captain if I have to."

Crossing my arms and staring her down, "You'll take it to your captain and what? Tell him that a woman from the group has been murdered and mutilated, another was stalked and threatened, and you don't think he'll see cause enough to require protection details for these women? What exactly do you think your captain will say about that?" I was asking rhetorically, but when she opened her mouth in retort, I jumped in, cutting her off. "Or should we be focusing on the men's deaths first? Maybe that's the key to all of this."

If there was anything to my line of thinking about Mattie, then she would want to keep the focus off that part of the investigation.

She started nodding, "Of course not. Living people take precedence. Whoever killed Laura needs to be off the street. That was a particularly violent crime where the other deaths could still have been accidents." She took the bait, hook, line, and sinker. I felt certain that neither of them had hurt Laura, but she and Mattie had to have something to do with the 3 dead men. Maybe the 4 men missing from their college, too? From what I knew about the men who had been murdered here in NOLA and suspected about the missing ones, it left me questioning whether I really cared. I knew enough about Mattie to know that she wasn't planning on being at home tonight. Alice had no intention of letting her go alone, and I had no intention of letting either of them out of my sight.

"I think we need another interview with Dr. Raines. I want to figure out if the threat was part of this investigation or something else entirely."

I'm still not sure of my suspicion of Mattie, but more information couldn't hurt anything. The last time I saw her with the doctor, it was clear they weren't friends, but maybe that was for a reason. At the very least, we had to do our best to keep her safe. Whatever was going on seemed to be marking the good Doctor as the next target.

Alice wasn't giving up so much as was just placating me, biding her time. "Alright, but you take the lead with the interview. I think she will be more forthcoming with the FBI than the local police."

Together, we started out of the office. I grabbed the files on the women. As we left the station, the sunshine beat down on the back of my neck. The drive to the hospital's annex building was quiet, and that made me more uncomfortable than just talking to Alice about what we were both pretending wasn't going on.

I liked Alice, and what's more, I respected her as a detective. Maybe she was blinded by her duty to her sister, but I couldn't say I didn't understand that. Mattie drew me in, too, and before I even knew it, I was ready to help both of them. The silence was finally broken by Alice's stomach gurgling loudly. I laughed, thinking of how Mattie had joked about keeping the city safe from hangry Alice.

"Sorry," she whispered. I waved her off, chuckling, "My fault. I brought you a Po' Boy, but I forgot it in the office." She glanced over at him suspiciously, her warm brown eyes narrowed.

"You brought me a Po' Boy? Why?" It was my turn to squirm, "Well, Mattie ordered you one during brunch and then forgot it, so I brought it in with me."

She looked back at the road, but I could see the questions running through her mind.

"She doesn't forget things like that," she said softly to no one in particular. Maybe she would know what could shake up her sister so dramatically that she ran out on me. I wasn't above snooping for answers, obviously, and when it came to this woman, it was really the only way to get them.

"She did. She asked me to brunch, and we were having a great time until she got an envelope from that Lucian guy, then she ran out white as a sheet." Alice signaled and pulled over into a parking lane without saying anything else. She pulled out her phone and sent off a text quickly. Then turned in her seat, propping her knee on the center console to stare at me, "Lucian came by?"

I shook my head, I wish he had, because if I had seen the two of them together, I might be able to make up my mind about how I feel about her 'friend'.

"No, he left it for her, like he knew she was going to be there. It was weird. Who the hell is the guy?"

She waved him off casually, "What was in the envelope?" she asked.

I shrugged. "She didn't show me. Whatever it was freaked her out, and she left in a hurry." Alice seemed to ponder that for a long moment. "Maybe you're a bad date?" She asked dryly.

I chuckled, "Thanks for the knock to my ego, but I promise that I was a gentleman, and we were having a good time."

Minus the fact that I had flat-out accused her of murdering Dan Reynolds. Other than that brief blip, we had laughed and talked. I enjoyed myself more in an hour with Mattie than I had with any of the handful of women I've dated in recent years. Alice was looking past me to the cars going down the street. I reached out and put a hand on her forearm. She was clearly lost in thought about Mattie and Lucian's correspondence...I wonder if there was more to this guy than a friendship. Maybe he was helping her to get rid of people, for a price.

"Alice, if he's dangerous, I'll help you both. If Mattie owes him something, we can help her."

She laughed loudly, "Oh, he is dangerous…very dangerous, but not to Mattie. Don't go kicking over rocks if you don't want to see underneath, Will."

That was the first time she had addressed me by my first name. It felt weird. If she believed that he wasn't a danger to Mattie, I would follow her lead, but is it a possibility that the man was helping her group in a more hands-on way?

"Okay, is he a threat to Dan Reynolds?" Alice pondered over the question for only a split second, her dark almond eyes looking directly into mine.

She was deadly serious when she answered, "Yes. If he thought he was a danger to Mattie, then yes, Lucian would get rid of him."

Okay, so maybe this Lucian guy was the one taking out all of the men, with Mattie and Alice covering for him. Except then, who killed Laura? They wouldn't protect this guy if they thought he had harmed a woman from the group. There wasn't any evidence that Dan HADN'T done it and gone to ground. Maybe Lucian tracked him down later and killed him. I loved this idea because it would mean that neither Alice nor Mattie would be implicated in the reports when I caught up to him. I would do that for them.

"Do you like him as a hit man?" I asked, waiting to see if she would cover for him, too. She smiled darkly, "Oh sure, he could be, Bennet, but he's a prince of New Orleans. We would never catch up to him. Too many people to hide behind and too easy for him to disappear. Evidence would disappear, and lawyers would be paid off. Hell, he has I don't know how many Judges in his pocket."

At least she didn't cover for him, and he was a good suspect if we could get some evidence that would stick. New Orleans might be a haven for him, but the federal government had more reach than a Prince of NOLA.

"So, you had brunch with my sister?" She asked, turning back in her seat and signaling her intent to pull back into traffic. Now it was my turn to get grilled. "Yes."

She looked over quickly. "Just yes?" Her voice was incredulous over my short answer.

"Yep." Putting her on a bit, "You want anything else, you'll have to talk to her. She and I have nothing to do with this investigation. That's the private section of my life," I said matter-of-factly.

I wasn't going to spill to Alice about how fascinated I was by her sister. Gesturing to the hospital annex we were pulling up in front of, "How about we do some work instead of talking about my dating life?"

She signaled to pull in and looked over. "Oh, Bennet…you know I am going to hear all about it later. I was just giving you a chance to explain your side first, but that's fine. Mattie's version will be more salacious." Her Cheshire grin was completely ridiculous and contagious.

Chapter 17

Mattie

A few hours of sitting in my office, surrounded by the smell of paper, leather, and glue, should have been enough to clear her mind of anything for the moment, but I was still running through a million ideas of how Dan's driver's license had ended up in the swamp.

Option one: Dan had dumped it there on his way out of town after killing Laura.

Option two: Dan was somewhere under the water after killing Laura, with several people who could have put him there.

Option three: someone had killed Dan, and maybe Laura too. The key was the words carved into Laura's arm. "Liar in lace."

I pulled out my phone and opened the messages from Alice to look at the crime scene photos she sent me before. There was a new text that just said, 'Lucian left an envelope?' Will is a blabbermouth. I noticed a voicemail notification at the top of my screen. Pushing play, I could hear the frustration in her. It broke my heart to think of all the pressure on her shoulders. She was always a people pleaser, and I knew that if I was removed from the situation, it would be better for her. Maybe if Officer Brian Kemp worked out, I would finally be able to move on before I ruined her life.

"…be good. Love you." I clicked save on the message. Never deleting a single one had become a ritual. Someday, it might not be so easy to hear her voice, even when it's angry, frustrated, ordering me to bring home milk. So I kept each one.

I was studying the photos, zoomed in as much as possible. I reached over and turned on my printer. Quickly sending the photos over to print, I took a notebook off the shelf to my right. Sometimes I had to visually see facts before the connection appeared.

Unlike Alice, who always seemed to do everything in her head. I started making notes of what I knew about Dan, Laura, Hannah, and even Will. All the info could be relevant if it were in the right context, but I wouldn't know it until I could see it physically in front of me. I had been hunched over my desk, making notes for a while, when I felt someone coming up behind me.

I held still, waiting to see if I could sense who it was. My sense of smell was dulled like this, but still better than most people's, and I didn't really recognize it. I kept scribbling swirly doodles while I tried to focus on who they were. I was waiting to see what their intention was, but it was killing me. The predator side of me didn't like anything coming up from behind.

Turn around, Mattie. Now.

Kaida said urgently, she wasn't known for her patience. I held my breath, closing my notebook with the photos tucked inside. I reached for the knife I use to cut old bindings. I had it wrapped in my hand at the same time Brian loudly said, "Hey Mattie, I'm just trying to track down your sister!"

He was smiling broadly, casually leaning against the door frame. He must have been there for a full two minutes before he spoke up, but he was acting like he had just walked in. I turned to meet his gaze, trying to figure out why he was here, of all places.

"Why would she be here?"

He stepped into the room, and I internally bristled. This was my space, and I was not a fan of him being in it. He ran a finger along the shelf at eye level, appearing to be looking at the titles but keeping his gaze on me.

"Well, if she isn't at the station, she's with you. That's just a given with you two, isn't it?" His voice was casual, but there was a volatile tone underneath. Something about the way he said it made him sound jealous.

"Well, we do live together, so between home and work, she doesn't have a ton of free time to be elsewhere. Do you want me to have her call you?"

"Shouldn't that be the other way around, Mattie? After all, we have been getting serious for a while now." Now I was starting to question how much Alice wasn't sharing, since that last time we had a Brian download, she said it was only a few casual dates, a couple flings in the back of her SUV, and some boring make-outs that ended too quickly for anything else on Brian's end. But either way, Alice liked Brian, so I would tolerate almost anything, even this weird behavior from him. "Absolutely, dude. You guys talking about getting a place soon? I will warn you, though, she has a midnight snack problem and hogs all the hot water. I could use the peace and quiet after 15 years living together." I tried to be as calm and casual as possible with a smirk on my face.

Brian was young, fresh-faced, with cropped blond hair and a weak jaw. He topped out at 5'11 and 170 lbs, but in this small space, he felt larger and more imposing.

"That's more like it, Mattie. You need to know your place in her life now. Alice deserves the best, and I'm the best for her." The smile on his face as he turned to face me amped up the creep factor to 10.

I balked at his comment about my place, but managed not to physically react. I could ignore that for the moment.

Umm, sure, dude...if 'the best' meant you couldn't keep it up long enough to get it out of your pants, Kaida added in a snarky tone.

She wasn't usually a fan of any of the men Alice dated, but she had disliked Brian, viscerally, from the very beginning.

"That's not our business, but yeah." I thought back to her.

"But it's Alice's life, and she is almost 30. She might actually be thinking about settling down." I could feel Kaida cringing in my head.

I hoped, as my best friend, that I could confidently know she wouldn't be keeping something like this from me. I didn't believe for one minute she said anything to him about me having less of a place in her life. I was the one who pulled away, and she ran after me. A fact I was always grateful for. Right now, this weirdo was the only one trying to set boundaries between me and my sister.

I got up with the knife in hand and slid it subtly into my back pocket, just in case, while watching Brian. He was still studying my office, in particular, an old photo on my desk of Alice and me in front of our college dorm building from before the curse. I needed him to leave; every instinct I had wanted to get away from him.

I'm getting the same instinct, we should go...creeper vibes all the way.

"Well, if you don't mind, I have a meeting I'm late for, Brian?"

"With the FBI agent?" he said lazily, cocking his brown eyebrow.

How the hell did he know about Agent trouble and me?

"Um, no, with my department head. But if I hear from Alice, I'll let her know to get a hold of you." I walked over to the door and gestured for him to get out. He walked towards the door with a smile lighting up his face as he put back on his patrol cap and rested his hand against his gun.

I don't like him.

No shit, Sherlock...he is a creep. I tensed, the hissing in my head was growing louder by the second. For whatever reason, the gorgon thought Brian was a threat, and I was beginning to agree.

"Just remember, Mattie, Alice is MINE." He tipped his cap and left the room. I shut the door behind him, letting out my held breath and leaning against the door, waiting for my adrenaline to calm down and my brain to catch up. He was threatening me. Threatening me over who was first in my sister's life.

I pushed off the door and crossed to my desk to pick up my phone and call her and tell her all about the Creepasaurus Rex that just left my office. I had no more than unlocked the phone when it began ringing with Agent Bennet's number flashing. I ignored it and pushed Alice's name. It only partly rang when she answered, sounding frantic, "Mattie!" Where are you?" I could hear the worry in her tone, and Will was talking in her other ear.

"Where is she? Is she okay? Tell her to come to the station. No, tell her to stay put, and we will come pick her up." His voice muffled as he tried to get closer to the phone and talk over Alice; both things were sure to annoy her.

"Alice, what's up? You, okay?" I asked.

"No, we were at the clinic interviewing Dr. Raines in the cafeteria when she got a call from security for the building," Alice explained.

"Is she okay? She's safe, right?" The last thing I wanted to worry about was something happening to Hannah just as she was crossing from casual acquaintance to friend. I figured she's earned the title of friend, seeing as she thought I was killing people and was totally cool with it, I guess.

Terrible therapist, but a good friend.

"She's fine, but her office was vandalized while she was meeting with us. Someone broke in and painted the wall with a message written in what appears to be blood," she said, with Will still trying to talk over her into the phone. I could hear her grunt as she pushed him away and hushed him.

"Just stay where you are, Agent Bennet, and I will be there to get you in about 30 minutes. Don't go anywhere without an officer." I looked at the clock and it was about 5 pm now, "Alice, I need to get home." I paused, hoping she would hear the implication in my voice.

Will must have heard because suddenly there was a scuffling sound on the other end, and then he was on the phone.

"Mattie? Stay right the hell where you are. I'll be there in 30 minutes. I swear to God if you push me on this, I will arrest you just for shits and giggles." He sounded so frustrated, I was sure his hair was a mess from running his hands through it over and over again.

"Got your handcuffs, Agent Trouble? Cause I'm okay with that threat usually, but it has to be invited, or it's just creepy." He paused, his breath audibly caught in his throat, before chuckling softly. "Maybe next date, Mattie. You at work?" His voice was suddenly husky.

I was going to get home faster if I played along.

"Yeah, just send Alice. We have to get home for the night anyway, so you don't need to waste your time." He was going to argue, but seemed to think better of it. "Alright, be a good girl and stay put."

Whew, and there he went and pushed my lust button. All of a sudden, the seriousness of the situation went out of my head, and so did the fact that I ran out on our date just this morning.

New kink: unlocked.

The feminist in me wanted to rage, but Kaida was just purring away, quite pleased with herself.

I find it offensive that you think I would let him do that to me... if anyone is going to be tied up, it's going to be Agent Trouble. I would love to have him at my mercy.

She was always such a flirt. Thank the Gods that I controlled what we actually said...most of the time.

Alice came back on the line, "I'm texting you something. Don't move," and she hung up. She must be seriously worried because there was no way she hadn't heard that comment from Will, and didn't tease even a bit. Staring at the far shelves, my brain started counting the books and sorting them by color while my mind wandered. With the new threat against Hannah, how much longer could we pretend that my existence, my vengeance, wasn't the reason there was a target on the group? Had following Kaida's lead to these women's lives to be turned upside down?

Well, that's a cheery way to put all the blame on my shoulders, little monster.

Anger colored her voice. "I made my choices, too, Kai...but maybe there were different paths we could have taken. Paths that wouldn't have cost other people so much." I do love Kaida, but I wonder what my life would have looked like if I had searched for peace instead of justice.

We have sacrificed plenty. Our whole lives have been a sacrifice.

She was right, we had made many sacrifices, but so had the people who loved us. Could we compare wounds by who bleeds more? "I'm just thinking out loud, Kaida. I think I should be doing a better job of being the logical one, the one who keeps us safe. You can keep us wild, and we'll have a better balance. I promise." She huffs but doesn't respond as my phone buzzes with a message. I opened it and clicked on the image. It was a wall, presumably in Hannah's office, painted a light, calm green color that had been ruined by the bloody words painted on it.

"Blood is thicker than water."

Well, isn't that just wonderful? Hannah had a target on her back, and we have no idea who has their sights on it. How much longer until this person makes their way through the whole group?

Chapter 18

William

The psychologist's office was a chaotic mess. The walls were smeared with blood, the furniture overturned, and papers scattered everywhere. Alice and I stood in the middle of the chaos, lost in our thoughts. My eyes darted around the room, searching for any clues that could lead somewhere. But my mind was elsewhere, trying to figure out a way that I could excuse myself first and beat Alice to getting Mattie. One of us was going to get the chance, and I wanted it to be me, so I could corner Mattie about this morning and the envelope.

Dr. Raines, visibly shaken up by the vandalism, stood close to Alice and me as officers and techs moved about the scene. In spite of how shaken up she was, when Alice had called Mattie, her eyebrows arched into her hairline when I took over the phone, Alice might not have said anything right now, but I'm sure I am going to hear about it sometime soon. Dr. Raines definitely suspected I might be having a relationship with Mattie.

Alice was methodically searching for any evidence, hoping to incriminate Dan Reynolds in this latest escalation. As nobody had seen him since before Laura's body was found, it was becoming less likely that he was involved here. It made sense that he would want to go after Laura; at least there was a motive.

Here, he had no connection, other than Hannah knowing her. The entire city was keeping an eye out for him, and we had no idea how he could have made it past security and into the office. With each passing second, the tension between the three of us in the narrow hall grew thicker. The building was crawling with officers taking photos and dusting for prints. It had been quickly taken over when Alice called it in. A patrol officer, the same one who had come to report to Alice the day Laura Turner's body was found, walked up to our group.

"Ma'am, the cameras were disabled internally for about 20 minutes." He addressed Alice, but he kept glancing over at the doctor with a nervous air, "Seems they knew exactly when you were going to be out of the room, Dr. Raines."

He was polite to the doctor, but it was obvious he was checking out the statuesque woman. She wore her hair in a short black bob with a smart, professional black dress and high heels. She was absolutely stunning, but there was a time and place, and after she had her office vandalized and been threatened, wasn't it, so I shooed him off with a wave of my hand before crossing my arms and turning back, blocking both women from the chaos with my body. Hannah was chewing on the edge of her thumbnail nervously, "You had better get going. We both know that Mattie won't be patient for long."

Alice checked her watch for the 10th time; she was nervously tapping her foot while I took statements. Ever since we had hung up on Mattie, she seemed ready to bolt.

"How long have you and Mattie been friends?" I asked, curious about their relationship. They had been photographed together at that meeting. I saw them at the cafe together, but other than that, they didn't seem like two people who would meld.

Hannah Raines was educated, professional, and poised. She was stunning, but she gave off an air of calm certainty that must make her a great therapist. She chuckled darkly, tucking her short hair behind her ear, "Mattie doesn't have friends. She came to the meetings for a year before I knew her name. If this situation with Laura hadn't happened, I don't know if I would even know her phone number." She looked apprehensively at Alice, either afraid to say too much to me or too much to her.

This incident had shaken her up. "Listen, Mattie is a very kind person, but she is extremely guarded. She doesn't open her circle, but she cares about those around her. Maybe too much…" She trailed off again, staring at the wall where a message was left.

The bloody words were painted rather than slashed on the wall. Her choice of words caught my attention. What did the doc mean by Mattie cared too much? I studied her profile for a minute till I noticed Alice out of the corner of my eye; she had backed up to the wall behind us, looking pale as I had ever seen her. There was a worry and fear in her eyes that screamed it was about more than just getting to the library to pick up her sister.

She met my gaze, "Agent Bennet, I am going to go get my sister now. I would feel better if she were home with all this going on." I nodded, and she quickly took off down the hall.

She weaved in and out of officers and techs, passing Officer Kemp, he grabbed her by her elbow, and I started towards them, she just brushed past him with a glare, but didn't say anything. He watched her go for a moment. When he turned, the look of fury on his face was shocking, reminiscent of the last time she had kicked him out of her office. His face transformed back to happy-go-lucky just as quickly, reminding me of Dr. Jekyll and Mr. Hyde. If I hadn't been watching closely, I could have sworn it was just my imagination.

As much as I wished I could go with Alice to get Mattie, I still had some questions for the Doc that would be easier without Alice around. There were some parts of the investigation I needed to work out without either of the sisters around.

"So, Doctor, when we spoke earlier, you said you didn't have any info on your brother's whereabouts. We haven't been able to link him to the city either, but we're still exploring other avenues. This, however," I gestured at the room behind us, "this screams of escalation, and it's personal."

She nodded, already putting that together herself, "You know I won't tell you anything about Mattie."

"Why do you think I'm asking anything?" Head tilted to the side, I wondered just how good a therapist she was. She stood taller, straightening her shoulders, and pulled on the small pendant she wore around her neck, "You know, yesterday I pondered for a while if the messages were retaliation for the men's deaths… If someone figured out our group was connected to them. If that's true, then, out of all of us, Mattie is in the most danger."

She looked strongly at me to convey her message. She waved her hand to have me step a little further away from people who could overhear, "How involved are you two, Agent? Since you arrived here, you've found a way to mention Mattie in almost every sentence."

Did I? Hell…I thought I was more subtle than that.

"You aren't subtle. I was standing right there when Alice called Mattie. My question isn't what would you do for Mattie, but what wouldn't you do?" Her brow arched as she searched my face for an answer I didn't know how to give.

I have a job to do, a calling, but now, I've been pulled into Mattie's orbit, and I don't want to escape. "Why would she be in the most danger?" Rolling her eyes, she smiled sadly, "If you haven't put that together, Agent, then you aren't as observant as I thought."

My mind raced. Was she telling me that she thought Mattie had killed those men? She admitted that they were all connected to the group, even though we had only been able to verify two of the men's connections.

"May I go now? I have to speak with my bosses about this before I can go home."

"Yeah," I waved her off, "your security detail will wait for you and then escort you back home, and an officer will be outside all night.

She nodded, "Thank you."

Turning to walk down to the elevators, "Oh, Agent Bennet?"

She stopped and faced him again, "The person who did this? They messed up the message." Blood is thicker than water was painted in thick letters across the whole wall of her office. Whomever had done it seems pretty confident that Hannah would understand the intent of the message. It was a common saying, one my own mom had used a hundred times when my brothers and I were fighting.

"Oh yeah? How?"

Her face was deadly serious, the sharp angles of her cheekbones more severe as she pursed her lips angrily.

"The saying goes, 'The blood of the covenant is thicker than the water of the womb.' It's from a Scottish author. It means the bonds we choose are more important than our familial ties. They meant it as a threat, but I intend to take it at face value. Those women are my family, I will fight to protect them, and so will Mattie. You have to decide which side you are backing."

Without waiting for my response, she turned and walked out of sight, the echoing click clack on her high heels on the floor fading with her. I really wasn't sure what she wanted me to do with her suspicions that Mattie might be the killer. Did she want me to stop her, or help her? If she was right, what exactly was I going to do?

Chapter 19

The car ride back to our home had been silent except for the playlist Alice always listened to on repeat. The Spill Canvas playing filled the car with memories of teenage angst. I sat with my hands tucked under my thighs and tapped my foot repeatedly.

Finally, she broke the silence, "So were you a good girl?" I laughed so hard at the break in tension that I started choking on the air. After a full minute, I leaned on the center console, invading her space.

"Aren't I always?"

She was grinning big and wide, too.

"I cannot believe he said that out loud at a crime scene! I was ready to die standing there, unable to look at my partner at an active scene."

I sat back in my seat and fanned myself dramatically, "You? How about me? I was so hot and bothered, I was an arson threat to the library antiquities room."

She laughed again and looked briefly at me before turning back to the road.

"So you aren't mad?" I was curious how judgmental she was going to be about the situation.

"Mad? No. But I am concerned for you, Mattie. If it were literally any other guy, I would push and prod you to go for it. The only guy you have hooked up with in ten years is Lucian, and that's almost just as sketchy

"

as you going after the one guy who might be able to connect the dots on your little partner's crime spree." I opened my mouth to retort, but she was exactly right.

William wasn't an idiot, and he was going to notice something eventually. If it wasn't the people that disappeared around me, then my excuses for never being around him after sunset would certainly set off some alarms. It had crossed my mind as every other thought since he cornered me outside the church after I found Laura. There couldn't be a future with him without revealing my curse. If he couldn't accept the darkness, there was nothing I could do about it. Will didn't seem like he would accept the supernatural, let alone me and Kaida doing illegal shit, and we couldn't stop. Stopping would lead to going crazy and dying in a short time.

"I've never slept with Lucian," I said quietly, deflecting.

She looked back sharply, her perfect brows arching over those almond-shaped eyes, "Seriously? Why not?" I shrugged my shoulders.

She really is clueless... they're both dancing around each other.

"Probably because he'd rather sleep with you." Lucian was the definition of a dark prince, his ebony skin decorated in piercings, while he dressed like he walked out of a period romance but forgot the shirt. Dreadlocks and a charming smile drew people to him, and there was no way that Alice didn't notice how pretty he was, even if she couldn't admit she was drawn to him, too.

Her jaw dropped open, "Are you kidding?!" She sounded genuinely shocked.

Clueless, dear sister...

She had porcelain skin, dark eyes, and hair to match. She was curvy but petite and always looked like a bad-ass with her pantsuits and gun, but was shocked that he would have noticed?

"No, he just flirts with everyone. I thought you guys were hooking up for years." I put my hand on her shoulder gently.

"He's like my brother, for lack of a better way to put it. Plus, he has been half in love with you since you arrested him for selling those gris gris bags two years ago." She looked flabbergasted, opening and closing her mouth over and over again like she was going to deny it or offer a retort, but also thinking through everything he had ever said to her.

Then that feline smile came across her face, and I knew it was over for creepy Officer Kemp.

Thank the goddess. I was going to bite him if he didn't go away soon.

Thank the goddess, alright…there was more at work here than just desire. Lucian and Alice needed a push; someone should get their happy ending.

Our ending isn't set in stone yet. Don't ruin it for yourself, Mattie.

She cranked the music to full blast and rolled her window down. Lucian Corbin had better start running because he is in trouble now. Riding around with the music blasting was good for the soul, so we just sat with our thoughts. For a moment, we were kids again, and it was balm for the soul.

"How was Hannah? The threat must have shaken her up?" I asked, as we pulled off the main road onto dirt.

"You should call her; she'd like to know that you care." Our last call still had me a little rattled. Even sitting across from her at the meeting and the diner after, I hadn't answered my question of how much she knew versus only suspected. Let alone what she was going to do with that info. Our long driveway stretched before us as dirt flew up behind our SUV.

"Of course I care."

Alice was studying me now, "It's not obvious to other people, Mattie, sometimes you have to say it out loud."

I was about to say something about being pushed to share my feelings for the 100th time when my senses went haywire. The hissing started in my head, louder than it had ever been when I wasn't in my other form. The hair on the back of my neck was standing up, and if the sun had not still been shining in the car, I would have thought I had changed already.

You need to go back. There is something at the house. Run.

Kaida sounded frantic and was pushing forward like she could take control of us. Just to be safe, I shoved my sunglasses on and grabbed Alice's arm.

"Stop the car, now!" I was being loud and alarming, but Kaida was too worked up for me to control myself.

Alice slammed on the brakes, sending dirt flying around us about halfway up the drive. I was unbuckled and threw open the door before the car stopped rocking.

"Stay the fuck here, Alice!" I slammed the car door and started through the grass towards the house. I was taking the shortcut through the trees to approach the house from the side. I looked up at the sun, suddenly very aware of how close six thirty was to nighttime, and how far it still was. Whatever had set off Kaida was still there, and both sides of me were all worked up. The house was just through the tree line, and all looked fine from where I was standing. I could see a few of my statues in the distance, covered with vines, standing guard around the house.

I ran across the lawn, hopping over the low fence without opening the creaky gate, and looked through our side door. Everything inside looked fine, so I started around to the garage, set off to the side. Just as I was about to round that part of the house, I sensed someone coming up behind me. I spun around and grabbed the person by their throat, pinning them to the wall beside the patio. My adrenaline was racing through my veins and heart, ready to beat out of my chest. It took a full second before I realized it was Alice.

She had left her jacket and kicked off her shoes at some point. Her gun was held loosely in her hand. It was pointed in my direction, but her finger wasn't on the trigger.

"What part of stay put didn't you get?" I hissed at her, releasing her from the wall.

"The part where you aren't the boss of me," she stuck her tongue out. "I'm an actual trained officer, and I have a weapon."

I crouched down at the end of the patio, looking towards the outbuilding, "Give me an hour, and we can have a competition of whose weapon is more effective." She moved up behind me, clicking the safety off on her weapon, "Mine. It works 24/7," she whispered behind me.

Despite being on the razor's edge of anxiety, I couldn't help giggling at our antics. "Just stay here for a minute. If I don't come back, you can go full Die Hard."

I didn't wait for her answer before I raced off, rounding the edge of our patio towards the garage. Kaida had finally stopped hissing in my head like a crazy person, so I could concentrate. Looking at the garage I had just painted, a message was scrawled across the wall in dried blood.

That's a vibe. Apparently, the swamp puppies weren't a good enough deterrent, Kaida drawled dramatically.

"All clear, Alice!" I yelled out.

I was certain whoever had vandalized our refuge had left a while ago because the blood was already dry. I stepped up to study the slashing letters as Alice ran up with her gun drawn.

"Holy shit," she whispered, lowering her gun and putting it back into her holster.

There, written in bloody big slashes, was a threat to them and their existence in New Orleans. The words 'shed your skin and I'll still find you'. Someone knew more than they should. Alice was already pulling her phone out of her back pocket. "I have to call this in."

I looked at her and said, "You can't. At least not yet."

She glanced up and then groaned, "Oh shit, we'd have a whole crew crawling all over this place."

I nodded solemnly, "Not to mention the statues?" She glanced over her shoulder at the one you could see clearly at the edge of the garden, "Yeah, that would look weird." She walked back to the house and started pulling the hose around. "What are you doing?" With a big yank, she got a kink out of it, the front of her hair coming loose to fall around her face, "Cleaning this up, obviously."

"You can't destroy evidence, Alice," I stated, like she was losing her mind. Maybe she finally was and I had broken her brain with stress. "Do you have a better suggestion, Mattie? We can't have your hottie or the precinct out here, so we don't have any other option." I turned around and stepped back to take a few photos from different angles. I texted Lucian quickly, requesting that he watch over Alice and me at the house. We needed backup, and the illegal kind was the only kind we could ask for. My phone buzzed with a reply almost instantly. He only responded with a thumbs up and a crow emoji.

The sun was setting now, painting the sky with shades of pink and gray. "Alice, go inside. I got this." I said firmly.

"No way, Jose. Sorry, it's partner time tonight," she said stubbornly.

"I have a partner. She'll be along for the ride, and unlike you, is very hard to kill."

She was already walking back down the drive, stopping so suddenly that the dirt at her feet dusted up. Her shoulders heaved as she took deliberately deep breaths. Without turning around again, she held up her arm, flashing me the middle finger.

"You know what, Mattie? You both fuck off." Her anger was coming off her in waves. I started to follow, confused why her sudden outrage was directed at me.

"What the hell, Alice? You know this is dangerous. I'm asking you to stay safe."

Tread carefully, little monster. She is no gorgon but she is just as terrifying.

She stops walking and turns slowly, pointing her finger at me. She stomps towards me again, "Safe? Mattie, I haven't been safe once in 10 goddamn years, hell, maybe not ever. Helping you cover up crimes that could cost me my career, living with Kaida who could kill me just by accident, living in foster care, my whole family dying and leaving me alone at 2… Fucking 2 years old."

Alice never talked about the house fire that killed her parents and brother when she was a toddler. It was an accident she rarely revisited, choosing to look forward rather than dwell on the past. I knew that my curse had put her in a bad position, that any sane person would have run far, far away. Not Alice. She kept showing up for me every day, no matter what it brought. Standing there with her finger stabbing at my front while her whole chest heaved in anger, it finally set in that Alice had paid a higher price for my curse than even I. I pushed her hand down and pulled her into my arms, wrapping her in a hug.

"I am so sorry. So sorry…Alice, I have no excuse. I'm an idiot." Her tears soaked into my shoulder as she relaxed and squeezed back.

"I'm not sorry, Mattie. You didn't choose this life, but I did. I may not have known everything that would happen, but I did know that whatever came, I was signing up with you. No regrets." She pulled back first, wiping her tears away, and turned to go get the car and compose herself. Wetness finally trickled down my cheeks as I scraped a good chunk of blood off the wall of the garage, putting it in a tissue from my pocket. I know she said no regrets, but there was one thing that would make me regret this whole life… if it cost me Alice, I wouldn't be able to go on.

I went inside to change my clothes. Pulling on jeans, a black tank top, and a zip-up hoodie with an oversized hood. I felt the change wash over me just as the sun sank below the horizon. One minute I was me, and the next Kaida looked back at me.

Welcome back, friend. Now we have to get out of here without Alice, I thought to her, looking up at the mirror over the dresser.

Our eyes flashed a luminescent green. I had taken my hair down before the sun set, and now it writhed around Kaida's face. Little flicking tongues teased at the nape of our neck and ears, she reached up and patted one of the little danger noodles on his head. It nudged at her fingers before nipping it lightly. We were immune to their venom, but this one was always a little feisty. Grabbing my sunglasses, Kaida slid them on, pulled up the hood over our hair, and headed for the door. Looking across the hallway, Alice's door was shut.

She was probably showering and changing after the long day. She was going to be pissed when she saw us gone, but finding us would be another matter. We quickly made it the front door, leaving my phone on the sideboard so she couldn't track it. If anyone looked at my location, It would show I was home with my cop sister all night.

We grabbed the car keys to Alice's SUV and left. Driving into the quarter in the darkness was disconcerting, and the guilt was eating at me now. Thinking of William's face when he was sitting across from me at breakfast, that cute little side smirk with a dimple was the best part of my day. If things continue the way they are, it will probably be the last great moment I get with him, even if my lusty self wishes things were different.

"If that was the last moment, we should have spent it naked," Kaida said, her lisp curling around her words.

She parked a block from the cemetery gate and got out, listening for anyone moving around. It was still early for the partiers by quarter standards, but our nerves were shot.

Can you behave for like five minutes? It's been a long day, and now we are running around town...I could really use a full 8 hours.

"No. That would be boring. Let's find Lucian and see what those photos were about," She said, moving into the shadowy back part of the cemetery. We took a seat on Granny Corbin's marker and waited.

Chapter 20

Mattie

The moon had taken over for the sun, and the shadows settled into the graveyard like spirits themselves. Kaida leaned forward to look at the gate again, her impatience growing by the second. I had never been a particularly patient person, but when I was in my gorgon form, it was worse, she had no chill.

"We need to get going….I want to hunt," She said into the darkness.

Yeah, sure, but hunt who? No, we need to get Lucian if we are going out. I'm really not looking to lose my head because you're too impatient to wait for backup.

Whispering to her in the darkness was easy when we were alone. Sometimes I felt like she actually listened if I said it out loud. I could feel her rolling her eyes at the very thought.

"They will hurt Alice. Someone came to our home. They threatened us, and her too. You are mad at me because of her."

I'm not mad at you. I am mad at myself.

I could feel her shoulders relax. It had been a long time since Alice had really blown up and even longer since I had seen her shed tears. We needed to have a conversation when this thing with Laura was settled. A real one, about what can and can't happen from now on. Alice's peace of mind needs to be taken into account, and as much as I hate to admit it, maybe it is time to finally settle what happened the night I was cursed. Maybe if I had the answers to that, I could start to heal.

"I am just saying that she is going to be in danger until we catch the person behind this, whether it is Dan or not." Kaida hissed, scanning the darkness for anyone else. We usually had the place to ourselves, but every once in a while, some group of drunk kids would wander this way. Better to be safe.

You know something I don't? You can share with the class.

If she knew more than she was saying, I'm going to strangle her myself. There were many times were I felt like Kaida knew more than she shared, but unless it involved Alice, I let her keep her secrets. She huffed wordlessly and started searching the shadows for anything.

Lucian will be here soon. He promised.

I say loudly, hoping it acts like a prayer and makes him appear. My apprehension is worse now. The night is dragging on, and not having my phone is giving me anxiety.

"You are worried about the boy. You don't need to be, he will be okay." I know it was smart to leave my phone at home because of Alice being nosy as hell, but I wanted some way to communicate with Lucian if something did go wrong. It was my turn to huff at her.

Lucian is not a boy. He is a grown man who can take care of himself.

But I was worried, it was stupid. He was one of my few friends and he seemed to be taking hits left and right. No one really knew about our friendship, though…that would keep him safe. I was lost in my thoughts, staring into space, when a throat cleared behind us. Kaida jolted up, startled that someone snuck up on her like this. She was still in my sunglasses, hood up, but moved away quickly into the shadows anyway. Silver glinted on his pierced, full bottom lip, shining in the moonlight when he smiled broadly, "Hello, gorgeous."

Shit he scared the crap out of me! Ask him if he has a damn death wish? You don't sneak up on us like that!

I chastised, trying to catch my breath.

Don't flirt with him. I'm not in the mood.

"I am from another time, dearest. Men were expected to worship women like a goddess. This one understands that." She really just couldn't help herself. His smile grew, swinging his legs, he hopped up on the top of a grave cover. "See, Mattie dear, Kaida and I have a special relationship. You don't always get to be the boss of everyone." I scoffed while the gorgon purred happily. Seriously, for the personification of a women scorned, she was the opposite of a feminist sometimes. She ran a finger over his shoulder, "Yes little monster, someone else finally understands how controlling you can be. If he wants to worship me then he can."

He isn't worshiping you. This is just his personality.

He stopped spinning the ring on his dark finger and looked over at her in the shadows, raising a brow and tossing his dreads behind his shoulder, winking her way, "If you want someone to worship you, then I will be first in line." He said it cheekily, but I noticed that the humor didn't reach his eyes. This was not the point of the evening and I didn't need her getting a bigger damn ego.

Building a temple to you will probably put Alice off, I pointed out.

While she loved both sides of me, the day Alice wises up and decides to make Lucian hers, he would have to be hers alone. "Oh yes. Alice might not like that. She does not share." Kaida hissed out a sigh and leaned against the wall next to us, inspecting the long black nails on my hand. "If he ever worked up the courage to actually talk to her." She spoke to me but looked right at Lucian. Kaida was nothing if not a girl's girl. She loves Alice, and she is going to make sure those two eventually end up together.

Now he looked crestfallen; he talked a good game, but Lucian was sure that he would never be good enough for someone like Alice. He always asked after her, and I knew he watched out for her when she was out working a case, especially at night, but he hasn't spoken more than a handful of times to her.

Okay, Kai don't be so hard on him. He might be cocky on the outside but the poor man has a chewy caramel center. Ask about the envelope.

She changed the subject to something safer, "So where did you find the license?"

He perked back up, finding his metaphorical footing, "West side of the bayou. Headed inland. A cousin said there was a rental car down there in the trees. I thought I would check it out to see if there was any clue to when he left it there, but it doesn't appear he intended to leave it there."

Too much to hope he just got unlucky and got eaten by a big ass gator? Kaida repeated my question out loud.

He chuckled, "Don't think so, Cher. Not with what I've been hearing around town. Another woman has been threatened, and your place is being targeted as well." She nodded along, "We didn't think so… We aren't writing him off as dead quite yet." Pulling the tissue with blood out of our pocket and stepping out of the shadows to show him, "This is from the house. Do you have the license?" He reached behind him and pulled a baggie out of his leather satchel. He leaned forward to hold it out. Kaida grabbed it and was looking it over when I realized he was staring intently, "What?" She asked.

He smiled again, "You really are quite beautiful like this." I met his gaze through her eyes carefully. There wasn't an ounce of fear or apprehension. His gaze was genuine and warm, everything Kaida wanted to see reflected in her from a different pair of eyes. My heart cracked a little from the loneliness she felt all the time, to be the only one of your kind...to be considered a monster or a curse. She put on a brave face, but there were times when the sadness in her broke my heart. "If there were more men like you, Lucian, this curse would not exist." She was so earnest with her words. I could hug him just for giving her this one moment where she didn't feel like her existence was merely tolerated, but because someone liked her for her.

I was loath to admit how many times I thought about how I could have done something that night Catherine came home crying, or the night I was attacked. Since nothing could be done about the past, I had to keep on living. All I could do now was pray to the gods for more Lucians in the world and a lot less Dans . His smile fell away, and there was sadness permeating the air now. We all knew how the curse started and why it existed. While I had made friends with my demons, it didn't mean that I hadn't wished there was no reason for it to even exist.

"You know I'm not the only good man out there, another could be much closer than you think but you won't find one if you aren't keeping those eyes open." He glances over his shoulder at the crypts a few feet away, like he senses something. Following his gaze, I don't feel anything there.

"Keeping these eyes open seems like a bad idea if I am looking for a good man. As Mattie keeps reminding me, our garden has enough statues." He and I both chuckle. Nothing like a little self-deprecation to lighten the mood. She pulled open the baggie containing Dan's license and sniffed deeply. The gorgon hissed loudly, her snakes wriggling under our hood. Lucian startles, not moving away, but instead holding perfectly still.

"This is the same blood as from the house. The blood is wrong though...dead blood."

Awesome, that's just awesome, I think sarcastically, *the blood from the house is the same as the license. Probably the same as the blood painted in Hannah's office, too. That's a lot of blood.*

Lucian reaches behind him and pulls out a note in another baggie, handing it over. We grabbed it, angling it towards the light to read.

"Free yourself of the lies," Kaida read it out loud. It was scrawled on a piece of torn paper.

"Where did this come from?" Lucian jumps down off the grave cap and moves back a few steps, fear grows in my stomach.

"It was on Alice's SUV the other night. When she slept at the station." The fear turned to anger so quickly that I couldn't even think through the fog. I saw red, I felt red, I WAS red, and that anger wasn't going anywhere until I found the person responsible. Someone had left the note on her car while she was sleeping inside the station, threatening the most important person in our lives.

"This is done. NO ONE goes after Alice… I will put a stop to this right now." Kaida stalks out of the cemetery, following her instincts and senses, not really paying attention to the direction. There are no footsteps behind us, but I know Lucian won't be far behind. He knows better than to get in front of a monster and her hunt. The snakes are writhing against my cheek and the back of my neck, pushing out of the strands of my hair, worked up by our combined anger. They have no idea the target they just painted on themselves.

Chapter 21

William

Sitting in my SUV around the corner from the cemetery entrance, I watched Mattie's figure enter about an hour ago. She pulled up in her sister's car, but there was no sign of Alice. I almost texted her to see where she was since she swore, she would be with Mattie tonight. Mattie had a hoodie on and sunglasses covering her eyes even as the sun had set. Her idea of a disguise made me laugh; a criminal mastermind she was not. I could pick her out in a crowd by a mile, but then again, my eyes could find her anywhere it seemed. I could just make out the shadow of her sitting in the darkness.

We both sat waiting for something to happen.

What the hell was she waiting for? The darkness settled in, and I was seriously contemplating giving myself away and marching in there to ask why the hell she was wandering around at night when someone was after the people around her.

My phone rang and I checked it; Alice was calling me.

"Alice?" I answered, "Bennet, is Mattie with you?" She sounded flustered and worried.

"Why would she be, Alice? You swore she never goes out at night. That you were enough of a detail to put on her." Even if I didn't already suspect Mattie and Alice of the first three killings, I was sure that they didn't have anything to do with Laura or the threats, so that meant they were in danger. I liked Mattie despite everything I suspected and didn't want her hurt, or worse.

"Bennet, seriously! I know. I'm sorry, I thought I could get her to see sense, but we had a fight, and she isn't herself right now."

There was a confession in her tone if I looked for it, "Is she okay?" I asked, still staring at her form in the shadows. Alice was quiet for a long moment.

"Can I trust you, Bennet?" I looked away from Mattie and down at the console of the car that Alice was speaking through, "Trust me as Alice or as Detective Hester?"

She scoffed, "Are you William right now or Agent Bennet?" She asked incredulously. I was about to answer when Mattie's shape jumped, startled, and moved away further into the shadows.

"Gotta go, Alice. I got her back." I hung up and pulled out my gun from it's holster. Forgoing my jacket, I slipped out of the SUV and closed the door softly. Slipping along the shadows, I heard Mattie talking to someone, "Men were expected to worship women like a goddess. This one understands that," she said, her voice had an edge to it, and a bit of a lisp. There was another shadow of a person sitting down, swinging his legs. He was just barely visible, but Mattie was further in the shadows of a crypt.

They were speaking softly, and I was just far enough away to catch every third word, except for her loud outburst. There was a third person they both replied to there that I couldn't see. I was crouched down behind one of the other grave caps, trying to keep Mattie in my sights. She moved towards the man, and he handed something over, which she took. Her tone seemed pissed off now. Then I heard a snake hissing. I was startled and looked around my feet.

Last thing I needed was to get bitten by a damn snake in a cemetery. Mattie was pacing now, and the shadows were playing on her features. I could see the glint of her sunglasses still. Why the hell was she wearing sunglasses in the dark? There was no one here to recognize her. The guy in the shadows called her beautiful, I could pick up on the flirty tone in his voice. I was pissed, was this why she ran out on breakfast? Why was she giving me the slip? She already had a man, but spent her day flirting with me? Wait, did she just say Alice? The man responded, but the only word I caught was Alice. I was straining to hear anything. I wanted to move closer, but between the snakes and the darkness, I was better off waiting till the guy left.

Suddenly, Mattie was moving towards the gate, fast; she was moving somewhere furiously. I looked back at where her companion was, but he had disappeared. I scrambled up and back towards the gate. Looking both ways, I saw her moving towards the river and the warehouses to the right. I followed about a block behind. It was a struggle to keep up; wherever she was going, she was moving fast.

"Shit" I said under my breath.

I holstered my gun and started lightly jogging to keep up. Was she going after someone? I was going to accidentally catch her in the act. Well, that would put a damper on trying to woo her…But I couldn't just let her kill someone…could I? I ran around the next corner looking for her, but she disappeared.

Breathing hard, I slip between two of the warehouse buildings and spot her at the far end of an alley with her back to me, just standing there staring at the ground. I stepped forward quietly to see what she is looking at. She bent down and touched a puddle by her foot…curious. I start to move in and ask her what the hell she is doing, when my path is blocked.

A large black man steps in my way from between two doors I didn't even notice before.

"You should go back," he says. His voice is deep and threatening. He is just slightly shorter than me, but muscular, with dark dreads pulled back into a ponytail. Silver jewelry flashes in his ears, lip, and eyebrow. He looks like a pirate dressed in an open black shirt and tight leather pants. I recognized his voice from the cemetery. He waves with one hand and pushes me with the other on my shoulder. I grab his wrist to shove him arm away when he spins me around and pins my arm behind my back. He pushed my face into the brick wall and cut off my view of Mattie. I wasn't expecting him to be so strong, or quick.

What if this asshole was who was killing the men for the group? Like a hired hit man? I loved that idea far more than arresting Mattie as a killer.

"Listen, Mon Cheri, I am trying to save your skin. You need to go back.

Don't come this way. Don't look behind you," he whispers, extremely close to my ear.

"I know Mattie. I'm trying to help her." His dark gaze meets mine, and his hand loosens a bit, but he keeps me pinned, his breath a whisper uncomfortably close to my ear.

"I know. I've seen you, Agent Bennet. Why do you think I'm trying to help you?" I pull my arm loose and turn to face him, looking past his shoulder for Mattie. She's already gone, must have slipped away during our little scuffle.

"Who the hell are you?" He smiles with blindingly white, straight teeth. The glint of the light reflecting off his lip ring. He bows with a mocking air, "Lucian Corbin, at your service." Ah yeah, the asshole who ruined our date. The one Alice had said could be the killer.

There was a file on Mr. Corbin at the station that Alice had put together for the trafficking case she was trying to push as the cause of the original three deaths. He was a known criminal following Mattie around the cemetery at night. I pushed past him to go after her again, and once again he reached out and grabbed my arm.

"You don't want to go there, friend. You need to go back to your car and leave. Go to your hotel and lock the door tight." I shook off his arm aggressively, "Get out of my way before I arrest you. We are not friends. I'm going to follow her because she's in danger out here alone."

I pulled out my handcuffs and pointed them at him, "I would take you in for questioning, but I have her to follow tonight."

I was striding quickly away, trying to ignore the infuriating man, when he started to laugh. It was a low chuckle at first, and then it took on a sinister air that raised the hair on my arms and gave me goosebumps. I looked back and he was still just standing there.

"I can promise you Cher, that they are just fine. It is you who will be in danger. Then I will have Mattie angry at me, and Alice too. Can't stand for that Cher...non, that would be bad."

He started stalking closer, and I reached for my gun, drawing it and pointing it at the man when he suddenly opened his hand and blew dust in my face. I coughed at the invasion, my head instantly spinning as I fell. My knees hit the pavement hard, toppling over, my head hit the ground with a thunk. My body felt completely numb and I was struggling to keep my eyes open as panic set in. Lucian walked over and crouched down beside my head.

"Now now Cher, don't you worry. Lucian will care for you tonight. Mattie can deal with you as she sees fit tomorrow. I won't risk my pretty face just to be rid of you. And by the way, Alice is the only one allowed to handcuff me. You should have left when I told you to."

I couldn't keep my eyes open. As they closed, his grin was the last thing I saw. I could hear Lucian pick up my weapon and move it elsewhere. I felt him digging in my pockets for my wallet and keys. Great, the guy was going to rob me, too. Just a fantastic end to the night. I was losing consciousness quickly, but felt Lucian tug me up and over his shoulder.

He grunted, "Oof trop de beignets. Skip that tomorrow, Cher…maybe tomorrow we will talk again and be real friends. I don't have many friends, and if you are going to hang out with my girls, I would like to be there. My dearest Alice likes you, so you must have some redeeming qualities past your horrible listening skills."

My last thought as I passed out was that I would definitely get beignets, and punch Lucian in the face, several times. Darkness and silence wrapped around me.

Chapter 22

Mattie

We moved through the shadows, anger and a need to protect Alice driving us. We had a clue now, and that was everything. Footsteps sounded behind us, but stopping and facing them would be more of a risk than letting Lucian deal with it. He had our back. We needed to keep our focus on what lay ahead. The scent of the blood was stronger now, easier to follow. Shining in the moonlight was a dark puddle. This was almost too easy to find. We'd been searching for clues for days now, and suddenly it was right here, in the first place we look? Bending down and looking closer, already knowing what it was.

"It's blood," She whispered.

Yeah, I guessed that. Poke it.

"You want me to touch it?! That's disgusting." She recoiled her hand and cringed inwardly.

Really? That's where you draw the line? Who knew you were such a delicate flower? Don't bitch out on me now.

She hissed loudly. "If I could bite you, I would."

I get that impression, but then, who would take you to flirt with Agent Trouble and Lucian? She hesitantly dipped a finger in the dark pool and raised the blood to our nose. *anything?*

"It's the same blood as before. There is so much, they are surely dead." She stood up, a look of disgust on her face.

Can you tell whose it is?

"I'm a mythical being but not an oracle. I can find the body though…I think."
   I wanted to laugh initially, but was a bit shocked at her admitting that maybe she couldn't do something.

It will be okay. We'll figure it out.. together, as always.

"Pretty man has caught our follower." She hissed out, looking behind us. I saw the shape of Lucian with a man pressed against the wall. Stalker or homeless guy, Lucian would send him on his way easily.

He seems like he has it handled. Let's keep going.

We turn and keep walking. He would catch up when he's done.

The night dragged on as we searched for the source of the blood, but as dawn started to paint the sky pink, I finally called it.

Babe, we're getting nowhere. This whole chase seems like it was designed to confuse someone us.

We headed towards the docks to wait for the sunrise. "That would mean someone had intimate knowledge of what we are."

Yeah, it would, but so did the whole 'shed your skin' line on the side of the garage.

We found ourselves at the edge of the water in the park, all alone. The water was a delicately painted reflection of the sky, with the light dancing off the high points. Something about sitting in the brief silence that had fallen on the city was calming.

"Good night, Mattie. We will try again tomorrow night. and the next night, and then the next, for as many nights as it takes."

The curse lifted, and my skin relaxed. I felt the change back to my normal self washing over me, Kaida falling silent and calm inside me. I pushed off my hood and moved my sunglasses up and into my hair before sighing and relaxing back on my hands. Together, we spent the night following the scent from the alley, and it led us to the edge of the water.

Presumably where our mystery suspect had gotten in a boat and gone inland, up the river. I don't know whose blood it was, but none of the options cleared anything up. A series of dead ends…with nowhere to go from here, I decided that the best course of action for now was to just take a break and rest for a moment. Sometimes, doing nothing was better than running around blindly hoping to find something.

I really tried to live by the belief that the universe will show me the way when I need it, but what if it's too late for that? Sensing someone approach from behind me, I stiffened, but relaxed again as I smelled Alice's familiar perfume of citrus and oud. She walked up slowly and sat down next to me, crisscrossing her legs, laying her head on my shoulder.

"Hey, Houdini." I expected her to be way more pissed, especially if she has been out looking for me all night.

"Hey," there are so many things left unsaid, but that's how it always is with us. We don't always need to say we're sorry or yell in anger. It was a simple transaction of love that helped us to always move past whatever was between us. I couldn't imagine a world where Alice didn't forgive me for almost anything, and there was nothing I wouldn't forgive her for either. Reaching into the pocket of my hoodie, I pull out the two baggies Lucian gave me and set them on her knee. She doesn't move to touch them, just staring at them for a long minute.

Then, she sits up and looks closer at the note from her car.

"You got a threat too?" I shake my head, "No. You did…Lucian took it off your SUV the other night when you slept at the station."

Her head whips up to look at me.

"Lucian stole evidence right off of a police car? In front of the station? What was he even doing there?" I sigh and sit back on my hands again.

"He watches out for you when he can, mainly when I'm not around to do it. He didn't think you would tell me about it if you found it." She was turning the license over in her hand, inspecting it in the morning light.

"I wouldn't have… but you don't need to make him watch over me."

I smile, "I didn't even have to ask. If you would just look, hon, you might see that there's more to him than you think." Alice sets the license down and looks at me, our eyes meeting.

"And how did you come upon Dan Reynolds' license all covered in muck and blood?"

Sighing again, "Lucian. He really can be helpful when he wants to be…" She starts to stand, "Great, so we can put together an arrest warrant for him."

I reach out and grab her wrist, "You know he didn't do anything."

Shaking her head, she pulls away, "No, I don't. I know it wasn't YOU, but it could have easily been him."

I stand up too, "Alice, Lucian didn't kill him either. Not that he wouldn't have, but he just tracked him and found a car rental in his name that was left out in the swamps, and that license was left out there too." I take the baggie from her and put it back in my pocket.

"Come on, let's get home. I'll fill you in on everything we found last night. You're probably exhausted, and I know I am."

Looping our arms together, we started toward the car, "I just got to town. Parked your truck a few blocks away."

Oh yeah, I had taken her SUV last night, and my keys were hidden upstairs… apparently not well enough. "I'm surprised you didn't follow me last night and try to chase us down."

She scoffed, leaning into my shoulder again, "Some of us can just trust that the other one will be safe and responsible. We don't have to act like crazy stalkers because we don't believe the other one will do the right thing."

I rolled my eyes at the heavy sarcasm, "Oh yeah? You just trust me to do the right thing and be safe?"

She giggled, "I said some of us, not me. No, I called Bennet last night, and after a dressing down about saying you would stay home, he hung up on me quickly, so I figured he was trying to follow you. When did you give him the slip?"

Oh fuck…fuck…fuckity fucksticks.

"I didn't, Alice. I never heard or smelled him either."

Thinking back to the events of last night, I tried to remember sensing someone. I never did, but the memory of Lucian staring off into the darkness pops up in my head. Then there was the guy that Lucian tangled in the alley… "Fuck, Lucian Corbin, I will kick your ass!"

I let go of Alice's arm and started running to the car. Hitting the unlock button, I slid into the driver's seat and started the car just as Alice ripped open the passenger door and jumped inside.

"What the hell did Lucian do?"

I pulled out with the tires squealing, "Last night we were hunting down a lead, and he was watching my back. Someone came into the alley, and I thought it was the person who tried to tail us last time, or just a homeless guy, but they got into it with Lucian before they could get close enough to me. Normally, Lucian would just convince them to take another route or maybe threaten them to back off… but if it was Will, there would be no convincing him to walk away."

I bang my hand on the steering wheel, feeling frustrated again that I left my phone at home, preventing me from calling Lucian to find out what happened. Alice had her phone to her ear. Finally, I heard Will's voice directing her to leave a message.

"Nothing. Straight to voicemail, but hon, it's still early, maybe he isn't even up yet."

Listening to the little voice in my head, I thought it through.

"No, if Will was following me last night, he might have seen something, and if he did, Lucian would never let him walk away."

Alice looked at her phone as it dinged with a message, "Oh! It's Lucian. He said to meet him at our house."

Oh, thank the goddess, but Alice looked more concerned, her lips flattened, and her brow furrowed.

"What?" Alice looked over. "He texted from Bennet's phone." Well shit. I punched down the accelerator and sped towards home as fast as I could.

Pulling into the driveway sharply and hitting the brakes, there was a flurry of dirt flying up from the tires as I jumped out and raced towards the patio where I could see Lucian sitting in one of our rocking chairs with a cup of coffee in his hand and another sitting on the railing, steaming in the morning light. He smiled as Alice and I approached, "Where the hell is my partner, Lucian?"

Alice yells across the yard, quickly walking toward him. He puts his hand to his heart in feigned injury, "Oh Mon Ami, please don't tell me you have fallen for the Agent's charm too? I will die of heartbreak if you tell me this is one of those situations where you two are going to fight over him. If you are going to fight for a man, I will happily volunteer."

He waggled his eyebrows suggestively and smiled at Alice's frustrated expression. I feel a smirk trying to come over my lips, but I tighten them and look at him as sternly as I can.

"So, it was Will who was in the alley last night? Please tell me you just pick-pocketed him and gave him the slip?"

I really, really, was hoping he was going to say, 'of course and then I came here to wait for you' and offer me the cup of coffee but it was still sitting there, black as sin, and Lucian knew I took mine with cream and sugar clearly wasn't for me. He shrugged and leaned back in the rocker while Alice and I climbed the stairs and stood next to each other directly in front of him.

"Cher, I tried. I really tried to get him to go the other way, but the handsome man wanted to dance, and who was I to refuse?" He pauses to take a sip of his coffee.

"He was quite determined to catch up to you, so I put him out."

Alice went still, "You killed him!" she screeched, outraged.

I relaxed and leaned against the railing. "No, he means he knocked him out. Devil's breath?" I asked, silently praying that I'm not going to have to kick his ass. "He's probably still sleeping it off at his hotel." I said, hope in my voice.

I have my doubts about that little monster.

Kaida waking up for to add to the party with sarcasm was the last thing I needed. Lucian stiffened and grimaced, looking guilty as he glanced toward the garage and sipped at his coffee again.

"You drugged a federal agent?" Alice rubbed at her forehead, looking even more frustrated, with us both. I followed Lucian's eye line to the garage, just as I heard the quiet yell for help coming from that direction…oh no…he wouldn't!

Oh yes he would. He was supposed to protect us. You can not be mad at him for doing exactly what we asked.

"We most certainly didn't ask him to kidnap anyone…at least I didn't." Kaida giggled softly in my head. I got up and quickly walked toward the sound. Alice followed closely behind, her hearing not good enough to pick up anything yet.

"What did you do?" She shouted back at Lucian. He collected the other coffee cup and followed behind.

Shrugging his shoulders casually, "What was necessary. These two are too stubborn for their good. I am helping Love, I promise."

He said, easily passing Alice and catching up to me. "Maybe you should let me go in first?" He asked.

I reached for the knob, hearing Will inside yelling about how he was a federal agent, and how he was going to arrest the absolute hell out of Lucian.

He will smooth everything over…or we could just turn him into a statue. I would enjoy keeping him.

I'm not sure Kaida or Lucian were appreciating the fact that we had jumped into the deep end without a floaty. Will was not going to be 'smoothed over' or just forget about Lucian now. This was a powder keg, it was set to explode, and take us all with it.

Will was sitting inside, probably tied up, making threats that only grew more colorful and louder as Lucian opened the door with a huge smile on his face. Then, he mostly closed it behind himself, the crack allowing us to listen easier from outside.

"I swear to God, when I get out of here, I'm going to rip you limb from limb. Charging you with murder is going to be the highlight of my fucking day, Mr. Corbin."

Oh, he was beyond pissed! In the time I knew him, I hadn't heard him curse. I kind of wanted to watch him fight Lucian, he deserved to take a punch or two in the face for this.

I want to watch that too. Kaida purred.

He could have dumped him in his hotel, and Will would have woken up confused, but none the wiser. The mind gets creative when it fills in blanks, and no one likes blanks in their memory. Lucian's laughter drifted out the door as Alice moved in closer to listened next to me, "Mon Cheri, I tried to get you to go away. I tried to reason with you, but you are as stubborn as my friend Mattie. I like that in a person, and since she likes you, I did you the favor of bringing you here instead of dumping you out in the swamps to feed the gators."

I winced at the threat, feeling Kaida smile, *keep Lucian from feeding him to the swamp puppies. I like them but I like Agent Trouble more.*

Lucian absolutely would do that, but that wasn't the way to win over Will.

"Great if he didn't already like Lucian for the snake murders, he certainly would now," Alice whispered.

I glanced over to her.

"He thinks Lucian is the one who killed those men?" She winced, and guilt was all over her face.

"I may have helped him with that theory." I started to open my mouth to yell at her, but she cut me off.

"It was better than him going after the theory that it was you! And I told him he wouldn't ever ACTUALLY catch him. Lucian could get out of any trouble, and of course I would help him make a great escape and disappear long enough for Bennet to give up."

I started to say that throwing Lucian under the bus was underhanded, but Alice knew that already. She would never let him actually go to jail. So I shut my mouth and went back to listening to the conversation in the garage again.

"I've brought you a lovely cup of coffee to knock away that cobweb feeling in your head, so if you'll be civilized, I'll untie you and we can have a chat before I drive you back to the city."

Silence drew out, we strained harder to hear if maybe Will was whispering some more not-so-veiled threats or if maybe Lucian had just drugged him again.

"Are you helping Mattie?" He asked, sounding calm.

"Oui. I am not a threat to her or Alice, Agent." After a few long seconds of silence, we heard Lucian move across the garage toward Will.

"Here, we shall drink coffee and become friends. You can't not become friends when one brings you coffee," he drawled casually.

"You drugged me, stole my phone and wallet, and then left me tied up in a garage till dawn. It will take more than a cup of coffee to make us friends. Not to mention, I'm pretty sure you are a murderer." Will said it so matter-of-factly and calmly. It was impressive how he could keep his cool in this situation.

Lucian started laughing loudly, "Well, I don't know who you think I killed..."

Will interrupted him. "I think you are killing the men who hurt the women in Mattie's S/A group, for money. I think you're blackmailing her and threatening her so she won't tell me anything, and apparently stalking her too."

Lucian immediately laughed so hard he had to gasp for breath, and I can't help but smile as well. Kaida was laughing hard in the back on my mind, the idea of Lucian being a hired hit man was funny, but thinking that Lucian would blackmail and threaten me was beyond hilarious. Lucian blows out a big breath, still trying to control his laughter, and I could picture Will inside drinking his coffee with a bitter scowl.

"Cheri, you make me sound so much more bad ass than I really am! My sweet Alice would chop off my balls if she thought I was blackmailing or threatening her sister…that's not even the worst that would befall my pretty face if I tried that with Mattie. I assure you, my friend, that I do have some brains in this head, at least enough to know better than to play in a den of snakes," he says.

I wondered what the hell Lucian is up to, because his choice of words was not an accident. He pretends he isn't whip smart, but he is a little genius, and wouldn't be dropping hints like that for no reason.

Sometimes we need a push dear, and sometimes we need a shove.

"Cher, you come in now?" He calls out for me, and I look at Alice.

She shrugs and gestures for me to lead the way. Pushing the door open, I step inside. The small windows don't let much natural light in, but the light bulb above us is on and illuminating the garage in yellowish light.

I wave at Will wryly. He is leaning against the workbench while Lucian is sitting in the same chair in the middle of the room that Will must have spent the night tied up in. His usually tidy, wavy hair is mussed up, and his white dress shirt is covered in dust and some mud. He looks like Lucian rolled him out of the alley and down the streets. His empty holster is strapped across his shoulders. Lucian must still have his gun.

Will's holding a cup of coffee, his eyes barely glancing at me for a single second. Alice comes in behind me and his eyes dart up and check her over carefully. A bite of jealousy washes over me. It's not that it isn't gratifying to know he cares about her, but he had barely even glanced at me. Then his blue-gray eyes meet mine before he finally lowers the cup and speaks.

"Did you know it was me at the cemetery?" Lucian and I both go still and look at each other.

"Nope, don't look at him. Answer me," he snaps sharply. He's really mad, but his calm voice is deceptive.

I did not know it was him either. Just so you know...but that makes sense now.

I shake my head hard enough to shake a bit of hair in the front loose.

"I didn't know you were in the cemetery at all." He quietly studies me for a long moment before he nods and sips at his coffee again.

I would rather he yell or stomp around because, like this, I have no idea what he's thinking.

"Alice, how did you guys find us so quickly?" He asked her, and I'm hurt that he doesn't think I would tell him. I guess I haven't given him the impression that I would be very forthcoming with information, so why not trust Alice more?

We could try being honest.

Honest? Yeah, I can see that working out fine. Well I am the monster you are trying to catch. Oh, and I would really like to go on another date sometime. Doesn't seem like that's going to go in our favor, I think to her harshly trying to stifle her into being quiet.

Alice glances over at me and then Lucian briefly, "You're at our house."

She gestures around, "In our garage. And Lucian told us where you were before we even realized you were gone."

She was clearly trying to shelter Lucian from more of Will's anger, but Lucian just kept leaning back in the chair, balancing it on the back legs and drinking his coffee like it was just totally normal to kidnap someone and have them accuse you of being a hit man. Of course, with Lucian, this could be a regular Tuesday for all I know. He was an enigma. Will was looking around the garage with renewed interest, his gaze landing on the tarp in the back of the room that covered two statues we had left in here for storage. Eventually, Lucian would take them out to the swamps and dump them for us, but it had been a while since he made any trips for statue disposal.

Oh yeah...we should do something with those. Maybe more clamanatis!

Inwardly wincing, it's clematis. I cleared my throat to bring his attention back to me. He looked my way as I walked closer to him. "I swear no one in our group hired Lucian to kill anyone."

Lucian coughed, "Cher it's..." I held up my hand to silence him.

"He would never threaten or blackmail me. Lucian could never hurt me." Will's eyes softened as I spoke, and I reached out to take the cup from him, setting it on the workbench.

Kiss him. Come on Mattie, just a little bit closer.

I took his hand ignoring Kaida's unhelpful distraction. I didn't need her commentary, I wanted to kiss him, had wanted to since that first day but I needed him to go, for his sake and mine. He looked past me at the others for a second and then pulls my hand hard as he wraps his other hand around the back of my neck. His fingers push into my hair, and he leans in, "I have to do this first." He whispers against my lips and then presses his mouth to mine, and just like that, everything else fades away.

Fucking finally.

Chapter 23

Will

Waking up in the dark garage I was pissed off as I looked around the dark room and tried to piece together my memories from last night. My head was pounding, and my mouth felt dry as hell. I couldn't remember a hangover that ever made me this miserable. As soon as that prick from the alley came back, I was going to bash him in the head and then haul him to jail. I don't care if he knows Mattie; in fact, that makes it worse for him. There wasn't much in this small space. I was in a chair in the center of the room with a big set of doors behind me that, guessing from the sliver of light creeping in, open to the outside. There was a smaller single door across from me as well. Small windows were behind me, above a workbench, but they were too high and dirty to see much through them other than sunlight.

The door cracked open, and the aforementioned asshole walked in smiling, carrying two cups of coffee. The sunlight streaming in hurt my head, and he turned on the naked light bulb hanging above me, which stung my eyes even more. He's talking while I do my best to ignore him and pull at the rope binding my wrists behind my chair.

"...I did you a favor by bringing you here instead of taking you out to the swamps to feed the gators."

I stop and stare at him. Is he seriously threatening me right now? As soon as I get my gun back, I'm just going to shoot him. Thinking back to what Alice said about him, he's the best suspect for the murders, and I really don't care if he is guilty or not right now. I just want him to not be here.

"Now, I've brought you a lovely cup of coffee to knock away that cobweb feeling in your head. So if you'll be nice, I'll untie you and we can have a chat before I drive you back to the city."

Is he offering to just let me go after all this? Why the hell did he attack me and drag me off to his creepy shack if he was just going to let me go? Maybe he's insane. I did have cobwebs in my brain- okay, I'll get loose, drink the coffee, and if it's poisoned, I guess I'm dead. If it's not, we go back to town, and then I arrest him. Somewhere in the middle of all that, I'll hit that smug smiling asshole right in the mouth. He's still holding out one of the cups with a snarky grin on his face. I nod at him and lean forward so he can untie me.

"You're helping Mattie?" I ask, curiously. His smile grows as he finishes the knots and steps away to hand me the cup. I take it and stand up, leaning on the workbench. After so long sitting my legs feel weak and wobbly so I stretch them out one at a time while I watch him.

"Oui. I am not a threat to her or Alice, Agent."

Well, he sounded sincere, but how was I supposed to believe a criminal? Maybe he was blackmailing Mattie and that was what was in the envelope at the diner. That would make sense. He has the gall to wink at me and then move over to the chair, with a sweep of his long steampunk style coat, he takes a seat, crossing one ankle over the other knee. He's completely at ease after kidnapping an FBI agent. It's unnerving and I want my gun back. I set down my coffee and rub the raw part of my wrists while he watches me.

He raises his cup in a mock cheer, "Here we shall drink coffee and become friends. You can't not become friends when one brings you coffee," he drawled casually, and then took a long sip. I can definitely say I can't ever see myself being friends with Lucian Corbin. So far, most of my thoughts are of ways to get back at him.

"You drugged me, stole my phone and wallet, and then left me tied up in a shed till dawn. It'll take more than a cup of coffee to make us friends. Not to mention, I think you are a murderer." He lowered his coffee cup, uncrossed his legs, and leaned forward to meet my eyes dead on. A smile on his face and humor dancing in his dark, thick lashed eyes, he said "Well I don't know who you think I killed but..."

I raised my hand to stop him and say, "I think you're killing the men who hurt the women in Mattie's S/A group for money. I think you're blackmailing her into not telling me anything, and apparently stalking her too."

His reaction will be everything my gut needs to know. Evidence be damned. How a man reacts to that kind of accusation is enough for me. I'll work backwards after he's behind bars. He sets his cup down calmly next to the leg of his chair and then his shoulders start to shake. He's still staring at the ground when I realize he isn't breaking down, but cracking up. His laughter fills the small space, and he leans back clutching his stomach. A full minute of roaring laughter spilled from him before he wiped away a tear from his eye. My gut and I are at a loss, I've done a lot of interviews over the years, but that was a first.

"Cheri makes me sound so much more badass than I really am! My sweet Alice would chop off my balls if she thought I was blackmailing her sister...that's not even the worst that would befall my pretty face if I tried that with Mattie. I assure you my friend, I do have some brains in this head, at least enough to know better than to play in a den of snakes," he says.

He said snakes like a reference to the killings. My gut says he isn't lying, so if he isn't the killer, then why is he emphasizing snakes? He has a mischievous smirk on his face now, "Think harder Agent."

He whispers like someone will hear him, then, I realize why when he picks up his cup, leans back in his chair, balancing it on its back legs and winking at me. "Cher, you come in now?" He spoke loudly, and I watched as the door pulled open.

Mattie walked into the room in jeans and the same hoodie she was wearing last night. She had her hair half tied up and her sunglasses perched on top, as usual. I've never actually seen her without sunglasses on her. I quickly look her over, the dark smudges under her eyes showing just how tired she is from her midnight wanderings. I see Alice follow in behind her. I check her over as well to make sure my partner is okay. A quick glance tells me she is well rested and unharmed, but nervous as hell. I take a drink to give myself a second to think about last night and start to wonder if she knew it was me following her and sent Lucian to scoop me up and keep me out of the way. Whatever she was up to last night, she made sure that neither Alice nor I could follow.

Only way to find out is to tempt fate.

"Did you know it was me in the cemetery last night?" I ask Mattie. She stiffens, and out of the corner of my eye I see Lucian freeze with his cup halfway to his mouth. She looks at him and my temper finally snaps. It's been a long day and a half and I'm not really in control of my emotions anymore. Her looking at Lucian sends me off the deep end.

"No, don't look at him. Answer me." I snap sharply and her green gaze shoots back to me. She shakes her head and a few pieces of hair from up top fall out to frame her face. My fingers twitch, wanting to push them back behind her ears, but I stay still.

"I didn't know you were at the cemetery at all," she says, then bites her lip, giving away how nervous she is. Lucian is still watching us like we're an episode of a soap opera, just smiling away at all this back and forth. Punching his stupid face will be the highlight of my day. I do my best to ignore as I look at Alice. "Alice, how did you guys find us so quickly?" She glances down, guilt all over her face, before she looks at her sister, then Lucian, then back at me before speaking. "You're at our house."

She gestures around, "In our garage. Lucian told us you were here before we even realized you were gone."

Looking back over at the wannabe pirate, he's just staring at Alice and sipping from his cup. He winks at her before he looks back toward me. Alice rolls her eyes and turns partly away. Lucian looks at me, then darts his eyes toward some tarps covering large shapes in the dark corner of the garage. The girls don't see it, but he's clearly trying to draw my attention to that corner. While I'm studying the shapes, trying to make out what could be under them in the shadows, Mattie walks over to me as she clears her throat to get my attention.

The sway of her hips, the swing of her hair, those blazing green eyes that hypnotize me. It was like she moved in slow motion. Finally, she stands right in front of me and speaks.

"I swear no one in our group hired Lucian to kill anyone." Lucian coughed and I glanced over to me.

"Cher it's…" Mattie holds her hand up to silence him and I look into the gorgeous green eyes again. Something about her overrides all my systems. I can't help but believe what she's saying. If she's lying to me, it could mean the end of my career, but I'd say fuck it and leave anyways just to make this girl happy. I don't know how she stole so much of my faith so quickly.

"He would never threaten or blackmail me. Lucian couldn't hurt me." Without breaking eye contact she reaches out to take the cup from me, setting it on the workbench. I can smell her lilac and vanilla scent. She always smells like books to me… books and rain. Taking my hand, I look past her at the others for a second.

At this point I don't care if she is casting a spell on me or if I'm still under the influence of whatever Lucian drugged me with. I'm going to figure the mystery of Mattie out, today, but before I do I need something from her. Something to separate the before and after. I let go of her hand to slide mine around her waist, pulling her in close so she's flush against me. I can feel her breasts pressed softly to my chest, our lips just inches apart. I wrap my other hand around the back of her neck and dig my fingers into that long dark hair. She's so close now I can feel her heart racing. Her pulse dances against my chest and her breath hitches, waiting.

"I have to do this first." I whisper against her lips and then press my mouth to hers. It takes a second, but she sighs and melts into the kiss. She tastes of sin, the kind of sin I would never ask for absolution from. I drown in her, needing her more than I need air. I pull away for a moment and she gasps in a breath before I'm devouring her again. My hand snakes around to cup the front of her throat. Using my thumb on her chin, I tilt her head up slightly for better access. She drags her teeth lightly over my bottom lip and I groan.

When I decided I needed to kiss her, it had been a defining moment. If the worst eventually came, at least I would have this one thing to take with me. I was drowning in her and I didn't want to be saved. Something shifted in the universe, and I was certain that I'd die before giving her up. The world started spinning again as we hear clapping, breaking the magic of the moment. Lucian was watching closely and was clapping, with a huge, dumb grin on his face.

"S'il te plait. Don't stop for us. Best show I've watched in a long while." I released Mattie and stepped toward him to get in the punch that he had asking for all morning when Alice stepped up and kicked the chair out from under him. He fell onto the dirt floor with a grunt, the wind knocked out of him for a moment. His eyes were closed while he recovered. Then he opened them and smiled up at Alice broadly.

"Alice, Bien-aimee I fell for you a while ago. No need to knock me back down." He said it with complete earnest. I couldn't help but laugh too. Alice's face finally cracked a smile, but when she looked back at me, she blushed.

Leaning forward, I offered my hand to Lucian. He took it without looking away from Alice. I decided to take advantage and get my just desserts. Before he could shake off her effect, I pulled my arm back and swung full force, hitting him in the jaw as hard as I could. Mattie and Alice gasped loudly as Lucian stumbled back. Alice ran to help him, and Mattie grabbed my arm to prevent me from throwing another punch, but I just wanted one good cathartic hit. Now we could be friends. He looked back at me, still smiling, rubbing his hand on his sore jaw.

"Feel better?" He asked.

"Oui, asshole" I smiled back. I could use a few more friends, even one as annoying as he is. Besides, he's friends with Mattie, so it's better if we're friends too. Mattie and Alice looked at each other for a long moment and then Alice nodded.

Whatever silent communication just occurred, it didn't go the way Mattie wanted and she sighed heavily before taking my hand and leading me out of the garage and toward the house.

Chapter 24

Mattie

Leading the way out of the garage and into the bright light of day was terrifying. I was coming out of the shadows both literally and figuratively. Alice wanted me to share what we know about the case, Lucian wanted me to share everything, and I just wanted to go inside and pretend none of this was happening.

You have to stop burying your head in the sand, little monster.

I wanted to rewind time and go back to when my life was just a series of simple choices. Everything was cozy shades of gray and now the hand grasped in mine painted it all in bright colors. Colors I hadn't seen in years, and I wasn't sure I was ready to yet.

That is because he is meant to be ours. Take a leap.

His hand was large enough to engulf mine, warm with calluses on his palm. His fingers weaved through mine, and it made me feel grounded. Suddenly he pulled me, and I was jerked to stop with him. He was looking back, Lucian and Alice had followed us out of the garage, but he was staring at the bloody words still painted on the outside of the garage. Hell, I had forgotten that was there with everything that was going on. Even though they had faded, the threat was still readable. Lucian looked back following his new pals eye line and froze as well.

You should have let Alice wash it away...

She's right...again. I should have just let Alice spray it off yesterday.

"Merde..." Lucian whispered, and grabbed Alice's elbow as she pushed past him to go around the house, presumably to get the hose like she wanted to in the first place. Will looked back at me expectantly.

"I can explain..." He just cocked his eyebrows, waiting for an explanation.

I can't believe he actually expects us to explain. It is what it is.

Doesn't he know that's just an expression? He dropped his hands and crossed his arms, still just staring silently, waiting. Lucian came up to stand next to him and stared too, but he was looking past me to where Alice was pulling at the tangled hose, trying to get it far enough to reach the garage. She was grunting with the effort, it was the only sound, and it was grating on my nerves.

"Alice! Just leave it...I'll paint over it later!" I yelled out at her and she dropped the hose with a huff, shoving her hair back off her face as she walked over to our awkward group.

Will watched me silently for so long that Lucian finally broke, "First Alice is threatened and now you? At your own home? How could you not tell me?" Lucian asked, sounding actually hurt.

I put my hand on his forearm to comfort him, opening my mouth to remind him that I did text him when it happened, and all he responded with was an emoji of a crow.

Will broke his silence, "What do you mean Alice was threatened? When? By whom? The same person threatening Dr. Raines?" I sighed and glanced back at Alice before taking the note in the baggie out of my back pocket again and handing it to Will. He looked it over carefully and then turned it over and looked harder like he might see something we didn't.

"Where was this?" he asks softly.

Lucian pipes up to 'help', "On Alice's SUV, a few nights ago outside the police station."

Alice is staring at Lucian, studying him. For the first time she sees what has been obvious this whole time. Lucian is a flirt of the highest order, but he means what he says. When he says he cares for her, he really means it. I know he's in love with her, but I'm staying out of their mess.

Well mostly...

Will is still inspecting the note in his hands.

This is your chance, Mattie. I can tell, he will believe.

Kaida starts hissing in my head again and I gasp touching my temple. Lucian and Alice break their staring contest to look at me, concerned.

Shaking my head and ignoring Kaida, I meet Will's gaze.

"Free yourself of lies" he reads out loud.

"Any idea what lies they mean?" Alice shakes her head, signaling that she doesn't want me to do this. I know what my secrets have cost her; how can we ask her to keep more when it's her that's in danger now?

"It means me." Alice grabs my arm and pulls like she can hide me behind herself, but Will reaches out and puts his hand on my opposite elbow to stop her, "What do they mean by lies? What is Alice lying about for you?"

He's watching my expressions. Looking into his eyes, I could drown in that cozy, warm, safe shade of gray blue. He looks so serious, but nothing in his body language says he is unsafe to us; nothing raises my hackles and yells at me to protect. Somehow my instincts know he's okay.

Do it Mattie. Make the leap. I know it will work out, Kaida says, her voice so serious.

Not a single joke or quip, not an ounce of sarcasm. If I trust this gut feeling it will be the same as jumping off a cliff without a parachute. Alice is still holding my left arm in her tightening grip, just watching the silent exchange. It's time to jump…and blindly hope it works out. I pull my arm away from her gently and glance at her, trying to relay all the love and appreciation I have for everything she has done for us. If not for her, we would have died a long time ago. Now it was time to keep her safe.

"You remember that background check you did?" Will nods and Alice freezes, wincing. I forgot she didn't know about that. Lucian is standing nearby looking casual, but from the corner of my eye I see as him move toward Alice, standing at her side right behind me, a symbol that he has my back.

He leans in and whispers, "Cher, are you sure you are ready?" Seems like suddenly he's second guessing forcing my hand this way. Without looking away from Will, trying not to break the spell that's making me feel brave, "You didn't give me much choice. You started this, Lucian."

He chuckles softly, "And I will happily finish it for you, love. There is a boat in the water 100 yards away, and some very hungry swamp puppies that will rid us of the problem."

I glanced towards the tree line, "I thought you wanted him to be your bestie?"

Lucian smiles, "I do," winking at Will, he puts his ring covered hand on my shoulder, "I always have a back up plan or two…but I think it will be okay Mattie. Something in me knows it will be."

I can't look at Alice right now, she's overwhelmed by her anxiety and fear, and I can taste it in the air. Will look at Lucian, leaning in by my shoulder, a twitch in his jaw flickers.

"And here I thought we were friends now" he says tightly.

"Mon Cheri we are friends for life now. For as long as you live, I am your friend. How long you live is what is up for debate." Lucian shrugs his shoulders, steps back to stand next to Alice, and wrap an arm around her shoulder pulling her into his side. Surprisingly, she doesn't fight him and leans into him just a little.

Will glances over at the two of them and then back at me.

"You're talking about the guys from your college?" He asks quietly, like he is trying to keep it a secret from the two people next to us. I nod sharply so there is no mistake.

"That's just the first part of it." He waits for me to finish what I was saying, but I just stand there, silent. I don't want to say it out loud. He's one of the few people that isn't put off by me. He actively chased me even. Once he knows the truth, he's going to look at me and see a monster. I don't mind being one because she and I serve a purpose. We have a reason for being, and it works, but the thought of Will, with his soft gray-blue eyes seeing me as a monster; that might be the thing that finally breaks me.

It changes nothing, my friend. You will still be you, I will still be me. We will continue to do what we do for survival.

When he understands everything, he will reject me, he will reject us. I shared my biggest fear with her because I knew she wouldn't placate me like Alice or defend me like Lucian. I have no choice but to continue to love this part of myself. Loving the darkness is the thing that keeps me alive. I accepted a life I never asked for and together we turned a curse into a chance for more. Will stepped closer and took my hand back in his, weaving our fingers back together.

"Did you kill them?" His words are an invitation for me to tell the whole truth. I breathe deeply and feel the tension from Alice and Lucian behind me. Both will step in if this goes badly.

"Yes." I say it succinctly, staring at the ground under my feet. Alice steps up to put her hand on my shoulder comfortingly, "It wasn't her fault."

It wasn't…I had no control and that was part of the curse, but I would have done it by choice if I had the option and she knows it. Will looks between us, thinking hard. He grunts, dropping my hand and aggressively sliding his hand through his hair, pacing back and forth in front of us.

I can't help but flinch, not that I think he will hurt me, but because Kaida feeds on anger, even revels in it. I understand it but it still makes me uncomfortable. While I know Will won't physically hurt me, there are so many worse things he can do to Alice, to Lucian, and me. I can't help but think this was a terrible idea. He's still pacing and working though things.

Looking past Alice, Lucian and I make eye contact, "Promise me?" I whisper to him, almost inaudibly.

The shine in his eyes dims as he realizes what exactly I am asking of him. I know he would happily help me get rid of anyone who was a threat to our lives, but I can't do that to Will. If everything goes to hell, we have a contingency plan in place. Shortly after the first time he met Alice I realized what he felt for her. I made him swear to me that if things fell apart, he would do everything he could to make sure it all landed as far away from her as possible. There was nothing I could do to make up for dragging her into this, but I would make sure she was safe and happy in the end.

"Forever une déesse," he said, his voice full of confidence, crossing his right arm over his chest to thump his fist against his heart. I scoffed and rolled my eyes at him.

You are being so dramatic. Nothing bad is going to happen. No need for secret plans or killing anyone.

I took Alice's hand, looking down at hers in mine. I couldn't look at her, if I looked, she would know. She would see what I'm willing to do for her, and she would try and stop me. A tear slipped down my cheek and splattered on our joined hands. I would let myself have that one tear, but no more than that. This was just a consequence of being who I am, and I won't apologize for that. Will stopped his pacing, "You killed four men at 19 years old?" I nodded silently but Lucian ruined the moment by gaffing loudly and then trying to cover his smile with his hand when Will looked at him.

"What?" he asked.

Lucian took Alice's free hand and pulled her towards the porch, "I'm going to need a nip of something in this coffee if we are going to do this! Will?" Alice walked with him quietly, her arm through his elbow, up to the house.

"Am I going to need it?" he asked loudly, raising a single brow. Lucian chuckled to himself and Alice elbowed him hard in his side. He huffed, clearing his throat. "Depends on what your stance is on goddesses and curses..." he rolled his wrist to admit Alice to the house ahead of him and followed her in, letting the screen door slam.

I could feel Will's eyes on me and it was making me even more nervous.

"Was he talking about you? I took high school French...It's pretty hard to believe you are just friends when he refers to you as a goddess, even in front of Alice." I took off for the shade of the porch so I could sit. I hope to all the gods and goddesses that may be, that I can get a coffee before we have to finish this. Waving my hand for him to follow, "Yes, Lucian loves his pet names, but we're just friends."

Sitting in my favorite rocker, I finally look at him. His hair is disheveled and dusty, his chest peeking out of his unbuttoned and roughed up shirt. His sleeves are rolled up and showing off his firm forearms. He has tattoos decorating what looks like his entire right arm. I couldn't see them closely the night I watched him in his hotel. Reaching over, I slid his sleeve a little higher on his elbow and admired one of his tattoos. It had intricate scroll work, a large circle with runes around it, and a raven disappearing around the outer edge of his arm. I wonder what else completes the art piece. He sits still letting me inspect him.

"So Will, do you believe in the gods?" I ask without looking at him.

"Depends on which names they go by, Mattie" I lift my hand to shade my eyes and look at him. Really a curiosity, this one. "I figured you for a good Catholic boy." He locks eyes with me while leaning back in his chair, crossing his arms. "I was, once upon a time. The world changed how I viewed things and made me question a lot about religion. What about you Mattie? What beliefs and philosophies do you have?"

Kill or be killed is a good philosophy, Kaida hisses.

You aren't wrong, but maybe this is our Perseus moment, Hon. Maybe if my ancestor had been honest, things could have turned out different for her. She was quiet now, like she was pondering it.

I smile, "Oh I know the gods and they know me." He closes his eyes and sighs. "So, you killed those boys from your school and Alice helped cover it up?" I couldn't hold back a laugh.

"No, a friend killed them, but I was there when it happened." He opens his eyes and looks at me, wondering if I'm being honest, or just protecting Alice.

"If you didn't kill them then why say you did?" Alice and Lucian chose this opportune moment to interrupt, walking out to the porch with two cups each. Alice leans in and hands me a coffee with a sad smile while Lucian holds one out to Will with a big grin.

"I swear to god if you drugged this Lucian," he growls at him.

"Will, dear, I am insulted!" Will takes a sip and sputters instantly, "Although I did doctor it well enough for you to be a little more receptive." He hops onto the railing and sips his own cup, then sighs contently.

Will finally catches his breath and takes another sip, easier this time, since he expects the copious amount of Irish whiskey that Lucian put in his coffee. He looks back at me, ready for me to answer him. Alice and I are having a staring contest over the rims of our own cups. She wants to deal with this her way but it's too late. She isn't safe.

"I didn't kill them, but it was my fault."

Alice slams her cup down just as Lucian starts to speak. He shuts his mouth as she glares at him.

"It wasn't your fault. You're not responsible for what she did that night, and you won't pay for it." Will looks at her and then back to me.

"Who is she?" Waving my hand nonchalantly, "Irrelevant. I'm responsible for the others."

Of all creatures that can feel and think, we woman are treated the worst.

Kaida whispered the paraphrased quote from some Greek philosopher, all her guilt and sorrow about that night coming through. It wasn't your fault. You can't help what we are any more than I can.

"Responsible? Or you personally killed them? How many?" he says suspiciously. I don't have to think back or count, I've kept a running tally in my head since the early days of the curse. Each person was the price the universe paid me as penance.

"26," I answer matter-of-factly. Will sputters his coffee again, turning his wide eyes to me. His gaze filled with disbelief and horror, "You've killed 26 people?" He shouts, not believing me. Lucian smirks at his reaction and takes another sip.

"You have been busy Cher." Alice is staring into her black coffee that she no doubt hates, like she might drown in it.

"Men. I killed 24 men." Will is looking at me like I have snakes in my hair or something. Saying it out loud feels like a weight off my chest that I hadn't noticed was there until now. Giggling, I drink my coffee again; it might be the last cup I ever enjoy so I may as well savor it.

"Alice, please say something. There is no way this is possible," He demands of his partner, who's casually leaning against the porch railing by Lucian.

"She has, and two women." She drinks again. They were special exceptions…turns out no matter what we were taught, anyone could be a predator. Women just hide it better.

"I killed them all. Just not the first four."

"So, what, did you learn from the other killer? This is so twisted." He was mad now. Alice tapped my foot with her own and nodded her head towards the door. "Excuse me a second." I set the cup on the little side table and followed her inside, leaving Will sitting there dumbfounded with a Cheshire Lucian. He is such a shit-stirrer.

Inside the front hall Alice turns on her foot and throws her arms around me. She squeezes the life from me better than any constrictor, but I squeeze back just as hard. I know she's afraid of what comes next, and so am I.

"You don't have to do this. Lucian will knock him out and we can disappear. He offered while I made coffee." I smile warmly; of course he did.

I can't hear them talking so Will must be processing all this. Pulling away to grasp Alice's face between my hands, "Alice, something is telling me to do this. Kaida wants me to go for it.

My instincts are screaming that I can't stop what's coming, that I can't keep you safe. That I can't keep Lucian safe, or the girls, and I won't be able to keep myself safe either. Too many times I've felt like I'm being hunted, and for the first time, I'm actually scared. I don't know what to do except get him to help. I promise that no matter what, I have no intention of being a martyr, but I won't reject his help if he'll give it."

She studies me for a long minute before huffing and resting her forehead against mine.

"Whatever you made Lucian promise, he wouldn't tell me. Whatever it is don't push me away, I won't forgive either of you." I know she thinks she means it, but she will forgive him. as for me? Well, I won't be alive to forgive. My Lucian contingency is a last resort, a hail Mary, but it still stands.

"Alice, just do me a favor?" She hums waiting for my request.

"Don't stay with that douche-canoe, Brian."

She startles back and laughs hard. I grin at her, "Seriously, you don't have to run away with the voodoo boy and have beautiful caramel babies, but just, not Brian." She wipes her eyes and squeezes my hand while we walk back out to the porch. "Lucian come on," he hops off the railing and follows Alice back inside to the living room.

I square my shoulders and step back on to the patio.

"If I tell you a story, do you promise to listen till the end? Then, if you want, you can ask whatever questions you may have," I say while climbing back into the rocker and facing him. He stares and stares like he is trying to decide if I'm serious.

Finally, he nods. I pull down my sunglasses and shove them on my face as I sit down and start to gently rock my chair.

"Kaida, I need a moment, just let me do this part alone please," I think to her.

You are never alone, little monster, but I will keep quiet.

Chapter 25

William

This whole morning felt like a million days rolled up into a few brief hours. It started with me screaming at empty walls, tied to a chair, and fighting with my new favorite asshole. Then finding out this girl…this impossible girl with sparkling green eyes, who wore heart shaped sunglasses and ripped jeans, was a serial killer. Not just any serial killer…The most successful serial killers in U.S. history, male or female, if she was telling the truth.

Oh, and I was falling for her fast and hard.

Half of me wanted to kick myself for kissing her but the other half couldn't muster up even one ounce of regret. Mattie was inside talking to her sister while Lucian sat across from me, grinning like a cat. He sips obnoxiously loudly on his coffee and then leans in to whisper, "You're welcome my friend."

You're welcome? For what? Did he want Mattie to go to jail forever? To ruin Alice's career and likely her life? Processing it, no, he didn't. He had offered to dispose of me to the gators earlier and I think he was totally serious about that. So, what was I welcome for? Because so far, he had kidnapped me, pissed me off, and now ruined everything with Mattie.

"For what?" I was exasperated with him.

"You were going to get nowhere with Mattie unless I helped. Sometimes a push here and a shove there for a friend who can't get out of their own way is needed. I saw her watching you outside your hotel and was curious, so I hung around and watched her. For just a few moments cher, believe that there are bigger things in this universe. Big things that connect you two, like a thread from opposite sides of the world that has been pulling you closer and closer together. Now, there's enough slack to wrap that thread around you both, if you let it."

He moved his hands closer and closer together and then whirled one finger in the air and tied a bow with the figurative thread as he spoke.

"I see this thread for you and her, just as I have seen it for myself and Alice. This is my gift Mon Cheri, and you shall see, I am never wrong." He smiled big again and looked over at the door where Alice was waving for him to come inside. He looked back and tapped one finger over his heart and then pointed it at her while he turned to walk inside.

"Just believe her, Will. Try." He muttered softly.

Mattie walked back out of the door and our eyes met. She was breaking my heart with her tears still glistening on her lashes. I know she's killed people now, but she's still Mattie…My Mattie.

"If I tell you a story, do you promise to listen till the end? Then you can ask me anything you want." She settles into the empty rocker and watches me. I guess she's going to tell me her villain origin story…I should record this, but I can't, Lucian still has my phone and my gun. Whatever she has to say has GOT to make more sense than my imagination. I nod gently, rather than speaking . I don't trust myself to speak without asking a million questions. She sighs and puts on those familiar sunglasses before leaning back and rocking in her chair.

"Once upon a time there was a beautiful apostle who lived in a temple by the sea."

Okay that wasn't where I thought this would start. She was serious, so I try to keep my face neutral.

"A god tricked the apostle. He did something terrible to her and she was punished by the goddess she served. She was punished for being hurt, by someone else. For being too kind, too beautiful, for being alive I guess."

This was the story of Medusa. I knew it well, my brothers and I had all loved Greek mythology and spent countless hours acting out the tales of the Odyssey and the Iliad. "She hid in the caves by the sea and lived alone for shame of her punishment. She was angry, and when the moon rose each night, she sought revenge for what was done to her. By day she was herself, but more...then he came for her, seeking a monster and finding beauty instead."

I nodded along as she went off book, this wasn't the story I knew anymore. I wonder if this was a creative metaphor for what happened to her.

"He was charming and kind. A great hero of old. He wanted to rescue her. For a time, she believed in his goodness and thought she could be happy again."

Sighing, she stopped rocking for a moment and composed herself. I could see that she had tears welling up underneath her sunglasses. The hitch in her voice giving away that this story meant a lot to her, even if it wasn't accurate to the legends.

"When he found out that the beauty and the monster were one in the same, he ran. He spread the legend of how he had slaughtered the monster, but the only thing he did was break her heart and leave her pregnant with a daughter." Glancing over to make sure I was paying attention, she found me watching her, completely enraptured. She continued her story.

"A daughter who passed down a curse over the next 3000 years, mother to daughter, every generation. The acolyte became as well known as the goddess who cursed her, and as feared as any monster of myth. She was an original story of female rage and vengeance. She became a symbol for women everywhere who could relate to her story, who knew her pain as their own. My own mother told me the story while she tucked my sister and I into bed at night. To her it was just a fairy tale like any other...to me too, until Catherine was taken from me by the curse." She paused and wiped at the tears trying to escape under her sunglasses. I couldn't stop myself from reaching out and taking her hand in mine, intertwining our fingers.

My heart settled and the tightness in my chest that I hadn't realized was there relaxed. She stared down at our joined hands. Silence stretched between us while I waited for her to continue. The sun was all the way up now; the scent of food cooking inside wafted through the breeze that carried Alice and Lucian's voices. She was laughing at something he said, probably to distract her from our conversation out here.

"I didn't know what had happened to her back then, but I do know she was attacked, and just like Medusa, her curse began. She killed herself soon after that. She must have thought she was insane after her first time turning, I know I did. She left me alone in our apartment and checked herself into a mental hospital. No one there knew what really happened, but when the sun rose the next morning she was dead and so were three men. All of them from snake bites, in the same room where she slit her own wrists. I didn't have any family left so I went into foster care, met Alice, and lived my life as normally as possible, until I was cursed as well."

She won't look at me at all. I don't know why, but I need her to. I reach up and cup her cheek with my free hand, turning her face towards mine. Her breath feathered over my face as I pulled off her sunglasses and gazed deeply into her eyes. Those sparkling green eyes that captivated me the first time I saw her, are glowing now.

Wait… her eyes are literally glowing! It was easily noticeable now that I was this close. I pull back a bit as she reaches for her sunglasses, but I hold them back out of reach.

"Anything else?"

She chokes out a half-hearted chuckle, her voice watery.

"This wasn't enough? You aren't ready to run?" She asks. I shake my head leaning in once more to kiss her forehead lightly. When I fully sit, she is still leaning forward with those eyes closed. For the first time I don't see her as gorgeous, fearsome, or strong. I see her fear and vulnerability etched into every feature.

"Question time now?" I asked, wanting to know if that was the end of her twisted fairy tale.

She smiled sadly, "No, you haven't heard how the curse awoke in me."

I don't know what kind of analogy she's trying to make, calling whatever made her kill those people a curse, but it clearly means something to her.

"I was nineteen. Alice and I went to a party. We just wanted to have a good time, to dance and sing off-key. I still remember laughing and twirling around together. I think it was the last time I had any innocence. If you asked me back then I would have told you that my innocence was already long gone, but it wasn't… That was the night it was taken from me."

She chokes on her words, painting a tale that I think I already guessed the ending to.

"I still don't know what happened. Alice said I was there one minute and then suddenly I wasn't. I woke up the next morning in the woods outside campus. My clothing was ripped up and dirty; I had no underwear on and no memories of where I got the bruises and marks on my body." She looks me dead in the eyes, her pain obvious.

"They were everywhere. Bruises shaped like hand prints…a lot of them." I sat back and clenched my fists, trying to stop a rage like I've never experienced from spilling out. Pulling her legs up, she crisscrosses them before swallowing hard as she tries to compose herself before continuing. Now her voice is coming out without emotion, like she's telling a story that she's completely dissociated from.

"I called Alice, she was already frantically looking for me. When she pulled up in the car, how bad it really was, was written all over her face. She wouldn't look at me the whole way back. We got a hotel room off campus and I showered, scrubbing myself for hours. Alice told me that police were looking for me and four guys who didn't come back to their frat house that night. We hid the whole day in that hotel and it was getting dark."

I see someone out of the corner of my eye. Alice is standing in the doorway watching us closely, tears in her eyes.

"That was the scariest night of my life." Alice says softly. Mattie scoffs, "Really? I would have thought the next night was a thousand percent worse."

Alice half smiles, "No way. That was a cake walk." Mattie looks back at me and takes another deep breath.

"The first time was…unique. The pain was excruciating. It was like every inch of my body was on fire and freezing at the same time. Everything from my hair to my nails ached." Mattie looks past me; her eyes locked on Alice as continues.

"I changed. I met my monster, Kaida, and nothing was the same after that." Alice pushed past me and squatted down between Mattie's knees, taking her hands in hers.

"We met her, and she was magnificent." I stare at the two of them, confused. Who the hell are they talking about? I think back over Mattie's story. In her version of the myth, Medusa was only cursed at night…is Mattie implying that she's Medusa? Oh God, she must have had a breakdown after her attack. She attached herself to the myth and used it to justify killing. But then what the hell is Alice doing feeding into her delusion? Mattie smirks at her sister and then looks back at me.

"If we don't hunt, if we don't protect those who can't protect themselves, then the urge drives us insane. I had two options - to die or to live. I chose to live and do what needed to be done."

I have to put a stop to this. I can help her to get treatment, to get through what happened to her. If she's really this sick, she won't be held fully responsible for what she's done.

"Mattie…" She stands up and shakes her head at me. Moving past Alice and I, she walks into the house and up the stairs without looking back. Alice watches her until she's gone, then she holds up her hand, stopping me from speaking as I open my mouth.

"Give her a minute. I know this sounds insane, trust me, I get it. Voodoo boy sounded insane too when he told me about the thread he sees between you and Mattie. Think we are crazy if you want Bennet, but stay, she wants you to stay and see for yourself. If that sun sets," she throws up her thumb behind her at the sun sitting halfway up in the sky, "and nothing happens, you can take us all away in shiny handcuffs. Lucian will probably think you're just flirting with him, but what's new?" I studied her.

She was totally serious about seeing her sister turn into a gorgon of myth when the sun set.

I looked up at the ceiling of the covered patio, it was painted a light blue like the sky. I heard the screen door slam closed and then I realized Alice had gone inside to sit with her sister. Whether it was all true, or completely nuts,

Mattie believed it and was probably drained after revisiting all that trauma. I felt weird going into their house without an invite, but my stomach growled, and I wasn't going to die of starvation waiting for one.

I opened the screen door, walked in, and took in the space surrounding me. A long hallway stretched back to what was the kitchen. A room on my right was a cozy little living room with a fluffy green couch covered in blankets and pillows. It faced a TV with an antique gold frame around it. Books were stacked on shelves that framed an old fireplace which held only unlit candles now. There were nick knacks and picture frames dotted among them.

I stepped into the room, momentarily forgetting my stomach to take in the space that was cozy, and utterly feminine. I picked up the first picture I saw, it was of Alice and Mattie with their arms thrown over each other's shoulders while they held up their opposite hands with peace signs. They were young, maybe sixteen, and looked so happy and free. The next one was of Alice and Mattie sitting on the same porch we had just left, except this version looked like a death trap to match the haunted house vibes the cottage had once given off. They were both dusty, wearing paint splattered overalls.

Mattie had her head resting on Alice's shoulder while they smiled at whomever was taking the photo. I placed the first frame back and moved to the other shelf. The books were ranged from dark romance, fantasy, classics, and horror. There was a whole shelf of just Greek mythology, with a very old version of the odyssey in the middle. I gently pulled it out and opened it to the title page. It was in Greek, the print year was 1860...this was valuable, but it had tabs in it. There were markings on the pages in several people's handwriting. Pencil, pen, and ink. Several people had written notes in a few different languages.

As I flipped through carefully, I came upon a note written in English. Scrawled in pen were the words, "curse or gift?". Closing the book and putting it back on the shelf, I heard Lucian clear his throat behind me.

"Hungry?" Looking back, I see him leaning against the room divider, arms crossed and his invincible smile still plastered on his face. I swear the guy never loses that dumb grin; I hate that I actually admire him for that.

"How did you get pulled into this madness? Alice?" His smile broadens at her name, but he shakes his head no, his dreads swinging wildly.

"I met Kaida one night. I was out walking the streets on a…let's say, errand. I heard something and a shadow moved in the corner of my eye. As one who likes to move in the shadows I was intrigued, so I pursued. Imagine my surprise when instead of another man of the night I discovered a living breathing goddess of justice."

He pauses for dramatic effect but actually seems to believe what he's saying. His eyes zone out as he thinks back, "I didn't stare, but bowed to her and she whispered a secret in my ear. When I looked up, she was gone, and before the sun was up the whole of the quarter was talking about a man dead by snake bite. I kept walking the streets that night until we came upon one another again. It was close to dawn, and she was taking care of some business and ran into a problem, so I offered my assistance of course. When the sun finally came up, painting the water, Mattie was standing in front of me. I bought her breakfast, and she told me her story. We've been the best of friends ever since, she and I.

My lovely goddess and I are kindred spirits. We both are not made for this world, but here we are." He was totally serious. He believed he met a real creature of myth…Lucian was a little weird but he wasn't insane. Maybe he was telling the truth.

"I was raised by a woman of old magic in a city that's so steeped in myth and legend, I've learned never to discount anything. Mattie is the best of the monsters that roam these shores. I can promise you that." He crosses his fingertips over his heart.

I hear a creak in the floor from upstairs and the soft closing of a door before water rushing through the pipes in the walls. Lucian gestures for me to follow and we walk down to the little kitchen where breakfast is laid out on several plates on the dinette table. There are only two chairs so we each take one silently. "You're serious?" I finally asked him.

He looks up from his plate, setting down his fork and leaning back in his chair. He stares at me with his head cocked to the side.

"Deadly. I refer to Mattie and Kaida, the gorgon, as separate beings and in some way, they are. In others, they live and breathe as one. They both only want to make the world a better, safer place. Something they were not afforded. They have separate ideas on how to accomplish that, but they work it out together. I know you're thinking she's not a crazed killer, and you are right. They don't kill anyone who doesn't deserve it, they live by a code they agreed on years ago." He tucks back into his food while I think through what he has said.

"Okay so if it's all real and she's cursed, why not just hide out? Why kill people? Or try to break the curse?" Lucian is nodding along and then looks over my shoulder as Alice comes in. He jumps out of his chair and signals her to take his seat, carrying his plate to the counter instead.

"You think we didn't try to break it? There's generations of cursed women in her family and we've never found any evidence that it even can be broken."

She starts filling one of the empty plates with food, "Neither of them has a choice. It's a curse for a reason Will, if they could just ignore it and hang out at home don't you think we would have done that? Catherine learned the hard way that if you fight it, you go crazy. The voice inside her head drove her insane and she killed herself, but not before killing innocent people too."

She leans forward and curls her finger at me to do the same, so I follow suit. She whispers, "I don't agree with bringing you into all this. No matter what Lucian sees between you two… if you do anything to harm her, I don't care who you are or where you run - I will kill you with my bare hands. It will not be quick, and it will not be kind. I'm not the creature. I'm much worse, and when you're dead and I've bathed in your blood, I will simply smile and enjoy my revenge. You remember that this is not a threat- it's a promise."

She stands up, picks up two forks, and walks out of the room to go back upstairs. She pauses in the doorway and looks back at Lucian, giving him a smile and a wink before leaving.

"Gods, every time I think I've fallen as far as I can for that woman…" Lucian says, holding one hand over his heart and watching all moony eyed as Alice leaves us alone again. I guess we're just going to wait the day out and see what sunset brings. I'm not sure I believe anything the three of them are saying, it sounds insane.

What if it's true? What if there's more out there than I ever imagined and like Lucian said, coming to this city was always my destiny…that she was always meant for me?

Chapter 26

Racing up the stairs, my heart was pounding harder than I could ever remember. Memories of Alice and I at that party the night of my curse played in my head. I picture us laying together under the covers in the hotel room whispering to each other…the first time I changed and saw myself in a mirror. I was horrified when the voice started and now I can't imagine living without her.

You know I feel the same, Kaida whispers from inside me.

Raising my hand, I put my fingers over my heart and whisper back, "even if I could wish away that night, I'd never wish you away. We are one in the same."

I can't believe I told Will everything. This could be the end now that he knows. Lucian doesn't think so, but he's ever the romantic and thinks that we can bring him over to our side, or maybe he just thinks this is the only way to keep Alice and I safe. Kaida has gotten nowhere close to the answers we need while whomever is killing people and sending us threats is getting closer and closer. If Will asked, I'd assure him that we'll catch them soon, but even I don't feel that confident about it. Someone is closer than they should be, and our home has been infiltrated at least twice. The fear eats at me. They're calling out the people closest to me and don't seem to be stopping.

Alice isn't safe, Hannah isn't safe, and I certainly don't feel safe, even with Kaida here. I stop pacing in the hallway and go inside my bedroom, shutting the door. Stripping off of my clothes, I throw them in the hamper and start the shower in my bathroom. Staring at my reflection in the mirror, I take some time to study the bags under my eyes. I've gone too many nights without sleep. I start to take out the braids weaved through my hair. The kinky curls frizz out among my otherwise wavy hair, making me smile. Even now, I look like a gorgon with a bad hair day.

I don't have bad hair days, little monster, she hisses.

"Oh of course not! After all, you're a goddess, and I'm just a mere mortal." I step under the steaming water of the shower and it stings at first, but after a minute I adjust it to be even hotter. Reaching for the shampoo I start to lather up. "Do you ever wonder about her?" I ask out loud to Kaida.

Wonder about who? Athena, or your ancestor? Kaida asks back, her voice guarded.

She was sensitive when it came to questions about the past. Especially when it came to the real Goddess.

"I guess both. I think about her sometimes and I wonder if she was angry with Athena for what she did. If she hadn't been turned, she never would have fallen in love with Perseus and he never would have broken her heart and tried to kill her... but then again, she never would have had a daughter...wasn't her baby worth all those terrible things she went through?" Rinsing my hair and squeezing the water out before applying conditioner, I wait for a response.

I think if anything had been different, her daughter wouldn't have existed and neither would you, so for that she would have been grateful. To be grateful for a curse that took away half of her life and cost her someone she could have loved forever would be hard. None of us get to see all the paths we can walk and choose between them. We just step forward and hope that tomorrow will be better than yesterday. It's an act of faith to simply live. She was grateful for her daughter, I imagine, just not for the way she came into existence, and that is okay.

The thought was both reassuring and depressing. Athena never got the full story, maybe she didn't want it. Medusa didn't either. Maybe things would have been different if they had all the information. Maybe Catherine's story would have ended differently, too. Would it change how we do things if I couldn't hide from my memories of the night I was cursed? Would knowing change who I am? The other women in the survivors group didn't get to hide...they had to live through life with faith that it would be better tomorrow. Do I owe it to myself to live the same way? Would it change how I see things?

I have told you that when you are ready, I will show you...I just do not want you to regret it. I can't take it back once you have seen, little monster.

Changing the subject, I ask her, "What do you think of Will's reaction to everything? He didn't slap cuffs on us and haul us away, so that's something. It doesn't mean he believes in any of this or that he won't eventually arrest us, but at least he listened." Rinsing out the conditioner I turn off the water and step out. Alice is sitting on my bed staring at the ceiling as she adds to the conversation. "Lucian doesn't think he will. He's making breakfast and keeping an eye on him, but he said something weird about you and Bennet..." she says, without taking her eyes off the ceiling.

Moving into the room, I open the dresser drawer and pull out clean underwear, slipping them on, because if I do end up in jail or dead before the day is done, I'd rather do it in clean undies. Skipping the bra altogether I move to the closet and start sorting out what to wear. Clothing is like armor, and today I needed better armor than most days.

"Is this about magic threads?" I shout out to her from the closet. Sitting up, she peers around the closet door.

"He told you about them before?" she asks.

"Of course. Lucian didn't exactly react normally when he and Kaida met the first time, and after he explained about his own peculiarities it made more sense. He thought the connection was leading him to me that night, but it wrapped around me and led straight to you."

Pulling out a pair of moto pants and a tank top that laced in the back like a corset, I threw them on the bed before looking back at Alice. I promised myself long ago to stay out of their story, but it was getting too delicious not to meddle a bit. After all the snake jokes Lucian made this morning, he was asking for it.

"I saw him the first time he spotted you, Alice. He stopped dead in his tracks, not breathing, not looking at anything but you. I hadn't even pointed you out as my sister, and he said, 'There you are'. I tried to get him to explain but he said he couldn't, that you had to be the first to know. I have seen him match make for his cousins and some friends over the years…with the one they were meant for. Once, on a drunken night with him, I was talking about my curse and how I had a destiny to do what I do but he just smiled and said he wasn't so sure. Then, a few months ago, when I was taking care of Carol's husband, he had insisted on coming along. It was done and we were leaving; he looked at my chest and said 'Finally'. I get the impression that Lucian knew Will was coming and he's been playing a long game this whole time to get us together."

Buttoning my pants and pulling the shirt over my head, I turn around and see Alice laying down on my bed now. Her brain is buzzing…a tense and swirling mess of thoughts.

Her voice cracks as she finally speaks, "He said the threads are connections between two people."

She pauses and licks her lips, "Some are friendships, some are close family, some are for darker reasons, but in rare circumstances, people have threads that go to only one person and those lead to their soulmate. We were in the kitchen, and he said that people don't notice when half of their soul is missing, but he always does. He always felt someone out there waiting for him and sometimes he would grab the thread and pull it, so she would know he was waiting on the distant end."

I lay down on the bed next to her on my side and she turns over to look at me. "Then he said the craziest part…that one day he was following his thread, and there I was. That I was the one at the opposite end."

I pushed her hair behind her ear and whispered, "And are you?" Alice closes her eyes and sighs, rubbing her hand over her heart.

"I think so." Then she starts giggling.

"We are so fucked." I burst out laughing. After a minute we both calmed down enough to talk again and Alice spoke.

"I thought you and Kaida would be the craziest part of my life…now, my soulmate just dropped in."

"There is no better man out there than Lucian. He might exist in the shadows of the city but down to his core he's a good man. I trust him with my life…and yours," I promised her. The last thing I want is for her to ever feel like choosing herself means leaving me behind. Alice deserves more, and I know Lucian will live the rest of his days making her happy if she lets him.

We both stayed there in the silence, hiding from all the changes that are waiting for us downstairs.

"Will is a good man too, Mattie. I know we haven't known him long, but my gut says he's honorable to the core. Everything is going to be okay."

I smirk at her, "He's…too good for a monster."

My stomach chooses that moment to growl in hunger. I haven't eaten since yesterday and I'm starving, but after that emotional explosion this morning, I am also exhausted. I laid still, trying to decide which of my bodily functions is going to win, but I didn't have to wait long. Alice sits up and slaps my thigh while sliding out of bed.

"I can't sleep thinking you're so hungry you might eat me. I'll run down and grab us something and then, we nap. With a little food and lot of sleep, everything will look better, Mattie." She slips out the door and closes it behind her. I count her steps away and down the squeaking stairs. Voices drift up from the kitchen, but I can't make out much as my eyelids get heavier. Rolling over I plug my phone in on the nightstand and then pull a fuzzy blanket over me. I'll just close my eyes for a few minutes.

I'm not sure how much time has passed when I hear the door of my room open as Alice slips inside. I can't bring myself to wake up and eat anything, so I just snuggle down in the blanket and let sleep back in. Slipping into bed, she pulls up the blanket and wraps an arm around me as she slides in closer. The smell of warm cedar and pine washes over me. The arm around my middle is way too big to be Alice's.

Do not open your eyes, little monster. Just enjoy this, Kaida whispers, her voice sounding as tired as I feel.

I have to say something, he's in my bed.

"Will?" I whisper, afraid to ruin the moment and have him pull away.

"Shhh, go back to sleep." He murmured tiredly into my hair, his breath tickling my neck.

"But, Alice." I wonder where she went off too and how Will slipped past her to get in here.

"She's sleeping too. Everyone needed a nap. Now go back to sleep Mattie…We have a lot to talk about later."

Cracking one eyelid open, I see the time projected onto the ceiling by my alarm clock. It's 2:00 pm, I'd been asleep longer than I thought. Warm and cozy next to Will, sleep pulls me back under, and I let it, slipping into a dreamless moment that I hope will go on forever.

The next time I'm pulled into consciousness, 'Bleed' by Connor Kauffman is blasting from my nightstand. Sliding out from under Will's arm, I reach for the phone to check the caller ID. Will grunts in his sleep and tries to yank me back under the covers. When I resist, he scoots to follow me and wraps his leg over mine so I can't slip away. I can't help but giggle while reaching up to pull my hair away from eyes. It's Hannah calling, the clock says it's

6pm. Only about an hour till sunset now. I swipe to answer, "Hannah?"

Heavy, frantic breathing sounds come through the phone.

"Mattie! Carol is dead!" She yells, her voice trembling with fear. There's a shuffling sound and a man's voice whispering angrily at her before she cried out like someone hit her. Shooting up, I am wide awake, my heart beating wildly, "Hannah? Hannah, you there?" A few seconds pass before I hear her breathing into the receiver again.

"Mattie, I need you to listen. He says he knows what you have been doing, and he is going to punish us all. If you want to see any of us alive again you need to meet him. Don't bring the agent, don't bring Alice, don't tell anyone." She's breathing heavily, and her voice is monotone like she is reading from a script. I reach behind me and shake Will, but he's already awake. He grabs my hand and leans in to listen too, so I put her on speakerphone.

"He wants to meet you. Come to the warehouse district tonight at midnight. You will get a pin texted to you. Come alone and he'll let me go and leave the others alone too."

She pauses for a second like she is listening to someone. The silence stretches for so long I think we lost her, but the call continues counting down, "Mattie don't come! Blonde hair, brown eyes, 5,10, wearing a badge!" She screams out as the phone is pulled away from her quickly and a slap rings out and we hear her cry out in pain.

She's being punished for trying to help me.

The phone is still connected, so I shoot my shot, "I'm coming for you. Hurt her and I'll punish you worse than anyone before you."

My words are calmer than I feel inside. My skin is already starting to tighten; sunset isn't far away now. Anger and anguish are raging inside me. I don't know who he is, but I am going to find him and get Hannah back. Her only crime has been trying to save me, now the monster is going to save her.

Tossing the phone back on the nightstand and pushing off the blanket, I pull out of Will's arms and try to stand. I forgot that I still haven't eaten, and now another whole day has passed. Darkness fogs my vision and my head swims. I can't stay standing long or my knees will buckle, so I sit back down on the bed and hold my head between my hands, breathing deeply as I try to calm down. Will comes around the bed and kneels between my legs, his face just on the other side of my hands.

The sun is setting dear. Be ready and we will fix this. It is almost my turn.

Kaida says, her fury is palpable inside me, just as much as her excitement to finally reveal herself to Will. He pulls my hands down and studies my face.

"It'll be okay. Alice and I will get her back." I don't know why he thinks after everything he's heard today that I need him and Alice to save Hannah. Pulling away from him, I speak up.

"Will, I don't need you to save her. I'll have all the help I need in about 30 minutes." He gazes in my eyes for another second before sighing and hanging his head down. Sitting back on his heels, he looks at the ground.

"You really believe that, don't you? You, Lucian, Alice...you all really believe that the sun is going to set, and you're going to transform into some mythological monster. I don't know what you want from me Mattie, but I have to be an Agent now. I have to find Dr. Raines."

He sounds so defeated, like he thought we were all just tired and hungry so when we woke up, it would all be just a temporary delusion. Pushing away from the bed, I snagged my sunglasses from the dresser, put them on, and walked into the hallway.

I yell out, "ALICE! LUCIAN! UP AND AT EM. I have a Doc to save and a killer to catch!"

Will is standing in the doorway to my room watching me go with a blank expression and sadness in his eyes. If he's decided we're all crazy then he is in for a rude awakening in a few more minutes.

"Think what you want, Agent Trouble. I wanted to ease you into this, but it appears you're getting the same crash course as everyone else. Welcome to the party." I don't wait for his reply; I head downstairs, hearing Alice and Lucian coming from her side of the house as I start munching on some bacon that was left out on the kitchen table.

Reaching into the fridge I pull out two energy drinks and set one at Alice's seat at the table. Lucian beats her to the kitchen and immediately starts making a pot of coffee. I know I'm being messy by stacking a fried egg on toast with some bacon and taking a huge bite, but it's hard as hell to eat once my fangs come in, so I want to get something down before I faint.

Alice enters the small kitchen with Will on her heels. Wordlessly, she pulls a plate from the drying rack and sets it on the table, shoving my shoulder lightly. "Crumbs Mattie, seriously?" I take another huge bite, chew, and swallow it before I mumble, "Fangs, Alice. They're a bitch to eat with."

Will is standing silently in the doorway, watching us. Alice reaches into the fridge and pulls out the orange juice.

"You're going to want something stronger, my love." Lucian says, before going for the bottle of whiskey we keep under the sink. He sets four glasses on the table before pouring a three fingers in each. My skin starts to tighten as Kaida begins hissing with impatience. Glancing up at the window, I see the sun is starting its decent beneath the edge of the horizon as I finish my makeshift breakfast sandwich. Taking one of the glasses, I throw back the whiskey, savoring the burn of it over the rising panic in my chest. I head toward the living room but Will is blocking the way, so I smoosh past him. He reaches for my waist, but I pull away. "Where are you going now?" The lines around his eyes show how frustrated he is, his mouth set in a grim line. Alice speaks for me, "She doesn't change in front of people if she can help it. It's best to make sure no one is standing close enough to get bitten."

I make it into the living room just as the change washes over me. My skin tightens everywhere and my face shifts to accommodate my fangs. My hissing little snakes tickle at my ears and neck.

Kaida reaches up to check our sunglasses are on properly before turning around to go back into the kitchen and fill everyone in so we can make a plan.

Please be on your best behavior.

Will is standing in the hallway with his mouth hanging open in shock.

Lucian steps over and puts a hand on Will's shoulder as he greets Kaida.

"Good evening, gorgeous. We have some work to do tonight, eh?" Breaking away from Will's stare, she nods to him, "Yes we do."

"He is still staring. Does he not like us? I was hoping that he would like us." She says internally, sounding like her feelings are hurt. She loves Lucian because he isn't afraid of us, and all his flirting, so we're both disappointed to to smell the fear wafting off of Will. We have bigger worries right now. At least he knows we were telling the truth, the rest can wait.

He'll be okay. It's just a shock.

I really hope I'm not lying to us both.

Carol Shanks is probably dead and now Hannah has been taken. We aren't some idiot in a horror movie that's going to run off into danger with no help and no plan just to end up dead. Kaida doesn't even look at Will, our face turned away, but I feel the shock in his gaze. I've been there, I know what it feels like for the earth to shift suddenly. I can at least sympathize with him in that.

"Oh, now you've hurt her feelings, good luck there Mon Cheri" Lucian says to Will who stumbles behind us.

"Mattie…Mattie…I didn't…" He trails off reaching for me but one of the snakes by my shoulder, the green one I love so much hisses at him and snips at his hand. Lucian knocks his hand out of the air between us.

"Non, not Mattie's feelings, Kaida's." He gestures his hand at us from head to toe.

"I told you that she and her monster are the same, yet not. William, meet Kaida. Now no touching, unless you want to end up dead you stay back a ways, and NEVER look her in the eyes." He advises sternly. Alice is sitting at the table looking at her phone and drinking her energy drink.

"Good evening sis," She greets us both.

"Carol Shanks is dead," Kaida says, like ripping off a band-aid. Alice is watching us carefully now. She sets her drink down and looks at the guys standing a few feet away.

Will finally shut his mouth, but he is still just staring, like if he looks hard enough, I'll change back. Shocker, I don't.

"How did the killer find her?"

We look over at Will before answering, "Hannah, she has been taken. The killer has her. She is the only one who knew where Carol was hiding, so I am guessing she was taken so they could find her, and now she is being used as bait to get me to the warehouse district tonight."

Alice slides her phone across the table; an email is pulled up. Pushing my way forward in Kaida's mind, I get her to take the phone and bring it closer. It's anonymous, sent to her work email. All it says is 'free yourself of the lies or I'll do it for you'.

"This was in my inbox," she says calmly. Will steps up, "You think it's Dan Reynolds? Making threats against you and the rest of the group?"

Shaking our head hard, "No, Dan Reynolds is dead. Has been for a while, and we do not think he murdered Laura. Well, maybe he did…but he is definitely dead now."

Will and Alice both freeze and stare at us, "What?!" Alice asks.

Tell them about last night, I say, needing to feel useful right now.

Waving her hand in Lucian's direction, Kaida speaks. "Before we were interrupted by Will, and Lucian ran off to play kidnapper, we were tracking the blood on his driver's license that Lucian found out in the swamp. It led us to a large pool of blood in the alley. It was dead blood, and from the same person. It smelled the same as the words painted our garage. We think Dan has been dead for a while. Whoever took Hannah is 5 '10, has blonde hair, and brown eyes, and…" looking at them again she stops talking.

Our shared mind begins racing, putting things together like a puzzle. Kaida imagines a face in our her mind, but it takes me a moment to catch up with her. Oh fuck…he was right in front of me. That's why we were so freaked out at the library. That's how he got onto the property… "And what?" Alice asks quietly. She's watching us connect the dots and work through who it is.

Kai, you have to say the quiet part out loud. She needs to know...

Kaida winces, "You do it...I don't want to..." Alice stares, her wide eyes watching us internally argue.

I get it Kai, but you...

Will clears his throat, "And a badge." His face is pale as he answers for us, "Hannah said they had a badge. Alice, who was on watch outside Dr. Raines' house last night?" Alice quickly pulls up the assignment list on her phone. Scrolling through it, all the color drains from her instantly. Her skin looks ashen and drawn before she gags, claps a hand over her mouth and jumps up to puke in the sink. I step back quickly to let her get by and Lucian shoves Will aside to gather up her thick, black, hair and hold it back for her. She's dry heaving and gasping, trying to answer Will's question.

He moves to the table checks the list for himself, but Kaida says it before he can, "It was Officer Brian Kemp."

Alice heaves again, tears streaming down her face while Lucian rubs her back soothingly. He murmurs something to her, but I don't think she can hear anything as her eyes glaze over.

"I knew something was wrong with him, I felt it, and now we will make him pay. He thinks he knows what we are, but he has no idea what we can, and will do," Kaida says to Alice, a fury unlike any before in her voice.

We don't need any more statues though. I want him to suffer...

We Look over to Alice, who's leaning into Lucian's arms with tears on her face, looking more fragile than ever.

"I swear to the goddess Alice, we will make him pay." The words are layered as both Kaida and I speak them together.

Will is watching us, his jaw is tight and that twitch is back again on the right side as he grinds his teeth.

"If we do this right, we can make him pay for it all. We can make this all go away and keep you both safe too." Now everyone is staring at him in silence. Alice, Kaida, and I equally shocked that he would do this for us.

Lucian leans against counter, grinning away like he knew all along that Will was going to suggest this.

Chapter 27

Will

From the moment I headed to the living room to try talking to Mattie away from prying eyes, my world had started spinning counter-clockwise faster and faster until there I was, staring at Mattie...Kaida...both of them, in the kitchen. The words "If we do this right, we can make him pay for it all. We can make this all go away and keep you safe too" came out of my mouth, like I didn't even have to think them to say them.

I could still see Lucian and his dumb smile out of the corner of my eye, holding onto Alice, but I couldn't tear my gaze away from Kaida and all that she was. If you had asked me what magic I believed was out there yesterday, I would have laughed and walked away without giving it a thought. Magic was the only explanation for Mattie and Kaida existing...and I don't mean her curse. Something brought me here, led me to her. I don't really get it, but I can't deny this feeling in my chest that says I am doing the right thing by jumping in headfirst.

I was face to face with a creature of myth and I didn't know what I was supposed to say. Lucian, Alice, and Mattie had told the truth. In my gut, I had known they were being honest about everything, but my brain couldn't process it till it was right in front of me. The setting sun was still glowing beyond the horizon and the kitchen lights were casting their own warm glow from above her. Mattie was the most beautiful woman I had ever seen, green eyes and full lips, with high cheekbones and freckles dotting across her skin. No matter how cynical she was, those freckles made me think of her as young and innocent. Kaida wasn't innocent, she was dangerous. Where Mattie's features were soft, hers were sharp. Her firm features highlighted the way those small fangs dug into her full bottom lip. I couldn't help but smirk at them, they were cute. She cocked her head curiously at me, studying me as I looked at her. I could feel Mattie behind her gaze too.

Looking over at Lucian, who was still rubbing Alice's back while she composed herself. I beckoned Kaida with my finger to follow me to the back patio. I thought she would say no to being alone with me, but this was a predator, and predators don't back down. She nodded and walked outside with me following. Looking back at Lucian, he caught my eyes and winked, mouthing silently, "GOOD LUCK!"

Shaking my head at his antics, I let the screen door slam; Kaida stiffened in front of me and the little snakes woven through her hair started hissing loudly and turned their heads toward me. Suddenly I was being judged by a dozen sets of eyes. I expected her to maybe be defensive, but she shocked me by turning around and leaning in close. I froze as the snakes closest to me flickered their tongues against my face and neck. Breathing evenly, I tried to meet her eyes behind the lenses so she could see I wasn't scared of her. I wasn't, I was scared of the whole world being flipped upside down and shaken like a dirty martini, but not that Mattie..or Kaida, would hurt me. No matter what she looked like on the outside she was the same woman who had just been sleeping next to me in the cocoon of fluffy blankets upstairs. The same woman who collected romance novels and gardened in the flower beds around their yard. They were like two sides of the same coin. Kaida had no more control over this curse than Mattie. They were both victims of circumstance and fate, just making the best out of the hand they were dealt. Kaida wasn't a monster, even if she said differently. "Agent Trouble, it is so nice to finally meet you." She grinned and whispered close enough that I could feel her breath brush across my face. I couldn't help but smirk back at her. Apparently, that day in alley at the crime scene I hadn't met Mattie, but her alter ego, and she had a thing for nicknames.

"What would you like me to call you? Your highness? Princess? Oh wait…my goddess?" She hummed appreciatively and smiled back, flashing deadly fangs. "Kaida is fine. We aren't two beings. Just two minds in one. Sometimes it can be confusing, but you get used to it." Reaching for her hand and intertwining our fingers in mine, I found myself admiring her light green skin and long black nails. "You're the same person, right?" She nodded looking down towards our hands. "Same person, different minds, but connected. I know this is not something you thought you would ever be a part of, but if you can help Mattie, Alice, and Hannah, I will do whatever it takes to keep out of the way for you and Mattie."

I was shocked that she felt the need to promise me anything to get my help. I'm going to make sure of them are safe, regardless of how this turns out. Honestly, I'll be surprised if we aren't all dead by sunrise.

"Kaida, you're part of her. Mattie…Kaida…my goddess…it doesn't matter, I like ALL of you. I'm sorry I didn't understand before, I should have believed you."

She was staring at our hands and scoffed lightly, "I understand this is crazy. She did not choose this."

She uses her other hand to gesture to her own body. "But we don't hate who we are. Monster or not, the people in our life have to like both parts."

The vulnerability in her voice hurts me. After listening to Mattie spilling her guts yesterday, the horror story of how this happened to her, they both need to know that it changes nothing for me. Looking past the glasses, past Kaida, "Mattie, I didn't know you would be here, but I'm happy I found you. You're the strongest women I've ever met, and I am not walking away. I wish we had hours, weeks, months, to get to know each other and do this the right way, but we have to do what we can to stop Kemp and get the FBI off your back before it's too late." Pulling my hand away from hers, I reach my hand out towards her cheek. Kaida startles back, adjusting her sunglasses on her face.

"You can't! There are ways to survive the venom, but not being turned to stone. I do not know how to undo that…I do not think there is a way at all." Her voice venerable as she cringes away. Pulling her closer, I whisper.

"Shhh. I won't take them off, I promise. I just need you both to know

I'm not walking away. I'm here to help." She watches me, still as stone herself, like she's waiting for me to shout 'gotcha!' I can't explain it any better than she can. After I saw her as a Gorgon something clicked inside me and everything I had questions about didn't matter as much as making sure they are okay. We sit in silence a few more minutes before the door squeaks behind us and Lucian pops his head out. "Sorry to interrupt, but Alice is done with her freak out over her psycho ex and now we need to know what we're doing." Rolling my eyes at him, I sigh and start for the door. Kaida reaches out and stops me.

"You are serious? You will help us?" I don't know how to make it any clearer to her so I lean in close and grin.

"I'm all in, my goddess. I am here to serve you." I place a soft kiss to the edge of her lips, making her gasp quietly. Grabbing her hand, we can go inside and join the others to make a plan.

Inside, Alice has another glass of whiskey in front of her at the table and Kaida is standing with me near the fridge. Her eyes focus on our joined hands and then shoot to her sister's.

"You okay?" She asks. Kaida is silent, likely conversing with Mattie in her head, with two of her fingers pressed to where I kissed her. I guess both sides of her needed a tete-a-tete about what I said outside. Somehow, I think convincing the gorgon of my sincerity will be easier than convincing Mattie.

"Yes...We are fine." I release her hand and step up to take two of the whiskeys from the table, handing one to Kaida and shooting the other quickly. I winced from the sudden burn, but it wasn't bad stuff.

"So, Officer Kemp has taken Dr. Raines. He may have killed Carol Shanks, and Laura too. We can assume he is behind all the threats as well. The question is why? Alice, anything you can fill us in on?" She tightens her fingers on her glass and a green tinge reappears on her face.

Lucian moves in to hold her shoulder. Breathing loudly through her nose and out her mouth she says, "I know he hates Mattie...He puts on a good show, but I always got the impression he didn't get us. He knows about her group, and he never said anything specific to set off any red flags, but he was always saying things like, 'innocent until proven guilty' or 'there are two sides to every story'. We only went out for a short while and it was sporadic because of our schedules. He's been trying to rekindle things between us for a while now, but I'd been put off. I was just trying to salvage our working relationship. I told him as much right after we found Laura and he didn't take it well."

I was nodding along. I knew how hard was to see something when you are too close to it, so I understood.

Kaida interrupts her, "He showed up at the library the same day Hannah's office was vandalized. He set off Mattie...made us feel jumpy and on guard. Neither of us understood why but he was warning her that you were moving on from her and things were getting more serious between them. He said that you were going to move in with him."

Alice's eyes fill with tears again and she reaches for her sister before pulling back, remembering she can't.

"I wouldn't keep that from you, either of you. He's a son of a bitch." Mattie's phone dings. Kaida's slender green fingers pull it out of her pocket.

"It is from Hannah. A pin for a warehouse by the water." She hands the phone to Lucian.

"Know it?" He takes the phone and zooms in on the map, studying it. Shaking his head he hands it back, "Non, but give me twenty minutes and I can get us a dozen or so people watching the place. I don't want them too close if you are going in, but they can let us know who is coming and going until we arrive."

He pulls out his own phone and starts typing away to whomever he has that owes him a favor. I am going to have to look into Lucian Corbin a bit more later, because he is a huge question mark.

"I can call the captain, but without any proof it'll be impossible to convince him to go after Kemp. Maybe Lorraine would be willing make an anonymous call after we have him in custody," Alice says. Not wanting to rock the boat, I speak up. "Maybe let's keep this to as few of us as possible. The captain isn't your biggest fan, and he is unlikely to believe anything from me either without evidence. The last thing we need is for anyone to see Kaida. We don't know what exactly he wants Mattie for yet, or what he is willing to do to Hannah, but we can assume he isn't going to let her go if she's seen him well enough to identify him. Whatever he's up to, it feels like his end game."

Lucian puts his phone away and leaves the room. A few moments later he returns with his long coat and a satchel. He sets both on the table and reaches into the satchel, pulling out a few small cloth bags and an old Colt revolver. Alice and I both raise our brows.

"I'm going to assume this isn't legally obtained?" Alice asks as he tucks it into the back of his pants.

"Non my love. But then again, neither is the powder in those bags, but Will can attest they work all the same." Kaida was tucking one of the bags into a jacket pocket.

"What is that stuff?" I asked, but wasn't sure I wanted the answer. He shrugged, "Devil's breathe is something I have perfected over the years to keep certain people away from places they shouldn't be." He kept transferring things from his satchel to the many pockets hidden in the coat as he spoke. Kaida fills us in where Lucian was being deliberately vague.

"Lucian uses it sometimes on men in the quarter if they get carried away. Before they can do anything stupid, he knocks them out and they wake up with a terrible hangover, but still breathing."

Turns out, Lucian is one of the good guys too. Alice puts her hand on his forearm, and looks up at him, smiling.

"That's what you are doing skulking around the quarter at all hours?" She asks, sounding impressed. He smiles back.

"That's a side gig when I'm not busy trying to take over New Orleans." Kaida coughs to cover a laugh band rolls her eyes, but keeps her mouth shut. She's much more obvious with her feelings than Mattie. Everything she is thinking or feeling is written on her face. If Lucian wants to make us all believe he is a criminal mastermind, she's going to go along with it. I drop it for now, but when things calm down, I have a few ideas on how I can get Mattie or Kaida to spill his secrets.

Catching Alice's gaze, I ask her, "Are we going in as cops or not?" Alice opens her mouth to answer but Kaida interrupts.

"Neither of you are going in at all. You are a support team. We are going in to deal with Kemp alone and then Lucian will get Hannah out. Then, you will all leave together and we meet you back here." Anger flares in Alice's eyes and I can see her gearing up to argue.

"Lucian knows how to hunt with me and stays out of the way. Alice, you know we will be fine. We will take care of him and come home safe." While I agreed with her stance on being safe, there was one problem with her plan.

"Yeah, but we need him alive. If he's alive after all this, he will have seen you. If we want to convince anyone that he murdered Laura, Dan, and Carol too, then keeping him alive is the best bet."

Both women look over to me and then back to one another.

"Fine, alive" she hisses out, the snakes in her hair hissing and wriggling like they're just as irritated at the prospect as she is.

"You are more trouble than you are worth, Agent Trouble" she says under her breath. I can't help but smile at her frustration toward me. Mattie isn't bloodthirsty, I guess this is Kaida's instincts.

"I'll try my best to make up for the trouble when this is over." She looks back at me and I wink cheekily at her. Her cheeks flush a darker shade of green, and I puff out my chest at having made her blush. In all the ways Mattie guarded her emotions, Kaida was open. Probably because she didn't feel the weight of their secret anymore, but it made it easy to tease her.

Feeling a huge amount of pride in myself, I walked over and leaned close, one of the little snakes, a lighter green one, rubbed its head on my neck.

"A few hours worshiping on my knees should make up for it, right?" I whisper quietly, keeping my voice low so it stays between just us. Kaida shoves me away lightly and sits down at the table. Her blush had spread across her chest and neck now. Lucian was watching with a grin on his face again. The guy was thrilled at where this was going, but so was I, so I guess I owed him one. He pulled out two black velvet bags and handed one to

Alice and one to Kaida.

"These are in case of emergency. They will kill pretty quickly. You can't breathe any in, so just open the bag, toss it, then run quickly. I'll bet Kemp is working alone, but keep it close, just in case."

Pointing at the bag I ask, "What is it?" Lucian looks over at Kaida and winces guiltily, "It's her venom, powdered and weaponized…and a few extra things I added." I furrow my brow at that, looking between the two of them.

Alice shakes her head and walks out, coming back with her service weapon, and mine. She hands it over with my holster and badge. I Strap my holster on and drape my badge around my neck. Alice sets hers on the table next to Lucian's things and sighs.

"I'm going to go change." She walks toward the stairs and Kaida starts to follow but she waves her away.

"I just need a few minutes. I'll be right back." Kaida sits back down and rests her head on the tabletop. Her snakes are swishing back and forth, agitated. Lucian and I both just watch in silence.

"Carol Shanks has a baby…a little girl. If she is dead, that baby is all alone now," she whispers quietly. It takes a minute for me to put together why she is so sad. She admitted that she killed Carol's husband herself, so now the baby is an orphan, like Mattie. She's feeling guilty.

"Kaida, you tried to help her to get away, right? Mattie tried to intervene, to find any other way of helping first, right? He was hurting her, and he would have hurt that little girl too. We don't know for certain that anything has happened to Carol, so let's worry about Hannah for now and then we will do whatever we can for them." I try to reassure her, but it falls flat. Guilt makes everything fall flat when you're in the depths of it. Lucian puts his phone on the table and slides it to her, "Cher, we need you both to focus on this. We will save tomorrow's worries for tomorrow." She tips her head to look in his direction and then nods.

"Okay." Alice comes in dressed in new clothing, totally different from her usual business attire. Black jeans, a black long sleeve top and a black jacket with an oversize hood.

"I borrowed some of Mattie's things. If he's watching, he'll think I'm her."

It was a good plan since they were built similar, but he would assume that even though he said to not bring her, that Alice would follow Mattie anywhere she went.

"We take both cars. Alice and I in one and you two in the other." Kaida watches us, biting her fangs into her bottom lip. She was busy thinking or maybe talking to Mattie. She points to Lucian first, "I will go in the warehouse and try to engage Brian. Lucian, you find Hannah and get her out. Do not wait for me." Alice clears her throat, "Fine but you get twenty minutes, and then we come in. We'll wait nearby until you leave the building. Lucian, you take Hannah back here and wait for us while we clean up the mess with the cops. Hopefully we can clear everything up quickly and be back by morning, but don't count on it. Arresting a fellow officer as a serial killer is going to be a mess." I nod, she's right.

We don't just have to convince the department that Kemp killed the women, but also Dan and the other men that I was sent here to investigate.

It might not be so easy to pin the whole mess on him, but hopefully we'll have all the proof we need once we save Hannah. Kaida pushes away from the table and opens the drawer at the end of the counter. Pulling out three knives, she slips one in each boot and one into a scabbard that she straps onto her forearm.

Coordinating the plan is easy enough since it's just get in and get out without Brian seeing Kaida directly, but the prospect of him not being alone is concerning to me, and Alice as well. Lucian and Kaida load up in her truck first and as we watch them drive away with the dust blowing behind them, I throw my arm around her shoulders and squeeze. Alice sighs and leans into me for a moment. "So you and Lucian were in your room quite a while," I say teasing her about their disappearing act.

"Yeah. While there were two lumps under the blankets in Mattie's room… curious. You don't ask me about my weirdo, and I won't inquire about yours, deal?" I can't help but laugh at her while nodding.

"Deal. I wish we could be more helpful with this." Climbing in Alice's SUV, I buckle up in the passenger seat.

"You didn't shoot Kaida, or arrest Lucian, or arrest me. You're helping us catch Brian and pin everything on him, so I think you're more helpful than any of us." As we pull out of the driveway, I study her and note how her shoulders are more relaxed, her face not at tight with worry.

"You're really okay with Kaida? I won't tell either of them what you say, but I worry about Kaida too…for a monster she has a very delicate heart." For the first time in years, she has someone to share the burden of worry for Mattie with. I appreciated that Alice had been there for Mattie long before I could. Now I had her back, and Kaida's too.

"No, surprisingly I am more okay now that I know the full story." Alice watches me out of the corner of her eye. I must give off an honest air because she doesn't question me any further. Probably because I was being honest, with her and myself. I wanted Mattie no matter what, Kaida was like the whipped cream on top.

The open land outside my window quickly got eaten up by houses and then the city as we made our way into the quarter towards the warehouses. Seeing Mattie's truck, Alice parked across the street, and we watched the shadows move with no idea where our people were, but crossing our fingers and offering up our prayers that they would be okay. Alice reached over and took my hand in hers, "I just need this. Calms my nerves…they will be okay. She always is but I am still always anxious about it."

Squeezing her hand, "Okay. Distract us. Tell me what you thought when this all started." I was curious how she dealt with all in the beginning, and we have a few quiet minutes while we wait.

"The night Mattie disappeared, I was searching everywhere. I lost her while she went to find a bathroom…five minutes and our lives changed. Isn't that always the way of it? Five minutes was all it took for me to crawl out of my bedroom window while my family's home burnt down. Five minutes for the fire to make their escape an impossibility. Five minutes was how long the neighbors could hear them screaming for help." Tears welled up in her eyes.

I knew Mattie and Alice to have been in foster care together, but I never could have imagined the story was this horrible. No wonder she's so dedicated to protecting her chosen family.

"Five minutes is all it takes for any of us to have totally different lives whether we want it or not. After searching non-stop, Mattie called me, and I went to get her. I booked us into a hotel under an alias, far from the campus. It was already known that the guys who hurt her were missing, but no one cared that I couldn't find my sister. No one but me was even looking for her until someone at the party told the cops she was with them. We hid at the hotel, and when she changed that night, I spoke to the gorgon for the first time. No matter how badly I was freaking out, she was my sister in every way but blood. We didn't know anything, but Kaida filled us in on what she could. As far as I know she never told Mattie what happened that night, she protects her from that memory, she can tell her, but Mattie doesn't want to know. So that night and the next day we made a plan, one that changed our lives." She shrugged like it was all so simple.

She had changed her whole life to accommodate a curse her sister was bound to. Mattie couldn't walk away and had to live or die by her choices, but Alice could have left. Instead, she just accepted the craziness and moved forward. I couldn't help but wonder if I loved anyone enough to just walk face first into the blaze. No questions asked, no looking back at what would be lost, just one foot in front of the other into the fire, hand in hand.

Mattie's face popped up in my mind...Shit...Until her I didn't think so, but like Alice said, five minutes was all it took for my whole life to come crashing down around me and now here I was breaking the law and all my own rules just for a chance to help her.

"Is this the part where you run?" She asked, sounding halfway serious.

I squeezed her fingers again, "Only if it's to her." I answered honestly because I had already decided if Mattie was walking through fire I would be by her side. Silence filled the car while we both sat with our own thoughts.

"I have the keys to Brian's apartment...it's only a few blocks away," She says, staring out her window. I smile, "Maybe we go and let ourselves into your boyfriend's apartment really quick, legally since he gave you a key, and see if we can find any evidence?" She smiles and throws the car into drive, pulling away from the curb.

Kaida and Lucian must see us leaving because my phone buzzes in the cup holder. Picking it up I read her text out loud.

"Is everything okay? We only have an hour till we go in." Alice rolls her eyes, "Tell her yes, we are just checking up on a lead. If you're not vague, she will try and involve herself and someone needs to be watching the warehouse."

Typing out the message, leaving it as ambiguous as possible, I send it off to the troublemakers. The blocks fly by and before I know it, we are walking up a flight of stairs to a second-floor apartment. Alice unlocks the door and peeks inside, "It's empty." She pushes the door the rest of the way open and lets me in behind her. She loops her hair tie around her keys and hangs them on the door handle before turning to see me watching her, "An alarm, if someone turns the knob, we'll hear the keys jingle." She walks down the hallway and I look back at the door, impressed.

Looking around the plain living room, I take in the bland beige couch and overly large TV taking up the wall across the room. It's sitting on what is supposed to be a coffee table with a couple gaming consoles. There are no books anywhere and no pictures on the walls. Moving into the small kitchen, I open the fridge, there's nothing much inside. I open the freezer and spot an empty baggie, pulling it out I examine it. There's a brownish red stain inside, opening it, I take a whiff. It smells of stale blood.

Gagging, I turn to look for Alice, she is standing part way down the hall looking pale as a ghost.

"You'd better come see this." She waves me over. I put the baggie back in the freezer and joined her.

Stepping inside the bedroom with a queen bed pushed under the window, I see the closet is open and all the hanging clothing pushed to the side. Looking back at Alice, she nods, gesturing with her chin to look inside. Using my elbow, I push the closet door open further to look inside. Taped to the back wall of the closet were the surveillance pictures taken the day I arrived in New Orleans. There were more from outside the girls' houses, some of Alice outside the police station. Creepily enough, there was one of Alice sleeping in the station and another of her sleeping on the bed in this room. In every single photo of Mattie her face had been crossed out with a red marker.

There were post it notes tacked to the wall with the names of people in the photos. Laura's name was crossed out and a copy of her police report was taped to the wall below it. There were photos of a woman next to a news article about one of the snake bite victims, Carol Shank's Husband. I spot a note in different handwriting from the rest on the outer edge of the creep collage, so I move in closer to look without touching anything. A woman's handwriting loops across the post it note.

'Don't look her in the eyes. Stab the betrayer in the heart to kill her.'

Pulling down the note, I hand it to Alice; she looks it over before crumpling it up and shoving it in her pocket. She pulls her phone out and calls Mattie. I hear Mattie's voicemail.

"Fuck." she curses, turning and running out.

"Would that kill her?" I yelled out behind her, suddenly panicked that he knew what Mattie was and how to hurt her. Alice doesn't stop as she unties her keys and stomps out, "No but it would slow her down. That isn't his handwriting, so who knows about her and why are they helping him?"

We both run to the SUV and head back to the warehouse as fast as we can in worried silence.

Chapter 28

Pulling up to park the truck a block away from the warehouse, the streetlights tried their hardest to cut through the black of night. Jazz music played loudly a few blocks up from us, but down here by the water it was eerily quiet. Lucian sat quietly in the passenger seat the whole way here, looking more serious than we had ever seen him. He was clearly thinking about the change between him and Alice, so we left him to his thoughts and kept to our own about Will.

If I wanted a soundboard he would listen and vice versa. Right now I just wanted to concentrate on stopping Brian and getting Hannah to safety, then I could hyperventilate over Will and his quiet acceptance. It should comfort me that he was so accepting of Kaida, but it was like he had no self-preservation, and that scared me. No one came close to me in this form…sure Lucian flirted with us and called us beautiful but when Will leaned in, his eyes sparkled with intensity, without any fear. He touched and kissed Kaida, like he liked her just as much as me.

"That is because he does. This is the real you. We are one and he sees that," Kaida thought to me, keeping our conversation private. *Of course you'd say that,* I whisper. Lucian breaks the silence and looks over at me before checking the time on his watch. Smiling at us he says, "She likes him, non? Good of her to finally admit it. You have better taste than her."

Hey! Not all of us have the fates guiding us. Some of us have to do it the hard way. Not to mention he was hunting us down just two days ago.

I don't like being ganged up on.

He's only saying that because he likes you best.

"He better like me best. I AM the better half after all!" Lucian smiles and tosses his hair over his shoulder, the silver of his earrings glinting in the dim glow of the streetlights.

"I like her better than you most days, darling Mattie. Somehow her bite is preferable to your bark."

Lights flash behind us as I spot Alice's car pull away from the curb. They make a U-turn and drive away.

Check on them Kai.

We flash our headlights at them, making sure they see us, but I'm sure they already did. Kaida shoots off a text to Will asking if everything is okay. My phone dings quickly, "gotta lead. Be right back. Xoxo." I smile inside and roll my eyes at him. Whatever they're up to, they clearly don't want backup.

I guess they'll be back as soon as they can.

Kai nods in agreement. "I do like him more than you, you are always wrecking my vibe. The oracle is good for my ego."

Wait, what did you just call Lucian?

He's looking over at us with wide eyes, questioning. He didn't know why he could see the threads of the universe, just that his grandmother had been able to do the same. So for him, it was just something he never questioned, at least not out loud. "What did you just say about me?" he asks.

Kaida responds in our head. "I called him an oracle. Did he not realize? How else do you think he can see the weave? He is one of the chosen of the Moirai. I assumed he knew." She sounded genuinely concerned that she may have given away a secret.

No, he didn't know!

I say, frustrated that she knew this whole time and didn't say anything. I wonder what else she knows but is keeping to herself. Kaida answers Lucian, "I called you an oracle, a chosen of the Moirai. I knew what you were that first time we met. Your grandmother knew what she was, I just assumed she told you about your history. She should have prepared you and your cousin better."

Lucian had a dozen cousins, but Kaida clearly was thinking of one in particular. "She never explained exactly, just said it would feel like a curse, but it was a gift. Wait?! You said she should have told me and my cousin? Which one?" Kaida smiled at him, "For some reason she didn't tell you, maybe because I was destined to do so. If she did not tell her either, I have to think there is a reason. She will find out on her own when it is time."

Lucian looks like he is going to argue, opening and closing his mouth several times before he balls up his hands into fists and stares out the front window of the truck silently for a long moment before looking back at us.

"The Moirai were the weavers of the universe, right? I didn't think they were actual people, but I never would've believed that an actual gorgon was walking around New Orleans if I hadn't run into you either…If you're real then so is the first gorgon, Medusa. By that reasoning Athena is too…all of them are. I guess the Moirai are too then. That's a mind fuck I didn't need today."

He was right of course, if one was real then the rest being real made sense, but without any proof, it had been easier to just ignore the idea. That was a door to be opened later, when we didn't have a psycho killer to catch. Reaching over to pat his arm, "There there poor Lucian, we will have an existential crisis later, with tequila. Right now we have to stop Brian. I have waited a year to kick his ass, and I am looking forward to it even more now.

"Kaida's voice fills with excitement and I can feel it vibrating through us.

Next time you info dump on people, let's run it by me first so we don't hurt them.

He smiles back at us, "I spent an entire year wanting to break his nose, so I'm in!"

We both hop out of the truck and start down the block, Lucian steps away quickly, melting into the shadows and disappearing. We need Brian to think I came alone, and Lucian needs to focus on getting Hannah out safely. Kaida pulls the hoodie up over our hair and snakes, making sure it drapes down on our forehead, adjusting the shades over our eyes so we don't end up with another statue. Just before we get to the side door, I feel someone's eyes on us, and the hissing starts to warn anyone off.

Hey this isn't helping the sneaking so make them stop!

Kaida looks over our shoulder for any sign of a threat. Nothing moved in the shadows but our snakes were still quietly hissing.

We have to go Kai, it's probably one of Lucian's people still keeping watch.

"Someone is following us. Another threat, so I am sorry to inconvenience you, but I am trying to make sure we do not die." Well thanks… *Okay well let's avoid that threat until we get Hannah safe.*

"It is not the pretty one. I know his smell, this is different." She says sniffing the air and trying to guess who it was. Nothing to do about it but be ready I guess. Opening the heavy metal door, it creaks loudly, echoing in the space. I hope Lucian finds a quieter way in or we'll lose the element of surprise. Towards the back of the empty space there is someone tied to a chair. Any normal person would have missed her, but our eyes are better than that. So many nights in the shadows have proven that.

The light above her suddenly illuminates and shocks her awake. Hannah jolts her head up and looks around the empty, dark, space quickly. She has a few fresh bruises on her caramel skin and some dried blood on the side of her face, but otherwise she appears mostly unharmed. There is another lumpy shape lying on the floor a few feet away from her under a tarp.

Whoever turned on the light had clearly heard us come in, but I am not the surprised. Kaida moves into the shadows.

"I came Brian! Now let Hannah go!" She yells out, copying my voice almost exactly. Hannah's face turns my way as much as she can manage.

"Mattie go! He's going to kill us!" She yells back trying to warn me. Ignoring her, Kaida keeps moving forward, looking for Brian.

"Brian, come out now and talk to me. We don't have to do this. Alice is waiting for you." From ahead of us we see someone move slightly, "Alice is here?" He steps out near the tarp and Hannah. He isn't fully in the light, but he looks rough.

Normally he's a clean-cut guy, dressed in his uniform or polos and khakis, but his clothes are dirty and rumpled. Dark blood is dried to his shirt and pants, hand prints of it swiped on his thighs. His hair is messy like he's been pulling his hands through it over and over again and his face is tight and drawn like he hasn't slept in a while. I guess being a psychotic asshole has taken a toll on him.

We tried to smile placatingly at him, slowly moving forward.

"No she is waiting for you at the station. She is really worried about you, and Hannah too. Maybe we could go there so she does not worry." He walks closer, the light illuminating him a bit more. Shaking his head back and forth, his lips move like he is talking to himself. Pointing his finger harshly towards Hannah, he mumbles loudly.

"No no no, she is a betrayer. A liar. She can't be around Alice. I have to stop her before they corrupt her." He walks up to Hannah and puts his hand around her throat, and she freezes in place, eyes darting wildly.

"Come out Mattie. Come show us the monster you really are."

The way he said it with extra emphasis on the word monster stopped us dead in our tracks. Holy shit did he really know about Kaida? Panicking a little at how he could have found out anything…My phone dings in my pocket and I try to reach for it, but Brian tightens his grip on Hannah's throat, and she winces in pain. Kaida holds up our hands in surrender. A shadow moves along the catwalk above us and I sigh in relief.

That has to be Lucian. Now all I have to do is get Brian away from her so he can get her out.

Kaida refocuses on Brian, watching him as we slowly move,keeping to the shadows.

"Brian, how about you and I talk for now. We can circle back to Hannah. The police and FBI already know it was you who killed Laura, Dan, and Carol. They even think you killed those men the FBI are investigating…" She keeps her voice low and quiet, minimizing her lisp, walking slowly. He growls angrily and Hannah squeaks in pain as he squeezes harder on her throat.

I need him to let her go, now.

"You killed those men! I only took care of the liars!" He's visibly worked up now. We stop moving and focus on him as he pulls his own hair at the scalp, letting go of Hannah's throat. She gasps for air.

We circle behind them and he turns his back to Hannah, watching me.

"It doesn't matter what I did, or what you did. Only what they believe." We try to goad him into moving toward us.

I'd rather he comes after us than her.

"They believe you are a monster and that is all that matters."

He steps towards us quickly, "I'm not a monster! You're the monster! She told me!" He stops before he reaches the shadows, but we're already moving again, luring him away from Hannah. Glancing at Hannah again, she was putting things together, but I never thought she would look at me as a monster.

He keeps stepping toward us as he speaks again.

"I just have to get rid of you and the other liars and then Alice will be mine. She won't fight it once you aren't around to poison her." He pulls a gun out of his waistband, and chambers a round as Kaida throws us to the side to duck behind some boxes.

"Alice doesn't want you. She didn't want you even before she found out what you've been doing. Why do you think killing us is going to make her change her mind?" She says calmly, seeing Lucian move into our eye line. There was no way he got down from there so fast so silently…He bends down to whisper in Hannah's ear, unties her, and puts a blindfold over her eyes. Whatever he told her got her to get up and follow him. He led her by her hand through the dark. They're close to the same door we came in when Hannah trips and her feet scuff on the floor loudly.

"Mon dui…" Lucian mutters, picking her up and swinging her into his arms, he bolts for the door. Brian sees them and turns, firing blindly in that direction. I swallow a panicked scream as Kaida jumps at him, pulling at his arm to knock the gun away. It hits the ground and slides away screeching against the concrete. The door across the room makes a familiar creak and then a slam, signaling their escape.

"Finally, I can be me." Kaida hisses. Standing tall and imposing, she releases Brian and pushing our hood back. With a deep breath I let myself sink back and let her take full control for what is to come.

We need him alive, remember? For Alice?

"That is a body over there. It is pretty fresh…. I think it was your friend Carol." She hisses, turning her eyes toward the tarp. Yeah, she is probably right but this is what Alice asked of us, so we'll try our hardest to keep him alive. *'Leave him alive'* I say to her. Kaida looks away from the tarp, but not before I feel the tears welling up, the guilt eating at her. I had no idea that she would feel like this…I should have known, should have prepared her better.

Brian is watching her, the fear wafting off of him. It stinks like sweat and decay, worse than anybody we have come upon. She starts to circle him like a shark as he pulls a small knife out of somewhere and brandishes it. The little snakes push their way out of our waves, hissing and snapping out at him. If Kaida was any closer, he would be bitten, but she keeps a little space.

"Why did you kill Laura? And Carol? They never hurt you and they had nothing to do with Alice." He laughs, a crazy unhinged look in his eyes. I barely hold back a wince.

"I had to kill them! They were spreading lies and you would go kill the men they lied about. You would kill them and eventually you would come for me." He moves while talking to keep facing me, but looking above my head.

"Oh? And why would I have come for you Officer Kemp? Were you doing something you should not have been?" He cackles like a jackal and lunges towards me, swinging the knife, but we side step him and hit his forearm out of the way easily.

"You would have figured out what I do to women in the quarter. The ones who say no...who don't mean no. I just give them something so they don't say no...they don't say anything ever. They don't even remember."

Our snakes hiss and swish. Kaida bares her own fangs and hisses at him, "Did you put your hands on Alice?"

My anger was growing by the second at the thought of him violating my sister. "No, Alice is sweet. She isn't a liar like you, like the other whores in this damned city. She loves me and she's going to be mine now. I just have to bring her to the woman and then she will be mine." He falls apart in front of us, his eyes wide and crazed. I should be gratified that he's so destroyed, but I wonder who the hell the woman he is talking about is.

He is coo coo for cocoa puffs obviously and has been hurting women since long before Laura.

"He cannot be saved. We need to be make an example of him before he hurts anyone else. I know that Alice and Agent Trouble want him alive, but this one is worse than anyone we have hunted before. This is what we were made for, to get revenge for those that cannot. Mattie, we cannot hold back here. This is our purpose." She says in our mind, speaking only for me.

Thinking over her words, she had a point. We were made to stop people like this. But she was wrong about what our goals were...it was never about vengeance. It was always about getting justice. Will and Alice can do that just as well as we can this time. Maybe they could get justice and answers for the victims. Answers that would die with Brian if we did things our way.

We have the ability to get them justice AND answers Kai, so we have the responsibility to try. At some point we have to grow...

Internally, she sighed, understanding my thinking. "As you wish, little monster."

In the moment we internally discussed our plan and its complications Brian had moved. Now we were backed up to the wall with few options for escape. That feeling of being watched crept over our skin again, and this time it couldn't be Lucian. It felt slimy, and set off Kaida's instincts. Looking up into the gallery for any sign of someone, Kaida was distracted for a second and Brian saw his opening. He lunged and swiped with the knife. The sharp blade caught us on the top of our right shoulder and sliced its way across our chest. The stinging pain seared as he tried to push the knife into our heart.

As shock settled in, I couldn't even feel it now as Kaida caught his hand between ours and tried to push it away. Our snakes were writhing and lunging forward, trying to bite him, but their venom wouldn't save us in time. Panic crept into my thoughts. Were we going to die at his hand? I didn't know if a knife to the heart would actually kill us, but I didn't want to find out. Kaida tried to angle our elbow up to knock the sunglasses off of our face. I'd rather have him as a statue than end up dead.

"NO! NO! NO! You won't get me!" He screamed angrily and squeezed his eyes shut tightly, still pushing hard at the knife clutched between our joined hands. The tip pierced the skin above our left breast and blood was streaming. I cried out in pain, Kaida echoing my cries as it punctured. We only had a few seconds to gain the upper hand, or we were going to find out just what we could or couldn't survive.

With a loud bang the door at the far end of the warehouse slammed open and gunshots rang out. Kaida flinched in pain.

Brian's grip loosened on the knife; he let go and stepped back, shock written all over his face. He was staring at us, reaching for our sunglasses. His fingers barely glanced them as Kaida stepped back. Blood bubbles over his lips as he smiled at us. New red stained his shirt quickly. He stepped back and crumpled to the floor in front of us. Looking up where he had been a moment ago, I met Alice's gaze from the doorway. Her gun held up pointing in our direction, her chest heaving with heavy breaths. Will was following her in, his own gun drawn. He took one look at Brian and then at me.

"Alice, check him!" pushing past her, he rushed across the room. He stopped right in front of us, his hands moving gently, touching the knife still lodged in our chest. I couldn't bite back the shriek of pain when he touched it, "Shhh baby. I know it hurts. Just give me a second and I'll get it out." Brushing back the tendrils of hair that had fallen across my forehead in the struggle, being careful of my glasses.

He kissed Kaida hard, crushing his lips against hers. She had a split second to pull our lips across her fangs, so she didn't nick his. He gripped the knife handle and pulled it out quickly. We gasped in pain as he dropped it to the ground in front of us with a clatter. He slapped a hand over the wound to stem the bleeding. "You're okay. You're okay. Alice is okay. Lucian's okay. Hannah is okay."

He had one hand over the wound and the other wrapped around our waist, our head cradled against his shoulder. The snakes were nuzzling him gently, happy to have him nearby.

"Took you long enough, Trouble."

"We got here as fast as we could," he whispered against the top of our head. We squeezed him back, but the adrenaline was leaving us quickly and the searing pain in our stomach we'd ignored while the knife was sticking out of our chest, now hurt like a bitch. Alice was bent over Brian's crumpled body. He was staring up at the sky, unseeing, while she checked his pulse. Running her fingers over his eyelids, she closed them, and her shoulders slumped as she started to cry. I pushed Kaida to the back and took control, moving away from Will, ignoring his attempts to grab onto me for support. Clutching our hands to our stomach, we wobbled towards her, dropping to our knees right in front of her. I reached out to grab her hand.

"I'm so sorry. I tried to stop him; I held Kaida back. We tried to do better Ali." I chanted the guilt almost as encompassing as the pain at this point. The guilt wasn't that he was dead, but that we had broken our promise; that we had disappointed her.

She was staring at his body. "Don't apologize, I know you both tried your best. This is on me...I should have seen it sooner; he was a psycho. You should have stoned his ass." She said it like it was a joke, but I could hear the tight pain in her voice. Even if he was crazy, Alice didn't take his life lightly.

My vision darkened on the edges, and I groaned around the ache in my stomach. Alice looked at us finally and saw all the blood on us. She gasped, lunging forward, careful of my snakes.

"Holy shit Mattie, why didn't you say you were stabbed? Will! Why did you let her get stabbed?" Coming up behind us, he pulled me back to lean against his chest.

"Yeah, I let her get stabbed!"

I smiled at the two of them bickering, Kaida was so exhausted, she didn't fight to take back control. We just both smiled, tired.

"Hush now children, no fighting. If Will is to blame for the stabbing, then Alice is to blame for the bullet." They both stopped grumbling and looked down, Alice grabbed my shirt and shoved it up. I knew this pain was familiar, thinking back to having Alice shoot me so we could figure out just how sturdy I was. Sure enough, there was a bullet wound in my lower abdomen pulsing out blood in time to my heartbeat.

"Fuck you shot her!" Will stood, scooping us up and cradling us to his chest. He was rushing for the door with Alice chasing behind us.

"HOLY SHIT! I'm so sorry! I didn't mean to hit you!" The metal door banged open, and Will was running towards my truck.

"What the hell did he do to her?" Lucian yells out from the cab of the truck. "Well, he used her as a pincushion and Alice shot her!" Will yelled back, jostling us into the truck, making us groan in pain.

"I didn't shoot her on purpose Will! Mattie will be fine tomorrow; trust me this isn't her first bullet wound."

She was right of course. It sucked, but I would be okay in a few hours. Until then, Alice would be swamped with guilt, just like she had been the first time she shot me. She didn't need Will making her feel worse.

"Lucian, shut the door and get me home. I don't want to listen to them bitch anymore." He reached in and clipped our seat belt on before he pushed our sunglasses up on our nose more. I was grateful he adjusted them for us because right now I couldn't feel my arms, let alone move them.

"Okay you two, I will take her highness home, and you can clean up this mess. Personally, I'd rather not deal with the legal side of this disaster." Lucian mock saluted them and with a quick kiss on Alice's cheek rounded the hood to the driver's side. "I'll even let you pick the tunes tonight Cher."

I rolled my eyes at him as Will stepped into the open door and leaned forward to kiss us again. Before his lips met ours, Kaida pushed forward to speak. "Be careful Trouble." He smiled and leaned in to plant his kiss.

"Never have to be around you. I'll see you in a few hours, my goddess."

He stood back and let Alice push in. "Don't even apologize again, Alice. It was an accident. Go be a detective and solve your big case."

She pats our knee, "Ha! you thought I was going to apologize? What for? I was the one who got the bad guy!" She studies our wounds, Kaida smiles to reassure her that we'll be fine. She smiles back and slams the truck door closed. Lucian pulls away quickly and drives towards the house in silence. We lay our head back and the darkness washes over as the quiet seeps in.

Kaida softly whispered to me,"Rest now Mattie. We are safe."

It feels like only a few seconds pass before we're jostled by Lucian picking us up to carry us inside.

"Shh, close your eyes. I have you. You are both safe." Normally Kaida wouldn't let anyone close while in this form, but we're too tired and too hurt to do anything about it. Besides, Will just smashed through any boundaries we had in the last few hours.

I let myself relax and slip into sleep.

Chapter 29

Will

Hannah hadn't seen us carry Mattie out when we got back to the SUV where Lucian stashed her. She watched me silently with pursed lips, the dried blood on her head a minor concern. I changed into a clean shirt and waited for her to start asking questions.

She still just watched me, the last 24 hours had to be traumatizing for her, but her stern gaze and steel spine implied that she wasn't ready to fall apart in front of me. She looked me in the eyes and finally asked, "What do I say about Mattie…when the police get here?"

Asking her to lie would be a lot on top of everything she'd been through, but she said that Mattie was family to her, so maybe asking her to omit certain things would be acceptable.

"I don't know what you mean. Mattie Cutler was never here, Okay?" I sounded as serious as I could. She didn't argue or question it, just nodded back. We sat in silence in the back seat, both of us watching Alice pace in front of the vehicle with her phone to her ear. Soon, more cops than either of us could imagine would take over the area. Then the press, and the lookie loos. Chaos was coming soon but right now we could take a breath.

"I knew what she was doing" she says softly to the dark, not looking at me.

I studied Hannah, she had been kidnapped and beaten but still managed to look collected and professional as she stared straight ahead at Alice through the windshield.

"You knew she was doing what?" My stomach twisted with anxiety, maybe we couldn't get Hannah to go along with our story. Lucian had put a blindfold over her eyes but maybe she saw more than she was supposed to, and then we all, mostly Mattie, were fucked.

She scoffed and rolled her eyes, rubbing at the crusty blood under her nose. "Having our own avenging angel wasn't a bad thing, Agent Bennet…I never looked down on her for doing something about what we couldn't fix ourselves. I would do anything to thank her for the peace she brought some of us. To slay monsters for others is a selfless thing." I smile at her, the woman was made of steel, and after hearing her say that, I'm confident that she'll keep what she thinks really happened here a secret.

"I like that…avenging angel. It describes her well. I'm sorry that my people, the people that were supposed to protect you and the others, couldn't or just didn't do enough."

Reaching over to take her hand and give it a squeeze, she squeezes back and says "Where the universe finds a void, it does something about it. She did the best she could…make sure she knows that." I nod looking back at Alice as she hangs up her phone, slipping it in her pocket and walking back to the door.

"Just make sure you stick to the story to keep Alice and Mattie safe."

Opening the door to meet her and join the chaos, I'm about to close the door again when she leans across the seat, holding the door open.

"He called someone. She came to the door twice…the first time I thought she was Mattie. She looked similar from behind, something about the way she stood, the way she spoke, but I couldn't see her face. They talked for a minute and then she left, and he was more agitated than before. That was when he killed Carol…He stabbed her over and over again." She was crying, the tears streaming down her cheeks leaving marks on her dirty skin in the dim lit car light.

"I tried to help her. To help Mattie…I didn't want to call her. Will you tell her it wasn't her fault? It wasn't."

I patted her arm comfortingly, "She knows, Hannah. It wasn't your fault either. It was only Kemp's." Shutting the door softly I turned to find Alice waiting.

What feels like only a moment later the dark warehouse that we had kicked our way into a few hours ago was surrounded by flashing lights of a dozen police cars. It had started to rain. I stood to the side of the commotion, talking to John on the phone to fill him in on the recent developments.

The moment we called in the shooting to the head office Alice also called Internal Affairs and requested they send someone straight there for an officer involved shooting. She gave me her weapon, and I put it in the car right away. We followed every protocol as more people started to show up. After a few more cars showed up to secure the perimeter and the ambulance was treating Hannah, I wrangled a few cops.

"Head to this address and photograph everything. I want the secondary scene contained." Sending them off to comb through Brian Kemp's apartment. A short time later, they sent the photos to my phone. They were finding plenty of evidence that he had been stalking the women of the S/A group, killing them and the men that they had accused. Suddenly the scene was thrown into more madness when the captain showed up and jumped out of his car, instantly screaming.

"Hester! Where the hell is Hester!"

I stepped away to leave a message for Shaw about what was happening here while Alice gave her statement. She was standing a few feet away with the IA officer; a tall woman with short blonde, cropped hair. She was the antithesis of Alice but was nodding along with her, respectfully. An officer shooting another officer was a huge deal, but the way everything was laid out, Alice was justified in every way.

We had coordinated our stories before calling it in: saying we got an anonymous tip about weird activity down here at the warehouse, and when we were investigating, we spotted Hannah tied up. Officer Kemp had a knife and was strangling her so we stormed the room. He wouldn't release Hannah and tried to stab her so Alice shot him. It wasn't cut and clean, but it was good enough for IA after they saw the pictures in Brian's apartment and spoke to Hannah. Alice met my gaze with an eye roll and a cocked brow as the captain stormed up to her and the IA investigator, trying to shove between the two.

Pausing my conversation with John's answering machine, I gave her a look asking if she wanted my help or not. She looked from me to him again and then nodded. I said into the phone, "John, this is a mess here, but I will call you in the morning with some answers. Just know we got our guy. I gotta go," hanging up with force.

I slid the phone back into my pocket and pushed off the wall to stride over to the Captain. I step between Alice and him, and he quickly pulled in the finger he was jabbing her way, having to crane his neck to look up and meet my eyes. I can feel Alice close to my back. If there weren't so many Officers here, I would give her a hug. This close to the captain, I towered over him by a full head.

"Is there a problem captain?" He turns a color of reddish purple. He might actually have burst a blood vessel in his face as he sucks in a breath to start his rant anew for me.

"Damn right there is! I have a dead officer, and I want this woman arrested! I don't care what they are saying about him, Kemp was a good cop, and they were privately involved before this. It's damn suspicious."

He leans around to yell at Alice again, "What did he do? Hurt your feelings? Dump you? You decided to get even?" Spittle flying from his mouth to land on my arm, before she or the IA officer still watching can say a word in her defense.

I step closer to him and lower my voice, "You think your officer was a good cop? Right now it's looking like he murdered at least 6 people, maybe more. He took a 24-year-old girl, from your city, and killed her. He cut her so deep that her head was almost removed. Then he desecrated her body and dumped in on the steps of a church. There's a dead mother laying in that warehouse that Dr. Raines SAW him murder after he kidnapped them both. She saw him stab her over 50 times. Now there's an orphaned baby because of Kemp. You think this is all make believe so Detective Hester can get revenge against a man SHE broke up with?" If he could have popped like a pimple, he would have exploded when I poked him in the chest, "You might want to think how all this plays out to the brass, the FBI, the press, and the city officials before you go around spewing shit like that." He stands there, gulping like a fish out of water for a moment before he turns on his heel and storms off.

Taking a breath of muggy air into my lungs to calm down, I turn, and am met by Alice holding up her hand in the air. I look too long, trying to figure out what the hell she's doing, raising her hand like she has a question. She smirks and lifts up my hand and slapping it against hers. The knot in my chest loosen.

"I was just looking for backup, not total destruction, but beggars can't be choosers. Thanks Bennet." She's grinning again, and doesn't look as worn down as I'm sure she feels. She pulls out her phone and looks at it a second before looking back at me.

"I'm so sorry, my sister is really worried about me. Can I take this?" She asks the IA Officer, who nods nicely.

"Yeah of course, Detective Hester. We are done for now. We can meet with your rep in a few days and review your statement, but I don't have any red flags, considering all….this." She waves her hand over the open door of the warehouse as she speaks.

Techs are dusting and photographing everything at the scene. Alice nods and walks off to answer the phone, hopefully getting us both an update on Mattie. My phone dings too and I pull it out. It's a text from Mattie, but the photo is of her tucked in her bed covered in the same fuzzy blanket from yesterday. She's still Kaida, but out cold. The snakes woven through her hair are asleep across her pillow and cheek. There was no blood on her now, so Lucian must have gotten her cleaned up. Returning the phone to my pocket, I rub a hand over my exhausted face, shaking off the exhaustion so I can keep going.

Carol Shanks' body was indeed found under the tarp at the back of the warehouse and was currently being loaded in the ME's van. She'd been carved up so badly and violently, we couldn't tell if Kemp had been trying to write something on her too, or if he was mentally too far gone at that point. Watching everything unfolding, another detective walks up and speaks to Alice as she is walking back toward me. He stops her just close enough for me to overhear.

"You did good Hester. I knew Kemp was off… though I didn't know how much." She pats his shoulder, "I'm not worried Oliver. I know I did my job, anything else can be answered tomorrow. I really want to get home now." He pulls her in for a hug and let's go, walking away just as fast.

She walks the short distance to me. "We can go. We gave statements, the apartment is being combed over, nothing else to be done tonight." I nod and follow her to the SUV, climbing in the passenger seat.

"Lucian texted me." She nods, driving us away from the chaos.

"Yeah, I reminded him to send you proof of life. The bullet was through and through, she's resting now." The memory of Mattie and Kaida in that warehouse is going to haunt my nightmares for years to come. I had followed Alice in when we heard her scream, rushing through the door. Alice fired three shots before I had even seen Kaida behind Kemp.

When he fell away, I was so relieved, but only for a split second and then the glint of the knife sticking out of their chest caught my eye. I grabbed her and kissed her, to distract her and myself, from the sucking sound the knife made as I pulled it out. A couple inches deeper and it would have been buried in her heart… I was grateful that it was still beating. After Lucian drove off, Alice reassured me that all the other times Mattie had been shot she'd been fine, like it was a totally normal thing to say. Apparently, after the gorgon told her she was pretty tough, the girls had taken it upon themselves to test that theory in a multitude of creative ways.

"I've shot her, stabbed her, poisoned her, and one time she jumped off a really big cliff. She broke both her legs, but she healed as soon as she turned back into Kaida. We never cut anything off though, because that seemed like a bad time to find out things don't grow back…" The house is illuminated by our headlights as we pull in, but the sun was starting to come up as well.

Nobody clarified what time exactly Kaida changes back into Mattie, but close to sunrise seems like a pretty accurate guess. I expect if I'm around long enough, this will all become normal to me, too. We both haul our weary bodies out of the car and into the house. Lucian is asleep on the couch, his legs too long, so they're draped over the side with one arm folded over his eyes. Alice walks in the living room to drape a blanket over him, with a kiss on his forehead that is sweet and tender, she waves me on to the kitchen. Shaking my head, I point towards the stairs and start up them.

Clearly, I was running on pure adrenaline, because 20 minutes ago I was fine, and now I'm not sure I can make it all the way upstairs. Maybe I can convince Lucian to carry me up. Smiling at the mental picture of the tall man giving me a piggyback ride, I drag one foot in front of the other enough times that I get to the top. I round the balcony edge and head straight for Mattie's cracked door. Peering inside, I see her sleeping, wrapped in blankets. I pull off my loose tie and toss it in the chair in the corner, then undo the buttons at my wrists. I pull the bottom loose from my pants and undo the buttons up the front.

There's a choking feeling in my throat, my chest tight as the light from the sun filters through the blinds of the window. Kaida's form wavers and then she seems to fold in on herself, changing back to Mattie. From green to light creamy skin, freckles dot across her nose and cheeks that are softer and fuller now. The fingernails on her hands, which are tucked together under her face, shrink and change back to the blue color she had painted them a few days ago. Watching the gentle rise and fall of Mattie's chest, I can't seem to look away in case she isn't breathing the next time.

In one breath she was the woman I loved again…Wait love?

Pausing as I remove my shoes, I stop to stare at her again. There in the bed was this woman who had been through trials of unimaginable pain, and she still smiled. She laughed with Lucian, made sure her sister always had food and the poor excuse for coffee she loved. She did everything she could to help a group of women she never let herself get too close to. She was willing to sacrifice herself over and over again, but never asked for someone to help hold her up. She could have gotten angry and bitter over her curse, could have self-destructed, but instead she turned it into something beautiful. I don't know what I would have done in that situation, but most people would have gone a different, darker path.

Athena might have cursed her, but to me she's stronger than the goddess herself… I went and fell in love with this woman without even realizing it. Maybe I did realize it when she looked at me that first day outside the station with judgement in her gaze, or seeing her in the crowd of the church, her eyes filled with derision. Maybe it was over breakfast at Monty's, the first time I heard her laugh out loud. She drew me in like a spider in a web and I was caught before I even knew what happened. Plopping down at the edge of the bed, I sigh and flop back next to her softly so as not to jostle her. She stretches out with a yawn and turns to face me. Laying side by side in the quiet of the morning we just look into each other's eyes silently for a moment. Brushing her hair back and behind her ear, I cup her chin and pull her face closer to mine, "Feel better?"

She looks at me like she's memorizing my face before nodding, silently. Her eyes blaze and burn into me. I have to choke back the words I want to shout from the rooftops. Swallowing hard, I continue to drown in her green eyes, her freckles, her lilac and vanilla scent. I'm just about to release her face when she closes the distance and presses her soft and full lips against mine. She slips her tongue against mine and I can't hold back the groan that slips out as I slide my hand to the back of her head, holding her tighter against me. She scoots closer, wrapping one leg up and over my hip so we're pressed fully against one another. Her tongue slips further in between my lips and tastes me deeper. I'm drowning in her and I don't give a shit…I would drown in her kiss forever if she'd let me. Pushing my other arm under her waist, I slide my hand up under her shirt and trail my fingers up the length of her spine. She trembles under my touch, and with a final soft kiss, she pulls back. She opens her eyes and looks at me lazily. Her eyes sparkle, then she grins as she sits up and pulls her shirt over her head, tossing it off the bed. She looks deep into my eyes, but I'm trying to remember how to breathe as I take in the sight of her hair tumbling messily over her bare shoulders, her breasts, barely contained in a sheer purple and black bra. A large angry, red, scar runs from the top of her right shoulder to her breast, and a matching, smaller scar is over her heart on the left side.

The gunshot wound is almost fully healed on her stomach. Reaching forward, I trace the one on her heart with a finger. She watches me quietly with curiosity. I reached forward with my other arm, wrapping it around her waist and pulling her closer, tucking her underneath me. Leaning over her, I run my hand flat across the top of her breast and down her stomach to the bullet wound. I look down at it before I kiss the top of her shoulder and down across the top edge of her bra to the other side. Gently pressing my lips to the healed knife wound, I look up to see her watching me intently, holding her breath as I follow my hand with my lips until I get to the bullet wound, tasting her skin before I press another light kiss to it. She huffs out the breath she was holding, and I look back to her face to make sure she's okay. She's flushed across her neck and cheeks, and breathing as heavily as I am.

Meeting my eyes, she nods and lifts her hips in silent command. I grip the waist of her jeans and panties and pull them down her thighs, slowly exposing her. I pull them all the way off and toss them as she grips the sheets tightly. If she still had her little talons, they would be in shreds. Smirking at the thought, I put my hands between her knees and push them apart so I can admire my prize. She's already wet as I lean in to run my nose up her slit taking in the smell of her.

She moans, "Will…" her flush covers her whole body now and her skin in more heated under my hands as I hold down her hips, dragging my tongue up the center of her in one long lick before circling her clit with my tongue in little slow circles. She gasps and covers her mouth.

"Now now, my goddess. I earned those sounds. Don't hold back on me." I say, my voice low and husky before I suck her clit into my mouth and flick it a couple times. She can't hold back her gasp this time, and then moans hard enough to send shock waves down to her core. Her fingers sink into my hair and she pulls hard enough to sting, but I continue to feast on her like she's the last meal I'll ever have. She lifts her hips to meet my mouth, a silent plea for more. I use one hand to hold her down and the other to sink two fingers into her warm folds. Thrusting them slowly in and out, I tease her clit to the same rhythm. She wiggles violently as her orgasm builds in time to the moans slipping from her throat. Nipping her clit lightly, she comes with a silent scream, arching off the bed and pushing herself firmly onto my face and fingers. I continue to lick and suck until she's spent. Pulling my fingers out, I catch her staring, so I pop them in my mouth and lick them clean, never breaking eye contact. Being able to see those eyes uncovered is its own gift.

Being here with her in the morning light is something I wouldn't trade for the world. She sits up and pulls my hand to bring me closer. Reaching down, she undoes my belt and pants, pulling them off. I raise up to help. She takes my cock in her hand; it's pulsing hard and heavy with all the blood in my body. I can't hold back the groan that slips out as she strokes me slowly. She lets go and slips out from under me, pushing my shoulder to turn me onto my back.

"You came to save me last night." She has me entranced as she straddles me, her wet pussy pressed tightly against the underside of my throbbing cock.

"You kissed her. That was stupid and dangerous, but you did it anyway." Grabbing onto her hips, I lift her and press my tip to her entrance.

"I'll always come for you, and I kissed YOU. You're her, and she is you. It may be stupid, but that's what I want, from today until the end of days." She's holding herself up as my fingers sink into the softness around her hips. Her eyes close and she sinks down on my cock, taking it to the hilt, stretching her open perfectly, and we both moan softly. Until the day the darkness claims me, I will remember this image of Mattie, hands on my stomach as she rolls her hips, riding me. I can't hold back as my hands find their way down from her breasts, to her soft thighs. I don't take over, letting her do what she wants with me. The pleasure rolls over us both as I struggle to string together coherent thoughts. It takes everything I have to hold back from flipping her over and fucking her hard enough to get it through her head that I want her AND Kaida. I'm a selfish man who wants it all. She tosses her head back, her eyes closed, hair streaming down her back. Reaching up, I wrap my hand around her delicate throat, squeezing firmly. Her eyes shoot open and the movement in her hips becomes harder and more erratic as she chases euphoria. Our gazes clash and lock, bright green with gray-blue as she clenches down on me and cries out raggedly. I pull her to me as stars dance in my vision and I cum with a deep groan, filling her and marking her as mine.

Mattie collapses on top of me, too spent to move, gasping quietly as she comes down from her high. I lay there staring at the ceiling fan slowly spinning above us and stroking her back while the world resettled and we caught our breath.

"I don't know what to say right now…but I can't stand the silence."

Smiling, I pull away and look up at her, pressing a soft kiss to the side of her head, "Silent moments are the best. Silence is where you figure out what you are thinking, or not thinking." She buries her head in the crook of my neck and nuzzles in with a sigh. I can feel the upturn of her lips against the skin. I pull out of her now and reach down for the covers as she slides off to lay next to me. Normally I would suggest cleaning up, but I am too tired for anything at this point. I want to spend as much time as I can with her, but if I don't rest, I might die. Pulling her against me again, I close my eyes and start to fall asleep as she brushes her hand softly against my chest.

As I drift off, I hear her whisper, "There you are…I think I found you."

Chapter 30

Mattie

The sun is high in the afternoon sky, and the day is blazing hot as usual. Rocking in the chair on the front porch, I enjoy the breeze as it tries to find its way and the sting from the hot cup of tea in my hand. Running my finger down the arm of the outdoor rocker, I realize it's overdue for a good sanding. It's one of those things that we put on the back burner while we were fixing up the house. Just a few short years ago we were buying this place, which was an absolute disaster, and it was just Alice and me. Alice and I had been together through our childhoods, the complicated teenage years, leaving for college, and then dropping out, bouncing around and struggling more than we ever did in foster care. Through it all, it was Alice, Kaida, and I against the world. Then one day, Lucian strong-armed his way in and just stuck around; finally, Alice noticed he was waiting for her all this time.

Smiling and sipping my cup, I can picture their lives falling into place so easily. He could move in here with us or buy her the house of her dreams. He'll never question that we're family first and everything else is second, he'll probably pack her lunches, while wearing a frilly apron, so she doesn't starve while on shift. I make a mental note to get him a super frilly one for Christmas because he will think it's as funny as I do.

I can picture a whole life for her if she would just grab it, but after this morning I'm struggling to do the same for myself. I've slept with people before, no more than a handful over the years, and even liked one or two of them, but nothing came of it. Yet, there was a moment upstairs this morning where Will's fingers were wrapped around my throat, his other hand branding my thighs with bruises of his fingertips. Our eyes met, and I could see them brimming with love. He didn't say it, but I could feel it filling up the space between us…I felt it in the air last night when he pulled the knife from our chest, too. I almost wanted to say it but had to swallow down the words that were too big and too soon for us.

He was the first person I had let this close, and he hadn't promised me forever, but he promised he was there for me, for her, for everything that I am. If that isn't love, then what is? If you show someone all the dark parts of yourself and they love you for them, isn't that what great love stories are about? Thinking back through the old legends of love that my mother would read to me as bedtime stories, they all share a common theme…where love exists, it's usually followed by disaster and heartbreak. Of all the evil I have done, all the lives I have taken, all the darkness I have inside me, the thing that would finally break me would be to ruin someone like Will. The deepest, darkest, most selfish part of me knows that I won't be able to let him go.

The screen door creaks and I don't look, expecting Alice, but the breeze catches on Will's dark woodsy scent. His hair has gotten longer while he's been in the city, and it flops across his forehead now. His face is covered in stubble that says he hasn't shaved in a few days. He's shirtless but wearing a very wrinkled pair of dress pants. I take my time admiring him from his bare feet up to his chest, broad-shouldered and pleasingly covered in chest hair. I always liked a man who looked like a man. He has a blanket thrown around his shoulders while he stands there smiling at me like I'm sunshine incarnate.

"Morning, gorgeous." He crosses the patio and leans down to kiss the top of my head. He snags the cup out of my hands, stealing the warmth. He takes a sip before making a disgusted face.

"I thought you were done trying to poison me." I can't hold back a laugh, and I take my cup back to sip it myself, "It's just tea. For relaxing." No matter what my head says, he sets off the butterflies in my stomach with a simple smile, and I don't want to lose that.

"Tea is for old ladies and the British. We need coffee." He opens the screen door and bows mockingly for me. I smile and shuffle inside, hearing the low voices of Lucian and Alice coming from upstairs.

I make my way down the hallway decorated with the attempts at embroidery that Alice and I had tried, photos of our adventures, and one really ugly painting Alice had done after two bottles of wine. It was supposed to be a tree, but in the end, it turned out looking like a giant black dick in the forest. Of course, I was going to mat and frame it for our home. There was still plenty of space to make a few new memories now that the world isn't falling out from under us. It was funny to think that back there on the porch I felt lost and alone, certain that the best thing for Will would be to walk away, but then he came out and lit up my world with fresh sunshine I didn't realize was missing. Suddenly, my face hurt from smiling constantly, the weight on my chest and shoulders was gone, and I slept deeply when he was around. Starting to make a fresh pot of coffee, I see Will enter and watch me from the kitchen doorway. Without looking his way, I spin around to take out the cream and sugar.

"Tell me a secret no one knows about you." I want to know everything about him. He smirks, watching me.

"A secret, huh?" Crossing his arms in front of his chest draws my eyes, and I can't hold back from a little ogling.

"I love to bake…mostly sourdough bread, but I make an amazing pie with Thanksgiving leftovers every year for my brothers and I to enjoy. It's my contribution to a little tradition we have where we go out the night after Thanksgiving and have beers, a bonfire, and eat cold turkey sandwiches. Now, it's my leftovers pie. We've been doing it for years." His eyes sparkle with mirth at the memories of himself and his brothers. It sounded like the nicest version of the holiday that I could imagine.

"Alice and I usually stay home, eat pot pies, drink a few bottles of wine, and pass out watching serial killer documentaries. Not quite as Hallmark channel as you guys." He was caught up in the memories while I got out a little pan and the eggs to fry up a couple.

"Next year, you both can come to my mom's. She would love to have you over and would probably enjoy the serial killer documentaries. Now you have to tell me a secret," He teased me. It is sweet of him to invite us, but there is no way for it be a reality…I think his mom would notice if halfway through dinner I changed, and Kaida couldn't be trusted to behave at a bonfire. It would be a disaster, but it's nice to dream for a second. I try to suppress the urge to roll my eyes but fail miserably, "Aren't you tired of my secrets?"

Walking over, he grips my hips from behind me and wraps his arms around my waist so his front is tight against my back. He leans in to whisper in my ear, "I won't be tired of them, even when they all belong to me." A shudder runs through me at the husky quality of his voice as it tickles the back of my neck. He presses his lips there before letting me go to fetch a cup for his coffee, "How are you feeling after last night?" I try to shrug my shoulders, but tense up when no snarky comment emerges from Kai. I realize that my head is quiet; I haven't heard anything from my other half since Lucian brought us home. Holding up a finger so he will wait, I pause.

"Are you there?" I ask out loud and think as loudly as I can. Nothing but silence greets me, and panic starts to claw its way up my throat.

"Hello? Kaida, is everything okay?" I ask again, pulling down my shirt top to look at the mark fading in the skin over my heart. What if it hurt her? What if I was too far gone and it was her or me? Would she have sacrificed herself for me? Hyperventilating, I lean against the counter, my legs struggling to hold me up. "KAIDA, FUCKING ANSWER ME!"

Will is watching me silently with worry all over his face. He looks like he wants to reach out and comfort me, but doesn't want to get in the way or startle me. This morning, he promised he wanted us both, but what if all that was left was me? I heard the footsteps on the stairs, stomping down, one set followed by heavier ones following. Alice appeared in the doorway with Lucian hot on her tail, both disheveled. Alice's lips were swollen, and her hair was mussed with a blush she rarely showed painting her whole face and chest. She was only wearing Lucian's shirt, and Lucian was standing there behind her, every inch an ebony god incarnate. His arms were painted with tattoos, and his pierced nipples glinted in the light. His low-slung jeans were not even buttoned in their rush to get down here. Both of them looked around for the invisible enemy who had interrupted them.

Normally I'd be crowing from the rooftops that it was about damn time, and my monster would be right there with a smart-ass comment for one of them about how even if she wasn't invited to join, she could have admired the view at least. The tears started before I knew what was happening, and once they were flowing, there was no stopping up Niagara Falls. Sobs wracked my chest, and I collapsed, Will barely catching me before I hit the floor. Alice was trying to reach for me and muttering to Will to find out what had happened, but he was too busy soothing me to answer. I clutched his arm and cried into his chest, sitting across his lap on my kitchen floor, devastated that Kaida was gone. It made no sense, but here I was. With no warning, my brain felt like it swelled, a familiar pressure I hadn't noticed until it was gone. Kaida must have slipped so far back into me that I didn't know she was even there…

Good goddess, little one. You are nothing if not dramatic…tell Agent Trouble to get back to work distracting you so I can rest.

I choked back the sobs as relief flooded me and I wiped at my face messily, "Rest?! I thought you were gone!"

Well, you are still stuck with me, little monster. Feed yourself and get some rest before tonight…I will need to be at my best when it is finally my turn with Agent Trouble.

She sounded so casual, but I could hear the pain in her voice, the exhaustion. What we went through rattled her just as much as it did me. "Forgive me for caring about you."

I love you too. Always have and always will.

The tears welled up anew at her usage of the saying my mother would use when I was little, the one Catherine had told me before she left the apartment that night she first changed, the same saying that Alice and I would say whenever we separated.

"Always have, always will," I whisper back to her. Alice freezes and puts a finger under my chin to get me to look at her. Still sitting in Will's lap, she scoots as close as she can on her knees.

"Is she okay?" I nod, still not steady, maybe from the scare, maybe still adrenaline crashing from the mess of last night. Will is running his fingers through my hair, scraping lightly across my scalp. If we weren't in the kitchen with our friends, he might just pull a moan from me. Alice holds up a hand in the air like the royalty she is, and without missing a beat, Lucian steps in and takes it, pulling her to her feet and against his chest before settling them both in one of the dinette chairs. They are the craziest separately, together they may be totally insufferable.

Pulling away from Will, I stand and hold out my hand to help him to his feet. He takes down three more mugs and fills them all before setting them on the table in front of us. The eggs I had been making had burned in the pan while I was preoccupied, so I settled for coffee. Lucian reached forward and snagged a cup, taking a large gulp before sitting in front of Alice and twirling one finger around a lock of Alice's hair. She took the cup and doctored her coffee. I reached for one of the untouched ones to realize that Will was already putting cream and sugar in my cup.

Pushing it over, he leaned back against the counter.

"Stop winking at me, Lucian, or I'll punch you again." We all look at Lucian who is holding back a grin and trying to look innocent, which we all know is bullshit.

"I was just going to ask if you got any sleep, William. I was worried you were still tired, Mon Cheri." Alice and I both hold back smiles and exchange glances. Neither of us got a lot of sleep apparently. I'm looking forward to that information download, but then I'll have to share as well, and that's not as appealing. I want to keep this morning's memory locked up tight in my tiny vault of perfect memories. I need to get moving if I'm going to tick things off my list today. Standing up to go upstairs, "I need to get going if I am going to get done by sundown."

Now they all look my way with a mixture of confusion and worry.

"Where are you off to, darling?" Will asks, just throwing out pet names now.

"I have to go see Hannah…I don't think she saw anything last night, but she still tried to save me, she deserves me standing by her now." His eyes are sad as he looks from me to the others, "She might not know what you really are, but she knows you were the one protecting the women in your group. She doesn't care…she might not get your reasons, but she thought they were good enough for her to hide you. I'll get dressed and take you in."

I wanted to interrupt, but he waved me off, "She is under police protection, I can get you in the door and make sure no one listens in."

Damn, that did make sense. Alice stood from Lucian's lap and grabbed my hand, "Can we talk a minute?" I nod and pull her hand, leading her down the hall to the living room. Normally, the pocket doors in here stay open for airflow, but I pull them closed now so she can say whatever she wants privately. I turn around and am attacked as she pulls me into her embrace, toppling us both over the back of the couch into its pillowy softness.

It's only a second before I feel the tears soaking the front of my shirt.

"I walked into that warehouse, saw him standing over you with that knife, and I thought you were already gone."

Patting her back, I let her talk it out, "You had a knife in your heart! I shot you! I was trying so hard to keep it all together for you, but I was a mess. I threw up for ten straight minutes when I got back last night…All I could see was you under that tarp staring up with dead eyes."

Hushing her soothingly, "I'm okay. Hannah, Will, and Lucian, we're all okay. It's over now."

She shook her head thoughtfully before pulling away and sitting back to talk, "He had a partner. Someone came while he had Hannah, but she didn't see them…" Thinking back to Brian's rants about how 'she' had promised him Alice. "There's more- there was a note in his apartment in a different handwriting that told him not to look you in the eyes and to stab you in the heart to kill you."

I scoff, sitting up too, "Clearly only half right." Alice takes my hands between her own. I can hear the desperation in her voice.

"Maybe we need to go. Move on...I have a bad feeling that this isn't over." The idea of leaving our home made me sad, I don't mind the idea of moving on to somewhere else for a fresh start and this place would be a nice nest egg now that we did so much work on it, but looking around the room I couldn't imagine running because we had to. No, if we were going anywhere, it was going to be because we wanted to.

"We'll figure it out, Alice, but there's too much good here for us to run now. Plus there's two other people we have to run it by before we call a moving van and put up the for-sale sign. They might like a vote..." From outside the pocket doors Lucian's voice rings out clearly, "Fucking right we would! Thanks for that love!" We both look over at the closed doors, me smiling and Alice rolling her eyes in frustration. Privacy will be a priority if we move on.

"If we do move, let's get a lady cave...no boys allowed," I say as I throw my arm around her shoulder to pull her into my side. Snuggling down into the pillows and cushions, she sighs, looking at me.

"Or a she-shed...We get through this together, always." I hug her tightly, "I have no intention of trying to do anything without you. Soulmates come in more than one form, Alice, and you were here first."

Chapter 31

William

Wrapping my arms around Mattie's waist, I rest my chin on her shoulder.

"Let's stay here for a breath." She huffs, leaning back into me, the weight of her in my arms feels surreal after everything we've been through.

"Hannah is okay. Alice is okay. You can take a moment." Mattie turns around, wrapping her arms around my neck, standing on her tip toes, her green eyes burning into me. She just watches me like she is trying to read my mind. Whatever she sees, she doesn't fight me.

"Fine. Alice is taking the day off, too. We have to go see her tomorrow, though." Nodding, I pull her against me and kiss those pink lips. I'll take her wherever she wants to go.

Taking her hand, I lead us back upstairs. The world feels like, for a moment, it held its breath while we all retreat to our respective rooms. Everyone cycles through going upstairs to get cleaned up and Mattie joins me in the shower, to conserve water of course. I told myself that I would behave, because the noises we heard coming from Alice's room proved that privacy in this house is a mere illusion. It's going to be a while before I get the sound of Lucian begging her- loudly- to let him come out of my head.

I say a lot of things to myself, make myself a lot of promises, and then the sight of bubbles running down her bare back takes all my ideas and washes them down the drain with my promises. What starts as deep kisses and wandering hands becomes more when Mattie drops softly to her knees and takes me in her mouth. Leaning my head back against the wall, I dig my fingers into the mass of her hair and push it back out of her way, groans slipping from my lips as hers move up and down my length. I look down at her, to capture the moment in my mind, when her green eyes glow brightly back at mine, I can't anymore.

I pull her up, and next thing I know, I have her pushed up against the wall, and I am buried inside of her. The feel of her skin against mine clouds everything else, my fingers digging into her toned thighs, holding them around me, lost in the moment until the hot water suddenly runs out, the shocking us enough to get back to cleaning up and joining the others downstairs. Lucian comes down in nothing but a very short, blue, fuzzy robe that obviously belongs to Alice. Alice was drinking a glass of wine when he appeared and sat down for dinner. After a laughing fit that made her wine go down the wrong pipe, she dragged him to the living room, where they hid until dark. They cuddled up on the couch to watch bad TV while I took Mattie upstairs to get the sleep she desperately needed.

It was around midnight when I felt something brushing softly against my cheek. Trying to push it away, I startled at the feeling of scales against my hand. Opening my eyes, I find Kaida leaning over me, watching me sleep, so close that one of her snakes was rubbing affectionately against my face. She reaches up to rub her own black tipped finger against my stubble, "Hello Trouble."

I can't help but smile at the nickname, "Hello Goddess." Her smile is thrilling, her small fangs pressing into her full bottom lip.

"I need to talk to you about something." Leaning up, I press a soft kiss against her lips, needing to feel them again. She pulls back with a shocked look on her face.

"Stop." She pushes her hand against my chest, holding me down, and the urgency in her voice gives me pause.

"Are you okay?" Moonlight streams through the window, bathing us in just enough light for me to see the little furrow between her brows, just like Mattie when she is worried. Kaida sits back on her heels on the bed, and I push up to sit against the pillows.

"No… Trouble, I am not. Mattie is resting, so this is between the two of us." I nod, but I'm not comfortable keeping secrets in this weird three-way relationship.

"As long as it doesn't hurt anyone, I'll keep it that way." Kaida looks toward the door like she's checking there's no one listening in. She turns back to me, those silly heart-shaped sunglasses masking her eyes.

"Mattie is still in danger. I know someone else was at the warehouse. Someone is coming for her, and I do not think I will be able to keep her safe." The panic grows in my chest.

"Who's coming for her?" She smirks sadly, "I have lied to her for a long time, for a good reason, but Mattie would not think so…nor would Alice."

If Kaida was keeping something important from Mattie, I could see Alice taking her side; practicality wasn't as important as loyalty to those two. Whatever secret, whatever lie Kaida is keeping from them, she's willing to risk them turning against her, making her the monster in their story. Her face is turned towards the light, stunning in its sharp angles, fear on her features.

"You should tell her, Kaida, secrets always come out. It would be better coming from you." Her face turns my way, and then she looks down at the bed, staring into the space between her knees, "I cannot…" Her voice trembles, making her seem so much more vulnerable.

"I just need you to promise me something…promise me that you will love her?" I reel back like she hit me, it feels like she's saying goodbye, like she's going away. "Kaida, what the hell is going on?"

She lies back down on the bed with a sigh and pulls my arm so I will lie behind her, "You will understand soon enough…" The sadness in her voice, an echo of Mattie's, breaks my heart. I hadn't even told Mattie about how I felt about her yet, but I decided not to let another moment pass for Kaida.

"I'll protect both of you. I'll love both of you. I promise you that from now, until we return to the stars." Squeezing her closer to me, the snakes slither across my face and neck, settling into the spaces between us and relaxing like my words brought them comfort.

"Oh, Trouble...I wish we had met you so much sooner." I hold her quietly, thinking, her breathing eventually evens out, but I can't seem to find sleep again until the sun starts to rise, lighting up the sky.

The next morning, everyone is on a divide-and-conquer path. Alice and I are going to drop Mattie at the hospital and make sure she can see Hannah. Then we have to go to the station and see what shit show has dropped in our laps in the last 24 hours. I was fielding calls from John about what happened. I was waiting to see what the local cops put together before I gave John any real conclusion to close my case so I had to get to the station anyway. Lucian was off to do whatever it is he actually does during daytime hours. Even Alice looked confused when I asked, and she tried to question him, but he and Mattie just laughed at their private joke and went about their preparations for the day.

The hospital had several guards outside of Dr. Raines' room. The guy at the door stopped Alice, "We had several reporters try and sneak through already, and one almost got into the morgue. Trying to scoop the story of the killer cop...Are you doing okay? None of us believes what the captain is spewing. I was at Kemp's apartment all day yesterday. You were clean."

She smiled at him and patted his arm kindly.

"Just keep doing your job. That's all we can do." Following Mattie and Alice in the room, I whisper in her ear.

"What kind of shit IS the captain spewing?" Shaking her head as Mattie greets Hannah with a tense hug, "No idea, but he's just digging himself into a hole by backing Kemp." Her lips were drawn and tense.

"Just gotta figure out who was working with him."

For a moment, Hannah and Mattie just stare at each other, the tension in the room stifling. Just when I think Mattie is going to run, Hannah opens her arms. Mattie throws herself into her arms and for a few minutes they both just cling to each other, whispering, tears streaming down Hannah's face. The trauma of her kidnapping and watching Carol Shanks be murdered had finally caught up to her. Something about Mattie being here allows her to finally let go. Mattie waves the two of us off without letting her go, "You guys go on. I'm going to hang out for a bit and then go get some of Hannah's things so she can leave tomorrow."

Stepping forward, I take her hand and place a kiss on her knuckles.

"Need me to come back and get you?" Hannah finally stops quivering and turns to watch us.

"No, I'll meet you at the station or maybe Monty's?" Alice and I wave goodbye. "Just text me, okay?" The secret Kaida is hiding from her is tying my stomach in knots, like I am waiting for the other shoe to drop. Alice and I drive to the station in silence, an indication of how nervous we both are. A block from the station, my phone dings with a text, pulling it out, I see John's name.

John: Inside the station. Meet me first before briefing the captain. Bring the detective.

Showing Alice the message, she goes pale, "Your boss is here?"

"I guess so. I called him from the scene…this isn't unusual if it's a big case. I'm going to guess my call was followed up by a loud one from the captain, so he flew out to back me up. The feds will be taking over for sure since this was a department employee." Patting her arm, I hope that I am not promising her more than I can deliver. John has always had my back, but then again, I have never had to lie to him about parts of a case. I believe he will hear me out, but I can't tell him anything about Mattie.

"Don't worry, Alice. John will hear us out. It's going to be okay."

Climbing out of the SUV, we make our way inside and I scan the room for John's tall, bald head. I don't have to look long as he is pulled up to Lorraine's desk laughing with her. They both have coffee cups from down the street, and I about fall with shock when the man I have known for years blushes at something Lorraine whispers in his ear before he throws back his head laughing. Walking up to them, Lorraine grins at me before getting up and coming around the desk to fold Alice in her arms and hug her tightly against her ample figure.

"Mon dui, this is such a mess, my dear! Are you alright?"

She pulls away from her to cradle Alice's face between her hands before glaring over her shoulder at me, "She should be at home resting! She looks tired…I'll call Mattie to come get you right now."

Alice pats her hands before stepping away, "Now, Lorraine, let's not sick Mattie on me. I promise I'm fine. I gave my initial statement to IA, and now we owe everyone our brief. The sooner we can put this to bed, the better." Lorraine rubs her hands together worriedly while John watches the whole interaction.

"Can I get you anything? I can call Sabine and have her bring you something to eat or a coffee?"

Alice smiles softly, "No ma'am, you leave Sabine at work. It's 9 am…no po boys yet, and I'm sure Luc or Mattie will be by with coffee and beignets just to check up on us." Lorraine sighs and clutches her hand to her chest dramatically, "Oh c'est ridicule. Lucian only comes here in handcuffs… unless" a gleam appears in her eyes as she looks over Alice again, and Alice blushes across her whole face. Lorraine flutters her hands excitedly, "Oh, finally!" Lorraine was smiling like a cat that got the cream.

"Anyways. Sir, it's nice to finally meet you. I'm Detective Hester. I've been working with Agent Bennet." She offers her hand to John with a sparkling smile.

This is a much friendlier welcome than I got, but I guess I was here to hunt down her sister, so between trying to throw me off the trail and an actual serial killer popping up, I guess I can forgive her. Alice is standing in front of him, the top of her head doesn't reach John's shoulder, he looks over at me with raised brows before taking in the pretty, petite, Asian detective. Alice certainly didn't paint the picture of a badass cop, but after everything that happened with Kemp, she's certainly being portrayed as one. He reached out and shook her hand vigorously, "Good to meet you, Detective. Bennet has had nothing but kind things to say about you in his reports."

Oh, now I understood the questioning brows. Tom must have been spinning tall tales about how I must have met a woman down in the Big

Easy. He could be completely ridiculous with the smallest bit of information, which is why he worked a desk job instead of being in the field.

"Detective Hester, can I have a minute with Bennet? I want to clarify some things before we talk to your captain." John asked, and she stiffened before turning to Lorraine, "Is he in yet?"

She nodded affirmatively with a grim tone, "He has been here since the shooting. Calling in favors and giving quotes to the reporters until the mayor called and put him under a gag order. He's fit to be tied that this is a conspiracy. Did you know that Kemp was his nephew?" We both looked at her, the shock on our faces giving away or answer, neither of us had any idea that Kemp was related to the captain. Sure, my not knowing makes sense, but why Alice never knew is more unusual.

Shit, that explained why he was so angry at the scene and trying so hard to disparage Alice. She shook off her revelation, shaking her head, "No, he never said anything to me about them being related. How was he assigned here if he's related to the captain?" Lorraine shrugged, "Captain called in favors back then and is certainly trying now. No one is buying it with how much they found at the apartment and that poor woman's statement."

Finally, I butted in, "Looking at files again Lorraine?"

She turned a withering glare my way, "Look here, boy, I like you, but I will throw you out if you sass me." I grin and raise my hands in surrender.

"John, there's a meeting room over here where we are set up." Showing him the way through the bullpen, I look back at Lorraine and wink just to be a pain. Letting him lead the way inside, I close the door behind me. I turn to see him watching me.

"You like it here?" He asks. I take a seat at the head of the conference table, avoiding answering right away. I did like it here. I liked working with Alice more than I did with anyone before. I liked the city. I liked Mattie, and I didn't want to leave. Would all of that be worth giving up the last ten years of my career? Maybe. "I do. Detective Hester has been a great partner. The city is fantastic, and I have made quite a few friends."

John starts flipping through the pictures from the apartment that are laid out on the table, a box with bags of evidence behind sits behind us.

"Good. I like you, Bennet, and you are an asset I don't want to lose. You seem happier here." Glancing up, he locks onto my eyes, smirking at me, "Tom been tattling?" I ask, knowing the answer, that man was a menace. He smiles, "Well, he did say you had a suspect that was a woman…a pretty woman…and then he heard nothing else. Also he said you weren't responding to any of his texts. I know he can be an annoying shit, but that's not like you. Then I'm called down here because you and your partner have apprehended the suspect. The lovely receptionist was happy to fill me in that while you have been down here, you have been chasing a killer and the pretty detective's sister. Seems like you've been busy."

Sighing and sitting back in the chair, I correct him.

"She wasn't a suspect. Just a person who was connected to a lot of the victims. Now we know it was because Kemp was obsessed with the SA group and with Alice. I did my due diligence. Until Dr. Raines was taken, we were at a loss, still looking for Dan Reynolds."

John walks over and starts pulling out evidence bags to look over. "Yes, Dan Reynolds. Where are we on that?"

A knock sounds at the door before Alice pops her head in, "May I join? I just picked up the reports on the inside of Kemp's car, apartment, and preliminary autopsy of Carol Shanks." John waves her in and she purposely takes the seat to my left, "We were just discussing Dan Reynolds." She takes one of the files out of her pile and slides it over to him.

"Techs found blood on Kemp's clothes that was a preliminary match for Reynolds. There was also a tip called in that a car rented in his name has been found dumped out in the swamp. We're sending a team out there to see if there is anything else…bodies that go in the water out there don't usually come back out, but we'll keep looking. There were also texts on Kemp's phone that were sent to Reynolds luring him to meet on the same night we discovered Laura's body."

John silently flipped through the file, his face set in a grim mask. Between the apartment and Kemp's phone, it was filling out to be a clean open and shut case. "Any similar texts to the three original victims, the ones you were sent here to investigate?" Damn it, I should have guessed that John would dig into what's missing before he accepted anything, but Alice leaned in and dropped another file on the desk, pulling both of our attentions back to her.

"No we think he had started to spiral by the time he got to Reynolds. He was more careful, but this is his duty schedule on the nights each man was killed. He wasn't on duty any of those nights and the cameras in his parking garage have him out of the lot each of the nights and his phone pings off towers close to each of the other murders. All circumstantial, but we also have a man in the quarter who is willing to testify that Kemp matches the description of a man who bought vials of venom at a voodoo shop."

I stare at Alice in absolute wonder and shock. She had taken a bunch of circumstantial evidence and some coincidences and somehow mushed it together into files that made the whole case look like a well-written report where Kemp's guilt would have been a forgone conclusion even if he hadn't kidnapped Hannah and killed Carol Shanks. Her testimony alone would have been enough to charge Kemp, but this was a whole other level that could keep Mattie safe. Schooling my face back to passive, I looked over at John, who was studying Alice with real interest.

"Between this and the IA report, this is good. This cleans everything up. Bennet, I expect you back in the office next Monday. Should give you enough time to pack and get everything wrapped up here for Detective Hester's case." I open my mouth to tell him that I have no intention of getting on that plane. I'm not leaving Mattie behind, and D.C. isn't the place for her. Too much security and scrutiny for her to be safe there. Another knock on the door and it opens suddenly, admitting two older men in suits; the IA investigator from the other night, and a very red-faced captain who marches in looking ready to throw a punch or two. His ruddy face and angry eyes zero in on Alice, and he steps toward her.

I push my 6 '3 frame up to my full height. Standing in front of his path to her, he stops and sweeps his gaze around to see everyone watching him in anticipation. I wave for Alice to move one chair over and slip around the table to take her chair, waving my hand at the newly unoccupied one.

"Captain, here have my chair. Hester was just giving us a breakdown of the evidence from Kemp's apartment and phone." He narrows his eyes like a bull ready to charge and then plops into the seat without a word.

The other men who entered introduced themselves to John as the mayor of the city and the police chief. John slides the files that Alice had given him over to them as they sit on the other side of the table. Both are avoiding looking at the evidence boards that are covered with photos of Laura, Carol, and Hannah's office.

"I was just saying to my agent that he and Detective Hester have done an excellent job of wrapping this up. It's a good case even if it won't go to trial. My superiors and I are more than satisfied and are glad to have this case closed."

The mayor smiles warmly in Alice's direction, "Yes, we came to the same conclusion during yesterday's emergency meeting. IA has cleared Detective Hester, and after she meets with the psychologist we will have her back on duty. That is, if you are ready for that detective?"

Alice looks briefly at me; her face is filled with worry. I know she and Mattie had a discussion yesterday about their next plans, but no decisions were made. Thanks to Kaida and Mattie, before the final decision, Lucian and I will get a vote.

"Thank you, Mr. Mayor, but I will be using my leave. I have 6 weeks accrued, and after talking to my family, I've decided to take some time off. This case has been a lot for me, and my sister was friends with several of the victims...we both are going to take some time."

The chief and mayor smile nicely at her and nod, "Of course. You take what you need and keep us in the loop if there is anything the department can do to assist you." The Chief offers and turns back to talk to John, but the captain shoots out of his chair and slams his hands down on the table.

"You're offering her assistance!? This slut should be in jail! She murdered my officer in cold blood- shot him in the back like the coward she is. She isn't welcome back in my precinct!" Spittle flying out of his mouth as he yells at the group.

The chief doesn't even flinch, "That's fine since it won't be your precinct much longer. There is sufficient evidence that your nephew killed at least 6 people, kidnapped and attempted to murder another woman, and was stalking another dozen. Don't think we won't be checking the records here and doing interviews with the other officers to find out if there was any complacency or negligence on your part involved in how long he was able to get away with this. I expect your retirement papers to be on my desk before that investigation is complete, or we will have a different conversation, Captain."

The chief finishes his draw down of the captain, calm and unperturbed in the face of his temper. Alice and I both look at each other, the laughter dancing in her eyes, little lines crinkle up at the corners, but her mouth remains a firm line painted her signature red. She is the epitome of professionalism, and if it weren't for all the time together, I would never guess that she is holding back her mirth till she's alone. The captain was getting the comeuppance he deserved, and it was long overdue. Neither of us nor John says a word while the captain and the chief stare each other down. He finally breaks and stomps out, slamming the door loudly behind him.

"Sorry about that, everyone, thank you for your report. Detective Hester, we appreciate your service. Take all the time you need to recover. Agents Bennet and Smith, we appreciate all your support in closing this case as quickly as possible. No need for more bad press in the city." The mayor stands and the chief follows, shaking everyone's hand before leaving.

Lieutenant Nelson stands and, with a quick nod, she takes her report and leaves with them. I'm thinking about excusing ourselves for lunch at Monty's when John says, "What are your goals career wise, Detective?" I look over to her and find her looking my way, raising my eyebrows, I shrug.

"I'm not sure right now, sir. I have a family, so I don't make decisions without their input." He smiles at her, clearly liking her answer.

"Yes, I know how that is. Married with a gaggle of girls myself. Well, while you're on leave, think about it, and if you would be interested in an offer, I'd like to speak to you about it." He hands her his business card the same way that years ago he handed it to me.

"You and Bennet work well together, and that's a rarity in itself. I'm too old to be chasing him around, and your paperwork puts his to shame.

Much rather leave the wrangling to someone else." He waves at me and starts, "Will, you have a bit of leave if you want to round out this trip with a vacation…Lorraine says you might want to stay in the city for a bit. I'll approve it right away. Detective, I hope to hear from you soon."

He closed the door behind himself. Alice and I stare at each other for a long moment filled with relief before she squeals loudly and clutches the card, jumping up and down in place.

"Did he just offer me a job on the same day that the captain was fired?" I smile at her antics, "Pretty sure he just offered for you to be my babysitter." She stops bouncing to grin widely at me. If I had to have a babysitter, I could do worse. "Well, if you get out of hand, I do have Mattie on speed dial."

Flopping back into her chair, "Did we do it? Mattie is free and clear?" Her relief is palpable, a weight that's been hers to carry for years now finally being shared.

"It looks like it. She and Kaida have to be more careful from now on, but yeah." I assure her that it's done. It wasn't how I thought this case would play out, and the idea that Kemp had an accomplice is still hanging in the air, but for now, we could both take a breath. Alice could do her job without looking over her shoulder, and if I had my way, then I would be around to watch her back, and Mattie's for as long as she would have me…maybe forever.

"I have to ask you something. I haven't talked to Mattie yet, but I am going to as soon as we have a minute. I don't think she should stay here in the city, but I'm not going to let her go anywhere without me following. You guys are a package deal, and I get that, so before I ask to stick around, are you okay with that?"

The wood grain on the table is all swirly as I keep my eyes trained on it, waiting for her response, "You love her?" She asks quietly. Looking up into her brown eyes, I see that they are crinkled with her smile, "I'm not answering that. Not because I don't, but because the first time I say it, should be to her. But I'm all in Alice. My help with this should be all the proof you need that I am not going anywhere."

She leans over to take my hand in hers, "I figured that out when I saw you kiss her as Kaida in the warehouse…I haven't so much as hugged her other form in all these years. They have always had rules and kept their distance, but you obliterated those walls. You kissed the monster without pause."

Squeezing her fingers and matching her stare, "If she's a monster, then I am madness, because I still want her. We all have monsters of some kind, and I want hers as much as she wants mine." Tears start to well up in Alice's eyes and she looks up to try and blink them away before giggling, "Fuck, Bennet. That was romantic as shit! Use that line, and she won't be able to get rid of you."

I grin back, "Yeah? Better than the guy stalking his soulmate around the city, getting into trouble so he can live out his weird handcuffs kink? Helping her sister so he can just be around her?" I ask, hoping to at least help out my new friend. If he hadn't drugged and kidnapped me, I might still be on the outside of this little family. I might owe him more than giving up my self-made promises to punch him at least once a day. Well, maybe not. If it wasn't yesterday's dumb ass thing he would do something equally punch-worthy tomorrow.

"I see what you are doing, Bennet. Trust me, Lucian needs no help…I'm pretty sure he's like a feral cat. I let him inside and fed him, so now I'm stuck with him." Her voice is resigned, but the humor and affection are there.

"Let's get out of here and get some food. I'm starving, and no one can begrudge us some lunch." Walking out into the sunshine today, I can't keep my eyes away from the steps across the street where I first saw Mattie.

Today, a woman is sitting on the top step, speaking on the phone. At first glance, I thought she was Mattie, but this woman has short shoulder-length hair, taller and slimmer than my girl. Climbing in the car's driver's seat for once, I check the mirrors before backing up and see her watching me with a familiar bright green gaze. I quickly turn around to take a better look, but the woman is gone already.

My mind is playing tricks on me…I just need to get some food and then go get my girl.

Chapter 32

Mattie

Sitting at a table on the patio at Monty's, I check my phone again for a text from Alice or Will. They were finishing up at the station and then heading this way, so I got over here quickly and grabbed a table in the corner. The waitress had already brought me a café au lait, luckily without any clandestine evidence as a side this time. Thankfully, with a hug and many many thank you's, Hannah was happy to drop the events of the other night and continue our relationship as better friends from here on out. I even agreed to take the number of a therapist friend that she recommended, planning to put it on Alice's bathroom mirror until she took the hint and made an appointment. The thought of making one myself wasn't totally disgusting to me either.

I do not understand why someone would tell a complete stranger about their experiences.

"Well, you can express your feelings about something to someone who won't be hurt or judge you for them, and then they help you work out what you'd like to do about them…actually, therapy would be good for you, maybe we could unpack those homicidal tendencies," I thought, looking around at the people walking by.

Humpf. I was created to have homicidal tendencies. I do not think being cursed by a goddess with a creature who shares your mind and body and kills people is going to be something a therapist can grasp.

She's probably right… I can't imagine how that would go over all too well. Therapists are supposed to be impartial but I imagine they would have issues with the whole killing thing. The guilt that was swirling within Kaida made me think it might be nice for her to talk to someone, maybe Hannah would be a good option. It probably wouldn't take much to convince her and she was pretty cool about the whole situation, all things considered.

While I had a minute to people watch and drink my coffee, I reflected on Will. I want to ask him to stay, or to go with us wherever we roam next. He isn't built like us, just the other day he said he lived at home until college and then the same apartment for 5 years before going to D.C where he moved into his current apartment and has been there for 10 years, all because he liked that it was a pre-war building and had an old Vietnamese woman who lived next door and fed him in exchange for fixing her leaky sink or taking out her trash. He's a man of steady consistency, and that is something I am not. Looking across the patio, my hand freezes with the cup halfway to my lips as I watch a memory pick her way through the crowds of people, weaving between the full tables. My breath suspended. She strides toward me with a wide smile on her face, the breeze ruffling her hair as she scoots past one of the tables with a warm glance at the person she bumps. She stops in front of me and pulls out a chair.

RUN! RUN NOW, MATTIE! Kaida roars in my head, my hands shaking, spilling the coffee over the edge and onto the tops of my thighs.

Crying out at the sudden burn, I stand up and wipe at my skin, not looking away from the familiar bright green eyes of my sister. I never noticed how much she and I looked alike until now. In the years of my grief over losing her, I had forgotten that. Her hair is shorter now, chin-length dark brown wavy hair swirling around her elegant face. With wide green eyes accented by sharp, arched brows, a straight, pretty nose, and cupid bow lips, she's stunning. Stunning, and apparently, not dead. I sit back down and just watch her, dumbstruck, as if she'll blow away and disappear forever if I speak.

"Hello, baby sister." She says, softly with a kind smile that doesn't reach her eyes. It's superficial like the sweetness in her voice. My instincts scream at me but I finally take a deep breath and blow it out, my mind racing impossibly fast while a low buzz of hissing continues in my head.

"Catherine…I don't understand. You died." She waves a hand to signal the waitress over, and she appears quickly, "I'll have the same as her. Thank you, darling! Now, where were we? Oh yes, the whole dead thing."

I just stare at her as she takes one of the beignets I ordered for the table and bites into it gracefully so as not to cover herself with powdered sugar. Wiping her mouth with a napkin, she looks back at me.

"Clearly not. We're not fragile creatures who die of silly things like knife wounds, now are we, Matilda?" Her brow arches, and a tenseness comes over her features. The stress she puts on her words is curious, but I only have a second to ponder if she was the one we sensed the other night.

"But I'm not here to talk about the past so much as I am about the future. Our future."

Mattie, we need to get away from her. We need to go find Will and Alice. I know you want to sit here and find out everything, but I promise, nothing she says will be good for you.

Kaida is full of panic, her anxiety affecting my own, but there's also the guilt spilling over into my feelings, the guilt I thought she felt about not saving Carol, about her little girl being alone. No it was something else. Sitting across from us was the source of her guilt, and she wanted me to leave before I got any answers. Years ago, I prayed the way only a scared little kid can, wished, and hoped for just one more chance to sit across the table from my big sister. To have just one more hour with Catherine. Now

I can't separate my feelings from Kaida's, my chest feeling like it's going to burst open. The waitress, Sabine, appears with a cup for Catherine, and she picks it up, taking a sip calmly. "I'm sure your monster wants you to leave, but that would be a mistake. I know something she wants to keep from you. A secret that will change everything."

She knows nothing. She is dangerous, we need to leave.

The hissing in my mind is giving me a tension headache so I try to concentrate on calming thoughts. We're in public, a very crowded restaurant, and Alice and Will are coming soon. Looking back at Catherine, I see her watching me with a serpentine grin on her face. She puts down her cup and leans forward, lowering her voice. "I can tell you how to break the curse."

The world around freezes and goes silent, our eyes locked. I can't focus on anything else. A way to get rid of the curse? Was that possible...even if it was, is it something that I want?

"What curse, Catherine?" I lean back and cross my arms. She startles me by laughing loudly, and for a minute, she looks just like our mom, the mom who used to laugh with her whole body and smiled more than anyone I've ever met, especially when she was with Dad. She is almost the same age as Mom was when she died. That thought makes my heart ache with a sadness I haven't felt in years. "What curse she asks? We both know that you're as cursed as I was. I can help you to break the curse and free yourself." She sounds so serious and genuine, but something feels off about how nothing she says changes the expression in her eyes; they're flat and cold.

"Okay, maybe I do have a monster, but I don't think of it as being cursed. My monster and I made friends a long time ago, and we work together to make the world better."

What I was telling her was true. Kaida and I had agreed to be together initially because anything else was mutually assured destruction, but as the years went on, we cared for each other. Yesterday, when I thought Kaida was gone, the only thing I could think of was that I didn't get to say goodbye. She's as much my sister as Alice is and we're a family in every way that counts. Catherine brushes her hands through her short hair and tucks it behind her ears.

"Do you really think you can keep this up? You'll hurt your friends soon enough. It's only a matter of time, and then do you think that your Alice will still stand by you? Do you think that man will ever love the monster who is half of you, or will he grow tired of having half a life? You will never be able to have children with him. Or do you want this life hanging over your daughters' heads too?"

With incredible accuracy, she had managed to carve out my heart and pick out each of my greatest fears with her cleanly manicured fingernails. It's my greatest fear that someday I would accidentally hurt one of the few people I loved in this world. I hadn't even considered the possibility of passing on the curse, until Will looked at me with a real future in his eyes. How could I commit to building a life, to having beautiful dark-haired children with him, when we knew what kind of curse would hang over them? I could dedicate every second of my life to trying to keep them safe, and I know it wouldn't mean anything. Bad things could happen to women regardless of anything they did to keep themselves safe. I would never sign my daughters up for this life. Catherine was right, there are things I would never be able to give him because of my curse… Kaida was keeping quiet, her guilt lessening with my every argument for our existence. She pictured Alice and me sitting together on the porch, images of Lucian sitting at this restaurant laughing with me, Will looking at me like I was his whole world. The final memory she sent me was one of her own, the moment I turned back from her to myself that very first time, watching the transformation in the mirror of that hotel bathroom. Alice was sitting on the side of the tub watching, too. It had been the craziest thing, but it was the moment I accepted my new reality. Nothing had changed since then; I didn't have to go without. Alice and I had made our own little family, and even though we never saw Lucian or Will coming, they were here now, and within days, our family doubled. Who's to say more wouldn't come along, and we would welcome them with open arms.

Thinking back to Will in my bed leaning over me, I could hear his voice whispering in my ear, 'she is you and you are her'. His love filled him to the brim, and it poured out of his very being and covered me. When the hard days came, he would love me, love all my darkness, because I would do the same for him. Looking up at Catherine, the love I felt for them all spilled out of me. I could see the coldness in her take over as her spine straightened, and she stood up from the table.

"I see that I'm not going to convince you, so let's try this. We are going to walk out the side patio and get into the SUV on the corner. You aren't going to scream or ask for help, or I will find your friend, Alice. I'll find Alice when she's alone, and I will snap her delicate neck. Won't be hard for my monster, and then I will hunt down your Agent and get him too. I'll break his heart before I bite him and watch him froth, choke, and die." She's pulling out a few bills from her fancy purse and setting them on the table. She finally looks at me and sees the horror written all over my face. I can't hide my fear of her doing exactly those things. This isn't my sister, not the one who read me bedtime stories. This woman was filled with darkness, the kind that wasn't a friend.

"Catherine. Kitty Cat...Why?" Using her childhood nickname was a step too far because she grabs my upper arm and digs her fingers down to the bone. She pulls me up out of the seat and pushes us towards the small gate exit on this side of the restaurant.

I told you to go. I told you to run fast and far, and now we have never been in more danger.

Kaida doesn't just sound worried. She sounds terrified. Is it because there is some truth to what Catherine said about breaking the curse? Concentrating on her voice, I thought to her, "Did you know she was alive? Is there a way to break the curse?"

Of course, she was. Suicide...how stupid. You have survived far worse, so I am surprised that you never put it together. There is truth to what she says, sort of. There is a rumor, but it is not something you will ever do; it's still just a story. No one has ever done it, and the cost is too high.

Catherine shoves me into the passenger seat of the SUV, slamming the door. "Why are you so sure of that?" I hissed at her, angry that she knew my big sister was alive and out there but kept it to herself. Of course, she was right that it was stupid to think she wouldn't survive slitting her wrists, but I had been a kid at the time and knew nothing of the curse, and by the time I did, I was so busy trying to survive I never really looked back at Catherine's story.

Mattie, the cost is too great for your heart to take. Be careful, little monster...She wants to hurt you.

Her voice was tinged with sadness. I can picture her face in my mind, the tears welling up in her eyes. Looking at the dashboard clock, I calculated the hours until sundown, but it's too many to be useful right now. Catherine gets in the driver's seat, pulling away from the curb. I look at the restaurant as we pass and see Will's face in the crowd. As if he hears my mental goodbye, he looks up and meets my eyes. Green and gray-blue clash together, and horror spreads over his face as he shouts my name. He jumps into action, launching himself over the short fence and he races after us along the sidewalk yelling my name. Alice is hot on his heels with her phone out recording, hopefully to get the license plate.

Catherine speeds up and runs the nearest corner before I lose sight of the two of them. Giving out a quiet prayer to the very goddess that started this curse, I ask her to bless their hunt and find me sooner rather than later. Looking out of the corner of my eye at Catherine, I think I am going to need any blessings I can get.

Chapter 33

Will

Walking up to the restaurant the girls love, I'm hungry enough to eat my own shirt and Alice has been hangry for the last hour that it took to extricate ourselves from the station. It was only at Lucian's insistence that we hurried up and met him so we could all grab lunch, which finally got us moving. Alice is chatting about some video she watched on these little cute dinosaurs they just discovered, because apparently, random conversations are the thing that distracts her from how hungry she is, but it makes me wonder if you can barbecue the little creatures. Alice walks up to the hostess stand to ask for a table, and I'm barely paying attention when I hear her mention Mattie.

Focusing on them, the hostess is pointing to the edge of the patio, and I follow her gaze as she frowns at the empty table, "She was just there with her friend. I thought she said they were waiting for you to join." She looks down at her station to check while I look around for her face in the crowd. "Yeah, here's a table for four."

A car catches my eye, and the prickle on the back of my neck has me turning around to see Mattie in it as it speeds by. As soon as our eyes lock, I can see the tears glistening in her lashes and the solid, grim set of her mouth. I can't see the driver clearly, but they're small, probably a woman. Yelling out to her, I hop over the closest table and start towards the fence separating the sidewalk, "MATTIE!" Alice spins around and sees the SUV I'm chasing. Hopping the fence, I take off at a dead sprint for her, "MATTIE!"

The driver runs the red light ahead and narrowly misses crashing as they turn right. Hitting their gas, they take off far faster than I can chase on foot. This is the threat Kaida warned me about, my gut certain that whoever just drove off with Mattie was what Kaida was so scared to tell her about. I spin and see Alice has her phone out, recording the car as it drives away.

"Will! Did you see the driver?" I bend over and rest my hands on my knees as I catch my breath in the middle of the street. A few cars honk their horns at us, but Alice pulls out her badge and waves it in the air.

"Hold your horses assholes!" She walks up and takes my elbow, leading me to the sidewalk and pushing me to sit down. The hostess runs up, "Oh my gosh! Are you guys okay?" She waves her off and pulls out her phone and dials it, "Luc? Someone took Mattie. No, we didn't see who was in the car. Yeah, I got the plates. Texting it over now. We have about five hours till sundown. I know. Sabine? The waitress? Okay, I'll be here." She pauses intermittently to answer Lucian's questions.

Hanging up just as a pretty young African American girl runs up to us, her curls pulled up into buns on top of her head, bobbing along. She was our waitress the first time I came here with Mattie.

"Sabine, this is Will. Lucian said you could help us." She checks us both out and then nods.

"Follow me." Alice gives me a hand up, and we follow the girl down the block and into a voodoo tourist shop. She rounds the corner into a back room as we follow. The little office is sparse, but she opens a laptop on the desk, "This is off the books, you didn't see me, you didn't see anything I do in here, okay?" she asks.

I finally found my voice: "No, I am calling in the FBI and police immediately. John is still in town, he'll help."

Alice shakes her head, "We can't. We can't have anyone out looking for her when the sun goes down. This ends two ways; either she kills whoever took her and the police find the body, or they find her and she hurts them in self defense. Mattie and I have had this conversation before. She said if I couldn't find her to go to Lucian. They apparently made contingency plans." Alice hands her cellphone to the Sabine. I can't believe she's suggesting that we just let one man do whatever he does and trust it works out. I like Lucian but that doesn't mean I trust him to find my girl.

"Yeah Mr. FBI, Mattie loves back up plans. She and Lucian have made back ups upon back ups. I helped with the one for taking Alice away to the Caribbean," The pretty young girl says while typing away at her computer without looking our way. Alice and I both freeze and stare at her, Alice finds her voice first and it's full of fury, "Excuse me?"

Sabine must hear the change in tone because she pauses her typing and looks up before blushing and going back to the computer.

"Sorry, forget I said anything." I look Alice's way before we silently agree that's not happening.

"Why the Caribbean, Sabine?" she asks, being deceptively sweet as she leans on the corner of the desk. Sabine bites her bottom lip looking guilty, her eyes dart my way and then she sighs, "Because that's where your money is, the house too. I helped them set it all up and get you both new identity. I picked it since you hate the cold."

Oh, now I'm intrigued. "What money?" The door behind us slams open and Lucian storms in totally unrecognizable, angry and fierce. I may be likened to a Viking but he looked like an avenging angel.

"Sabine, is everyone alerted? I want every single person to have that plate number and then I want all traffic cams so we can follow the car and see where it's going."

The girl shakes her head annoyed and rolls her eyes at him, "Not my first rodeo. I'm tracking it now. As soon as they stop, I'll have an address for you." Lucian nods and walks over to envelope Alice in his arms, presumably for comfort, but he should have gotten here before the master secret keeper Sabine spilled the beans. Alice holds up her hands to stop him and smiles that devilish smile of hers, "I have a house in the Caribbean? I have said maybe 10 words to Sabine, so how does she know I hate the cold? How is she making me fake papers? She's a kid, Luc!" Alice's voice is filled with frustration, mostly about Mattie not being safe, but right now Lucian is going to have to take the brunt of it. Of course, if he and Mattie really have been making plans for Alice without her knowing then maybe he deserves it.

Lucian glares over at Sabine who is holding back her grin while she types away and ignores us.

"It wasn't my first choice, but Mattie made the arrangements so." Thinking back, the day we made our plan to go after Kemp I remember Mattie making Lucian promise something.

"Mattie made you promise to make Alice go somewhere without her, didn't she? " I ask incredulously, happy for Lucian to be the one in hot water for once.

"Not in so many words. But if something happens to Mattie and Alice needs to disappear then she has a house and an account down there and I promised to get her there safely." He looks at Alice as he finishes his thought.

"I knew how you would feel about it, and I have no desire to fight a kitten dumped in ice water, so I took creative license with the plan. Poof, you go to sleep here and wake up safe somewhere else with a new life." Lucian says it all so casually I don't know if I should punch him or laugh.

"That seems like a pretty creative license. What if I don't want to go?" Alice asks, crossing her arms. Lucian mimics her stance, "That wasn't an option. I made the promise to her when we were barely friends. But we were friends nonetheless and I would not betray my promise to make sure you were safe and happy no matter what happened to her." While I hated the idea that the plan didn't seem to account for Mattie's safety or happiness, I had to admire that the man was willing to swear something that heavy to a woman he barely knew, for a woman he knew even less.

Especially if Alice was really his soulmate…if he took her away, even on Mattie's orders, and something happened to her, then Alice would never forgive him. He was willing to risk that all in the name of loyalty. Fuck, I hated when he did admirable shit and made me like him. Alice was studying him quietly, "What do you actually do Lucian?"

Sabine choked down a laugh, pointedly avoiding looking at any of us.

"A little of this and a little of that. I find people when they are needed… even if they don't know it." I open my mouth to tell him that's not exactly a real answer, but sassy Sabine beats me to the punch.

"Stop trying to be so mysterious Cupidon." She looks at Alice seriously, "He helps set people in the right direction…and some other less than legal things. But mainly the life advice part." No matter how serious our predicament or how bad I was in high school French, I recognize that his baby cousin called him Cupid. The big bad, mysterious, I am too cool to ever wear a real shirt with sleeves guy, is cupid going around setting up couples. I cover my mouth to stifle a laugh, but Sabine looks up and catches me, her smile sets me off even more.

Lucian glares at me, "You done now, Mon petit coquin?" She sticks her tongue out at him. Before I can answer, Sabine tenses, turning back to her computer screen with serious face.

"Got them, at one of the old buildings on Rue Toulouse." She spins the laptop around showing us a still from a security camera of them getting out of the car. I stiffen and move closer to look at the driver. It's the woman from outside the station that was watching me. Somehow, she beat us to the restaurant and got Mattie to leave with her…She has to be the woman that Kemp was referring to. The woman Kaida had been scared of, who told him how to hurt Mattie that night.

Alice's face drained of color, paler than a sheet of paper. Her nails are digging into the wood of the desk hard enough to make little moon shapes in the top. Lucian pries her hands loose and pulls her against his chest.

"Alice, do you know who this is?" I ask, pointing at the screen. She shakes her head no but doesn't stop staring at the screen like a ghost has come out, "It's not possible…" Lucian turns her around and shakes her shoulders firmly, "Love, do you know that woman?" She clings onto his vest breathing deeply in her nose and out her mouth to calm down.

"I've never met her. I couldn't, because she's dead…that's Catherine Wallace." She looks over at me, sadness pouring off her and filling the room with her desperation, "Mattie's real sister."

Chapter 34

Mattie

Catherine was speeding through the city with her arm draped on the steering wheel like we were out for a nice Sunday drive, it would have felt like it too, if she wasn't breaking every single traffic law. She hadn't looked my way directly since we outpaced Will, but I could feel her watching me out of the corner of her eye every few seconds. I couldn't tell if it was because she was shocked to be so close to me for the first time in fifteen years, or because she thought I would throw myself from the moving vehicle.

To be honest, I wouldn't have went with her if she asked, though I might have asked her to come home with me, but then she threatened to hurt the people I love. Now, I'm going to be a pain in her ass just because I can. Hearing the anguish in Will's voice as he chased down the car yelling my name, I wanted to climb out of my skin just to get back and reassure him I was okay. This is the second time in forty-eight hours that he's stuck panicking over my safety. I'm seriously starting to feel like a damsel in distress instead of a fearsome monster stalking through the night, and I don't need any more complexes until I get a therapist.

Fuck, somehow this was the breaking point that made me finally decide I actually need therapy. Great, now I was a therapy person....sighing internally.

Kaida was pouting in the back of my mind that I hadn't listened to her and ran when we had a chance. I wasn't pleased that apparently she knew a way to break the curse this whole time and didn't say a word. Maybe she kept it a secret because she was worried about what would happen to her?

Passing the turn for Bourbon Street, I can see the crowds of people gearing up for a night on the craziest street in town, but no one notices us. I knew Alice, she had already called Lucian, and he would be rallying the troops. He used a multitude of illegal things to track down things and people. He and his eclectic group could find someone in the city in a few hours, I just had to wait it out. I'd only been sitting at the restaurant for a few minutes before I realized that I had left my glasses in Hannah's apartment when I was fetching her clean clothes. I meant to go back and pick them up or get the pair that Alice carried around for me as soon as she got there, but now I was stuck with none and no idea if Lucian would find me before sundown. Things would get desperate if sundown came and I was still stuck with Catherine. She pulled up to a building on Toulouse and parked. It looked like one of the old factory buildings over here that hadn't been gentrified yet, with boarded-up windows and crumbling brick that nodded to its service years and years ago.

"You can get out now." Catherine opens her door and waits for me to follow, "Don't be difficult, Matilda."

Like a reflex, I roll my eyes at my birth name. No one has called me that casually since my parents died. It rankled me more than I liked. If this were a happy reunion, I probably wouldn't be so put off.

"If you want to be on my good side, don't call me that." I climb out and slam the door, looking around for security cameras in case Lucian can see me now. One above the last street light is pointing our way, I look directly at it and move my lips to say, "Be careful after dark. Three knocks."

Pushing my hair back with one hand to show off my lack of glasses that are usually perched on top of my head. Turning back to follow Catherine in the building, I hold 3 of my fingers up behind my back towards the camera. Begging the universe that he gets the message, and when they come, I'll have enough warning to not harm anyone.

The space inside is far fancier than I would have guessed from outside, a large bed pushed under the boarded-up windows looks clean and soft under a pile of blush pink blankets and fancy pillows. There's a little kitchenette set up and a fancy swoop-backed couch that belongs in a drawing room. My perusal of the space caught a stone statue near the edge of the decorated space of the room. It was a man curled in on himself, I couldn't see his face as his arms wrapped around his head protectively. My sister clearly hadn't spent all of her time lying low. This was the setup of someone who had been here a while and had been hunting. She was watching me, gauging my reaction, "Nice set up. Been here a while?"

She throws the keys on the little table next to the door and shrugs, "What's a while? I have been here long enough to make a friend or two," waving her arm nonchalantly at the statue, "and then your bestie had to go and ruin it for me. She has been a real problem…"

Sitting on the fancy couch and watching her, I look for the person I knew growing up. She always favored our mom, and in a lot of ways, I did too, but it wasn't as obvious until I was grown. I got my light skin and freckles from my dad's side, where she looked like a porcelain doll with a sun-kissed tan. She had always been beautiful, but now she reminded me of a viper; beautiful but deadly. Her eyes were the most alarming thing, while I knew that my own betrayed my every emotion and sometimes my other half's even more so, hers were flat and dead. They were bright green like mine, but in color only; there was no emotion behind them.

"If you have been here, been alive, why didn't you come back sooner? Alice and I have been here a few years, it wouldn't have been hard to track us down." Catherine crossed one lean leg over the other and sat back on her hands, "At first, it was because of what I was. Mom told me the legends about our family, but I don't think she ever really believed in them, just an old fable, but I learned she was very wrong about that. When Mom and Dad died, I hadn't planned on taking care of you myself. It was a stipulation in their will. I was young and I wanted to live my life…not be stuck with a kid at home."

The hatefulness in her voice feels like I have been slapped. "I just wanted to go on a date. One stupid guy asked me for drinks after work…another bartender. He was cute and played guitar, so of course I said yes. We drank and danced until nearly dawn." Thinking back to the night she was talking about, I remember being home alone and it getting so late I fell asleep huddled in a blanket, hungry and scared of the dark.

"Well, he got rough, and when I said no, he decided that my previous yes was enough to keep going. I was drunk enough that I couldn't stand and he left me in that alley all alone." A flood of emotions overwhelms me and Kaida. Guilt, remorse, sympathy, anger, we had heard this story before, and I felt horrible for her.

You were just a little kid alone at home waiting for her. Something bad could have happened to you too. Kaida whispers, apparently her anger is for me, not Catherine.

"After I changed, I couldn't come back. I'd killed people. I was a monster. I stayed away because it was what was for the best. Then you were changed too…If I'd been there, I could have helped you. Maybe saved you…" She pauses momentarily, sounding full of guilt, and stares past me, maybe being genuine for the first time. The tightening of her jaw betrayed her true emotion.

"Anyways, then I saw the truth of the situation. You didn't need me at all. You replaced me. I left and looked for a way to break the curse, I found it, and now here I am." She finished her words, taking on a manic tone at the end. Ignoring the implication that I replaced her with Alice.

"You found a way to break the curse?" I ask, my voice dripping with disbelief. "Oh yes, but it's not something I can manage to do by myself, and then I figured out that you were the perfect person to try it on." I stare at her, hoping she is going to clarify, but Kaida softly speaks in my mind.

It is too great a cost to your soul, little one. Think of this as Pandora's box, remember that story from when you were little? It was your favorite. I am begging you not to open it.

Her voice was so soft and drawn, exhausted.

Catherine watches me intensely as I speak.

"So you came to find me to see if your idea works?" She nods and then smiles broadly, "and when your little rescue gets here we'll get to test out my idea! It's going to be so much fun - far more fun than I would have had turning Alice over to Brian. He wanted her to himself and I told him he could have her, but I had no intention of letting her get away when I could use her for this."

Fuck, fuck, fuck…She was the one who had been at the warehouse with Hannah, the one who told Brian how to hurt me, the 'she' he kept referring to.

She wanted them to see me leave with her, to find us, to come here. She probably had figured out how long it was going to take for them to get here too. I needed to get away before she could get them here. It was always part of the plan with Lucian that if I needed help he would come and if he couldn't get to me he would get Alice far away. While I still believed that he would get Alice to safety I no longer thought he would be able to resist changing the plan for her if she demanded it. Every fiber of my being wanted Catherine far away from Will. I don't really care if both of them are angry at me but I'll be damned if I let them get hurt. Trying to sound casual and keep myself as relaxed as possible, "I am assuming that's Dan Reynolds?"

Waving towards the statue again, my sympathy for the man wasn't much after what he had put Laura through. I had killed plenty of people but I don't play with my prey and clearly Mr. Reynolds hadn't died a pleasant death.

"You told Brian how to kill me? Why would you want me dead?" She huffs, frustrated.

"Of course it's Dan. He was very helpful getting me information about you, watching you and your group, but his want for payback against that girl was too much for him so I had to find another way to make him useful. I found a way to do that and a new person to help me get to you. Officer Kemp was far too easy to manipulate and it was quite fun breaking Alice's toy. I didn't really want you dead. Stabbing you in the heart wouldn't have killed you anyways…I just needed you to be in enough trouble for Alice to come running. Then I would get the curse broken and we would be able to be together like we're meant to be. Once she's gone you'll see that I'm all you need. She's a poor substitute…Blood is thicker than water, Mattie."

Thinking back to the threat on the walls in Hannah's office I recognize the bastardized quote.

"You're the one who went after Hannah and broke into her office." Bobbing her crossed leg up and down she grins like a shark that smells blood in the water.

"It's shockingly easy to move about when everyone has a certain idea of who they are looking for. Mr. Reynolds made a suitable bad guy to keep the police busy chasing their tails." Catherine gets up and walks towards me, my whole body tenses in fight or flight mode and the hissing in my head starts. Not sure if it's because Kaida doesn't like having another one of her kind close to us or if it's specifically her, but it's not a comfortable feeling. Glancing over to the windows, the light is bright, like the sun is even with them.

"Before long the sun will set and then I'll be able to leave." I say pointedly. Catherine sits down hard and points over her shoulder at the windows, "This is me being nice Mattie. You won't get along with the monster. She doesn't care about you and she really doesn't want the curse broken. If you have any chance at survival it would be best that it's done before sundown."

She refers to the gorgon in her as though it doesn't listen to her and it makes me ponder if she and her monster communicate like Kaida and I do. Hers doesn't want her to break the curse any more than mine does, but I am guessing it's for very different reasons.

"Mattie, you have to understand that this isn't about hurting you. I'm trying to help you to be free. This curse wasn't meant to be ours to bear, but our selfish ancestors insulted the goddess and she punished them for it, then us for many, many generations." She reached out to brush my hair back and for a second I felt like we stepped through time and she was petting 10 year old Mattie…

"We can both be rid of the monsters and be free."

The thought of having her back in my life is tempting, but remembering how devastated I was not to hear Kaida after being stabbed, I didn't want that. I made friends with the darkness and I wasn't turning my back on half of who I was. Placing my hands on top of hers I try to look through her, to who she was deep inside.

"Cat, the night I was attacked…I wasn't changed into a monster. I wasn't punished, because I had done nothing wrong. Medusa might have lived the rest of her life bitter and angry, suffering in heartbreak and grief, but that wasn't what I wanted for myself. What happened was terrible but it didn't break me, the curse made me whole again. Kaida and I are one whole person." I pushed my hand to her knee trying to implore the big sister part of her to understand that we either rallied against our demons or we danced with them, and I had made my choice.

I was so focused on my hand resting on her knee that I didn't see her first flying towards my face until it was too late. It made contact at the crest of my cheekbone and I flew back, falling off the couch and landing on my ass on the floor with my hand held up to stave off another hit. Catherine flew at me scratching my chest and neck with her nails. They dug in and gouged at the delicate skin.

"You're an idiot. You think the curse made you whole, that it was nothing to be punished for something out of your control? Nothing to lose control of your mind and body? Nothing to hurt everyone around you? Do you know how many people I have killed? I have no idea, but the pile grows all the time. There's nothing I can do to stop it if I can't break the curse." She wraps her hands around my throat while I struggle to throw her off. She's just as strong as me, maybe stronger in her anger, and for once I am at a disadvantage.

"Cat" I hit her arms and try to pull away, "Cat you don't want to hurt me." She stops squeezing and looks down at me, her eyes were glowing bright green, but they change back to the dead glossed over reflection I was getting used to. With one hand she lets go and brushes the hair off my face sweetly before leaning in close. Our lips are almost meeting as she whispers, "I don't, but she does. She always gets what she wants."

We are not separate, Mattie. Neither are they, not really. When she says her creature wants you dead, she means it, but only because that is what she wants too. I don't do things without you, and neither does her creature.

She was right, while my impulses were harder to control at night, we operated as a team more than as individuals. We were always on the same page in the end. Catherine closes the distance and kisses the side of my face next to my lips, "I'll free you, and then you can hate me, but it won't last long. You'll help me be free, too. We're sisters. A sister for a sister is a fair exchange."

She is going to sacrifice you. Mattie, you have to get out of here. The way to break the curse is Alice. The cost is her death at your hands. And once you are free, she will do the same to you.

This is what she didn't want me to know before? That the cost was death?

Perseus could have broken the curse all those years ago. He just had to sacrifice himself for the woman he said he loved. He chose not to. Choice and love. What would someone give to the person they truly love? Would they give up their life? She doesn't understand that it has to be willingly given. If they do not choose it, then it will not work, and they will be dead for nothing. The curse is never really gone, because after that, you have to continue to live without someone you love.

Pandora's box indeed…So she figures she can get Alice here, and I'll kill her, and that'll break my curse? While Alice would give up her life for me a hundred times over, there was no way I would kill her. I would run myself through before I let it come to that, but I also couldn't end my life here and leave Alice and Will to run into Cat's trap without me to help them. The sun was setting soon and I could feel the skin start to tighten now. For once, it wasn't a relief that I would be changing because it meant that Catherine would too. Catherine pushed away from me, her face mottled by disgust. She went to the kitchen and pulled out a wine glass and a bottle from the fridge, pouring herself a glass of red while she stared at me sitting on my floor, still rubbing at my sore neck.

"Why do you think Alice would help break this curse? Alice is my family, but would she choose to die for me? Maybe. But will I kill her? Absolutely not."

Cat smiles and sips the wine again, "She thinks she loves you, though." I can't hold back the words that burst from my lips in certainty.

"She does." Now she's smiling like the cat that got the cream. Quietly, I hear three soft knocks on the metal of the roof. My heart races in my chest as the knot in my stomach eases a bit, and I restrain myself from looking up or smiling in relief. Without a clock, I can't tell how close we're cutting it, but if Lucian is on the roof, he will have me out of here in two ticks, and then we can make a plan to deal with Cat.

"That's the thing, though, Mattie. She might think she loves you, maybe she does, but is she willing to die for your freedom?"

I matched her glare for glare, "You wouldn't be doing this if you thought she wouldn't." Finishing her glass and setting it down a little too hard, I flinched at the sound of the glass breaking. Cat walked my way without a care.

"I guess we'll find out…" Lucian, hopefully, was listening to this and would keep Alice away. It would be bad, but he's tough and can handle her. My skin was uncomfortably tight now, so the change was imminent, but Cat didn't seem bothered by it at all. A knock at the front door made us both looked over, me in horror, and her in absolute delight. She crossed the room and opened it to admit Alice and Will, who walked in, hands held up to show they were unarmed.

Cat's face turned into a pout, "Oh, Alice dear, you didn't need to bring anyone extra. It's rude to bring a guest to a party they aren't invited to." Alice rolls her eyes and looks past her to check me head to toe. I wanted to shove her out the door, to yell at Will to grab her and run, but I knew he wouldn't, and he was too busy looking me over for injuries. I am sure the bruise on my face was the reason for the twitch of his clenched jaw. Trying to diffuse him, I wink and smirk at him, crossing my arms, "Okay, Cat, you got us all here. So, what do you want?" Alice is pissed off and her voice is wavering just a little.

Cat throws her arm around Alice and pulls her close. I tense up at her being so close to her when she is this close to changing.

"Well darling, we're going to have a little chat, and then you are going to help Mattie. If it works, fantastic. If not, then I'll leave and you never have to see me again." I meet Alice's eyes and try to silently communicate with her that she had to refuse to help. She had to leave me to deal with this, because the last thing I would do on this earth is hurt Alice.

Will was making his way around the room to come up next to me, "Hello, gorgeous. Starting to think you have a kink for getting rescued." He whispered low, trying to break the tension.

"Maybe your kink is being the rescuer. You certainly like your white knight routine. You fantasize about princesses in towers, Agent Trouble?" He rolls his eyes and takes my hand, "Tempt me, little goddess, and I'll get started on building you one tomorrow." Even in the dire situation, my thighs clench at the husky quality of his voice.

Catherine is watching the two of us, and the gleam in her eyes is new and terrifying. Seeing her stare, I squeeze his hand and ball my fist tight, "Put your tie over your eyes, Will."

He looks at us, Cat and I caught in a staring match.

"Mattie," he says my name softly under his breath. I move to stand in front of him so she can't look his way. "Now." The order as firm as I can be, yet sounding so desperate.

"Ali?" She looks my way, whatever desperation she sees there brings tears to her dark brown eyes. I sure hope she put on her waterproof eyeliner today, or she's going to be a mess.

"She wants to try and break the curse. It has to be a willing sacrifice; one made of love. It won't work because I would never let you do that. I need you to go. Go to Lucian and tell him to use the backup plan." Catherine smiles.

"Let her go, Cat. This is between you and me."

"If her love for you is so fickle and she wants to go, then fine. The curse won't be broken that way anyway.. It's about selfless sacrifice. Anything less is unacceptable." I wave at Alice to move towards the door, and just as she turns around, I feel the curse take over and the change wash through me. Will is still standing behind me, and I can feel the heat coming off him more acutely now. Opening my eyes carefully, mine and Cat's clash - she was beautiful as herself, but now she's the embodiment of Medusa. Her short hair doesn't cover her snakes at all, and they surround her head, writhing viciously in the air around her. She looks over at Alice retreating, and before I can do anything, she shoots forward to bite her. Gunshots ring out in quick succession, landing in Cat's chest.

One, two, three, four, five.

Five bloody holes appear, center mass, shot from above us. Looking up through Kaida's eyes, I see Lucian with a rifle leaning in one of the old skylights. Alice hits the ground and covers her head quickly, but something is glinting at her waist. Cat rounds on me, snarling, "You just couldn't cooperate! You couldn't just fix this! You never deserved to be free like I do." She rushes towards us; she is going to kill us. That's okay as long as Lucian kills her too. Just as she reaches us, Will steps in her path, facing us, his face set in grim determination. Horror washes through me as I realize that he is staring directly into our eyes, and I can see the gray-blue depths swirling as he studies our face. Catherine is screaming, but it's drowned out by the rushing of blood in my head.

Kaida, close your eyes. Close them!

I scream at her, but deep down, I know it's too late. Will clutches us around the waist and pulls us into his chest, and I hear Alice scream out angrily, a hard thud, and then silence. Pushing forward in my mind, I take over control of my body. Sadness, grief, and guilt all overwhelming wash over Kaida in waves, she relents control easily, slinking back into the recesses of our joined mind. Looking under his arm, I see Cat's head has been cut clean from her body and is rolling towards the couch. Her body slumps over, and Alice is standing there with a short sword. Blood splattered across her face and chest. Her face pales as she looks up, avoiding my eyes. Throwing the sword down she rushing for us both. I pull away from Will's chest and look down at his legs, which are already turning to stone.

"No, no, no, Will it's me, it's Mattie! I need you to stay with me." Panic washes over me, I grip his waist tightly and try to stop the stone with nothing but prayers. Will shoves a hand into the hair at the back of my head and pulls me away, his other hand clutches at my throat to tip my head back.

"What did you do, Trouble?" The tears are spilling over my cheeks before I can stop them, and the shudders make my knees buckle.

He holds me firmly upright, staring into my eyes. "I didn't even think about it. I saw her coming and did what it took to save you, both of you. I promised I would."

A sob is wretched free of my lips, and he pulls me closer, no longer being careful of my fangs, he crushes his lips to mine, kissing me with every bit of his soul because it will be the last time. The stone is over the middle section that my arms are around now, the hard feeling of stone beneath my fingers.

"I love you, Mattie. Know that I love all of you, and I will be waiting on the other side for you. I'll wait for forever to be with you again; gods be damned if they think they can keep us apart. Don't lose hope and don't stop loving me, okay?" Pressing my lips against his, I whisper, "You won't wait long. I'll walk into the gates of the underworld itself to get you back. I love you, William Bennet. I want you to stay. Please don't go. Please..." I begged with my tears falling and my lips pressed against his. I feel his hands harden, one gently encircling my throat and the other clenched around my middle. His final gasp for breath as the stone climbs his face echoed in the air, breaking my soul into a million jagged shards.

"I will find you again." He whispers with his final breath, and it's over.

Chapter 35

Mattie

Where Will had just been standing, clinging to me, a gray statue of him now stands. Pulling away from his stone arms where I was cradled, I hear a horrible keening sound, and it takes a second to realize it's coming from me. My chest burns, and my knees give out. Trying to catch my breath, I stare at him until I feel a piece of silk being draped over my eyes.

"Shh, Cher, it's just me. I am just keeping everyone safe." He tightens the cloth around my head, falling to my knees. Lucian sits with me, pulling my body back to lean in his arms.

"I killed him, Lucian. I killed him…" Lucian's arms tighten around me, and he gives my body a sharp shake, "Non, he died to protect you. Don't take that honor from him." Alice approaches and curls her body around my waist, hugging tightly. "I loved him. He loved me…he loved all of me…"

The two of them hold me down, hugging me tightly like I might disintegrate into the ashes if they let go.

He did love us, little monster. He did it because he loved us.

Kaida's sadness is just another drop in an overfilled bucket. She is pushing forward again, probably to save me from the overwhelming emotions, but I fight against her. Anger is a more comfortable place to be than sadness. The sound of her voice makes me want to throw up. Hours ago, I was thinking how grateful I was to not only love and accept this part of myself but to have found someone else who did too, and it cost him his life.

I was a monster, and I had killed the most important person I had.

All my nightmares had come true, just not the way I feared. I had asked Alice to help me once, and she refused; I didn't make the same mistake with Lucian. I had demanded an oath of him, and he said he would do what was necessary. Making up my mind, I push away from the two of them, feeling my way across the dusty concrete floor blindly across the space until I find the sword still lying where Alice dropped it near Will's body.

This isn't the answer, Mattie. You know it isn't.

She tries to take over again, to force me to stop, and it's a battle of wills that she is better set for, but my anger gives me an advantage. The handle of the sword is heavy in my palm. I scream into the darkness, "Shut up! This is your fault. It's your fault he's gone, and now I have a promise to keep." Standing up, I hold out the sword towards Lucian and Alice. I hear them scuffle to get up, and a second later, Lucian's hand grips mine over the handle.

"You promised me, swore an oath to me on your honor, if the day came that I couldn't fight anymore, that you would help me. I promised him I would follow. Time to hold up your end of the deal, Lucian." My voice was steady but devoid of any of the feelings roiling inside me.

There's only a moment of silence before Alice draws in a breath to lets loose on me.

"Fuck you, Mattie! You don't get to do this!" Alice's hand tries to pull the sword from my grip as she screams at me.

"And fuck you too Lucian. You will not do this. Fuck your promise and damn your honor. You help her do this, and I will never forgive you."

The anger in her voice shreds what little of my soul is left. The last thing I want is to leave either of them without the other… but I can't live in a world without Will. Lucian sighs, knowing what helping me will cost him.

"I won't do that to my friend, Mattie." Hissing at him with all the ferocity

I can muster, "I am demanding it as your friend, Lucian." He pries the sword from my fingers and lets it clatter to the ground, "Not you, Cher. William…In our short time together, I knew I wanted him as a brother. I knew he was meant to be a part of my family, of our family. You may hate me for not doing this and Alice will hate me if I do, but he would do worse if I even considered it. He loved you, Mattie, and I won't let his sacrifice be for nothing."

I try to stop the tears freshly falling and soaking the silk tied around my eyes. The darkness makes the gentle tone of his voice hurt even more. The sound of the sword clattering against the ground breaks open the floodgates of pain, "It hurts Lucian…it feels like I can't breathe, and I won't ever again. I don't know why they say it feels like your heart is broken…it feels like someone lit mine on fire." Alice stopped cursing the ground that Lucian walks upon, and I feel her slip her hand in mine.

"It won't be today, tomorrow, or maybe even months from now, but one day you will wake up and it won't hurt so badly. One day, it won't hurt to think of him. Pain like this is just love that can't be given to the person it's meant for. Love and pain are what make us human, what makes us not monsters. Please trust me, Mattie."

I know its weakness, I know she is right that the pain will dull and fade, but… "I can't do this." I cry softly to my creature, "Please don't make me."

I won't little monster. I have to say this now so you know that I never meant to cause you pain. I am so sorry. If I could have taken the curse away from you, I would have. I won't ever forget you.

"What?" I asked, the resignation in her voice chasing a bit of my pain. I squeezed Alice's hand hard as a darkness deeper than what the blindfold caused pushed in on me. It was suffocating as it pulled me under, and I could hear Alice and Lucian calling my name and shaking me, but I couldn't move or speak. A bright, bluish light blinded me, and I cracked my eyes open reluctantly and carefully in case someone was right in front of my face. Looking around, I could see I was in the woods somewhere; the blue light was the moon reflecting off the surface of the water in a lake just a few yards away. I sit up, cautious, since I was just in a building in New Orleans. I could tell by smell alone, I was no longer there.

"3,000 years and your guy is the first one to ever get it right…Astounding, isn't it? I'm just glad he isn't one of Zeus's progeny. Odin's a buzzkill at parties but the rest of them aren't so bad."

Spinning around, I see a woman sitting on a large boulder a few feet away. Her long brown hair trails down her back in one thick braid with a crown of golden laurels on her head. She has sparkly blue eyes and freckles painted across her sharp features. She's tall, even sitting down, wearing a long black dress with a dark blue leather under-bust corset strapped around her chest. She's watching me, her face awash in curiosity.

"Odin?" I ask skeptically. She waves her hand like batting away a fly, "Oh yes, your man is one of theirs." Looking around hopefully for any sign of Will, I catch sight of my hand and realize it's not green. It's pale white, and my nails are normal and short. Reaching up, I try and pat my favorite little green buddy and feel he isn't there, none of them are. I start to hyperventilate and look at the woman with panic written all over my face.

"What did you do to me?" She extends her hands in a gesture of peace. "It's okay, Matilda. You're fine. I told you before, your young man broke the curse."

Shaking my head I shout. "No, he didn't! It was an accident. I did it…I killed him!"

She smiles soothingly, "No, he understood that Catherine was going to sacrifice your friend to break the curse. So, he did it himself. He chose to put himself in harm's way for you in whatever way he could. The idiot didn't understand that he didn't have to die first."

It suddenly dawns on me that she keeps referring to things she couldn't know, talking about other gods like they were familiar friends. Here we were in the middle of a forest at night, and not in an old building in New

Orleans where I passed out.

Just like she was depicted in the books and paintings I had collected, she's pale as the moon, fierce as a wolf, and bright as a star. Suddenly, I am sure I know her. "You're Athena...the goddess." She smiles kindly, lighting up her face, and sits back down, patting the seat next to her. I move closer and sit next to her. "Sometimes I am...Sometimes I go by other names." I look at her, puzzled.

"Other names?" I ask.

She shrugs, "It doesn't matter. Mattie, I owe you something of an apology."

She stares up at the moon hanging above us before sighing.

"I know how the story is told, and it doesn't paint me in the best light. I won't say that my arrogance as a young goddess didn't sometimes backfire, but with Medusa, I thought I was doing the right thing. You can't even imagine how angry she was with me after I changed her...I thought it would keep her safe, that she could keep others safe, but I messed up by not explaining and letting ignorance drive the narrative. She was so angry at me, and then when she met someone and fell in love, I thought I was so smart. I thought that I had done it all right. Soon, she would be safe and loved in a way I couldn't provide. I thought wrong...He didn't appreciate my handiwork, and if there was anything left of her kind heart, he stomped it out. I didn't foresee my idea becoming a curse and being passed down. I kind of forgot about it for a few centuries, and then it had grown out of control. I had made a mess and didn't know how to begin to fix it.

I tried to do just that, then I stumbled upon you. I saw through your monster's eyes what happened to you. It should have stomped out your heart, too, just like Medusa. Instead, where there was pain, you found passion. Where there was loss, you filled it with a found family. Where there was hurt, you tried to help others without ever asking for thanks. You turned your pain into something beautiful and gave back by fighting for those who couldn't. I watched on, utterly amazed. You've been a bragging point of mine these last few years. You and your sister, Alice. A regular human woman who supported and loved someone others would have feared and hunted. She's a marvel, but not one I can take credit for."

She winked over at me, "Trust me, I would if I could, but she is already claimed. When I tried to reward you for all you have done in my honor I went to see the Morai. They told me to butt the hell out and stay away. I didn't see your young man coming along, and I certainly didn't see him falling in love with not only you but your monster as well. That was the surprise of the century, and as a goddess, it is very hard to surprise me."

She points over to the tree line, among the branches and I see a figure. My heart stops for a second before beating double time. The figure moves out into the clearing. My heart skips a beat as I see it's not Will, but my other form, myself as a gorgon. Kaida steps towards us and waves shyly. I'm frozen, confused, but that doesn't stop the tears as my brain catches up and I realize what's happening. I look back at Athena, pleading.

"Don't do this. Don't take her away. I've lost too much already…I need her." Her eyes are glazed with sorrow, but before she can say anything, Kaida reaches out and wraps her arms around me, sighing and relaxing into me, my favorite little green buddy nuzzling against my cheek.

"I have always wanted to do this, to give you the hug you needed. I am glad I got to say goodbye. When you were cursed, I was a creature of vengeance and anger. I didn't know anything about laughter, fun…family. Being a part of you has been the greatest thing to ever happen to me. We did so much good in the world." I wrap my arms around her too, squeezing like a python the same way Alice hugged me when I was sad, if I relaxed my grip even a little she would float away and be gone. I couldn't risk it…not yet.

"I got to flirt with Lucian, laugh with Alice, and fall in love with Trouble. I got everything and more with you. You could have hated me. I was a curse, a bad thing… and so was everything I represented, but I knew the second we were joined that you were different."

I soak in this moment, knowing it will be the last.

"I can't do this alone. I will stay cursed for a thousand years as long as you get to stay with me." Picturing a life without Kaida and without Will is too hard. I can't shake the pain gripping my chest as I struggle to catch my breath. She sniffles into my neck and squeezes me.

"You won't be alone. This was the trade - him or me."

Stiffening, I pull away from her. Her sharp features and blazing green eyes look back at me with a soft smile. My vicious twin is going to sacrifice her life for Will's.

"I can't let you do that."

She smiles sadly, "I am not asking permission little monster. I love him too. Hard not to with his puppy eyes and silver tongue. This was an easy decision." I knew she was just as invested in Will as I was and every moment they shared was just as important as the ones I spent with him. He was impossible not to fall for, especially if the fate's really had a say in it. I would do the same thing if it were me in her shoes. Looking over to Athena, I ask cautiously, "You can bring Will back?"

"Yes. As soon as you've said goodbye, I will give you this gift." I take in my monster, my sister, Kaida, one last time. Her snakes writhing through her hair, nuzzling against her cheeks and neck trying to offer some comfort. Her blazing green eyes rimmed with tears as she takes me in, trying to memorize everything about me too. Her red lips turned up in a sad smile of goodbye.

"What happens to you now? Will you just wait for another of my bloodline?"

Athena interrupts from where she is watching us, hands clasped in front of her, "No, you have broken the curse for everyone. True redemption, Kaida is the first to survive, so she gets to stay here with me. A reminder of a lesson I should have learned centuries ago." Kaida squeezes my fingers so I look at her again.

"I will be okay. Now go home before Alice has a panic attack." I giggle, my nose running embarrassingly. She's right that Alice will be freaking out, but I'm not sure how I'm supposed to leave her behind. She's been the other half of my soul for so long it feels like cutting off my right arm.

"Go, little monster. I have havoc to wreak on this world, and I can't get started till this sappy stuff is over." She shooed me off, but I can see the tears about to spill out of her too. I look back at Athena and nod that I'm ready. Releasing my hand and stepping back, Kaida is watching with tears spilling over her cheeks. Athena guides my face closer to her own, cradling it between her two hands. and presses her lips to mine softly. I gasp, but quickly relax, and the darkness creeps in again.

It's only a moment before I no longer feel her lips pressed to mine, but I'm being shaken harshly by a sobbing, sniffling mess disguised as my best friend. Groaning, I reach up and tear off the silk wrap around my eyes and push her off me, "Are you trying to hug the literal life out of me?" She looks up at me and gasps quickly before throwing her arms around my neck and climbing on me to straddle my waist and hug me with her bottom half, too.

Lying flat on my back with Alice wrapped around me like a python, Lucian appears above me, smiling, "Hello gorgeous." His smile falters, and he looks shocked at my face as he realizes, glancing up at the window, and then back at me.

"Yeah, I know. A little help?" I gesture to Alice barnacling me. "I need to get to Will."

Lucian grabs her under her armpits and pulls her off easily and up against his chest. He offers his free hand to help me up, but I am already scrambling across the floor to Will's feet. Using the statue, I haul myself upright. His eyes were still open and frozen like he couldn't bear to close them and not see me during his last moments. I press my lips against his stone ones. Please let this work. Please come back to me. A second passes, and I hear Alice struggling to pull away from Lucian and get to me, but he's holding her back. The moment is drawing on and on. "Come back for me, Will. Tell those Valkyries to fuck right off and come back." I murmur against the stone kiss.

Tears are pooling in my eyes again, and I think it hasn't worked…That I've been tricked. I felt a pull at the back of my head. Will's fingers tangle in the hair at the base of my skull, and then his other hand squeezes my neck, harder than before. It shocks me, and I gasp, my lips parting just in time for Will to slip his tongue in my mouth. Our tongues clash, and he groans, totally unsatisfied, as I pull away. Reaching for me again, he doesn't get a very good grip before he is knocked out of my arms and onto the ground. The pile of limbs that is Lucian and Will is hilarious, and I can't hold back the laughs or the tears that are bubbling up again as I watch Lucian wrestle Will into a hug as he laughs like a child.

This is a day for the record books. I've never cried this much in such a short amount of time. Lucian has Will pinned under him like Alice had me, but he is kissing his cheeks over and over again.

"Mon dieu! I thought you were dead and gone, my friend! Mattie was trying to off herself, Alice was mad at me, you went and died, so I had to deal with it all by myself! I aged 20 years in the last hour and my beautiful self can ill afford that."

"Hey!" Alice yells, "Get off of him before you kill him again, you oaf!" Lucian climbs off and pulls Will up with him.

"Sorry Mon Cheri, I got carried away."

Alice walks up and envelopes him in a hug before pulling back and punching him hard on the shoulder, "What the hell, Alice!?" He exclaims, rubbing his arm.

"Don't ever do that again!"

"Not a chance of that happening," I whisper to no one. All three of them look over at me before they realize it's dark outside and I'm just Mattie. Will breaks the silence first, coming up to tuck me against him, "What happened, darling?" Patting his warm, soft chest, the tears I thought were spent a thousand times over start burning behind my eyes again as I try to choke out the words. "I had to say goodbye. There's a cost to everything, and in this case, she paid it so you wouldn't."

Kissing the top of my head, I feel the first tears of his fall and mix with my hair. "I didn't want that. I never wanted her gone, Mattie. I tried to tell her the other night that I love you, both of you, for everything you are." His words are a balm on my soul, and I can't hold back the stinging commentary that Kaida would have thrown out, *Of course you love us, Trouble. That was quite obvious after that thing you did with your tongue and the white knight routine.*

But her voice doesn't echo in my head; there is no one to banter with. "I know that, Trouble...She knew it too. She was so sorry she couldn't say it herself, so I'll say it often enough for us both. Thank you for saving us. Thank you for loving us. Thank you for loving me...through all the chaos and disasters. I'll love you until the stars fall from the sky."

Hugging him tight, thinking of Kaida made my heart hurt and my head feel empty. After so many years of her taking up space and her unsolicited commentary, I'm not sure how to live without her. With Will beside me though, I feel in my soul that I'll be okay.

Lucian gathers Alice in his arms and tosses her over his shoulder. She shrieks and pulls at his dreads hanging down, "Lucian, PUT ME DOWN!" He smirks at us before smacking her on the ass, "Not now you viper, we have celebrating to do!"

Turning to grin at Will, Lucian says, "Did you know I own a bar on Bourbon Street? And the girls have never been." Will smiles down at me before grabbing me and swinging me into his arms, "Never been to Bourbon Street? That's something we have to remedy right away!"

We make for the door, and Lucian's cousin Sabine is standing outside with a few other people.

"Glad you're alive, Mattie!" She looks past us to see my sister's headless body on the ground. I avoid looking that way again. Whatever happened tonight, my sister died years ago. This was just what was left of the monster

Catherine had turned into.

"We got this." She gestures to a few men who start inside.

"Shame to lose so many of these old buildings to electrical fires." Lucian nods, and we load up in Alice's SUV.

"She's terrifying…how old is she?" Will asks. Lucian pulls the car onto the street and answers without looking at Will.

"Just turned 21, and gods help us all." I reach to front seat and pinch his arm, "Any god in particular?" He looks in the rear-view mirror, and even though his mouth is smiling, his eyes are deadly serious.

"Whichever ones help keep her safe." I smirk at his response and relax back into Will's embrace while we drive towards the bar.

"I'll put in a special request." We're all dirty, tear-streaked, tired, hungry, and absolute messes, but we were on our way to the first bar I had stepped foot at night in ten years. We'll drink, dance, and maybe even sing karaoke until morning. We'll celebrate that there is still breath in our lungs and a life to live after this.

Grief is for tomorrow, and the grief would come in waves for Kaida and even for Catherine. Life has a way of sending things that sneak up on you, love or loss, grief or happiness. It all comes in waves but when you have people worth fighting for, dying for, you make the choice to not waste a moment with the ones who make life worth living.

Dear god…I really do need to make that appointment with a therapist.

Afterword

Thank you so much for reading my scribbles and hopefully loving the journey. I couldn't have even begun this book without my loving husband's push, which became more of a shove off a cliff by the end. I have loved writing this story and giving a happy ending to one of my favorite legends. This has been one of my greatest achievements, the ability to say that I did the thing I had been talking about since I was 5 and writing my first stories. When I graduated from high school, the only thing I wanted to be was an author. Now I can genuinely say I have done it and I can't wait to see what I get to accomplish next. I hope each of you will come back and join me in this universe again, and maybe a different one based on my home in Montana.

Michael, you are weirdly talented at editing, and I needed every bit of help with my horrible grammar and sentence structure. Seriously, I didn't appreciate how many typos I had or things that needed to be reworded until he got hold of it. This is as much his project as mine. Not to mention the fact that if you didn't love me so thoroughly, so completely, that if it weren't for meeting you, I would have no love to write about. Everything I fell for in those stories is a part of you, and that's what makes us one of the great love stories.

Mattie's story meant more to me with every word typed, and she inspired me in so many ways. I based her on someone so important to me, and I wanted her tale to inspire anyone who resonates with her or with the others in this book to find their fire and fight back, however that looks to you.

The biggest thank you in this story goes to my muse, my friend, and encouragement, Marissa. If it weren't for you and some very long, late-night talks, I don't know that I would have gotten this book off the ground. What started as venting ended in this whole book, and with both of us better off than before. I am so proud and grateful to call you my friend, yesterday, today, and tomorrow.

Thank you to my sister, Kayla, who was my sounding board and first reader. Her feedback and healthy criticism were just what I needed to flesh out how to make this story a mix of myth and mystery. If it wasn't for our mutual love of spicy books, yelling into the phone at each other, and trying to top each other with crazy tales, then none of this would have come about.

To my very own Alice, Lisa H., just like in the story, we met quite by accident, and from that day forward, we were connected in weird and sometimes crazy ways. If there was ever someone to call if I'm stuck with a body on my hands, it would always be you. I know you'll read this and love how bad ass I made your character, but even she can't compare to how amazing you are as a friend, soulmate, and sister.

Thank you to my cover artist, Markee books, for creating just what I asked for and for being just as excited about this book as I am.

To M, L, C, and E -

You are the reason I have blood in my body, breathe in my lungs, and a will to go on every day. You will forever be my own happily ever after, even if that is sometimes bloody, covered in dirt, and a little wild. I would choose this universe with you four, always and forever.